Forward:

What you hold in your hand is the Third, and final revision of the Draoidh's Cearcall.  This book was first published as Voyage of the Dawn-Breaker, before being expanded in the first edition of The Draoidh's Cearcall.

The story demanded to be told, and here it is, every hard-earned page.

Now, maybe the characters will stop trying to stab me.

Also by Joseph L. Wiess

The Draoidh's Cearcacll  Series

The Draoidh's Cearcall

The Draoidh's Gambit

The Shadows Rise

Oath & Ember


The Lawkeeper Chronicles:

The Black Swan's Bond

The Sheriff's Oath

By Law and Flame

Oath & Ember

*The Draoidh's Cearcall*
ISBN: 979-8-9934166-1-8

**For my family,**
who taught me the meaning of courage
and love.

Dana – I miss you every day.

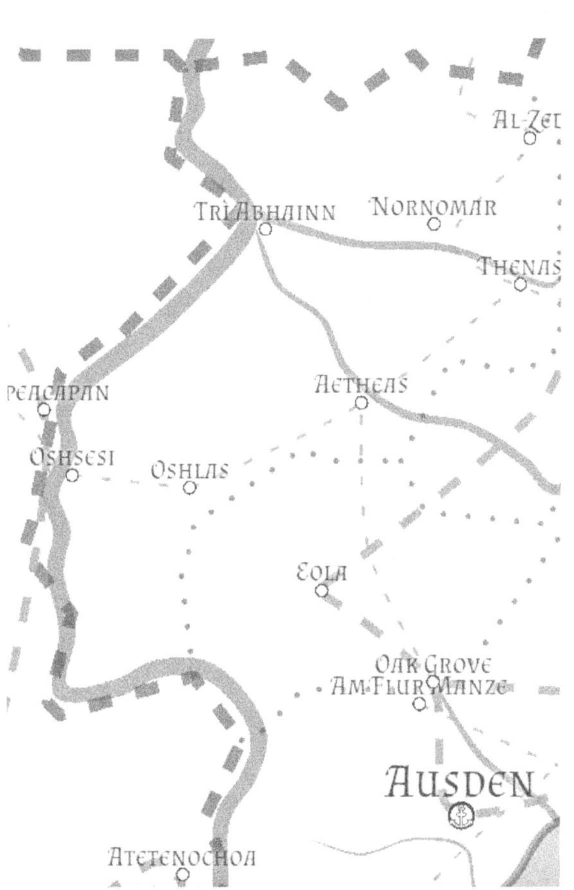
Al-Zet
Tri Abhainn
Nornomar
Thenas
Aetheas
Peacapan
Oshsesi
Oshlas
Eola
Oak Grove
Am Flur Manze
Ausden
Atetenochoa

# Contents

# Mid-Faoilleach

300 Years Post Founding

The clouds shifted, and the moon broke free, spilling argent light across a fortified village crouched upon an island where three rivers braided together. The waters whispered against the banks, their currents weaving a song of watchfulness. Above, a galleon hung against the night, her sails pulled tight against the spars until she lay adrift in the frozen air. The ship's timbers creaked softly, as though even wood and iron were holding breath.

Within the captain's cabin, lamplight trembled across polished maps and the sheen of a crystal orb.

Two men leaned over it, their reflections wavering in the glass.

"How long do we have?" asked the first. He stood a shade under six feet, hair dark but salted with gray at the temples. His eyes, brown as tilled earth, swept the forest canopy and riverbanks as though the land itself might yield its secrets. His cloak shifted hue with every pass of cloud across the moon: shadow, moss, stone, flame. Such cloaks were rare; only the First Dreamer wove them for chosen rangers. The fabric seemed alive, mirroring the sky's restlessness.

His companion, thinner, with shoulder-length white hair, raised his gaze from the crystal. "Three days." His voice carried like a whisper across grave soil.

Black leather clothed him, long as a duster, and the mage-staff in his left hand throbbed faintly with power, its runes reflecting the orb′s glow. The scent of resin clung to him, as if the staff bled sap.

The ranger′s mouth twisted. "It doesn′t look like much. Why is this place so important?"

"You know Rowena," the Draoidh replied softly, almost reverently. "She would not say much." At her name, the lamplight guttered once, and the crystal′s glow deepened, as if her goddess, unseen, had leaned closer to listen.

The ranger grunted, the sound of stone against stone. "Sometimes I think she uses that goddess of hers as an excuse. Where do you want us?"

The Draoidh extended a hand across the orb. The rivers shimmered in miniature, silver threads winding through a dark landscape. He touched one glowing patch. "That clearing. If we move quickly, we'll have time to prepare before they arrive."

The ranger's brow arched, the cloak at his shoulders rippling as though stirred by more than wind. He gave his friend a measuring look, then nodded. "Alright. Let's get going."

Beyond the cabin walls, the still night air thickened, as though the forest itself had overheard—and was waiting

.

# Chapter One
## The Staff and the Storm

The watchfires along the wooden palisades guttered as the villagers lifted their eyes to the heavens. From the parting clouds a shape descended, vast sails furled, hull gleaming in the moonlight, a ship that had no business in the sky. It broke through the mist like a vision from old tales and came to rest above the place where the three rivers met.

The waters below surged restlessly, braiding together in froth and current, as though the earth itself resisted being bridled.

Archers along the wall raised longbows in unison, their fingers trembling only slightly as they nocked arrows, fletching to string.

The air grew taut with the creak of wood, the thrum of tightened bowstrings, and the sharp tang of resin and river-cold iron.

From the ship's belly a line uncoiled and fell, hissing through the air until it struck the river with a slap and vanished into the depths. The villagers murmured. They saw shadows hauling it upward, hand over hand, as though the waters themselves yielded a tether to the sky.

Slowly, ponderously, the galleon turned until her prow faced the coursing waters, aligning herself with the current as if acknowledging the will of the rivers.

Timbers groaned in protest, anchors plunged with a heavy splash, and chains rattled until the ship settled into the embrace of the confluence. The smell of wet rope and tar drifted across the banks.

With a resonant crack, the gangplank extended, reaching shoreward like a wooden tongue. The Hîn-i-Balanath archers drew back to full draw, arrows brushing their cheeks, eyes hard. No command was needed; the village had seen invaders before.

A dozen figures crossed the plank, dark shapes descending into the tree line. The forest swallowed them without a sound, branches knitting shut as if to conceal what paths they took.

For an hour, the magnificent galleon lay still. Not a voice carried, not a footstep stirred.

Even the villagers ceased whispering, for it seemed the ship itself held its breath, and the rivers, the night, and every watchful heart held theirs with it.

"Do we know who they are?"

The question came soft but sharp from the silver-haired woman hidden in the shadows of the wall's highest perch. Moonlight slid across her pointed ears as they twitched toward the strange ship below, drinking in every creak of timber and hiss of anchor chain. Her eyes never left the vessel, as if willing it to give up its secrets.

"No, Bereth nín," her companion answered, voice low, report trembling in his gloved hand. He was lean, his body honed for the hunt, yet even he found his throat dry in the ship's presence. "No one has approached since the first group vanished into the forest."

Movement stirred below. Eighty men filed out in flawless black-clad formation, their boots striking the gangplank with the rhythm of war drums. The villagers on the wall stiffened. Some of the soldiers melted into the tree line, shadows within shadows. Others bent to the snow, shoveling and hollowing until white plumes rose like breath from the earth itself. The scrape of spades on frozen ground carried up through the night air, sharp as blades drawn from sheaths.

"What are they doing now?" the Bereth asked, though fascination already gleamed in her eyes.

Her companion swallowed. "Blinds, it seems. See how they cover the openings with tarps? They hollow the snowbanks, dump the waste into the river, and turn the white skin of the world into hiding places."

Indeed, the strangers worked with grim silence, their breath steaming, their motions mechanical. Snow fell in sheets into the rushing river, hissing as the current dragged it away. The blinds faced the village like patient, waiting mouths. When the work was done, the soldiers slipped into them and were gone, as if the night itself had swallowed them whole.

The Bereth lingered in thought before descending the stairs, her hand brushing the frozen wood. The torches guttered as she passed. "Keep lookouts posted. Report to me if any soul nears the gates," she commanded.

"As you wish, Your Majesty."

By morning the blinds were empty. The clearing lay pristine, the riverbank undisturbed, save for faint impressions where anchors had kissed the earth. No ship, no soldiers, no trace but the lingering scent of tar on the wind. Even the birds seemed uneasy, flitting restlessly from branch to branch.

Concerned, Allanagh turned inward to the gods. She knelt before the altar in her hall, the air thick with pine resin and the smoke of smoldering sage, and whispered prayers to two powers: the Forest Mother, who ruled her people's land, and the Veiled One, goddess of mysteries. Her auguries came muddled — branches casting runes that shifted in the firelight, water bowls that rippled with no wind, whispers threading through her ears only to contradict one another.

"The Forest Mother does not fear the strange ship," her priestess reported.

"The Veiled One bids us stay within the walls," said another.

Allanagh's silver hair gleamed as she rose, lips twisting in frustration. "I despise it when na Diathan hide behind riddles," she spat. The fire flared with her anger, sparks leaping like startled birds.

For two days trepidation pressed upon the village like a storm refusing to break. Allanagh's temper frayed, her words striking like blades even against her closest companions. On the walls, soldiers held their bows half-drawn, the oil-scented strings creaking in the frost, their breaths rising in pale ghosts. The river's roar deepened, the trees groaned as if burdened with secrets, and even the stones beneath the palisade seemed to hum with waiting.

On the third day, the forest exhaled— and hell came with the river's surge.

The forest grew deathly still, as though breath itself had been stolen from the trees. From the walls, the sharp-eyed Hîn i-Balanath leaned forward, their cloaks stiff with frost, eyes narrowing into the shadowed timber.

Then came the breaking: chilling howls rolled through the trunks, followed by explosions of raw power, and the ragged screams of dying throats. The chief among the scouts did not hesitate. His cry rang across the ramparts, summoning Bereth Allanagh Rionnag Shoilleir, speaker for Gwaith i-Taur[1], to the walls.

She arrived in time to see the tree line tear open. Grotesque, thick-muscled creatures stumbled into the clearing, harried by unseen foes.

---

[1] People of the Forest

Allanagh's eyes widened, her breath catching white in the air. "What is an Orcan war-band doing here?" Her voice trembled as she turned to Sloan.

"Unknown, your majesty," he said, lifting his gaze from the damp parchment of a report. "The scouts swore all was clear out to six leagues."

"Apparently not!" The words tore from her throat, sharp with fear, as more Orcan broke into the open. When their number swelled past eight score, her hand gripped the parapet until her knuckles whitened. "Is this what they were hunting?"

Sloan's jaw tightened. "If so, how did they foresee it?" His eyes tracked the ragged banners rising above the horde. He wondered if the strangers had enough men to hold.

Despite their retreat, the Orcan gathered into grim formation, ranks and files stamping the snow. Their battle-cry thundered against the palisade: "Blut und Sklaven für den Welterschütterer![2]" The sound shook loose frost from the timbers, echoing across the valley.

Allanagh's thoughts turned bitter. Had the strangers already abandoned them, slipping into the night with their ship? She swallowed hard. "Do they remain?"

"I believe so," Sloan murmured, though his voice carried little certainty.

---

[2] Blood and slaves for the World-Shaker!

Allanagh forced her gaze back to the clearing. The Orcan pressed forward, their tread pounding the earth like war drums.

Then—at some invisible threshold—the snowbanks erupted. Black-clad strangers burst forth in a storm of steel and fury, their answering cry tearing heavenward:

"Airson saorsa agus na Diathan![3]"

Caught unprepared, the Orcan froze in disbelief as the snowbanks erupted, and the strangers closed like a tightening noose.

The ambush was clean, disciplined, without a wasted step. Snarling, the Orcan turned, axes raised, their guttural growls shaking frost from the branches.

---

[3] For freedom and the Gods!

What followed was not a skirmish but a storm. For six hours the clearing rang with steel and roared with hatred. Snow turned to red-streaked slush beneath stamping boots; the river's voice swelled as if to drown the screams. Smoke and breath mingled in the frigid air until the forest itself seemed to choke on the struggle.

Neither side yielded—mercenaries in their black, moving with grim precision, Orcan pressing forward with raw, bestial fury—each consumed by a loathing older than the trees.

The draoidh lifted his gaze from the twitching corpse at his boots as a wolf′s call split the silence, long and mournful, rolling through the black timber. Hazel eyes swept the treeline, searching for any remnant of the foul Orcan that had dared march upon the Hîn i-Balanath. The stench of iron and smoke hung in the air, mingling with the raw bite of frost.

The ambush had unfolded cleanly, as planned, the war-band caught and broken by the tightening jaws of a pincer. With a low snarl of disgust, he loped toward the answering wolves, staff in hand. An Orcan lurched from behind a leaning pine, axe raised. The draoidh leveled his staff.

"Lúxar-Pyrith! Kaelor! Rûnath! Throgar![4]"

Lightning forked from the black pearl atop his staff and cracked into the beast, hurling it headlong into a trunk with bone-snapping force. The draoidh stretched his senses outward, touching bark and root. The tree shuddered, its limbs curling as though with wrath, and four branches wrapped the senseless Orcan, rending it apart until nothing remained but dripping tatters.

He exhaled, adjusted the brim of his weathered hat, and quickened his pace as the guttural cadence of Infernal war-cries drifted across the snow.

---

[4] Light burn, flash, crash, smash!

The clearing opened before him, scarred by fire and trampled earth. A crude campaign tent sagged in the middle, but it was not canvas that held his eye — it was the beast pinned between two towering Infernals. Nine feet tall they stood, their horned silhouettes backlit by firelight. Between them, writhed something no Orcan could match: a massive figure, tusks gleaming, fur matted with sweat, muscles ridged like stone. The ground seemed to recoil under its weight.

On the far side, the ranger emerged with his wolf-pack, breath misting from man and beast alike. The draoidh raised a hand in summons.

"Report." His voice carried the weight of command.

"Two Orcan squads destroyed," the ranger replied, his tone clipped. "Nat hunts the leader of the third." His eyes fell on the tusked creature straining against its captors. "By the gods, that's an ugly Ogren. Do you take it for their leader?"

The draoidh's shoulders rolled in a slow shrug. "That," he said, eyes narrowing, "is what I intend to learn."

The Orcan ran blind through the trees, lungs burning, heart hammering like a war-drum. He had faced kings and warlords, fought through campaigns that left rivers swollen with blood — yet nothing in all his years had carved terror into him like this.

He had seen his squad die, one by one, their flesh shriveling, their screams clipped short as the very shadows drank them dry. What hunted him was no mortal foe.

No matter how he darted through the undergrowth, she was there. She of the flame-red hair and the green eyes that glowed like emerald fire. She whom the shadows obeyed. The ranger' s companion — the one they whispered of already. Nat.

She slipped from darkness to darkness, each stride too fluid, too inevitable. It was not pursuit; it was a dance. Shadows curled with her movements, whispering of enemies long dead, of old wolves that never lost a trail. Fear tightened around the Orcan' s mind until even his own breath betrayed him, ragged and loud.

He stumbled, root catching his boot. The forest itself seemed to conspire against him, pitching him to one knee. The moment he fell, she was upon him. Tendrils of shade stretched long and thin, snaring his limbs, dragging him into the night that clung to her like a mantle.

Her voice was soft, cruelly tender. "It is time to die, young one."

His eyes flared wide – a hardened soldier reduced to prey. The shadow-blade slid clean between his ribs, black edge puncturing his beating heart. For an instant her eyes flared green, brighter than firelight. Then the Orcan collapsed inward, his life drained, skin shrinking against bone until only a husk remained at her feet.

Nat inhaled once, savoring the taste of fear that lingered in the air. The shadows coiled closer around her shoulders, as if purring their approval.

It took her but a few heartbeats to find them. She let the shadows gather thick at her heels, folding one clearing into the next until she stepped into the open ground where her companions waited. The night seemed to recoil at her passing; behind her, the dark closed like a door.

Her red hair streamed loose, catching the pale light like tongues of fire, an ember burning against the cold. The draoidh inclined his head in a half-bow, staff angled lightly across his chest.

"I take it your prey was not spared." His tone carried wry respect.

Her green eyes gleamed as she answered, voice low and edged. "That squad will trouble no soul again. The shadows feasted well." She turned then, gaze falling upon the hulking captive. The Ogren strained between the Infernals' grips, tusks gleaming wetly in the firelight. "And what beast have you snared in your forest weave?"

A chuckle rumbled from the draoidh's chest, warm against the cold night. "The leader of this band, if fortune has teeth."

From the walls the Hîn i-Balanath had watched the battle unfold, six hours of fury grinding beneath the winter sky.

They had whispered of tactics, compared maneuvers, and loosed shafts at any Orcan that slipped the noose, ensuring none came within two hundred yards of their gates. When at last the last cry faded and the field lay still, silence pressed heavy upon the village. The stench of blood mingled with snow, and smoke drifted in slow, accusing spirals.

"All healers, to the field," Bereth Allanagh commanded, her voice carrying. Below, a small contingent passed through the gates to tend the strangers. Out beyond, the black-clad mercenaries moved among the slain Orcan, stripping banners and spoils with cold efficiency.

"Bereth nín." Sloan's low voice pulled her aside. He extended the spyglass.

"What is it?" She brought the glass
to her eye, following his gesture.

Through the shifting haze she saw it
— not Orcan, not man — suspended as if in
mid-air, arms stretched as though bound
by unseen cords. Her breath caught.
"What is it?" she murmured, adjusting the
glass for clarity. She missed Sloan's
shrug, but when she lowered the glass her
silver brows were knit tight.

Without another word she handed
back the spyglass and gestured. Three
soldiers fell in behind as she descended the
wall. Sloan matched her stride, unease
written across his face.

"Allanagh—Bereth nín—are you
certain?"

Her silver hair caught the torchlight as she shook her head. "No. But we would be rude not to thank our benefactors." Her tone was iron. Sloan glanced at the others; he knew they shared his doubt, but her word was law, and they walked on.

At the gate they paused as the healer-party returned, bloodied but unbowed. Among them strode a golden-haired woman, eyes the same piercing blue as Allanagh's. She raised her hand, then broke rank to embrace her mother.

"Mathair—are you going out there?"

"I am." Allanagh's nod was simple, unyielding.

"Then I will come," her daughter said quickly, eagerness bright in her eyes. She fell into step beside Allanagh, voice lowering. "I have heard it whispered—their leader is a draoidh. I would see him with my own eyes."

Allanagh slowed, frowning. "That does not sound right. I have never known a draoidh to leave his woods, let alone lead a host." She studied her daughter's face, the certainty there. "Are you sure of this?"

Flur's golden head dipped, her voice firm. "Yes, Mathair. I am certain."

Allanagh said nothing for a moment, her gaze lifting to the waiting field. "We will see."

With that, she pressed on, step by step toward the suspended creature in the clearing.

They crossed the battlefield in silence. Allanagh paused mid-stride as two hulking shapes of stone and loam lumbered past, faceless and inexorable. With slow inevitability, the earth elementals drew the Orcan dead beneath the soil. The ground closed over them with a muted sigh, as if the land itself sought to forget.

A little further on, the Bereth watched in quiet astonishment as a pair of young girls — flaxen-haired, no older than ten — guided a tree-ent. Its roots churned the ground, overturning blood and ash until the battlefield looked like winter field again.

For long moments Allanagh could not name the disquiet prickling her skin. Then she realized — the girls were twins. For an instant she wondered if she had stumbled on dryads in disguise.

Her nerves tightened the closer they drew to the strange clearing. A guttural tongue, harsh and dissonant, carried through the smoke. She stilled her guards with a raised hand. Ahead, two armored giants hefted sacks of plunder as if they were feathers.

When one unlatched his helm, Allanagh felt her blood run cold. Black eyes glared out from a face too perfect, too cruel. An Infernal. She shrank back unconsciously toward Sloan, pulse drumming so hard she thought the soldier might hear it.

The Infernal′s gaze swept her way, and for a heartbeat she feared it could.

Beside her, Flur stared with unguarded wonder. "Mathair... I have never heard of Muinntir an Dorchadais [5]serving a draoidh."

Allanagh′s throat tightened. The words of caution rose to her lips, and she nearly ordered her daughter back with an escort. But memory stilled her:

Flur had already walked among these strangers, binding wounds and offering Saorsa′s grace.

"Please, Mathair," her daughter whispered, almost a prayer. "Let me not be wrong."

---

[5] People of the Darkness

The tips of Allanagh′s ears twitched at a soft chuff. She spun, fight-or-flight seizing her body, only to find a massive gray wolf standing behind them. Taller at the shoulder than any mount she had ever seen, its muzzle lifted, breath steaming in the night air.

"By the Mother..." Flur breathed, awe filling her voice. "Never have I seen a wolf so great."

Allanagh blinked. The beast′s jowls curled in what looked almost like a grin before it turned and padded forward, glancing back once as though beckoning. With dread pooling in her gut, Allanagh followed.

The hum reached her first — a low, bone-deep thrum that rose from the earth itself, vibrating through her soles.

The clearing yawned before them, and unease flooded her chest. It felt less like entering ground than trespassing upon a shrine.

Two more Infernals loomed in plate to her left. Wolves ringed the opposite side, their eyes glinting in the firelight. Between them stood a man, cloak rippling like water across stone, his stance as fluid and wary as the great wolf they had tracked. For a heartbeat she thought man and beast shared the same eyes.

A woman leaned close to him, whispering at his ear. Allanagh's breath caught. She had never seen such beauty. Tall and lithe, her curves carried like a weapon, her braids of fire-red hair tumbling nearly to her waist.

No armor shielded her, only a loose blouse and leather skirt — and yet it was her presence, not steel, that disarmed.

Green eyes lifted and found Allanagh′s. They sparkled, alive with knowing. She whispered something to the man beside her, and the spell rippled outward.

Sloan gasped audibly, shaking his head as if to clear it. The soldiers with them fixed their gazes on the red-haired woman, rapt as moths to flame.

Allanagh swallowed hard. The truth struck her like a blow. Sealgair Aisling — Dream-Huntress. Her unearthly beauty was no mortal gift. And for the first time since the battle ended, Allanagh feared she had doomed her people by consorting with these strangers.

"Be at peace, daughter of the forest." She heard behind her. "Nobody here will harm you or your people."

Another voice agreed. "You're where you belong."

When she felt two different hands rest on her shoulders and the peace of the gods flowed through her, stilling her racing heart, she slowly turned to find two women watching her.

The one on her right was wearing a green tunic with intricate brown and red spirals that adorned the loose collar and continued down the long sleeves. One large silver and gold spiral curled around her stomach and under her breasts.

She wore a knee-length teal skirt loosely wrapped around her hips, and her brown moccasins were of the finest elk hide, or so Allanagh gathered.  Her light brown hair framed her face in soft ringlets.

The one on her left was wearing a red silk tunic that fell to rest just above her knees.  Her auburn hair flowed over her shoulders and pooled down the center of her back while curling around to caress the underside of her generous bosom.  A silver choker adorned her throat, silver bracelets her wrists, and silver anklets drew attention to her bare feet.

Allanagh took a calming breath. "Lady Lilly, Sister Analise."  A cold chill inched its way down her spine.  "Why are you here?"

The brown-haired woman smiled. "The stars spoke of this moment. We chose to come and observe."

Allanagh almost fell to her knees as something flickered in the corner of her eye, and she glanced over to see two men standing directly opposite the horned hulks.

A six-and-a-half-foot giant, red-haired and green-eyed, watched the contest. The chain mail he wore over his gambeson caught the light as he listened to his companion.

His companion was shorter by a head and not nearly as muscular. His black hair barely crept out from under the wide-brimmed hat he wore.

Unlike his armored friend, he wore a white long-sleeved shirt, brown pants, and brown boots under a leather duster. He fixed his single, golden-tinged eye on the scene before him.

"Are they?"

"Aodh and Rennar, yes." Allanagh could feel the taghta's contentment.

Allanagh took a deep breath. "How close did we come to disaster?"

Lilly made a calming sound, drawing attention to her shirt's intricate spirals. "The moment approaches."

Up close, tree limbs and vines held the giant beast in place. It was at least nine feet tall, heavily muscled, and heavily furred, with huge tusks draping over a jaw that looked like it could grind bones to dust.

"What in the world is that thing?" She whimpered.  She would gladly take her daughter if she could disappear into thin air.

"It's called an Ogren." Lilly shivered in disgust.

A calm voice rose above the hum, distracting her from the monster.

"What brings you into our lands?" The man asked the Ogren.  A flat-brimmed black hat rested atop the head of white hair that fell about his shoulders.

From the neck down, he wore a black leather duster that almost hid the tops of his black leather boots.

"Am following my nature."  The Ogren tried to fight against the vines holding him in place.  "The strong prey on the weak.  Planned to destroy this place and make the Hîn i-Balanath Bereth and her people slaves."

Allanagh looked at the man. He towered over her by a head. His well-kept beard and mustache were as white as his hair. His face was careworn and ageless. She wondered how that could be so. His eyes hazel flecked with gold, caught her attention.

He looked at the Ogren. "So much for well laid plans."

The Ogren strained against the vines that entrapped it. "You were acting on your nature, the strong protecting the weak. There is no dishonor in failing."

Those hazel eyes pierced into the Ogren. "Who sent you?"

"Not telling." The Ogren growled as it strained to pull its arms down.

The man watched the Ogren's muscles knot. His right eyebrow arched slightly.

Without looking away from the beast, his left hand moved from the middle of the black wooden mage-staff to a spot eight inches higher, where he traced his fingers across a silver rune carved into the wood. "You can't, or you won't?"

He inquired as he reached into the right pocket of the duster and withdrew a gray seed, which he flicked onto the ground beneath the Ogren.

Magic flowed from staff to earth, transforming the numbing hum into a single pure note; A vine then spiraled, coiling around Ogren like a snake, stopping beneath his nose.

As Allanagh watched, it formed a violet flower and released a spray of pollen.

The Ogren instinctively drew in a deep breath, his face growing slack as the pollen made him more susceptible to interrogation.  The beast growled under its breath, hesitated, then opened its eyes. "Cannot."  As the two spells deepened their hold on him, the Ogren relaxed into the grip of the vines and branches.

"He will throw me from the great wheel if I tell."

A look of revulsion crossed his face; he recoiled. "That's not possible." The draoidh wanted to spit the foul taste out of his mouth. "Only Mathair Astinmah can deny people rebirth. I can name on one hand those she's refused."

"I just tried to versklaven [6]a village of her chosen children."

The man shook his head. "You were following your nature. Astinmah won't deny you rebirth because of it."

The beast tried to reach up, and when he couldn't, he growled in annoyance. "Your word on it, Maighstir Draoidh?"

---

[6] enslave

As the beast attempted to make its bargain, one of the Hîn i-Balanath dryads at the edge of the clearing changed. She grew almost two feet taller, and her lightly tanned skin deepened to a deep chocolate brown. Her teenage-looking body slowly matured into a lush, ripe woman with medium-sized breasts, wide hips, and long black hair with streaks of gray.
Her once-brown eyes changed to a startling vivid green.

Her twin watched the transformation, eyes wide in awe.  When the change was complete, she fell to her knees before the older dryad, who winked at her, before raising her right hand, making a swirling motion with her wrist.  Off to the east, storm clouds gathered, grew heavy with rain, and started drifting towards the fort-city.

One by one, everyone around the clearing noted the transformed woman, starting with the taghta nan diathan[7], those whom the gods had chosen as servants. Each sampled her prana and guessed her divinity.

The four sank to one knee before the forest goddess's avatar. The goddess's approach to the clearing's center held everyone's attention, save for the man and Ogren. She stopped at a respectable distance from the two and patiently waited for the staff bearer to decide.

Despite her role, she respected her servants' decisions.

The man briefly observed the Ogren, then nodded. "You have my word,

---

[7] the chosen of the gods

47

Mathair Astinmah shall not deny either you or the Orcan rebirth."

The beast sighed in relief.  "May I ask one more thing before I give the name?" Following a nod, the Ogren inquired, "May this one know who defeated him?"

Hazel eyes met Black.  "I am Rhyslin Darkblade."

The goddess glanced skyward, willing the clouds to stream overhead, blotting out the sun.

Taking a deep breath, Ogren stated, "I' ve heard of you, but never expected to fight you. The one you seek is Saldren Halber Drache."  The beast offered with its last breath.

The goddess nodded and snapped her fingers, willing the storm to hit with all the ferocity of a wild beast.

Rhyslin exhaled and turned to the brown-haired man and his woman. "Marc, would you and Nat please bury him with honor?" The ranger nodded. Rhyslin let go of the spell he'd sustained and managed only two steps before he collapsed.

He would have fallen if the goddess hadn't caught him on a cushion of air. The staff hung there for a glorious moment before it fell earthward, the goddess catching his staff before it hit the ground.

Once in her hand, the staff hummed like a child singing to its mother. The goddess responded in song, then addressed the others.

"Take him to Allanagh's cottage
and make him comfortable." The goddess
commanded, handing the unconscious man
off to the younger dryad.

Hearing that, Flur's ears pricked;
She immediately went to the dryad. "I'll
show you where to go."

"Just a moment, child." the goddess
brushed her fingertips across Rhyslin's
forehead, easing the pain on his
unconscious face.

"Thank you, my child." She
caressed Flur's right cheek, drawing a
timid smile from the woman.

Flur and the Dryad removed the
Draoidh from the battlefield.

Dismissing them, the goddess instructed Renner and Aodh, "Go tell Quetzalcoatl and Huitzilopochtli what happened here."

The two taghta nodded, vanishing into the shadows as they followed her command.

The goddess faced the ranger and Sealgair Aisling. "Seann Mdadadh-Allaidh, Neach Slanachaidh Bruadar." She formally addressed Marcus and Natolie by their titles. "Gather your troops and move them inside the walls. The Clann an-Coille will host them in the barracks."

The ranger bowed his head. "As you wish, Mathair." He gestured to one of the hulking Infernals, who lifted a brass trumpet and blew three sharp notes.

All around them, the black-garbed mercenaries gathered their kits and headed toward the sound of the horn.  When the soldiers stood in a loose formation behind the ranger, the goddess gestured to Sloan and Allanagh′s guard.  "They′ll ensure your comfort."

When neither Sloan nor the queen′s guard made a move, the goddess looked them over.

Seeing Sloan′s look of concern, Astinmah nodded in understanding. "Zered Sloan, I need to speak to my daughter alone. Will you entrust me with keeping her safe?"

"Where her life is concerned, I trust very few, be they gods or men."

The soldier eyed the goddess as he took a half-step toward Allanagh, stopping only when she whispered.

"I'll be okay, Sloan.  Just do it."

The soldier faced the goddess, choosing to obey Allanagh.  "Yes, Bereth nin."  Turning to the ranger, he examined him from head to foot.

With his eyes fixed on the knotted red cord at the man's right shoulder, he offered a salute, placing his fist over his heart and extending it.  "First Spear?"

"Ranger Commander, actually."  Marcus offered his hand.  "You can call me Marcus."

Sloan blinked at the implied informality. "Marcus ... Ranger Commander. If your men will follow us, we'll find space in the barracks for you."

"Lead on, my friend." The ranger commented as he followed Sloan. Natoli followed him, stopping as the goddess lifted a hand.

"Natoli, would you stay a moment?" As the Sealgair Aisling lifted a brow, the goddess continued her explanation. "The five of us have something important to discuss." She gestured to the two remaining taghta. First, she looked at Allanagh. The Hîn i-Balanath queen was still on her knees at the goddesses' feet, her head bowed, and her face hidden beneath her long silver hair.

"Rise, my daughter."

Allanagh looked up from the ground, her right hand moving up to tuck her silver hair behind her. "Is what the Ogren said true? Did the Ogren tell the truth about enslaving us?"

Allanagh felt the goddess's hand on her head. "Yes, I believe the war-band was sent to attack this village and enslave your people." Watching for Allanagh's reaction, the goddess posed a question. "Would your soldiers have succeeded in protecting the town and keeping you safe?"

"No." Allan admitted with a shake of her head. "The scouts did not show any Orcan within four leagues. We wouldn't have known about them until they were at the wall."

She paused and looked at the goddess. "Were you aware of their plans to attack?"

The goddess shook her head. "Their intentions didn't disturb the balance. Their attack and your defense wouldn't have created an imbalance any more than their killing some of you while taking some of you as slaves." She gazed down at the queen and read the thoughts roiling in her mind. "And no, I didn't send the mercenaries to help you. They came on their own."

"Why would they do that?" Allanagh inquired as she slowly rose to her feet.

"You should ask them." The goddess replied, as she handed the six-foot-long ebon wood staff over to the queen. Allanagh scrutinized the staff for a moment.

Ten silver runes ran the length of the staff, and the black pearl at the head was perfectly formed, without a noticeable defect. Was the staff humming to her?

"I would, except that their leader has been hustled off to my cottage by my daughter and is probably tucked safely in her bed." Allanagh looked toward the town, wondering what Flur was doing.

"Don't worry overly much," the goddess stated. "Will Mayana and Ilyriatri come here if you ask them?"

Allanagh shrugged, "Probably."
Gazing into the goddesses' eyes, she felt a bit of peace return to her soul. "Telling them you, Lilly, and Ana are here would encourage them to travel more."

The goddess blinked once and looked toward the village. "Then do so." A tender smile crossed her lips. "Should you need any help opening portals, I'll apportion some power for you."

Allanagh noticed Astinmah's cryptic smile and followed the goddess's gaze toward the village. "Oh, my sweet Flur. What are you doing?" She prayed that her daughter was behaving herself.

# Chapter Two
## The Tribute of Flame and Shadow

For three days and nights, only the slow, measured rise and fall of Rhyslin's chest proved he still clung to the living world. Shadows stretched long across the chamber with each passing dusk, and the rafters seemed to hold their breath above him. Now and then the air shifted—pine and hearthsmoke when Astinmah passed through, the cool musk of damp moss when Allanagh came, or the soft chime of prana when one of the taghta brushed the threshold.

Flur never left his side for long.

Tonight, she sat by his pallet, her fingers damp with the chill cloth she had wrung into the waste bucket.

A faint tremor shivered through her hand as she touched the cool rag to his forehead, yet his skin seemed to warm beneath her care. The water dripped into the bowl with a hollow cadence, and with it came a prickle at her nape.

Something was moving in the shadows.

Her ears twitched, betraying her tension, though she pressed her breath low in her belly, forcing calm. Not for herself— for him. She smoothed the damp cloth over his brow, every motion measured, every nerve alert to the new presence edging near. The chamber's silence thickened as two women entered.

The first made her blink twice: Allanagh's likeness lived in her bones, yet younger, dusk-brown of skin, chestnut hair rippling like polished grain, and green eyes alive with scrutiny. The second shadow at her side moved softer than a leaf falling, blue eyes too keen for her tender years.

Their clothes set them apart—tan blouses, turquoise skirts brushing knee-high moccasins. No green and brown of the woodland queens. No comfort of the known.

Flur rose halfway, shielding Rhyslin with her body. "Aunt Ilyriatri?"

"Afternoon, Flur." The older woman's step was as light as pine-needles settling, her gaze fixed on the draoidh. "Is this the one?"

The younger halted at her mother's side, her voice like the hush before rainfall. "Yes, Mathair. That's him. Can you not feel it?"

Ilyriatri studied Rhyslin's chest, the shallow lift and fall. Her brow furrowed. "Odd. Is he the reason for our summons?"

Flur steadied herself. "Mathair Astinmah invited you and Aunt Mayana here to work on the treaty."

Her aunt's eyes narrowed, sharp as flint. "You shade the truth, Flur Rionnag Shoilleir. Garion Cridhe Leòmhann's disappointment would be heavy upon you." She paced a step, then turned, skirts brushing the stone.

"Why should Mathair Astinmah
have us yield our freedom to this Saor-
shealbhan nan Roaintean Mòra?"

"That is not what is asked." Flur's
hand lifted, palm trembling but open.
"Mathair Astinmah offers us free travel
through their land, the right to dwell and
work beside them without fear."

"We have always had these rights."
Ilyriatri's voice cut like a raven's cry.
"Our blood, first-born of the gods, grants
them!" She pressed her hand against her
own breast as though steadying her heart.
"Forgive me, Flur. These days have been
vexing, and the forest Mathair's riddles
are no balm. I mistrust this treaty. Perhaps
too much.

There is one clause I cannot bend my mind around—why speak again of tribute? We buried such things centuries ago."

A low chuckle broke Flur's lips before she thought better of it. Her fingertips brushed Rhyslin's white hair as if staking her claim in silence. "The tribute is me."

Ilyriatri blinked. "I do not understand."

"What's not to understand?" Flur's brow arched. "I will be the tribute."

Her aunt's voice softened with disbelief. "What could have driven Allanagh to consent?"

"Because I asked her to," Flur answered. She let her fingers coil a strand of his hair around her forefinger, unable to resist. "Look at him. He's not Fire-Borne, but his prana burns steady as a forge. Can you not feel it?"

Ilyriatri hesitated, lips parting. She reached out, and the air itself seemed to recoil—then shiver under the weight of the draoidh's dormant power.

The younger one spoke, eyes bright as mountain sky. "I can feel it. Though he sleeps, his prana runs deep and unbroken."

Ilyriatri's head snapped toward her. "Vuuroena, what are you doing?"

The girl lowered her lashes. "Even in his silence, his thoughts ripple. He is calm, like a deep lake." Her eyes opened again, piercing. "Are you going to bond with him, cousin?"

Flur paused, her breath catching. She hadn't framed it so bluntly, yet the truth shimmered in her chest. "If he'll have me. He's a draoidh. Beloved of Mathair Astinmah. I want to learn from him. To serve him." She lifted her gaze, golden hair falling across her shoulders like sunlight on water. "Please, Aunt, tell me you understand."

Ilyriatri's resistance faltered. She let her senses stretch and shivered as raw power swept through her, a force greater than Garion's, greater than any she had touched. Fear, awe, and hunger braided together until she drew her hand back.

Vuuroena whispered, fierce with longing. "I understand, cousin. I would bond with him in a heartbeat."

"No!" Ilyriatri's voice cracked, sharp as breaking wood. "You are too young. You will not."

The girl bowed her head. "You're right, Mathair. Not yet." The prophecy she carried pressed against her ribs, but she swallowed it down. She leaned close to the draoidh, breath warm against his ear.

"Please help me when I call." Her fingers brushed his brow with reverence before she stepped back.

She turned to Flur, her hand extended. "Farewell, cousin. I wish you joy."

Flur lingered by the bedside long after her kin departed, the hush of their footsteps still clinging to the air.

The chamber felt heavier for their absence, the silence pressing against her chest like the weight of an unasked question. She dipped the cloth once more, wrung it out with practiced motions, and brushed it across Rhyslin's brow. His skin was cool, his prana steady, but even that rhythm seemed fragile when measured against the storm she sensed gathering beyond these walls.

"Mixcoatl's Suilean!" Marcus's oath rasped into the stillness. The ranger staggered back, nearly colliding with the two women as they swept out into the hall. They brushed past him with hurried grace, skirts whispering like leaves in a desert wind.

Marcus retreated into shadow, the folds of his cloak swallowing him until he was part of the stone itself. He watched, ears keen, catching half-finished phrases and the quickened cadence of their voices. Concern laced their words, sharp as flint. Concern for Rhyslin. His brows drew together. Why are they so invested in him?

The two disappeared down the corridor, their footfalls dissolving into the hush of the stronghold. Marcus exhaled slowly, then turned back.

Inside, Flur sat where he had left her, her hand moving absently as she lifted the damp cloth from Rhyslin's forehead. She looked dazed, as if her thoughts lingered on another shore.

"How is he today, Princess Flur?" Marcus asked gently, stepping from the shadows.

Her head jerked up, a blush warming her cheeks before she mastered herself. "Um... still asleep. I hoped he would waken by now."

Marcus's gaze lingered on her for a heartbeat, then shifted to Rhyslin. Even unconscious, the draoidh's chest rose and fell in a rhythm that tugged at the air, each breath drawing shadows nearer before releasing them again.

"I hadn't realized how much power he carried," Marcus murmured, half to himself, remembering the interrogation of the Ogren. The memory coiled in his gut. "Enough to burn through a lesser man."

He shook himself, then changed tack. "We expect the Dawn-Breaker tomorrow morning. Will you be ready to leave?"

At his words, Rhyslin's breathing altered — from the slow tide of sleep to a quicker, shallower pull, as though his spirit strained toward wakefulness. Marcus stiffened, watching carefully.

Flur smiled faintly, smoothing Rhyslin's hair as if coaxing him to rest. "I only need to finish packing." She hesitated, then bent close, brushing her fingers across his brow.

"Do you think he will be angry when he sees me aboard his ship?"

Marcus's mouth curved wryly, though his thoughts did not match his expression. Anger? No. Confusion, certainly. Concern, yes. And when he learns his goddess-mother interfered again... betrayal.

But he only said, "No, not anger."

Flur brightened, her relief as clear as sunlight breaking frost, and left the room with quick, eager steps. Her presence carried warmth with it, leaving the chamber colder in her absence.

Marcus let his shoulders sag, retreating once more to lean against the wall. The stone seemed to drink his weariness, shadows gathering thick about him like old companions.

He reached into his pouch, fingers curling around the stem of his pipe.

The thought of Saorsa mint stirred a pang of longing, but the healers forbade it. He grunted and let it go. Patience was the only balm he was allowed.

And patience, at last, was rewarded. Hours later, a deeper breath stirred the stillness, followed by a groan of pain. The shadows shifted with it, as if the stronghold itself roused. Marcus straightened, all fatigue forgotten.

Rhyslin was waking.

Rhyslin lay still, breath shallow, letting strength pool back into his limbs. When at last he pressed his palms to the mattress and pushed, every muscle trembled as if reluctant to remember the art of rising.

His body leaned forward, elbows braced, head cupped in his hands. The room tilted, shadows sliding like water across the walls.

"That was strange," he muttered, rubbing his brow. "Why did the spell fight me?" His lashes fluttered; vision swam. The mattress sighed beneath him, warm but foreign. "This isn't the Dawn Breaker, is it?" Already the thrum of a familiar prana stirred at the edge of awareness, steady as a heartbeat.

From the corner, Marcus stepped out of the shadows. His cloak shifted with the light, shedding its darker hues until it rested in quiet browns and tans, as if the very fabric obeyed the room's warmth. "How are you feeling, Rhys?"

"I feel like Ifrinn's been gnawing at me," the draoidh groaned, fingers combing through silver hair. His gaze sharpened, suspicious. "You didn't answer. Why aren't we on board the Dawn Breaker, halfway home?"

Marcus shrugged, though his eyes betrayed hesitation. "Because the Dawn Breaker had to evade a storm."

Rhyslin blinked, confusion flashing across his features. "Storm? I remember no storm." His brow furrowed, memory clawing backward. "The sky was clear... too clear."

Marcus nodded grimly. "What's the last thing you do recall?"

"The Ogren." Rhyslin's voice darkened. "I tried to let go of the power... but it clung to me, fought me. Then—" a shiver of vertigo sent him gripping the bedframe, "—nothing. Until now. What happened?"

"Your mother showed up," Marcus said flatly.

Shock tightened Rhyslin's shoulders. "Astinmah? When?" The very air seemed to constrict, walls pressing closer. His prana shivered with unease.

"Midway through the interrogation," Marcus explained. "She took over the eldest dryad. Matured her."

Rhyslin's breath hitched, then softened. "Poor Keisha... gods help her."

"That's not your greatest worry," Marcus murmured. He listed the names one by one, each a stone dropped into Rhyslin's chest: Mayana. Lilly Ann. Analise. Natolie. "All sequestered with the two Hîn i-Balanath queens. Plotting something."

Rhyslin exhaled, a whisper of defeat. "Why does this feel like being led to the pyre?"

"Because even wise men dread when seven women weave," Marcus replied, placing a hand on his shoulder. His voice lowered. "The storm broke the instant you fell—your mother's doing. Came so fast, Captain O' Cuire had no choice but to run before it."

Rhyslin′s jaw tightened, but he nodded. "The ship comes first. Always. But without her guns…" He shook his head, resolve setting in. "It will be a hard road if she doesn′t return."

Marcus grunted, unwilling to argue. His gaze followed Rhyslin as the draoidh searched the room.

"Now, where′s my caretaker hidden my clothes?"

When Marcus sputtered, Rhyslin only smirked. "I was unconscious, Marcus, not dead. I felt her hands. Each touch. Each cloth laid across my brow." He paused, memory flickering—a whisper, soft as a prayer, breathed by a young, dark-haired hin i-Balanath into his ear.

"There." His garments lay folded neatly by the bedside. "Someone even cleaned them." He dressed with steady care, every motion accompanied by the creak of weary joints.

His gaze fell upon the staff leaning by the wall. A grunt, and he pushed himself upright, staggering forward. Pain lanced his knee; his ankle crackled in protest. "Hush," he muttered at his own body, blood roaring back into long-starved muscles. Step by step, the world steadied.

When his fingers at last closed around the staff, the wood thrummed to life. Images surged—Keisha's transformation, her first breath in a woman's form, the song of power binding flesh to spirit.

"Oh, I see." His lips curled. "Marcus, your words don't do her justice." The staff answered in a soft trill, vibration humming into his bones.

"So, you sang for her?" he asked gently.

Another ripple, tender, proud.

Rhyslin chuckled, forehead pressing briefly to the wood. "Aye. I would have praised her too."

After communing with the spirit in his staff, Rhyslin adjusted the brim of his hat. The air around him hummed faintly, as though the woodgrain itself still whispered secrets from the communion.

"Come on, Old Wolf," he murmured, the words lined with resignation. "Let's see what Mathair's up to."

Marcus fell into step beside him, lips quirking. "Still feel like a condemned man?"

"Without a doubt." Sunlight flared against Rhyslin's hat as he tipped it lower, though the staff tugged his hand to the right with gentle insistence. He followed its pull, boots crunching over snow-hardened ruts.

The streets were sodden with melt and shadow; the unnatural storm had left the air unsettled, heavy with iron. Rhyslin shook his head as if dismissing the very sky. "It will take months for the weather to right itself."

"Can you mend it?" Marcus asked, though he already knew the weight of the answer.

"With the proper ritual and enough voices, perhaps. But I won't unravel the skies just to soothe pride." A breath left him in a curl of frost. "I'm not a god."

"Are you sure?" Marcus' brow arched, voice sharp with mischief. "Your mother would argue otherwise."

"That's what she keeps telling me," Rhyslin sighed, rolling his eyes, though a shiver of unease coiled in his chest.

They needled each other with barbs until they reached a three-story brick hall, its stained glass windows ablaze with green forest light.

Vines curled where no vine had been planted, and for a moment Rhyslin felt Astinmah's eyes on the back of his neck.

"This must be the place." He reached for the door—only for it to swing open on its own breath.

"You are up," a voice said.

A young Hîn i-Balanath woman stepped out, placing herself firmly between him and the threshold. Her presence pulled the air taut. She was youth still tempered with steel: black braid over her shoulder, desert-dyed leathers clinging to her frame, the scent of sun-baked sand carried in with her. One hand fell, steady as ritual, to the hilt of her sword.

Marcus stilled, shadow-sharp, watching.

Rhyslin met her gaze, noting the spark of resolve. A small smile touched her lips. "Why are you here, aon socair?"

The title washed over him, settling like cool water through his chest. Calm one. Very well, if calm was what she demanded, calm she would be given.

"I am here to see Mathair Astinmah," he answered, grounding his tone until it matched the steady weight of stone.

"She is here," the girl admitted, blue eyes glittering, "but you may not enter unless you pass me."

Marcus only shrugged, wolf-grin tugging at the corner of his mouth. Let's see where this goes.

Rhyslin felt draoidheachd coil around him like hounds straining on a leash. The shadows reached for his fingers; the trees beyond the street rustled though no wind stirred. He centered himself with a breath, tracing a grounding rune into the staff until the world stilled. "Before we begin," he said, voice steady as a river stone, "may I have your name?"

She dipped her head with a dancer's grace. "Vuuroena Seilmatt, daughter of Bereth Ilyriatri of Clann an Fhàsaich."

"Very well, Vuuroena Seilmatt, Guardian of this hall. First touch, or first blood?" His stance mirrored hers, staff angled like a blade, body braced in patience.

"To first touch. The Forest Mother would be angry if I broke you further." A half-curtsy flashed like a knife's smile.

"So be it."

He sketched a rune, and the ground answered. Shadows curled upward, fingers grasping for her ankle. She leapt, blade flashing, severing the darkness. The cut bled light into the snow.

"Dall!" she cried, brilliance bursting around her. He blinked, barely sparing himself, staff already rising as her point drove toward his chest.

He caught her blade under his arm, fingers closing warm and inexorable around her hand.

Her breath caught. She looked for a victor's grin, but found only the deep, icy calm of his hazel eyes. Prana coiled through her, her ears burning scarlet. Lasadh. Her sword blazed with heat, pressing against his ribs until he hissed and freed her.

"Reothadh." His voice dropped to winter's pitch. Frost spidered across her fingers and hilt. She yanked free with a cry, flexing stiffened hands, fury flushing her cheeks.

"What you are doing is not fair," she growled, circling back with a predator's grace.

"Life is seldom fair." His staff remained upright though his hands fell away, standing sentinel in defiance of gravity. Draoidheachd shivered in the air like the promise of thunder. "Pain will find us whether we choose it or not. We walk into it because we must. And when we cry out, our Mother will hear." His eyes pierced hers. "Astinmah will save you."

Her throat tightened. For an instant she swore he had glimpsed her dreams. Tears burned unbidden. When her sight cleared, he was there—so close his prana wrapped her in glacial calm. His hand rested lightly atop her head, fingers threading her hair.

"What do you know of Despoina's prophecies?" she whispered, her blade lowering. Her head bowed until it touched his chest, heartbeat steady beneath her cheek.

"Only what she shares," he admitted, voice a warm hush. His palm settled between her shoulder blades.

She trembled when his lips brushed the curve of her ear. "I'm scared."

"I know." His prana enfolded her, an embrace of winter stillness. She breathed it in, drinking calm until she steadied. Her hand rose, resting over his heart. His soul answered, vow written in its pulse.

"If I ask, will you save me?"

"If I can, I will." His words rang like iron, carrying truth into the marrow of the air.

At last, she stepped back. The blade slid into its sheath with a whisper. "Come with me. I'll lead you to the council chamber."

Marcus rejoined them, his eyes bright with things unspoken. He lifted the ebonwood staff and passed it back to Rhyslin. The draoidh's hand closed around it, weight and world settling into place.

*Chapter Three*
Tribute and Treaty Beneath the Ubhal

Upon entering, he stood at the entrance of a beautiful rotunda. Tilting his head back and looking up, he took a few minutes to examine the granite and glass dome that covered the four-square-acre garden. Light spilled through the panes in fractured beams, gilding the air with dust motes that danced like fireflies. The ancient ubhal tree intersected four equal quarters of the indoor garden, its roots swelling from the ground like the backs of slumbering beasts.

The ground cover was short grass, cool and damp underfoot, with flower beds interspersed throughout the space.

Subtle shifts of air carried layered fragrances—earth loam, rainwater clinging to petals, and the sharp sweetness of Rosan blooms. At four points equidistant from the ancient tree, the enterprising Hîn i-Balanath had planted smaller ubhal trees whose crowns tilted inward, as though bowing to the elder.

"The council chamber is this way." Vuuroena led them toward the ancient tree. Rhyslin could sense the sleeping dryad that lived therein, her slumber a soft hum beneath the bark, and suspected who had been tending the lovely garden.

Rhyslin took a deep breath and savored the scent of the well-tended Rosan bushes as they passed by. A gentle tremor in the air sent several blossoms opening wider as though to greet him.

Rhyslin brushed his fingers across the coarse bark of the tree trunk, circling the ancient tree, complete with the crafted wooden benches. Somewhere above him, a gentle sigh reached his ears, causing him to pause as dainty hands clasped around his, and a vine descended to snatch his hat.

"Greetings to thee, Mac Draoidheacd." The dryad squeezed his hand, her fingers curling under his palm. The bark around her pulse point warmed at his touch, tiny motes of light seeping from her skin into his. "You honour me with your presence." Her sultry voice would have sent tingles down the spine of a lesser man. Rhyslin knew how to handle dryads and had known since he was a child, growing up in Astinmah's grove.

Rhyslin returned the affection as he turned and looked up to where a busty red-headed dryad with cat's ears was leaning halfway out of her tree with his hat perched atop the wild curls. The glass dome overhead caught the flare of her hair, scattering red-gold across the rotunda like sparks.

"Oh, sweet tree maiden." He bowed at the waist, his free hand sweeping out to the side in an exaggerated court bow. Earthly royalty would have snickered behind their hands at his display. "How are you doing on this fine day?"

Vuuroena watched as the dryad accepted the bow at face value. "I am well." She nodded. "The Spréotha Daraen have built a wondrous enclosure for Dearg's grove."

She withdrew one hand from Rhyslin's and gestured all around her. The Rosan bushes seemed to exhale at her words, sending a ripple of fragrance outward.

Rhyslin turned in a circle, never letting go of the dryad's hand. "They have provided you with a Coille-Shìtheil." Turning back to the dryad, he rested the living staff on his left shoulder and reached up to retrieve his hat from her.

The busty dryad giggled as she leaned back out of his reach. Her laugh sent a rustle through the smaller ubhal trees, as though the grove itself enjoyed her play. "Dearg likes this hat." She used her free hand to push the Rhyslin away. "Do you think it looks good on me?"

She gave him a brazen smile as she puffed out her chest, emphasizing her ample endowments.

Vuuroena watched as Rhyslin continued to play the dryad's game. She couldn't believe that a nature spirit could be earthy and full of life.

"Yes, it looks good on you." Rhyslin allowed it, playing along with the flame-haired cat girl.  Then, Rhyslin turned the tables on the cat-eared dryad. "It's just such a shame, though." His words brushed the air like a cold current in warm water.

The dryad's eyes widened in surprise, and she leaned toward him as she watched his face. A Rosan blossom dropped a petal at their feet. "What is wrong with Dearg?"

She watched his jovial smile fade into a frown. "Mac Draoidheacd. Why are you sad?"

Rhyslin had set his trap, and the dryad had willingly stepped into it. The draoidh reached up and caught a lock of Dearg's lustrous red hair that had fallen from under the hat. The air pulsed faintly with heat as though the dome trapped summer inside. "My hat does look good on you, but it covers your magnificent hair."

Vuuroena watched as the dryad became putty in Rhyslin's hands, delighting in the feelings as he traced a strand of hair and tucked it behind her ear.

"Oh, Mac Draoidheacd, that feels so good." Her eyes closed as he cupped her cheek, and the grass beneath their feet shivered. "Dearg was resting when Mara-Astan graced us with her presence." Like Rhyslin, Dearg could set traps for her prey. She opened her eyelids to reveal liquid green eyes, which she batted at him. "May I go with you and meet her?"

Rhyslin used his thumb to wipe away a trace of the moisture around the dryad's left eye. His touch left a faint glow that sank into her skin like sunlight into leaves. "I would be delighted to take you to Mara-Astan. It will be the highlight of her day." The draoidh took a step back, watching as she stepped out of the tree and stood beside him.

Vuuroena couldn′t believe that the busy dryad only stood as tall as Rhyslin′s shoulder. The glass dome above them gleamed brighter, as though the hall itself approved her choice.

"Thank you, Mac Draoidheacd." Dearg handed Rhyslin′s hat back with a small bow. "I will be as silent as a dealan-dé."

The faint brush of wings whispered overhead, unseen, as though the promise had already taken root. A cool ripple of air stirred through the rotunda, carrying the resinous tang of ubhal bark and the sweeter breath of Rosan blossoms.

The dryad′s gaze slid from Rhyslin to Vuuroena, green eyes tracing every stitch of the young woman′s dress.

"Dearg thinks she must change her appearance." She circled Vuuroena with a feline grace, her bare feet brushing soft grass, fingertips prodding at seams, tugging at fabric as though testing its worth.

When her inspection ended, Dearg returned to Rhyslin's side. Her leaves rustled like sighing branches as they shifted—broadening over her chest into a short, low-cut blouse that left shoulders and stomach bare, narrowing below into a skirt of green fire that hugged her hips and rode high above her knees.

She tilted her head toward him, expectant, the scent of crushed leaves sharp in the air. "How do I look, Mac Draoidheacd?"

Rhyslin's gaze softened as he watched her pirouette, sunlight catching fire in her auburn curls. "You look as lovely as the fruits of your tree."

The dryad's face lit with joy, a blush of rose across her bark-pale cheeks. "Mathair will be pleased."

Vuuroena froze mid-step. A gasp slipped from her lips as color flared over her skin. Rhyslin turned at once, one eyebrow arched, curiosity alive in the air between them. "What is it, young one?"

Her hand fluttered upward, tugging her raven hair across her shoulder as though it could shield her face. "She's... well, her clothes are... very revealing." The blush deepened, and with it came a heat that seemed to press outward, rippling through the garden.

Rhyslin only smiled, his tone light as falling snow. "You must not spend much time around dryads."

Dearg giggled, leaves trembling—but her mirth stilled the instant Rhyslin lifted his left hand. The garden hushed with him. The dryad's shoulders curved inward; bark-colored lashes lowered. "I'm sorry." She bowed her head, contrite, the grass at her feet curling in sympathy.

Both men's attention slid back to Vuuroena. Her blush burned darker, her voice tentative. "There are very few trees where I come from." Her eyes caught the pond nearby, reflecting blue fire from its rippling surface. "Before coming here, I had never seen a dryad."

Her words carried the faint rasp of sand swept across stone. "The only spirits I knew lived under the desert—sand-walkers, hiding all day, covered head to toe even at night. A sand-walker would never be seen like this."

Rhyslin and Marcus exchanged a knowing glance. They had walked those deserts, felt that same barren silence. They nodded, their agreement grounding her confession.

"Dryads seldom conceal themselves," Rhyslin explained. He gestured to Dearg, whose leafy garb still shimmered faintly with light. "They reveal their bodies as thanks to Mara-Astan—for their lives and for their trees."

He pressed one hand over his heart, the other rising skyward, prana stirring like breath through the branches.

Vuuroena inclined her head in acknowledgment, though her cheeks still burned.

Dearg had lived her whole life in the forest, with water flowing freely, shade abundant. The girl's words struck her like drought. Her eyes widened. "A place with no trees?" She staggered back against her trunk, vines quivering as though stricken. "Oh, poor little one. I am so sorry."

Sorrow spilled from her in waves; the garden itself seemed to sag. She darted to Vuuroena and enfolded her in an embrace, leaves brushing against silk, sap-scent and moss enveloping desert-dry linen.

Vuuroena stiffened, helpless, her arms pinned to her sides. She shot Rhyslin a look, her eyes begging rescue.

The draoidh took pity. Stepping forward, he wove his fingers gently through Dearg's auburn hair, grounding her. "That's enough, Sweet Dearg."

The dryad released Vuuroena with a breathy sigh, bowing her head. "Yes, Mac Draoidheacd." She pressed closer to his side, smiling when he slipped an arm lightly around her waist. The ubhal tree above them released a contented rustle, approving.

"Come along, Dearg," Rhyslin coaxed. "Mara-Astan is waiting."

Vuuroena exhaled in relief and turned quickly, leading them on toward the council chamber. The dryad followed with lingering glances, green eyes mournful. "Do you think Mara-Astan knows about the treeless wastes?"

---

"Are we going inside, Mac Draoidheacd?" Dearg tugged on Rhyslin's duster as she watched Vuuroena.

The young spellblade stood in front of a plain wooden door, beyond which lay the council chamber. She stared at the door, wondering what her mother would think when she escorted the draoidh inside.

The oak grain seemed to waver in the torchlight, as if listening to her hesitation, the iron bands humming faintly with the weight of what lay beyond.

Rhyslin watched her for a few minutes before moving up behind her. "If you would like, we can enter without you." He was perfectly willing to wait as long as it took for her to work up her courage. The air about him stirred, prana faint as a slow tide, brushing the stone walls until moss curled toward him.

Vuuroena started as she felt his hand on her shoulder. "No. I am just ..." She didn't want to admit that she worried about how her mother would react. She had always worked hard to get her people to notice her as something more than just a girl who wanted to play with swords.

It had taken her learning how to be a spellblade to get her people to take her seriously. Her breath came shallow, the candle nearest the door guttering with each exhale.

Sensing Vuuroena's fear, Rhyslin leaned forward, resting one hand on her shoulder. "Fear is the mist before the dawn. It blurs, it bites, but it fades. Let it wash over skin and sinew. Let it pass, unheld. When it falls away, thought awakens, and calm stands in its place." His words seemed to draw the smoke in the sconces into stillness, the air pausing with him, waiting.

Vuuroena's brow furrowed as she listened to him. She wasn't sure that leading him into the council chamber was her biggest fear, but it came close.

Not only was her mother in there, but so were her aunts, both Allanagh, the one she'd met, and Mayana, the one she had only heard her mother talk about. If it were just the three of them, she wouldn't mind being seen as a worried child, but Astinmah, the forest goddess, was present as well. Her fear receded as she took a slow, deep breath and released it. The prana about her steadied, shadows drawing back from her face. She nuzzled her cheek against his knuckles. "Thank you, mo aon socair."

At her slight nod, Rhyslin withdrew his hand and watched as she opened the door and walked inside. The hinges creaked like old voices, the rush of warm air carrying the scent of resin and hearth smoke.

He had only known Vuuroena for a short while, but she had already impressed him. Not many young soldiers would challenge him to a duel. There weren't many spell blades that had her raw talent for draoidheacd. He gave her a few minutes to notify the women of his presence outside. She must have told them he was outside because when he entered the council chamber, he found the eight women staring at him. The chamber itself fell quiet, fire snapping once before dimming, as though testing his resolve.

Vuuroena stood in front of her mother with her head bowed.

Ilyriatri finished her conversation with Vuuroena and looked up to find Rhyslin standing there.

She gazed at him for a moment before taking her daughter's hand and pulling her back behind her.

Natolie saw Rhyslin's expression, then looked Marcus's way. Seeing the slight frown on his face, she lowered her head, a blush spotting her cheeks as she hurried to his side and dropped to her knees. Her movement stirred the rush mats beneath her, the whisper of reed on stone loud in the still air.

Allanagh blanched and slipped out of Rhyslin's line of sight. She was still raw from the Orcan raid, and she couldn't tell if his silence meant anger. The chill of his prana ghosted over her skin, making her shiver—it stirred a memory of Garion's quiet disappointment.

A knot of unease formed in her chest, the creeping sense that she'd done something wrong. Flur stiffened as well, the fine hairs at her nape rising with the same unspoken fear. The flames of the chamber hearth bent low, smoke curling toward the floor. In the span of a breath, she felt it—the sharp, helpless fear of prey caught in a predator's stare.

"No!" Allanagh tried to draw Rhyslin's attention back to her and away from her daughter. "Please, Mac Draoidheacd, don't hurt Flur. She — She — " She almost knelt as his eyes settled on her.

"I will not hurt women without due cause. Especially not one who watched over me for three days." Rhyslin's voice held disappointment and contained anger.

Without looking away from the Hîn i-Balanath queen, he spoke to Flur. "Go, stand by your mathair." The golden-haired princess nodded, shaken, and moved to stand behind Allanagh. Her skirts brushed the flagstones, the faint static crackle of prana clinging to her hems.

Sensing furtive movement to his right, he looked over his shoulder and frowned at Lilly and Ana. "Have a seat." Both froze, heads bowed, hands crossed over their chests. "When I'm through with whatever this is, we will discuss the proper roles of the chosen." From his tone, they could tell that they'd stepped beyond their obligations.

"Of course, Mac Draoidheacd, it shall be as you wish." The hearth-maiden of hearth-maidens turned to face him, cringing under his prana. The glow of the chamber lamps dimmed further, her shadow lengthening across the wall like a bent reed.

The bound taghta, on the other hand, scurried and knelt before him, her knees parted, her head bowed. "Forgiveness, please. Mac Draoidheacd." Her jewelry chimed as she fidgeted, each metallic note sharp in the silence, as if the chamber itself scolded her.

Catching sight of a familiar face, he ignored the taghta. "Mayana. Don't tell me you're part of this travesty."

The red-haired Queen of the mountain Hîn i-Balanath offered him a weak grin as she spread her arms out toward the others. "I had no choice, my protector. Mathair Astinmah summoned me." Mayana had come to him months earlier, requesting aid and protection from the strange people on the other side of the mountains. People, she said, wanted to invade her lands and enslave her people.

"I see." Rhyslin strode into the center of the chamber. The rushes underfoot rustled, the air parting like a tide around him. "At least tell me that you attempted to dissuade them from this foolishness."

Mayana's strained smile provided the answer he expected. She had tried, and failed.

Rhyslin turned from Mayana as he caught movement from his right side. "Don' t even think it, Mathair." He finished the turn, watching the goddess' s raised hand.

Astinmah, the forest goddess, Mara-Astan, daughter of Eru, caught in the act of tracing a rune in the air, looked embarrassed. The light of the torches bent toward her fingers, eager to obey, before she stilled them.

Rhyslin walked toward her, his mouth straight, determination in his voice. "Why do you seek to work behind my back?" It hurt him not to praise her, but she needed to know how much her attempt would cost her, both in his pain and trust. He could tell that she felt it keenly because she bowed her head in shame.

A breeze that smelled faintly of pine swept through, then faltered, as though the forest itself winced.

"I want what is best for you, my son." She always had, and Rhyslin appreciated her for it. As usual, she had taken over a situation she knew nothing about, and turned it to her own purpose, namely finding him a mate.

"Maybe what is best for me is —" The thought crossed his mind, but remained unsaid. He held his tongue until his anger faded away, leaving only the ever-present disappointment. The weight in the room lightened, the hearth flame rising as if relieved.

Rhyslin distracted himself by picking up a piece of parchment and reading it. The crackle of vellum was loud as thunder in the silence.

As he read, one brow rose—then the other. The fire crackled unevenly, a log splitting with a pop that made the shadows leap against the council chamber walls. "I'm – confused." His voice was low, strained. He read it a second time, though the parchment seemed to blur as though resisting his comprehension. The inked letters swam; the words refused to take root. He still couldn't grasp what he read. He glanced over at Marcus. "Didn't we wipe out an Orcan war-band?"

"Yes, why?" Marcus leaned in, the leather of his jerkin creaking as he reached for the pages. The shadows clung to him, as if his cloak wove him deeper into the wall.

"Because according to this" Rhyslin tapped the parchment, the sound echoing sharp in the stillness "the Hîn i-Balanath have surrendered to the Saor-Shealbhan and are offering me tribute." The air in the room thickened, as though the walls themselves held their breath. Rhyslin handed Marcus the document and pressed his fingers to his brow, pain flaring behind his eyes like a furnace banked too long.

When he read what the tribute was, he shook his head. A whisper of cold swept the chamber, lifting the edge of his sleeve.

How did they ever expect him to choose one woman from among many? The weight of it pressed against his temples, as though unseen hands tugged at him from every side. He massaged the spot between his eyes with the heel of his palm until the pain receded to a dull throb.

"This will never do." The quill in his hand trembled as if sensing his unrest. He reached into his bag, fingers brushing parchment that smelled faintly of cedar smoke and old ink. When he found it, he spread the sheets out on the table. The lamplight gleamed off the fresh vellum, promising clarity. "Shall we try again?"

The three women leaned toward each other, their voices weaving into a hushed chord. Their bracelets chimed softly, like the distant tinkle of river ice.

When they nodded, he said, "I want to rewrite this so that it makes sense." He gestured to the three Hîn i-Balanath queens and then pointed at the table. "Ladies, please have a seat and make yourselves comfortable."

He reached for a chair and sank into it. The wooden legs groaned as though under the weight of more than one man's burdens. The three women gazed at Astinmah before seating themselves opposite Rhyslin. For a moment, Flur and Vuuroena hovered, uncertain, the air thick with indecision. The hearth popped again, as though impatient. After exchanging glances, they settled with their mothers, roots drawing them back to their lineage.

Astinmah looked up at Rhyslin, and her heart went out to him. She saw the source of his pain and how it rippled outward into the chamber. She saw the tightness in his muscles, the tremor of his hand as it gripped the quill. A faint shimmer of light gathered at her shoulders, restrained divinity pressing against the mortal air. "Where would you like me to sit?"

Rhyslin fought the desire to grumble and covered his right eye with the palm of his hand. The vein behind it throbbed like a drumbeat, the firelight swimming red at the edges of his vision. "Honestly?" He threw it out as a peace offering.

Astinmah accepted, her breath releasing the faintest scent of myrrh into the room, hoping he would forgive her. "Yes, my son. I will sit where you wish."

Rhyslin eyed her, saw the sorrow that softened her divinity, and took her at her word. "I would like you to go sit under Dearg's tree. She wants to spend time with you."

Astinmah gazed at him for a minute, then nodded. Her light dimmed, gentling to mortal hues. She rose from her seat and held out her hand to the dryad. "Come, little one."

Dearg jumped up, her leaves rustling faintly, and took her goddess's hand before dragging her toward the door.

Rhyslin stopped them before they crossed the threshold. "Mathair, please let me take care of this first. I promise I'll talk to you after I'm through."

"Very well." Her voice was like velvet stretched thin. She wished she could help him, that he'd listen to her. "I'll be sitting under Dearg's tree."

The door closed softly, and with it the air in the chamber lightened, as if the walls sighed with relief. Rhyslin watched the two leave, then looked over his shoulder at the two taghta.

"What do you want us to do?"

"Stay." Rhyslin's voice was tinged with pain, his breath fogging briefly in the cooler draft that slipped through the stone seams. "I may need your advice."

Neither spoke as they moved to his side. Lilly picked a chair, wood creaking as she settled, her ankles crossed with quiet dignity. The air was filled with the chiming of Ana′s jewelry as she crawled to Rhyslin′s left side, her movement stirring the candle flames, and knelt with her derriere resting on her heels.

When both were in place, Rhyslin looked for Marcus and found him leaning against the wall near the door, a silent sentinel. "Marcus, would you do me a favor and find Torval and K′Tek?" His voice was low but resonant, drawing the shadows closer. He would need them to act as witnesses later.

Vuuroena watched as Natolie started to complain, her voice sharp against the hush of the chamber—only stopping when Marcus′s frown silenced her like a blade sheathed.

"Be silent, mo chridhe. In your hurry to make history, you forgot how many freemen are required to sign treaties that bind the Saor-Shealbhan to a particular action." His voice carried iron beneath it, striking sparks against the air. Unlike Rhyslin, he didn′t hide his feelings. His voice held barely controlled anger. "Come, let′s find our wayward freemen."

After casting a look in Rhyslin′s direction, Natolie followed Marcus out of the council chamber. Her footsteps seemed too loud, jangling against the stone floor. She needed to apologize to Rhyslin.

She had allowed Astinmah to fill her heart with pride and glory, and the air itself seemed to close behind her with a whisper of judgment.

Rhyslin rested his head in his hand as sharp pain wound through his nerves, making it hard to move. The chamber's light dimmed with his wince, shadows lengthening across the polished table. Then, as the pain faded, the air steadied, and he raised his head. His eyes fell on the three women sitting across the table from him.

He wondered if they recalled him from Rig Garion's kingship. He hadn't remembered them, and it was only when they were together that he realized who they were. The pain of loss hit him hard.

The torches guttered as though the room itself grieved with him. Garion had been his friend, a decent ruler, and a great family man. Shame followed pain as he recalled forgotten promises never kept.

"Á avatyar nin i rahtainenyar[8]." His whispered entreaty spiraled heavenward, and the rafters seemed to echo the syllables with a hushed breath. He was glad that Astinmah had left with Dearg. She would have seen through his shame and called him on it.

He shuffled the parchment, the rustle carrying like dry leaves in the still air, only looking up when one of the ladies delicately cleared her throat. Of the three,

---

[8] Forgive me my broken promises.

Ilyriatri thoughtfully gazed at him, her eyes holding a weight that pressed against his chest like a silent test.

"If you are ready to begin. Tell me what you want from the Saor-shealbhan nan Roaintean Mòra?"

Allanagh and Ilyriatri looked at Mayana, the mountain queen, who responded with a raised brow. Her silence rumbled in the room like distant stonefalls.

Allanagh cleared her throat and leaned toward Rhyslin. The fire behind her eyes flickered in the torchlight, casting her face in sharp relief. "Mayana said ..." she stopped and started again. "Could you please tell us about Mayana' s treaty?"

He had not expected to talk about Mayana's petition and had to think about it. He looked at Mayana and saw her nod, as steady and immovable as granite. "She has petitioned for Clann nam beann to join the Saor-Shealbhan as a member state."

Ilyriatri frowned. The air around her seemed to cool, sharp as the edge of a blade. "Mathair Astinmah didn't give us that option." She cast a dark look at the door through which the goddess had left. Not for the first time, she wondered what Astinmah had been thinking.

Rhyslin glanced at the door, hoping that his mother was enjoying her conversation with Dearg. "Of course she didn't."

He tried to hide the disappointment he felt, though the lamps above dimmed with his words. "She's always thought of me as a king."

Allanagh, her fear forgotten, leaned toward him. Sparks seemed to leap unseen in the air between them. Her people owed Rhyslin a life-debt, but she wouldn't let that lead them into slavery. "I wouldn't dare criticize a goddess, but you will have to convince me that joining you is the right thing." She had fire in her eyes as she stared at Rhyslin. "Why should my people join your Saor-Shealbhan? What do we get out of it?"

Rhyslin grinned, savoring her fire. The torches flared brighter, as if in answer. It was no wonder that she was a leader.

He glanced at Ilyriatri and tried to assess her intelligence. When he found her staring back at him, her gaze was like a steady current beneath the surface, and he saw fascination in her eyes. He wondered why that both thrilled and concerned him.

"There are many benefits to joining the Saor-shealbhan," he said, his voice resonating with the cool weight of truth. "You will be free to travel throughout the country; you will be free to work for whomever you wish, or you may start your own business, and you may live wherever you wish."

"What if we suffer another attack?" Allanagh's voice cut like flint on stone. The memory of Orcan war cries still clung to her words. "Will you come to our aid?"

She knew that they would; she just wanted confirmation.

Rhyslin was only too happy to give her that confirmation. The air warmed with certainty, his prana folding over them like a shield. "Once the treaty is signed, you'll be under our protection. Anyone who attacks you will face the full might of the ten companies."

"That's all and good." Ilyriatri lifted her right eyebrow. Her words rippled through the chamber like a testing wind. "What will your protection cost us?" She was very careful when she interrogated him. His disappointment had left with Astinmah, and his prana now settled over them like the surface of a cool lake, calm and assuring. She watched him as she considered her daughter's position.

Rana was correct. This man was exceptional, and that excited her. It had been a long time since she'd been interested in a man — almost too long.

Seeing the smile playing on her lips, Rhyslin leaned back, the chair creaking under him as though it knew the weight of what passed between them. He wondered what she was up to. "It will cost you nothing. In fact, by the time we pay for the land to build a fortress, the supplies to build the fortress, as well as equipment and supplies for the soldiers stationed there, we'll be paying you."

Hearing that, the three women held a quick conference, voices like low streams intermingling in the chamber. One that brought more questions.

"Will we be required to merge our armies?" came from Allanagh, her voice sharp with concern.

The draoidh shook his head. His refusal spread through the air like a quiet wind easing the heat of battle. "No. You may keep your military separate if you wish. We will give you as much or as little help as you need." He relaxed in the chair as Allanagh and Ilyriatri pulled Mayana into a huddle and interrogated her, their presence stirring the air like three elements converging.

When they were through, Ilyriatri stood. The air shifted with her, silks whispering like a question on the wind.

"What if one of your citizens breaks our laws, or one of our citizens breaks Saor-shealbhan law?"

Rhyslin wished that one of the legates were here. The thought of them seemed to stir the chamber's shadows; even in absence, law carried weight. Legates were the Saorsa's answer to the court. They took the evidence gathered by the law-keepers, appointed courts, juries, and determined if Council edicts held the power of law. Any of them would have answered Ilyriatri more concisely than Rhyslin could.

"All free people bear responsibility for their choices—and must accept the consequences that follow. We won't second-guess your court system. We just ask the same from you."

His answer must have satisfied them. "That's most enlightened." Allanagh kissed her fingertips.

Her gesture released a faint sweetness into the air, as though unseen flowers stirred. A gesture that was copied by Ilyriatri and Mayana, the sound of their silk cuffs brushing like water over stone.

The desert-born Hîn i-Balanath looked at him strangely, and again he saw the smile that promised him everything and nothing. A dry warmth lingered about her like desert wind pressing against cool stone.

"What if, at some future date, we wish to leave your Saor-shealbhan? What will happen then?"

For some strange reason, the thought of her leaving filled him with a strange mixture of sadness and longing. The candles quivered, as though the room shared his hesitation.

"When that day comes, we will allow you to leave. We won't try to force you to stay." He pointed to the stylized map on the wall, the parchment edges curling faintly as if the ink remembered old boundaries. "Joint military forces would disband and, depending on the terms of our contract, we will either withdraw to our forts or withdraw to our borders."

Allanagh looked thoughtful. The air seemed to cool with her silence.

"That is not what I expected." She turned to Mayana and Ilyriatri. "Can you give us a few mionaidean to discuss this?"

"Of course." Rhyslin used the opportunity to lean back. The chair groaned softly, echoing his weariness.

"Take all the time you need. I'll be right here." He winced as the pain in his head sharpened. A candle guttered as if in sympathy. He was thankful that it had allowed him to conduct the first part of the treaty negotiations.

His discomfort did not go unnoticed. The two taghta had been observing him. Their gazes pressed like warm hands against the air.

"How bad is the pain?" Lilly shifted in her chair to brush her fingers through his hair, probing for the source of Rhyslin's pain. The moment she touched him, the air grew taut, expectant.

He endured her touch, not pulling away as she found the tender bundle of nerves just behind his ear and prodded. The chamber held its breath.

"It's just another day. It comes and goes."

Lilly shook her head. The movement sent a ripple of unease through the stillness.

"Has Astinmah revealed what it takes to get rid of this pain?"

"She has." Rhyslin had not liked her remedy for his pains.

"And?" Her fingers found where the nerves bundled and deftly pressed down. His hiss became a sigh of relief, and with it the tension in the rafters seemed to ease.

"It's never going to happen."

Her fingers stopped, and he cracked an eyelid to find her staring at him. Shadows leaned closer around her.

"Why not?"

He was not ready to deal with that question. He cast around for the words to explain. "My pain comes from gathering too much ambient draoidheacd. In order to get rid of the pain, I must form life-bonds with several women." The very mention of bonds sent a low hum through the room, as if fate's loom pulled at hidden threads.

Ana suppressed a giggle as she stood and stroked the back of Rhyslin's head. Her touch was a spark against the fabric of the air.

"You find that distasteful?"

The tortured draoidh sighed when the bound taghta found the spot where most of the pain originated. Candles brightened, answering his release.

"Ana, you don't have to …" At her touch, pain receded, leaving the silence strangely tender.

"I don't have to, but I choose to, maighstir." Ana sounded pleased with herself. The title carried a subtle resonance that curled like smoke in the corners. "I live to serve."

"You don't get off that easy," Lilly admonished with a pointed finger. Her voice rang like steel on stone. "I'm still waiting for your answer."

Rhyslin just didn't have it in him to fight it. Instead of trying to trick her, Rhyslin shook his head. "I don't find it distasteful at all."

"Then why aren't you following your mother's advice?" Lilly raised one brow in challenge. A draft pressed against the map behind her, as though old boundaries leaned forward to listen.

Rhyslin could never explain it. Instead, he gazed around the room. The chamber answered with hushed silence.

"It's unfair to expect a woman to devote herself to a man like me, someone who is hardly ever home." He held his arms wide. The gesture lifted the room's weight like a plea. "Show me the woman in her right mind who would consider me a suitable partner?"

The two taghta hid tight smiles as they looked around the room. The flicker of their glances stirred the air like sparks catching kindling.

"You'd be surprised, Rhyslin," Lilly let her hand fall onto his shoulder. Her touch drew warmth into the space. "I see two women who would consider you a wonderful mate." She purposefully looked at Flur and Ilyriatri. Fate's threads seemed to hum between them.

"Three, more like," Ana pointed out, watching Vuuroena. Her senses detected fate's strands around the young spellblade, strands that shimmered like heat-haze.

Under the touch of both taghta, Rhyslin's pain diminished to manageable levels. The oppressive weight in the rafters loosened.

"Thank you." He opened his eyes to find Ilyriatri staring at him, her gaze bright with unspoken knowing.

"It was our pleasure," Ana responded as she came back to his side and again knelt. The sound of her knees against the floor was like an oath being sealed. Lilly echoed her assertion as she leaned back in her chair, the wood sighing as if in relief.

# Chapter Four
## The Tribute and the Bond

Mayana, Ilyriatri, and Allanagh spent almost an hour discussing what they wanted.

Vuuroena and Flur felt helpless as they watched the three old Hîn i-Balanath leaders cycle through ideas with ease, only to discard them moments later. The chamber's hearth crackled and dimmed in rhythm with their voices, as though the fire itself grew weary of revisions.

Rhyslin eyed the clock, wondering how much longer they were going to take. Draoidheachd curled faintly in the corners, restless, as if the room shared his impatience. To his amazement, he didn't have to wait long, watching as the three leaders reclaimed their places at the table.

Rhyslin saw the three join hands, offering support to the one they had chosen as their speaker. A hushed stillness spread, even the fire bowing to the solemnity of their unity.

Allanagh stood tall and proud, and looked straight at Rhyslin.

"Lord Darkblade …" When Rhyslin winced, a low tremor stirred in the rafters, like the wood itself rejecting the name. She took a deep breath and started over. "Maighstir Darkblade." The shadows eased back, soothed, and when that didn't elicit a wince, she continued, smiling. "We, Henneth Minui i-Ainu, formally petition to join the Saor-shealbhan nan Roaintean Mora as equals."

If Rhyslin had to guess, she was relieved the discussions were over. The air loosened around her shoulders, as if the weight of decision had finally lifted.

Giving a solemn nod, Rhyslin signaled his agreement. "Very well. When four freeholders are present, we will sign a preliminary agreement."

The hearth brightened, sparks leaping, carrying the word outward like heralds.

Allanagh and Mayana sighed in relief. Ilyriatri looked like she had expected nothing less to happen, a warm smile gracing her countenance. Behind her, the ubhal crest carved into the high beams gleamed faintly, as if catching hidden light.

"When the full council convenes, we will present your application and put it up for a vote. If a majority approves, the council will grant you membership." Rhyslin felt the knot in his stomach uncoil, the air warming as tension bled away. This had been the simple part.

Ilyriatri had watched him, amazed at how simple he made it look. Never had she seen a treaty signed without someone complaining. She raised her hand, continuing only when Rhyslin nodded.

"When does the next council meeting occur?" From what she knew of other kingdoms, she figured that they'd have to wait months.

Rhyslin pulled a calendar out of his pouch and consulted it. The parchment gave off a faint herbal scent, preserved with oils. "The next council meeting will be in three weeks." He checked the calendar again, verifying the date.

"So soon?" Allanagh couldn't believe her ears. A whisper of wind circled the chamber, echoing her disbelief. "How is that possible?"

Rhyslin grinned, understanding their confusion. His voice carried warmth, steady as the flame. "The business council meets every three months. We discuss and vote on preliminary contracts here. From there, the business council forwards major treaties to the Freeholders council. It takes place at the summer solstice." He waited for the three leaders to get over their shock.

The quiet seemed to lean toward him, eager. "If you wish to be present, you may attend as my guests."

Allanagh's only concern was for her people, and she had already decided her course of action. She approached Rhyslin with her arms folded across her chest. "I will take you up on your invitation." The floor beneath her boots creaked once, as though affirming her resolve.

"So will I." Ilyriatri joined Allanagh, her arms crossed under her breasts, her eyes meeting Rhyslin's. In them, he saw her determination, her strength, like the unwavering glow of embers refusing to die.

Rhyslin met her gaze, his own burning just as bright. The room seemed to hush, suspended between them. "Very well. When you are ready, you can send word."

He strode toward them, meeting them halfway. "Depending on your location, I can either send a cutter or ask Mathair to provide power to open portals."

If it came to the second option, he would enjoy a measure of satisfaction using his mother's power. The air cooled at her name, as if the chamber itself remembered her hand. It would be the least she could do for trying to entrap him.

Mayana chose that moment to join her bond-sisters. The three women stood together now, their unity palpable. "If you will send a ship to meet us at Garth i Loth-laeg at the appointed time, we will be ready."

Rhyslin ran his finger across the calendar and then used the quill to make a notation. The ink shimmered briefly, as though acknowledging the binding of intent. "It shall be done." When no one argued, he felt the anxiety flow away. Even the fire in the grate exhaled, settling to a steady glow.

All he needed were the two freemen he sent Marcus to find.

Rhyslin felt the seconds ticking down. The air in the chamber thickened with each heartbeat, the scent of resin from the torches sharpening as though the flame itself shared his impatience. If Marcus would just get back, he could move on to the next part, the part he was dreading.

As if they were waiting to make a grand entrance, Marcus and Natolie returned, the two freemen in tow. The door creaked wider with a hiss of draoidheachd, and the chamber seemed to inhale at their arrival.

The Hîn i-Balanath trio reacted differently to the entrance.

Allanagh paled, withdrawing, her aura flickering like a flame caught in sudden wind, as she saw the lumbering Infernal that followed Marcus into the room.

Ilyriatri leaned forward, her eyes lighting up like dawn upon water at the sight of the cloaked Hîn i-Balanath who brought up the rear.

Mayana, calm as always, had met the two before and offered both a half-bow, her serenity grounding the air between them.

Marcus walked up to Rhyslin and saluted, his fist over his heart, opening to an upturned palm as he extended his arm. The gesture carried a ripple of respect, echoed faintly in the timbre of the chamber's silence.

"Are we too late?"

Rhyslin returned the salute, the draoidheachd in the room answering with a subtle pulse. "You are right on time." He turned to the two freemen. "Gentlemen, if you will step this way, I have need of your help."

The nine-foot-tall Infernal took careful steps forward, each one sending a dull tremor through the wooden floor, as if the building itself adjusted under his weight. He stopped out of arm's range, mindful even of his breath.

"Seann-mhadaidh says there is
something for us to sign." He pointed at
Marcus.

"There is indeed." Rhyslin picked up
the rewritten treaty and handed it over.
The parchment seemed to hum faintly at
the prospect of binding hands upon it.
"The Hîn i-Balanath delegation wants to
join the Saorsa. You've spent three days
living among them." He brushed his
fingers through his hair, weariness stirring
the lantern flames. "If you feel that they'll
make good neighbors, let your sign be
your bond."

"I understand." The Infernal removed
his helmet, the motion releasing a wave of
heat that prickled against the skin of those
nearest, and looked around the chamber.
His eyes glowed dim, burdened yet steady.
"Where do I sign?"

"Anywhere on the bottom of the page." The order didn't matter, only the four signatures. Rhyslin handed K'Tek the quill and watched as the Infernal accepted it with care, claws held steady as if cradling something fragile.

"The Hîn i-Balanath have treated me as I expected." His voice carried sorrow, and the air dipped cold at the sound. Some had treated him with kindness. Others had reacted as Allanagh had, with fear and suspicion. That wasn't enough to stop him from signing the treaty.

Allanagh, hearing the sadness in K'Tek's voice, reassessed him. Her aura, once drawn tight, softened like thawing frost. She realized she had let her recent trauma color her perceptions.

Shame colored her face as she watched the massive Infernal, and the torches guttered faintly as though echoing her remorse.

Rhyslin turned to the cloaked Hîn i-Balanath standing behind the Infernal. "It's your turn, Torval."

Ilyriatri watched the cloaked Hîn i-Balanath, torn between thinking she knew who he was and denying the thought. The draoidheachd coiled near her skin, restless

It wasn't until he reached up and uncovered his face that she knew she was right. It had been years since they had spent time together.

She recognized Torval, though time had aged and tempered him, his presence carrying the weight of stone weathered by storm.

After he accepted the quill from his companion, but before he could sign, Ilyriatri stepped forward. Her voice wrapped his name like silk on steel.

"T'or'val." She drew his name out the desert way, each syllable sparking memory into the air. "Years have passed since our last encounter. Has time treated you well?"

Not expecting to hear his name spoken thus, Torval turned, his eyes falling on the woman who stood before him. The chamber held its breath. As he beheld her, his mind flew back to the past.

"Ily'ria'tri? I never thought to see you here."

A hush fell over the room, so deep the scratch of flame on oilwick sounded like thunder.

At Ilyriatri's side, Allanagh wore an awestruck expression. Never had she seen a Hîn i-Balanath of such stature or coloring. She couldn't help but glance between him and Ilyriatri, as if trying to place Torval's dark skin tone, her thoughts rustling like leaves.

Ilyriatri caught the glance and saw the look on Allanagh's face. She groaned, though she knew Torval wouldn't let it bother him. Her aura dimmed in brief irritation, then steadied.

Torval watched the emotions cross Ilyriatri's face and let out an amused chuckle that reverberated warmly against the stone.

"Ask, fair lady, and I will answer."

Allanagh, realizing she got caught, blushed, heat flushing her cheeks so strongly that the flame nearest her stretched taller.

"Where are you from? I have never come across one of us with dark skin."

"You would not know my birthplace, as it has been devoured by Anfalg i naur." His words fell heavy, like stones into still water. Turning to the table, he signed his name with a flourish that left the ink shimmering faintly.

"Will that be all, Mac Draoidheacd?"

Rhyslin accepted the quill with a nod and set it down on the table. The parchment seemed to settle, binding itself to their fates.

"You have my thanks."

Marcus glanced at Rhyslin but a moment before affixing his name to the treaty. The scratch of quill on parchment rang louder than it should.

"That was painless."

Rhyslin scrawled his name on the parchment. Shadows leaned in closer as he did so.

"True. I fear the hard part is yet to come."

"Ah, the infamous tribute clause." Marcus couldn't hide the amusement he felt. A faint breeze stirred as if the word itself called for witness.

"How will you handle it?"

"I know not." In truth, Rhyslin knew how he wanted to handle the tribute. He wanted nothing to do with it. The torches flared, then dimmed, mirroring his resistance.

"Le a diathan. Why am I constantly ending up in these situations?"

He pretended to shuffle the parchment as he tried to think of a way to escape what was to happen next. No escape came.

Finding none, he looked heavenward, shadows thickening above him.

"I know you orchestrated this, Mother." He could imagine the smile on her face as she wrote the tribute clause, her presence lingering like smoke on the air.

Turning, he picked up the second part of the treaty and waved it around. The parchment caught a faint draft, edges fluttering like restless wings, as if even the air knew what weight the words carried. "Out of curiosity, who invoked the tribute clause?"

When a blushing Flur raised her hand, Rhyslin blinked. The room itself seemed to lean toward her, torchlight softening around the golden-haired princess as though Astinmah's breath lingered in her aura. Of all the things he expected, this wasn't one of them. The pulse in his throat quickened, betraying him.

He thought about seeking help from Marcus, but the ranger had departed, leaving him adrift. For once, the seasoned draoidh longed for an ally's intervention and found none.

Rhyslin needed time to think. At least one night, if possible. Feigning tiredness, though his heart thundered against his ribs, he watched the blushing princess. "Might we resume on the morrow? I am more tired than I thought." His voice was steady, yet the draoidheachd in the chamber quivered faintly, responding to the undercurrent of unease.

Mayana, knowing him longer than the other Hîn i-Balanath, looked upon him with suspicion. The sharp tilt of her head and the glimmer in her eyes betrayed that she saw past his mask. The others took him at face value.

"Of course. You may stay at Allanagh's cottage tonight. We can finish tomorrow." She had never known Rhyslin to run from anything. The air near her lips shimmered with restrained laughter as she glanced over, saw the confusion on Flur's face, and hid a smirk. So, that's why Rhyslin was running.

In his rush to get out of the council chamber, Rhyslin neglected to grab his pouch, the signed treaty, his quill, and the piece of paper that had Flur's proposal.

The objects lay on the table, heavy with unspoken meaning, the quill's ink drop spreading like a dark eye.

"I can't believe that anyone would — Stupid, irresponsible people — of all the inane ideas." His muttered words carried into the hall, trailing behind him like shadows.

Astinmah looked up as he walked past her. Her gaze, cool and ancient, followed his retreat, though she made no move to stop him. She would have chased after him, but couldn't, because Dearg was re-braiding her hair.

The dryad's nimble fingers paused mid-braid, her moss-scented breath catching as Rhyslin passed. "What is wrong with Mac Draoidheacd, Mara-Astan?"

Dearg wasn't totally self-centered; she just enjoyed being the center of attention. Yet, even she felt the ripple of dissonance as the draoidh stormed past, the chamber's wooden beams creaking faintly, as though absorbing his agitation.

As she resumed re-braiding Astinmah's hair, she was already thinking about making her goddess a new laurel crown, vines and blossoms curling in her mind's eye.

Dearg frowned as she did something she rarely did. She stopped re-braiding Astinmah's hair and put on a brave face. The flickering firelight softened her bark-like skin, giving her the look of a child masking worry.

"Do you want to pursue Mac Draoidheacd and find out what's wrong?"

The forest goddess shook her head, her voice carrying the hush of leaves at twilight. "I think I will stay here so you can finish my hair." She glanced over her shoulder, the bronze of her eyes glinting. "When you finish my hair, I would like to take care of yours."

Dearg's face brightened, the chamber's shadows bending back as though to frame her joy. "Mara-Astan, Dearg would be honored." With thoughts of her goddess pampering her, Dearg concentrated on doing the best job she could, her fingers weaving rhythm and devotion into every braid.

Flur watched Rhyslin retreat from the council chamber. The blush on her face had subsided, leaving her confused.

She wondered if she had done something wrong. The chamber's high rafters seemed to sigh with her, the lingering warmth of torchlight dimming as if embarrassed on her behalf.

Unsure of herself, she walked over to the table where Rhyslin had left his supplies. After gathering them up and putting them in the pouch, she looked to her mother.

"Did I do something wrong?" She clutched the pouch to her chest, her thoughts somewhere between shame and pain.

The leather thrummed faintly against her skin, carrying the draoidheachd-stain of his touch.

"No, you did nothing wrong."
Allanagh hugged her daughter. "I think
Maighstir Darkblade found something he
didn't want to believe." Her silver hair
caught the lantern-glow, casting little halos
across the stone wall, as if the goddess
herself whispered reassurance.

The golden-haired princess tightened
her hold on the pouch, pouring all of her
heartbreak into it. "Do you think it would
be agreeable if I took his things to him?"

"I think it is only fitting that you take
him his property," Allanagh said as she
pulled her silver hair forward over her
shoulders.

The golden-haired princess kept
Rhyslin's pouch clutched to her chest for a
moment, then shook her head. This wasn't
like her.

She didn't pine after men, but Rhyslin was different, and she wanted to be his. With a nod to Allanagh, she left the council chamber and walked back toward the cottage she shared with her mother.

Behind her, the doors shut with a wooden groan, like the hall itself releasing her into fate.

Flur stepped through the front doorway and into the foyer of the small, cozy cottage that the villagers had let Allanagh and her daughter borrow for the duration of their stay.

With Rhyslin's pouch still firmly in hand, the golden-haired princess stared down the hallway that led to the bedrooms. Five days earlier, the cottage had been comfortable.

Now, the hallway seemed foreboding, cold, and made Flur nervous.

The hearth's banked coals gave off a tired sigh of smoke, shadows pooling along the hallway like doubts stretching long fingers.

Earlier in the day, she had waited for the draoidh to wake up. She had been excited, wanting to meet him. In the council hall, he had paid her the ultimate compliment when he said he remembered her taking care of him.

Flur watched Rhyslin win the three Hîn i-Balanath leaders over with his charm and knowledge. Then he read Flur's proposal and had excused himself from the council hall, saying he was tired.

Her heart replayed the word tired as if it had been aimed at her.

Flur clutched the pouch to her chest as she crept down the hall to the room she knew Rhyslin had retreated to, her room.

She stood outside the room, gathering her courage to knock on the door.

The timber under her feet creaked like an elder clearing its throat, urging her to speak her truth.

She was just about to knock on the door when it opened to reveal Rhyslin standing there.

For a moment, he stared at her. "Princess Flur. Please come in." He took a step back and swept his left arm out. "I'd ask what brings you here, but it's your house."

She held out his pouch. "You left this. I thought you would want it back."

Rhyslin took the pouch, setting it by the door. "Thank you." He couldn't help but notice the way she stood inside the door, as if she expected to be requested to leave.

The air tightened between them, thick with unshed words.

Flur brushed her hands down the front of her dress, smoothing out nonexistent wrinkles. "May I ask a question?" She waited for Rhyslin to nod before asking her question. "Why did you run away?"

Her voice wavered like a candle-flame tested by a draft.

For the first he could remember, Rhyslin was at a loss for words. He backed away from Flur until he felt the edge of the couch behind his knees. When he sat down with a thump, Flur took the chair opposite him and waited for his answer.

The wooden frame groaned beneath him as if registering his retreat, while the chair she claimed straightened, proud to hold her courage.

Rhyslin had never lied to anyone and didn't intend on starting now. "Would you believe that your proposal caught me by surprise?"

"No, I wouldn't." Flur looked into his eyes and fell into those hazel orbs. All she wanted to do was run her fingers through his hair.

Her pulse beat like a drum against her throat, echoing faintly in the draoidheachd-rich air.

Rhyslin's breath caught as he watched her. "'Tis true. I was not expecting a tribute clause, and it …"

"Sent you running for cover?" Flur fought the desire to reach out to him.

The air between them grew hot, as if the room itself teased him with her accusation.

Rhyslin coughed, trying to hide his thoughts. "In a manner of speaking." When the thought of spending time with her crossed his mind, he smiled.

"In a manner of speaking?" Flur almost laughed out loud. "You were in such a hurry to get away that you left your things on the table."

The floor seemed to chuckle with her, loosening the tension.

Rhyslin smiled, admitting defeat. "I would ask you to stay for dinner, but there doesn't seem to be much in the pantry."

Flur accepted the intended peace offering. "My mom and I frequent a small eatery nearby. Would you care to come along?"

Rhyslin weighed the benefits of accepting her offer, then nodded. "I would be honored to dine with you."

Within five minutes, the two were sitting outside the little cafe, eating a light lunch. The wind stirred, playful, tugging at Flur's golden hair as though it conspired with her boldness.

"Why the tribute clause?" Rhyslin leaned forward. He was curious about why anyone would sell themselves so cheaply.

Caught in mid-bite, Flur coughed up part of her bread. When she could breathe without coughing, she glared at Rhyslin. "Because I want to go with you." When he arched an eyebrow, she rolled her eyes. "I saw what you did to the ogren. I want to learn what you know."

Rhyslin eyed the golden-haired Hîn i-Balanath. "My skills … If all you saw was the interrogation, you haven't seen my skills in action."

When Flur gestured with her slice of bread for him to continue, he hid a grin behind his left hand. "What's there to tell? I can draw from the ambient draoidheacd and use it for gealdor."

Flur raised an eyebrow, finished her mouthful of food, took a sip of wine, and pointed her finger at him. "I saw what you did to the Ogren. You created a creeping vine out of nowhere."

Rhyslin shook his head. "It was hardly 'nowhere.' I dropped a seed on the ground and used draoidheacd to force it to grow.

The vines in the trellis behind them rustled faintly, remembering the echo of his will.

She blinked, awestruck. "That's amazing. All I can do is pray to Astinmah and heal people." She leaned forward. "Can you do that?"

"What? Heal people?" The draoidh had to think about it before he answered her question. "I'm no sagart. When I heal, it is by intent." He shrugged, snagged a piece of fruit, and took a bite. "I don't pray to Astinmah when I heal someone." If she only knew there were times when he didn't use draoidheacd at all, she'd have a fit.

Flur took another bite of her food as she watched him. Rhyslin had the feeling she was judging him for something he had done. He felt an itch form over his left eye and rubbed it with the edge of his finger.

After another bite, she leaned toward him. "Do you know the old ways?" When she rested her hand on his, Rhyslin blinked. What was this woman after?

The draoidheachd quickened in the air, curling around their joined skin like invisible smoke.

Moments later, he felt the warmth of her touch sinking into his skin and quirked an eyebrow. He had lost his train of thought. "What were you asking?"

Rhyslin could feel Flur's giggle along every nerve and held his breath.

"Do you know the old ways?"

Rhyslin turned his hand under hers, his fingers curling around hers. "I do." He traced her fingers with his. "I can tell by touch what is broken, what is out of place, what muscles are tense." He watched her face as he drew a spiral on her palm.

The air hushed, wine-dark silence folding over them, the spiral carrying weight older than words.

Her breath quickened, her skin warmed, her eyes dilated, a dusky glow crept up her throat, she licked her lips, and she softly moaned.

Even the breeze stilled, as if unwilling to interrupt.

It was too much, too quick. Flur pulled her hand away from his, heaving deep breaths. "Do you know how to make poultices and potions?"

"I know every root and petal and how to compound them to alleviate pain."

The golden-haired Hîn i-Balanath leaned forward. "Would you teach me the old ways?" Her unspoken please twisted around Rhyslin's heart.

"It doesn't require that you be a tribute to become an apprentice. All you have to do is ask."

Her blue eyes sparkled. "Can I go with you?"

Rhyslin pretended to think it over. "You can. If your mother agrees."

Flur froze as his words sank in. The firelight flickered across her hair as she quivered, her eyes narrowing, her voice turning cold.

"I don't need Maither's permission. I am past the age of majority."

The air thickened with her defiance. She poked him in the chest, and when he laughed, the hearth crackled in mirth with him. Flur growled, teeth clenched. "You're mean."

The draoidh chuckled, his amusement clear, the sound rippling through the rafters like a teasing wind. It made Flur that much angrier. She sought a way to retaliate, her own heartbeat drumming in her ears. Slowly, a toothy grin spread across her face as memory surfaced, her mother's story of how she had once brought her husband to heel.

Flur leaned toward Rhyslin and cupped his hands in hers. The warmth of her palms pressed against his calloused skin, and in that charged silence the room seemed to hold its breath. She gazed into his eyes, her voice serene and steady, carrying ritual weight:

"Rhyslin Darkblade. I, Flur Rionnag Shoilleir, ask the Lady of Chains to be witness as I give to thee, my soul-bond, my very self. In return, I ask that you teach me the old ways."

The air shifted, heavy with unseen chains; the scent of iron and roses lingered where no flowers grew.

At first, Rhyslin listened as if spellbound. Then, realization struck — his eyes widened, his breath quickened, and he yanked his hands back. The room shivered as if in protest. He tried to retreat from her.

"Do you know what you are —?" He could not believe what she had done. He could tell from her expression that she didn't understand.

Flur's eyes widened as she felt something heavy settle around her heart, a binding weight that was not entirely her own. She blinked as alien fear coursed through her, then resignation, but it wasn't hers. She gasped, seeing the haunted look on Rhyslin's face.

"What have I done?"

Rhyslin shook his head as the ethereal bonds wound around them both, settling into place with all the weight of an iron chain. Invisible links pulled taut, glinting in the mind's eye. "You've initiated a soul-bond."

Closing his eyes, he felt the tether digging into his soul, threads of draoidheachd twisting with strands of fate. This was what he had feared for most of his life, that a woman would invoke Ananke's name in binding, tying her very life to his. The gods themselves had leaned close to listen.

He had always thought that should such a thing happen, he could control it. But now he knew he had been wrong. There was no controlling such a bond. Should anything happen to him, it would echo into Flur as well.

"For better or worse, you are now bound to me, and I to you. I can only hope you don't come to despise it."

Rhyslin took Flur's trembling hand, the bond thrumming between them like a living thread, and brushed his lips across her fingertips. A faint spark flared at the touch, as though Ananke herself approved.

"Well," he said, with a weary tenderness, "that's one way to guarantee that you get to come with me. I hope you're ready to go."

# Chapter Five
## Chains of Ananke, Gifts of Astinma

The golden-haired princess stirred beneath the gauze of sleep, the hush of morning air curling warmly across her bare shoulders like the breath of a blessing. A single ray of dawn slanted through the latticed window, gilding her cheek with quiet fire. She stretched languidly beneath the covers, her fingers brushing the silk sheets with reverence, as though touching memory.

For a time, she didn't move. Not truly.

The world seemed to pause around her, the distant birdsong muted as though holding its breath, the scent of rosemary and lavender from the garden below rising upward but halting shy of the sill, unwilling to trespass. The silence pressed close, weighted, as if listening. When at last she rose, the air stirred gently around her legs, caressing them like a lover's parting hand.

She sat at the carved cedar vanity and took up her brush. With each stroke through her golden hair, the rhythm slowed until it was prayerful. Her breath fell into sync with the motion, her chest lifting and falling in cadence with the cedar's soft creak. She hadn't meant to count, but somewhere past thirty; she stopped trying.

The silence in the room grew aware of her, charged with expectancy, as though something ripened in the hush.

A warmth bloomed beneath her sternum, as unmistakable as it was unbidden. The stillness thickened, the faint smell of warmed amber rising like a hearth newly lit. She paused.

Without thinking, Flur turned in place, a slow, instinctive pivot toward the northwest wall, where no window lay and no light touched. Shadows there deepened, gathering into a veil. She faced it fully, spine straightening like a drawn bow. A pull, deep and certain, thrummed through her marrow, the air trembling faintly with it.

It was him.

Rhyslin.

The thought bloomed without words, and her lips curved before she knew they would. Not the polite smile of a queen's daughter, but something older, something sacred, born of marrow and vow.

She did not need to explain the why of her offering. The vow had risen like a tide, and she, a willing shore, had let it crash and remake her. Some women weighed their fate; she had known. If she had not spoken, he would have vanished, and the part of her that had never fully breathed would have withered.

She stood thus when the door cracked open. The smell of wind-pressed linen and crushed lavender marked Allanagh's arrival even before her voice.

"Good morning, loth nîn vell," the queen whispered, stepping into the sun-drenched chamber. Her voice held gentleness, but the silence she entered was not empty, it bent, aware, as though regarding her.

Allanagh paused, hand on her hip, catching the expression on her daughter's face. Her breath caught. That smile — distant, inward, radiant — she had once worn it herself, in a lifetime before thrones and treaties.

Two knocks, unheard. She moved closer and snapped her fingers sharply.

The pop cracked through the golden stillness, rippling the air like a stone breaking the mirrored surface of a lake.

Flur blinked once, the spell of reverie lifting. "Good morning, Mother," she said, her voice a sigh woven with blush.

"I saw you at Para's," Allanagh said, stepping lightly into the room, her gaze watchful. "With Maighstir Darkblade."

Flur smiled again, soft and secret. She moved to her chest of drawers and laid the brush in the shallow tray as though setting down a relic.

"And?" Though teasing, Allanagh's voice carried a cautious edge, motherly instinct outweighing curiosity.

"And," Flur said, turning, the light catching in her hair like fire through wheat, "I initiated a soul-bond with Rhyslin."

The breath left Allanagh's lungs as if the walls themselves had stolen it. The cedar beams above groaned faintly, echoing her shock. She stepped closer, urgency blooming in her posture, the air between them charged like a storm about to break.

"You spoke the vow?"

"I did," Flur answered, meeting her mother's gaze without flinching.

A beat passed. Then another. Even the silence seemed to recoil, folding in on itself.

Allanagh took a breath, bracing herself. "Do you understand what you've done?"

Flur gave a single nod, regal and sure. And in that moment, her bearing shifted, not just a daughter, but a woman enthralled by a deeper gravity, drawn into the orbit of another soul's fire. The faintest tremor of rose-petal fragrance lingered in the air, sharp with certainty.

"How did Maighstir Darkblade react?" Inwardly, she was cringing, and in her mind's eye she saw the treaty falling apart. She wanted to fall to her knees and pray to the gods for help.

Before Allanagh could speak again, a voice answered her question, low and certain:

"Maighstir Darkblade was so shocked he did not react as he should have."

The smell of beeswax seeped under the windowsills, and the light in the room subtly thickened — as if the air itself acknowledged his presence.

Rhyslin stood in the doorway, his eyes fixed on Flur, a quiet blaze rising behind them.

Flur rose and moved to him, her grace unbroken. She knelt at his feet, devotion shining from her face. "I could feel you from your room." She placed a hand over her heart, and the silence answered with a faint, resonant hush.

Rhyslin's eyes roved from corner to corner of the chamber, as though trying to divine the future hidden in the timber and stone.

But when Flur stretched out her hand and clasped his, the tremor in the air steadied. His heart slowed, his breathing evened, his gaze lowered to the woman kneeling before him.

He cleared his throat, voice roughened but resolute. "Good morning, my bond-mate."

If it was possible, Flur's smile brightened even as her blush deepened, the room itself seeming to glow warmer for it. "Good morning, my bond-maighstir."

Rhyslin returned her smile as he drew her to her feet, pulling her gently to his side. He turned to Allanagh, his eyes shadowed by wonder. "The last thing I expected when going out to eat was to be ambushed by a bonding rite."

All color drained from Allanagh's face and her knees were shaking. She had to grab at the bedposts to keep from falling.

The carved wood felt slick beneath her palms, as though the air itself had grown clammy with her dread. She would have, if the Draoidh hadn't crossed the room and slipped an arm around her.

The touch steadied not only her body but the quivering hush of the chamber, as if the walls exhaled with relief.

"Yes, that was my reaction last eve." His voice carried like a low note across taut strings, soothing even as it reminded her of what had unsettled him.

Allanagh held to him just long enough to get her bearings back. Her breath was shallow, edged with the taste of iron as though her body itself echoed judgment.

"Why?" She couldn't think of the right questions to ask. Her whisper trembled in the air, the braziers' flames flickering as if straining to catch the meaning.

"Why didn't I refuse her? or why did I let her?"

Allanagh could only nod.

A self-deprecating chuckle escaped him, and the sound stirred the still air like a breeze in closed drapes. "I would have tried to refuse her, except she took the vow in Ananke's name, and her desire turned ribbons into iron chains."

When he leaned closer and whispered in her ear, the chamber itself leaned with him, shadows tightening in the corners. "You are always welcome in our home, Naneth ven gwedh."

Allanagh gasped, the word striking her like a bell, and would have fainted had Rhyslin not guided her to the bed. The mattress dipped with her weight, sighing as if bearing witness.

Looking over to where Flur was standing, he raised an eyebrow. "Should I have checked you for these maladies before going to dinner last eve?"

Flur walked across the room, the boards creaking softly in rhythm with her steps, and lifted her hand to his shoulder.

The air thickened with her nearness, carrying a faint sweetness of lavender.

"No, my maighstir. I do not suffer from fainting spells."

The air seemed to thicken and Allanagh's spine stiffened as she sat up and glared at her daughter. The morning light through the shutters sharpened, as though siding with her indignation.

"I do not suffer spells, Maighstir Darkblade." She paused, each word heavy enough to make the silence vibrate. "At least not normally. Though this is not a normal morning."

When Rhyslin smiled, the air slowly relaxed, the droning of insects outside shifting into harmony, sounding like nature's instruments.

"Naneth ven gwedh? Honestly?"

Allanagh took a few moments to restore her equilibrium, her breath evening out while the world around her steadied.

"By my honor, I never thought to sway you by offering my daughter to you. It was —"

"Her idea." Rhyslin looked into Allanagh's eyes, seeing her honesty reflected like water stilled after a storm.

"I gathered that."

Rhyslin's mind skipped and reeled, like a boat on a choppy bay. Even the shadows seemed to sway with the turbulence of his thoughts.

Allanagh's mortified behavior raised a valid concern. "Even though it was unplanned, Flur's actions will not affect the treaty."

Without realizing it, Allanagh bowed her head. The air bent with her, carrying the faint, almost inaudible hum of reprieve. "Thank nan diathan for small favors."

"They seem to grant favors in unexpected ways."

Rhyslin assisted Allanagh to her feet, his grip steadying her as if he lent her the earth's own weight.

Once on her feet, Allanagh took a shaky step toward her daughter. "So, you aren't mad about what happened?" She didn't know why, but she didn't want Rhyslin mad at her.

Rhyslin barked out a laugh and rubbed his forehead, the sound cracking the solemn air like sudden thunder. "I'm still too much in shock to be mad. The treaties are safe."

Allanagh stared at him in surprise, while Flur simply smiled at him, her composure bright as sunlight through the shutters.

"Would you care for something for breakfast, my maighstir?"

Rhyslin nodded and reached out his hand for Flur's. The chamber brightened at the gesture, the bond between them rippling outward like warmth spilling through cold stone.

"I would. Would the same place be open?"

"Para's?" Flur tilted her head toward him. "I believe so." She curled her fingers around his hand, and the lavender of her skin warmed to his grasp. "Can Mother come?"

Rhyslin nodded, taking a deep breath of Flur's lavender drops. The scent seemed to ease the room, smoothing its earlier turbulence.

As the three left the cottage, the morning met them with a softer sky, the air fresher, the world itself lighter—as if in acknowledgment. It suddenly occurred to Rhyslin that he didn't have his usual early morning headache.

They paused along the way, when a speckled kitten leapt out of the bushes and attacked Rhyslin's right boot.

Allanagh started to shoo the cat away, but paused when a playful grin crossed the Draoidh's face and he moved his foot around, teasing the kitten.

The breeze shifted faintly, carrying the grassy-sweet scent of meadow clover as if the land itself exhaled with his smile. When the kitten pounced again, Rhyslin laughed, dug into his pouch, and dropped a small leather wrapped sphere on the ground.

The kitten pounced at it, then retreated, only to sneak up on the sphere and bat at it. When the sphere rolled away, the kitten yowled, the sound sharp against the morning hush, then chased after the object.

Rhyslin watched the kitten play. At his side, Flur watched attentively, noticing the small smile that danced across his lips, then disappeared like shadows at noon-time.

The faint warmth of buttered bread still lingering from the inn's hearth drifted on the air, a reminder of time passing. "If we don't hurry, breakfast will be done and we'll have to wait for lunch."

Rhyslin nodded and walked slow enough that both women could walk at his side. The earth seemed to soften its press beneath their boots, as though keeping pace.

They hadn't taken more than ten steps when a black and white spotted dog came running out of a shadowed alley and started sniffing around Rhyslin. The old draoidh paused and held out his hand, palm up, as the dog sniffed his fingers and then bumped his hand and whined. A faint musk of fur and wet stone rose as the creature pressed closer. Rhyslin blinked, wondering what the dog wanted.

The dog whined again, its tail wagging, as it bumped his hand again. When Rhyslin turned his hand over and started scratching the dog behind the right ear, it panted, its left foot tapping the ground. Rhyslin watched, bemused, as the dog angled its head in order to have the scratching fingers hit the right spot, then chuffed happily before walking back to the house and curling up on the porch.

Flur watched Rhyslin stand there in amused shock. The air around them felt strangely hushed, as if even the sparrows on the roofline waited to see what would happen next. After a few minutes, he shook his head. "That's odd."

"What's odd, my maighstir?" Flur half-turned toward him, her right eyebrow lifting slightly. The faint scent of mint teased the air, sharp and curious, mirroring his thoughtful mood.

"Two animals in less than half an hour." Rhyslin reached up and scratched his chin. "Usually animals run away from me, even when I'm around Marcus." His fingertips curled, almost as if he were itching to write a research paper over something.

Then, as if to make a point, four hummingbirds darted out from a flower garden as they walked by it, and circled Rhyslin's head, chirping at him, before darting off. Their wings thrummed the air with a high, glassy hum that shimmered in his bones. The draoidh tilted his head to the left and blinked.

The wind fell still for the space of a heartbeat, then stirred again. "That was strange."

At his side, Flur simply smiled, as if she knew the answer. Before she could speak, the two taghta walked up to him. The air seemed to brighten faintly around them, touched by the floral sweetness of their presence.

"What's strange, Mac Draoidheacd? They were telling you where to find a particularly juicy rose bush," Lilly commented.

"That's what's strange. Animals don't talk to me," Rhyslin murmured, trying to apply some kind of logic to it. The words tasted of iron in his mouth, as though logic itself balked at being bent.

The bound taghta, Analise, watched him for a minute, and then made a cheeky inquiry. "How's your head today?"

Rhyslin started to answer her, froze, his eyes narrowing as he thought it over. A hush passed through the street, as though even the sparrows on the eaves leaned in. "I haven't had a headache today at all." He paused, trying to recall the last time he had had a headache. "Come to think about it, I haven't had any pain since last …" His voice faltered, and a breath of cool lavender threaded through the air, softening the admission. "Mathair will never let me hear the end of this."

Ana cast a side-wise look at Flur, who blushed and looked down. Her golden hair fell forward like a curtain, carrying the scent of roses sharper now, betraying her emotions.

When the bound taghta looked back at Rhyslin, she was wearing a smug grin. "Maighstir Rhyslin, did you initiate a bond with the princess?"

Hearing that, Chantico's taghta, Lilly, gave a wolfish smile, sharp as flint sparking.

"No," Rhyslin whispered under his breath. The syllable carried the weight of disbelief, and his snowy hair seemed to stir though the air was still. "I didn't initiate the bond. Flur did." He was still in shock about that as well.

Lilly smirked, leaning in toward the draoidh. "I couldn't quite hear that. What did you say?"

"I didn't initiate the bond," Rhyslin said a little louder, his voice steady now but tinged with awe. "Flur initiated the bond, and she did so in Ananke's name."

Lilly chuckled, giving Rhyslin a quick hug that smelled faintly of woodsmoke and sage.

"Animals have always wanted to come up to you. Your pain has always kept them away." She turned to Flur and offered a half-bow, the air bending with her deference. "Congratulations." She looked back at Rhyslin. "You're right, Astinmah would never let you live it down." The wolfish grin danced over her lips. "But you still need to tell her—it's only right."

"I know." Rhyslin's grim tone earned him a playful smack on the back of the head by Lilly. His sigh brushed the morning quiet like a weary breeze. "Hey." He exhaled, then conceded, "You're right, Lilly." He looked at Flur.

"You might have to eat breakfast without me. I do need to go —"

"No!" Flur shook her head, her golden hair flying like sunlit flame. "You're not going to A' Mathair without me." Her rose perfume sharpened, almost metallic now, signalling her heartfelt feelings.

When he glanced at Allanagh, her grin said it all. "I wouldn't miss this for all the sweet bread in the city." Her words carried the warm yeast-scent of hearth and home, grounding the moment.

Resigned, Rhyslin turned away from the eatery and turned toward the council chamber. The light seemed to tilt, shadows stretching before their path. Before they made it there, several more animals crossed Rhyslin's way.

One was a flying squirrel which launched itself from a tree, its fur carrying the musk of bark and resin, and landed on Rhyslin's shoulder for a brief second before launching itself at the black pearl atop his staff.

The draoidh stopped and watched as the volans picked at the pearl, then turned to him and skittered. Rhyslin blinked as the thought of taking the black stone back to its den pulled at him like a whispered temptation.

Rhyslin shook his head in disbelief and waved the staff. "Go away, little one. This isn't for you."

The squirrel bared its teeth and skittered back, a dry chitter like crackling twigs, before leaping from the staff and gliding as close as it could to a tree before landing at the base.

In an instant, it was back up the tree and hiding in the leafy canopy, the branches rattling with its scolding.

"This is just too strange," Rhyslin murmured. "It scolded me for tricking it."

The bound taghta listened, her hands crossing over her stomach. She tried to keep from laughing, the sound trembling like a brook beneath stone, and nearly succeeded until, with the ruffle of black feathers and an imperious caw, a black raven descended. It landed atop the pearl and gazed down at Rhyslin with eyes like chips of night.

Analise's laughter rang out pure and joyous, and she dropped to one knee, overcome by the omen.

Flur watched everything in rapt fascination, even covering her mouth with one palm, when the raven landed and croaked at Rhyslin. Her perfume softened, settling into a steady bloom of rose and honey, mirroring her awe.

The draoidh grumbled under his breath, lifted his hand to the raven, which jumped onto it and stepped down his arm with regal weight before settling on his shoulder. The black feathers gleamed with hidden violet in the morning light.

"I think I preferred it more when you all tried to run away from me." His snowy hair rustled around his shoulders as he resumed his trek toward the council hall, the raven riding his shoulder like a herald.

With a determined look on his face, Rhyslin pushed open the door that he had entered only the day before, only this time, he entered with his bond-mate, the Hîn i-Balanath Queen, and animals in tow. The air inside stirred like a living breath, carrying the earthy tang of loam and the sweetness of sap.

Before he had even taken a step, the crow launched itself into the air with a rush of black wings, making a beeline for the giant Ubhal tree in the center of the rotunda. Its caws echoed sharp as struck flint against the vaulted green canopy.

By the time Rhyslin made it to the center of the rotunda, the crow was dancing around Astinmah, screaming at her.

The goddess looked up, golden-green light haloing her features as Rhyslin and Flur stepped into the boundary of her awareness. The air smelled suddenly of crushed apple blossoms.

"Good morrow, my beloved son." She paused, her gaze softening before it shifted to Flur. A note of spring rain touched the air with her recognition. "Good morrow, my daughter."

The draoidh walked over to the goddess and sank to his knees before her. His snowy hair slipped forward, catching the glow of leaf-filtered light. "Despite my every objection, and determination to never bond a woman to my soul. Ananke's iron bonds have bound me to my bond-mate." His voice was rough with surrender, anguish pooling in his eyes. "You have won, Mathair."

The goddess turned her attention from the crow to her son. Her presence bent the air, warm as hearthfire and cool as shaded forest. "It was never about winning or losing, my son. It was about living to your fullest. Ananke's life-bonds aren't punishments, they are rewards." She acknowledged when Flur knelt beside Rhyslin, the rose-scent of her devotion blooming in the chamber. "Has your pain not gone away? Has the natural world not sought you out, as it should?"

"It has," he whispered, the admission thin as falling leaves. "Next, I suppose you will try to place that damned crown on my head."

The forest goddess looked at Dearg, who was watching from her tree, her bark-skin shimmering with anticipation.

At her signal, the dryad scampered up into the top limbs of the tree. Branches swayed as though parting for her, until she gathered five apples, cradling them to her bosom as if they were newborns, then carried them down and placed them reverently into Astinmah's hands.

The goddess handed the fruit to Rhyslin, her fingers fragrant with sap and spring rain. He in turn passed them to Flur and Allanagh, his gesture both instinctive and weighted with unspoken meaning.

"I do not believe I will try to give you the crown." The goddess took a bite of the apple. The crisp sound rang through the rotunda like a bell.

A cool breeze wafted down from above the ubhal tree, carrying the smell of warm spring rains and new grass. Rhyslin raised his head, blinking, trying to decipher the layered meaning behind the gifts. The apple in his hand gleamed as though catching its own light.

"You are now opened to nature. When you leave this place, think about the meaning of the crown you despise. When you are ready, I will speak with you again." Her words shimmered in the air like a song carried on wind. Then, as quickly as she had transformed the dryad, the goddess was gone, leaving a sleeping Keisha nestled in her place, her breath rising and falling with the hush of leaves.

Rhyslin took a bite of the apple. Sweetness burst across his tongue, sharp and alive, the juice trailing down his lip like nectar. He wiped it away absently, his gaze lifting, lost in thought beneath the endless canopy.

*Chapter Six*
The Dawn-Breaker in Distress.

Rhyslin's peaceful contemplation shattered as Marcus entered the garden, his presence moving through the grove like a silent wave that stirred every bloom it brushed. The air shifted with him; petals quivered, stems leaned, and the faint hum of prana sharpened.

Instead of announcing himself, the ranger slipped forward with the grace of a shadow, his footsteps swallowed by the living earth, weaving between blossoms whose fragrance deepened in his wake.

High in her tree, Dearg, her eyes closed, felt his passage long before her ears twitched.

The air caressed her bark-skin as though in greeting, flowers bending subtly toward him as if compelled by memory of rain. A feline curiosity prickled along her spine, and with a supple coil of muscle she leapt down, the rush of leaves trailing her descent.

The busty, red-haired dryad landed near him, emerald eyes flashing, her cat-like ears twitching as her tail sketched an idle sigil in the perfumed air. She circled Marcus with the lazy confidence of one who ruled this rotunda, bare feet padding against moss that glowed faintly at her touch. "Gaur-thalun," she purred, her voice a whisper threaded with the song of roots. "You honor Dearg by not disturbing her flowers."

Marcus offered only a tight smile, but his hand moved with old familiarity, finding the spot behind her right ear. His fingers pressed gently, and she shivered as though the entire tree shuddered with her.

A rumble escaped her throat — part growl, part reluctant pleasure — as she batted at his hand. "Stop that, Gaur-thalun. Dearg is not a cat." Yet she did not step away.

An ivy vine uncoiled itself from the nearest trunk, stretching curiously toward Marcus, halting only when his raised palm met it with calm prana. When his touch fell away from her, the vine retreated, and Dearg bounded back to her tree with an indignant flick of her ears, though the lingering warmth still clung to her.

"What is it, Marcus?" Rhyslin's eyes remained closed, yet his awareness had never faltered; he had felt the ranger's approach the moment the air bent inward. Marcus, carrying the weight of years and the steadiness of a seasoned bowstring, drew the very grass toward him. Flowers tilted in his wake, the dome's breeze tightening into a current of urgent anticipation.

He gestured toward the sky, where the morning's blue dimmed with haze. "The Dawn-Breaker approaches from the North-East."

Rhyslin opened his eyes, their depth reflecting the green firelight of the rotunda. Marcus stood with hands clasped, utterly at ease among the living blossoms.

But beneath that calm, the draoidh read the taut edge of danger. "We expected her return today," Rhyslin said evenly. "You would not have come unless something is amiss."

The ranger's jaw worked before he answered, shaking his head. "The lookout says she's behaving strangely."

Flur, seated close at Rhyslin's side, tilted her head, raven hair glinting where sunlight spilled through leaf-dappled gaps. "In what way?"

"I don't know." Marcus's voice was flat, but his aura pressed heavy as ironwood. "The lookout couldn't explain it."

"Master Marcus," Flur spoke softly, her words carrying like ripples across still water. "My people have rarely seen a ship sail the sky. He may sense something but lacks the tongue to name it."

A grunt, half concession, half acknowledgment, broke from Marcus. The air about him stiffened as though a bow had been drawn to its last inch. "Fair point. Perhaps we'll know more at the wall."

The draoidh rose, fingers curling around the living staff that leaned against Dearg's tree. The staff hummed faintly, sap stirring at his touch. "Very well." He glanced to the dryad, whose green gaze was already on him. "Thank you for the ubhal, Dearg."

She ran fingers through her flame-red hair, the leaves above rustling as though echoing her pride. "Dearg is glad you enjoyed them."

Stretching upward, she coaxed a branch down with a gesture, plucking a ripe apple without looking. Offering it to Marcus, she inclined her head. "Fare well, Gaur-thalun." Then she turned and bowed with quiet gravity to Rhyslin. "Be safe, Mac Draoidheachd."

Marcus accepted the fruit, its skin cool and fragrant in his palm, and bit into it with an audible crunch. The scent of sweetness mingled with resin and moss.

"May the wind always bring rain to nourish your tree, Dearg Uhbal." Without further word, he turned and strode away, Rhyslin and Flur falling in step beside him.

Around them, flowers leaned into their passage, petals brushing their shoulders like benedictions.

From above, Dearg scampered high into her branches, her laughter low and leaf-tinged, watching until the trio vanished beyond the arch. "May the sky bless you, and the ground soften your steps," she whispered, her words sinking into bark and air alike.

Rhyslin, Marcus, and Flur made their way toward the nearest lookout station atop the wall. The air shifted as they passed, the murmur of the crowds thinning to silence, bodies almost instinctively opening up and making a path through which the three moved. The gaps closed behind them, as if by magic, as though the city itself breathed around Rhyslin's will.

Flur glanced up at him, uneasy at how naturally the people parted, wondering why they moved out of his way without realizing it. The grass at the edges of the stone path bent toward his passing, echoing the same deference. Footsteps behind her made her turn, smiling as she saw Ilyriatri and Vuuroena had fallen in with them. She slowed a step, falling back with the other women.

"How is he doing that?" She gestured as they passed through another gathering, the press of humanity rolling back like the tide.

"It's his prana." Ilyriatri pointed out as the crowd closed again behind them, her sand-colored skirt whispering against the cobbles.

"Those of lesser will move out of his way. The only reason you didn't know is because you are under the canopy of his will." Her words seemed to carry weight, as if the breeze itself thickened with them.

Upon reaching the wall, Flur eyed the stairs going up to the lookout station. The wind toyed with her hem, and she imagined the climb, imagined the eyes, the view beneath her skirt should the gusts rise. She decided to wait below, preferring dignity to curiosity. Still, she felt the sting of jealousy at how easily Rhyslin and Marcus took the steps, their bodies at ease with the climb.

Ilyriatri's hand on her shoulder pulled her back from her thoughts. The touch carried warmth, grounding, like dipping into heated sand at sunset. "Flur. Did you soul-bond with him?"

A slow blush crawled over her skin, heat rising like an ember beneath her cheeks. She turned, her voice quiet. "I did, tedel Ilyriatri."

The desert-born Hîn i-Balanath examined her niece, then nodded once, her satisfaction flowing outward like warm lavender smoke curling through the air. "I can sense your peace from here." She leaned closer, her voice binding the moment. "Did you vow upon our Lady of Chains?"

Surprised and a little dismayed by how her aunt had unraveled her secret, Flur nodded. Ilyriatri's lips curved with quiet triumph, and Flur could feel that satisfaction radiating through the bond between them, as palpable as sunlight through closed eyes.

Vuuroena's smile was bright, but her heart twinged like a harp-string stretched too far. She could not help but feel betrayed that her Aon Sociar had bonded with her cousin.

The breeze betrayed her disquiet, tugging more sharply at her dark hair, though she tried to hide the sting. "I'm happy for you," she said, and prayed Flur could not hear the faint fracture beneath her voice.

Once atop the windswept wall, Rhyslin's staff thudded against the weathered plank, the wood echoing hollow and alive as he scanned the hazy sky. The air was sharp with resin and pine, the mist cooling his skin, a warning of the storm rolling unseen.

Beside him, Marcus mirrored his motion, cloak snapping as he turned to the lookout whose rough-spun tunic whipped in the gusts.

"Where is she?" Marcus called, the wind carrying his voice and scattering it among the stones.

"Ennas," the lookout pointed with a calloused finger toward a distant cloud, a mile off. "Dancing in and out of the clouds for almost a quarter uair." His words were nearly lost to the rising gale.

Marcus followed his gaze. "There she is," he pointed, as the ship's keel sliced ghostlike through the cloud.

Rhyslin nodded, the curved keel visible against the grey. He waited, heart tightening, the flowers in the gardens below bowing under the downdraft of gathering storm.

Then the galleon plunged twenty feet, her keel scraping the treetops. Rhyslin gasped, the jarring nearness of collision sending a shiver through his spine. The world around him seemed to wince with him, branches creaking in sympathy.

"What is that pilot doing?" His voice sharp with concern, and his prana surged outward like a wave, staggering the lookout two steps back.

Instead of anger, the man calmly closed his eyes, wrapping himself in a bubble of prana that shimmered faintly in the air like heat over stone. He steadied himself, acknowledging the draoidh's raw force without fear.

Marcus swore under his breath as the sky-ship lurched right, then dipped her bow earthward, her sails snapping. "If Meron is drunk again, I'm going to—"

His curses were carried away by the wind as the vessel leapt upward in a violent gust.

Without turning, Rhyslin's command cut clean through the gale. "When she presents, check the spars, masts, lines, and sails."

The ranger nodded, pressing the long-glass to his eye. The metal chilled his fingers, the wind tugging at his cloak as he traced the ship from keel to masthead. "Nothing appears to be damaged," he reported, voice clipped. "Foremast and sails hold. Mizzenmast the same. Mainmast true." He swept upward, eyes narrowing. "Stun sails and booms are sound. Counter-sails set. Rudder holds."

As the winds at cloud-level strengthened, the Dawn-Breaker lurched forward. Her bow dipped hard, then fought to right itself. Rhyslin breathed the scent of damp rising, storm-wrack heavy in the air, the kind that pressed into bone and warned of thunder.

She was beautiful,  a three-masted galleon, meant to glide like a dolphin through sky-tides, not stumble like a drunk ox. Watching her jar sideways and tip left, pained him, as if his own balance had been stripped away.

He leaned into the wind, eyes fixed on her form. "If it's not the structure or sails, then it must be draoidheil." His frustration surged as the pilot failed to correct. "What is Meron thinking?" His jaw clenched. "Do you have your mind-stone?"

"Yep." Marcus kept his gaze steady. "Who do you want me to talk to?"

Rhyslin's eyes burned with worry. "Captain O'Cuire. Find out who's piloting her, ideally before she capsizes."

"Gotcha." Marcus reached into the pocket of his cloak, pulled out a reddish-gold crystal, and cupped it in his left hand. The stone's surface pulsed faintly, warmth bleeding into his palm. "O'Cuire." His eyes never left the sky-ship as she heeled starboard, timbers groaning, sails snapping. If she rolled, unsecured sailors would spill like seeds from a broken pod, dashed upon the forest below.

He repeated the call twice before the captain's voice bled through the crystal.

The delay coiled Marcus's temper tight, his breath hissing sharp. The air around him soured, tinged with brimstone and char, the acrid scent spreading like a warning. Finally, his voice cracked the storming silence. "Damn it, O'Cuire, I'm standing beside Rhyslin, and he wants to know why his ship is in danger of capsizing."

The anger flared, then eased as the ranger listened, his jaw tightening, his stance shifting. The brimstone dissipated into the damp, leaving only resin and salt. He nodded sharply, his voice clipped.

"Yes. Yes. I understand." He turned to Rhyslin, eyes shadowed. "Before they could run from the storm, Meron took a static strike. He's still unconscious. O'Cuire said it took them two days to wrest back control. They severed the connection between the crystal and the ship."

Rhyslin's breath hitched, his horror mirrored in the tightening wind, which rattled banners along the wall. "If they severed the connections, then why is she capsizing?"

Marcus bent his head, listening again to the humming stone. The color of his aura shifted, bright anticipation dimming into worry. "According to O'Cuire, Rembran offered to calm the elementals. They are not listening to him."

Rhyslin cursed, the sound heavy as lead. The air itself seemed to recoil. "Tell O'Cuire to level her and aim for the river. I want my ship down before the keel breaks."

His fingers curled hard around his staff, the living wood answering with a thrum. He leaned forward, eyes burning into the drifting galleon. "Come on, O'Cuire. Come on."

Every second dragged like a rope across raw hands. The salty wind whipped Rhyslin's hair into his face, the sting of it making him wish he stood on her deck, feeling the roll beneath his feet, steadying her with his own prana. The thought stabbed sharp as splintered wood, then dulled, he knew his presence would not change her state. All he could do was watch and wait.

From the distant sky came the rasp of wood against wood, faint shouts carried on the gale. "Come on, O'Cuire," he whispered, voice threading the storm. "Pull in the stun sails."

As if the ship itself heard, the handlers hauled with frantic precision. Ropes thrummed like bowstrings, snapping and singing as canvas collapsed. The air hung heavy with salt and sweat, taut with anticipation.

The counter-sails followed — their dance more intricate, a ritual of balance. Sailors lowered each with care, every creak of spar and boom echoing in Rhyslin's chest.

"They are running out of time." Marcus's voice was rough, like waves breaking on stone.

Rhyslin's knuckles whitened on his staff, the knots digging into his palm, each one a hard reminder of helplessness. The ship's deck tipped until she was nearly perpendicular to the earth, the forest beneath yawning wide to receive her. With a slow, agonizing sequence, each section of the starboard counter-sail came down, pulled inboard by straining arms.

The draoidh stood frozen, breath caught like a held chord. Then, at last, the Dawn-Breaker settled, her keel righting with a shudder. He fancied he heard her groan, not of despair, but of relief, a weary sigh of timbers spared.

"They did it." Marcus exhaled, the weight lifting from his voice, a ripple of calm replacing brimstone. Rhyslin's shoulders eased, though the lines of worry etched his face deeper.

On the deck far above, work continued as the port-side counter-sail was secured in mirrored fashion.

"It will take them days to reassemble it," Marcus noted, gesturing at the loose sails and scattered gear.

Warm pine and tar reached Rhyslin's nose, sharp and grounding. He released his grip, sighing. "Better a few days than to lose her altogether." His voice softened, though the ache remained.

Marcus touched the cool, polished surface of the mind-stone. It vibrated faintly, a thrumming pulse in the air. Closing his eyes, he listened, then opened them again. "O'Cuire asks where you want her to land."

Rhyslin barked a laugh, frustration and affection mingling. "Where does he think I want her? There's a perfect river below us, wide enough to cradle her. He need only take her down." He turned, boots thudding against the stair as he descended, the rough wood rasping beneath his palm. "Tell me when she touches water."

"Will do. Where will you be?"

"Breakfast." Rhyslin's reply drifted back over his shoulder, softened by the promise of simple comforts. Already the wind carried scents of fresh bread and bitter coffee, a reminder that life pressed on even when ships faltered in the sky.

Even as Rhyslin, Flur, and the rest of the Hîn i-Balanath women took their morning meal beneath the slanting light of the sun, his thoughts drifted far from the warmth of the table.

Marcus had mentioned something about the elementals—Ixa and Andros—suffering emotional turmoil. Rembran was trying to soothe them, but whatever had shaken them still echoed in the bond Rhyslin shared with the ship itself.

A faint salt tang haunted the breeze, out of place in the inland meadow.

His free hand tapped an uneven rhythm against the polished wood, fingertips whispering across the grain like restless wings. The wood itself seemed to thrum faintly beneath his touch, echoing agitation not his own.

He bit into a slice of honey-dipped bread, but even the sharp sweetness and the faint golden dust of open blossoms nearby failed to tether him to the present. The petals along the table's edge stirred as if in an unseen draft, shivering with his distraction.

Flur did her best to weave conversation among the women, her voice light as a sunray across still water. Yet when her thread ran thin, she folded her hands in her lap and sat as quiet as a thistle-mouse, casting small glances toward her bond-master. The bond between them fluttered faintly against him, like wings against glass, unanswered.

Ilyriatri watched him more openly. Her gaze held the weight of a mother-river—ancient, knowing, impossible to evade.

With a gentle certainty, she reached across and laid her hand atop his, stilling the insistent tapping. The wood beneath his palm quieted as though listening.

"You cannot mend a wind-torn sail until you're aboard the ship," she said softly. "And worry unspent becomes poison." Her gaze shifted to Flur, who blushed as though caught in a beam of truth. "Besides… you leave your bond-mate calling into silence."

The air hushed. Even the steady drone of meadow insects faltered, as if the world itself bent toward her words. The blossoms at the table's edge drooped under sudden stillness, waiting.

Rhyslin's shoulders slackened. He looked to Ilyriatri, then dipped his head once in solemn acknowledgment. "You speak the truth."

She leaned back, satisfied, a knowing curl lifting one corner of her mouth like a seal placed and sealed again.

Rhyslin reached out and took Flur's hand in his own, the warmth returning to his touch. The bond surged softly back into place, like a stream freed of stones. Light shifted through the trees, gilding the table, and the blossoms lifted again to the sun.

"Will you forgive me, my thoughts flying too far for your voice to call them back?" he asked.

Flur brushed her hair over one shoulder, a smile blooming like a morning lily. "Always, my beloved bond-master." She leaned toward him, the pulse of her bond brushing his skin like a soft breath. "What has you troubled?"

"Ixa and Andros. The elementals who hold the Dawn-Breaker's breath." His grip tightened, not on her, but against his own rising tension. "Marcus says they are experiencing distress. But until I walk her decks, I can do nothing but guess." He exhaled and gave his head a slow shake, as though trying to dislodge guilt itself.

The insects resumed their soft hymn, the meadow easing back into its song. The golden scent of honey returned, sharp and alive. Had he known the moment his spirit stilled, he might have recognized the intimacy between his soul and the living world—that they would rise and fall in rhythm with him.

Thirty breaths of the sun passed. Servers cleared the plates as tea cooled in the cups, steam unraveling into the air like faint, unfinished prayers.

Then Natolie approached, wind-tossed and alert, her steps as fluid as the river's edge. She dipped into a half-bow, sea-colored tunic brushing her knees, the scent of salt clinging faintly to her hair.

"The Dawn-Breaker is down in the river's heart," she said. "Marcus is guiding her toward shore. She floats high and proud—no hull damage we can see." Her smile, as always with Rhyslin, came with familiar ease, and carried just as much warmth toward Flur.

"Tell him I'll be there before the sand has passed." Rhyslin rose, the bench creaking in relief, and moved behind Flur's chair.

He paused a moment, letting his shadow fall across her shoulders, then drew the chair back with care, offering his hand. The bond between them hummed faintly, like a taut string awaiting its song.

"I hate to leave you, mo leannan, but duty calls me to her hull." His voice carried the steadiness of oaths spoken beside firelight.

Flur rose with his help, her fingers brushing his palm, soft as willow-leaves. She tilted up and kissed him lightly on the lips, a blessing more than a farewell. "We'll be fine. The four of us," she gestured with a tilt of her chin toward Allanagh, Ilyriatri, and Vuuroena, "plan to hunt the markets."

But the words did not loosen him. Dissatisfaction twisted his lips, and he pulled her in—close, possessive, necessary.

His mouth claimed hers in a kiss that seared like sunlight through morning frost, pulling her breath into his.

The air itself seemed to hush; even the bees at the windows slowed their wings.

Flur melted into him, her knees weakening as her bond sang like a struck crystal, flooding her with warmth, bright and stunned.

When he finally released her, she lingered in his arms, dazed and smiling, the scent of crushed blossoms rising faintly from where her skirts brushed the rushes.

"That was cruel," she murmured, lips flushed. "Now I'll be thinking of nothing but that kiss."

He turned from her, already walking, the air about him shimmering faintly as though scorched by his passing. "That was the intent," he called without looking back.

Behind him, the women laughed, their voices ringing like bells shaken loose from winter, scattering cold shadows and filling the hall with warmth.

# Chapter Seven

## The Draoidh's Crossing

Rhyslin stood on the sandy shore, staring at the mighty vessel drifting at the center of the river. At the moment, his thoughts were not on the ship, but upon the kiss he shared with Flur. All too vividly, he recalled her body against his, the feel of her lips under his, the taste of her breath, the sound of her murmurs as he released her.

The memory lingered like heat after lightning, the river wind cooling against his cheek as if to hush it away.

With considerable reluctance, he dismissed Flur from his thoughts. The source of his problem was where his ship was, or rather, where she wasn't.

It did no good to have her resting in the middle of the river, with the water lapping against her side in patient rhythm.

As long as she was there, he could no more board her than the sailors could replace the counter sails.

A pier would have better served her, but none existed. The river itself seemed to whisper this truth, a hollow lap against the hull, then silence.

Rhyslin turned to the black-clad Hîn i-Balanath standing a few feet away. He wondered if the man was making a statement, or if the lack of coloration served a purpose. "I have seen travelers up and down the three rivers. Why are there no piers?"

Sloan watched the river for a moment. The breeze ruffled the dark hem of his cloak, though he did not move. "We can pull our river craft up on the shore." He turned to Rhyslin and examined him with a killer's eye, as steady as a drawn blade. "A pier would make it far too easy for our enemies to cross the river and attack us."

Rhyslin's fingers curled around the worn wooden staff, seeking the calming silver-etched runes. His touch drew a faint vibration, like a sigh through the wood.

He shook his head. "I see your point, but not having one prevents me from boarding my ship, or others from leaving."

His frustration wasn't with Sloan. In fact, he found the black-clad Hîn i-Balanath to be much like Marcus, a soldier hardened by strife, scarred but unyielding.

Sloan watched the ship for a moment, remembering how many soldiers had leapt from ship to shore and spent cold days waiting for the enemy to show up, while his people stayed safe and warm within the walls. A faint ripple coursed across the river, stirred by memory as much as wind. "All of your ships traverse the air, like birds, yes?"

"Most do, but we have our own river craft." Rhyslin turned to Sloan. "The Saorsa has blessed us with many bodies of water to land upon, which helps with trade and transport of goods and supplies."

Sloan looked back at the ship. "Build your pier. We will need it when your ships stop by for visits." He shrugged. "If it becomes too much of a danger, we'll take it down."

"I may not need a complete pier." Rhyslin knelt down, almost ritually, and traced outlines in the sand. Grains shifted like tiny sparks, the earth shivering under his hand. "I need just a sturdy pole driven into the sand at either end of the ship." He drew the lines from the ship to shore. "Once secured, we can lower the gangplank and use it to cross."

Sloan held out his hand, rugged from many years bearing a sword, to Rhyslin. A tired smile played on his lips as he said, "I appreciate the fact that you are thinking of our safety, but as I said, build your pier."

Rhyslin stared at Sloan until the other shook his head, then gave a curt nod. "Very well. There's no time like the present."

Sloan drew in a slow, deep breath. The scents of cattails and warm sand drifted away into the forest to mingle with wild roses and the high crowns of Darach trees.

For a moment, the hush of the world pressed around him, as if listening for his decision. He hoped they weren't making a mistake.

As the sand shifted beneath his feet, he could well imagine that the river shared his misgivings—but like him, she would keep her own counsel.

Rhyslin turned to the river and watched as two men poled boats around the Dawn-Breaker. From the way they dropped lines into the water, he could tell that they were checking the depth beneath the ship's keel. In order to stay afloat, the Dawn-Breaker needed fifteen feet of water under her keel.

The river, stirred by their poles, sent back little eddies as though whispering its measurements for those who knew how to listen.

He looked around, trying to find Marcus, but didn't see him. Holding his staff up and waving it, he caught the attention of one sailor. "Have you seen Marcus?"

When the sailor indicated he couldn't hear Rhyslin, the draoidh muttered as he traced a sigil in the air. The silver lines shimmered briefly before vanishing like mist. "Have you seen Commander Tanner?"

This time, the man nodded and pointed toward the Dawn-Breaker. Rhyslin sighed. He knew where Marcus was, and now he had to figure out how to get to the ship.

He walked to the bank, dipped his staff into the water, and watched it become completely submerged. The current curled around the living wood as if tasting it, before tugging it deeper. It was too deep to wade.

Drawn by the displacement of the living staff, a catfish poked its head up and looked around. Rhyslin waved it away. "Go on, enjoy your life. You can't help me, anyway."

The fish, not caring one way or the other, flicked its whiskers and sank back into the water, vanishing with a ripple that lapped against the bank like faint laughter.

Rhyslin was about to give up, when he heard the whisper of wood to his right side and turned to find a lissome Hîn i-Balanath paddling her boat down the river.

The canoe's bow sliced the current with a hush, reeds bending as though bowing in her passage.

Her boat drifted to a crawl as she lifted her head and stared at him. "Is there a thing I can do for you?"

She brushed a lock of hair behind her ear. At that slight gesture, Rhyslin caught the scent of wild berries carried on the damp wind, mingling with the green musk of river reeds.

"Would you be able to take me to my ship?" He pointed at the galleon.

The girl looked from him to the majestic galleon, then turned her gaze back to him. "I would. It's not that deep. Why not swim?"

Rhyslin cleared his throat. "I'm not dressed to swim, and it's easier to ride out."

The wild berry scent intensified when she laughed, reminding him of a coyote calling to the moon. Even the water seemed to brighten with her mirth, glinting sunlight across the ripples. "I hear you, lazy man. Get in, I'll paddle you over to your ship, so you don't get wet." She held her paddle down and grounded it to stop her canoe.

Rhyslin sighed. She had every right to mock him. Nothing he could say would change her mind. Once he was aboard, kneeling awkwardly in the center, the Hîn i-Balanath used her oar to angle the canoe toward the Dawn-Breaker.

The craft rocked gently, answering every dip of her paddle. Rhyslin rode in silence as the river-maiden let her canoe drift to a halt next to the massive galleon and used an oar to push the tiny boat flush with the entry to the gangway.

Before trying to stand, he glanced at her. "My thanks, river-maiden. If you need anything, I'll do my best to repay you."

The giggle that followed reminded Rhyslin of soft rain falling into still pools. Even the river seemed to hush for it. "You don't have to do anything, Maighstir Darkblade. You spent good coin at my mother's eatery." She held the craft steady, watching as he climbed on to the gangway.

Then, with a cheerful wave, she set her paddle and let the river carry her away, her laughter trailing like droplets scattered across the current.

Rhyslin watched her go, then ascended the stairs to the main deck, each step a soft percussion in the ship's quiet rhythm. The Dawn-Breaker seemed to breathe with him, timbers flexing faintly beneath his weight as though measuring his intent. Before setting foot on the planks above, he raised his fist to his heart, then extended an open palm—invitation, not assumption.

The deck officer eyed him with practiced scrutiny, the river light glinting along the metal trim of his cloak clasp.

His hands brushed down Rhyslin's cloak in a search more ceremonial than suspicious, as if confirming to the ship itself that the draoidh carried no malice. He offered a shallow bowl of water, its surface trembling faintly with the ship's motion, catching flashes of sunlight in its ripples. "You may come aboard, Maighstir Darkblade."

Rhyslin dipped his fingers into the water, cool, metallic with the taste of the air, and washed his hands, then his face and the back of his neck. The ritual anchored him, leaving droplets to slide along his skin like tiny wards. The river's scent clung, iron and silt, before vanishing, drawing a thin veil between past and present. "Do you know where Marcus is?"

"When last I saw the commander, he was headed to clean up and fetch his bow." The officer returned the salute with measured grace, as though passing a blessing back into Rhyslin's keeping.

Rhyslin nodded and walked across the deck, exchanging quiet words with a sail handler here, a coilman there.

The boards beneath his boots held a gentle warmth, sun-soaked and salt-kissed, their grain rising like breath against his soles.

Each creak answered like a familiar voice, reminding him that even wood remembered service and strain.

Before he reached mid-deck, Marcus emerged from below, bow slung across his shoulder, the familiar lines of tension in his gait coiled tight as a drawn string.

Rhyslin intercepted him. "Before you leave, can you get me two work crews?" The breeze shifted at his words, no longer river-bound, but bending back from the woods.

It carried the scent of wildflowers crushed underfoot, sun-warmed bark, and the sharp smoke of hearth fires kindling noon-day meals—as though the land itself was listening to the bargain.

Marcus tilted his head, giving Rhyslin a long, measuring look. "What are they doing?"

"They're building a pier." Rhyslin gestured toward the shoreline.

Marcus followed his gaze, eyes narrowing. "That's a lot of trust to extend before the treaty is signed."

The breeze curled around Rhyslin's waist like a stretching cat, brushing cool fingers up his spine. The air dipped in temperature, a soft exhale of shared caution. "I didn't expect it either, but it'll speed our departure."

Marcus acknowledged Rhyslin's statement with a grunt and a nod. "The sounding party should be through soon. I'll find you when they return."

"Be careful when you do." Rhyslin's voice dipped into a wry forewarning, though beneath it lay a quiet gravity. "I may be in a delicate situation."

"I figured you might be." Marcus's eyes flicked toward the quarterdeck, where the Captain paced like a man waiting for a verdict, each turn of his boots sharp as punctuation.

"Have you seen Rembran?"

Marcus pointed toward the deck below. "He's wearing a groove into the floor outside the crystal chamber."

Rhyslin closed his eyes and sent his prana spiraling downward. The familiar tether of Rembran's mind met him taut with unease.

The spellblade's presence, usually a calm, dark lake, now churned at the edges, jagged with uncertainty.

Beyond the sealed door, the elementals pulsed like a storm barely held in its shell. Violent emotion, sharp as broken crystal. Rage. Fear. Sorrow.

Rhyslin inhaled slowly, and the breeze reversed again, stalling into a breathless pause, as though the world itself reeled from what he had sensed. Even the boards beneath his boots gave a muted groan, their voice uneasy.

"I'd wish you luck." Marcus drew a sigil in the air, its faint glow swallowed almost instantly by the sunlight. "But I think you'll need more than that."

Rhyslin opened his eyes and met his friend's gaze—wondering, suddenly, if Marcus knew more than he let on.

He said nothing, only nodded and turned toward the quarterdeck. The deck creaked beneath his boots, a familiar voice in timber, the planks bowing as if in recognition. At the base of the steps, the wind whispered once along the railings and then hushed, falling reverent, as though the ship herself understood what was to come.

Captain O' Cuire met him there, already descending. He raised a salute, shoulders tight, eyes bloodshot. "Welcome back, sir."

O' Cuire was dressed to standard: clean uniform, boots buffed, wind-breaker fastened tight. But he wore exhaustion like a second skin.

The grey streaks in his hair had spread like frost across the temple beams of his head, and his hands trembled faintly, though he held them steady at his sides. The air around him smelled faintly of brine and singed copper, clinging to him like the storm's ghost.

"I didn't mean to leave you without warning."

Rhyslin waved it off. "From what Marcus said, the storm struck without mercy. You did what you had to do."

O' Cuire exhaled, some of the weight leaving his posture. The rigging above them loosened in kind, cords sighing once as if sharing his release. "Thank you, sir."

Rhyslin's tone gentled. "Tell me what happened to Meron, and why it took four days to return."

"We took a lightning strike." The Captain glanced skyward at a blackened spar. "Static rode the line into the copper. Meron took the hit and dropped like a stone."

He swallowed, and the mast above them gave a low groan. "Andros and Ixa kept the ship steady before the storm, but they wouldn't answer to me or the lad. They'd have flown us all the way back to Am Manse Flùr if we hadn't severed the bond between crystal and hull."

Rhyslin remained silent, but the scent of beeswax lifted faintly from his coat, sharper now, honey-warm in the air. The wind stilled, and the rigging lines fell slack, no longer humming with tension. Even the footsteps of the crew softened, their cadence withdrawn, as if the ship herself had fallen into hush, listening.

"Did you check on them?" Rhyslin′s voice dropped low in concern.

"I did." O′Cuire′s face paled. "It looks like Ifrinn in there. The orb′s burning red and yellow. Like it′s bleeding fire." A single sail rustled above them, shivering once as if to say: truth.

Rhyslin gazed down at the deck, shoulders tight, breath shallow. The planks under his boots carried the faintest tremor, uneasy.

Whatever lay beyond that door wasn't elemental wrath alone. Something had torn the balance. "That's not good." Turning for the hatch, he nodded once. "If Marcus comes looking for me, tell him where I've gone."

"Understood, sir." O'Cuire saluted again, this time more reverently, the gesture mirrored in the hush of canvas above. "And sir—may Quetzalcoatl guide your steps."

Rhyslin paused a moment, then gave a single nod—one hand brushing the edge of his duster, as if warding or receiving. The beeswax swelled around him once more, and then he vanished below.

After descending the first flight of stairs, Rhyslin paused, allowing his eyes to adjust to the dim lighting.

A lantern guttered, flaring once, then steadied as if aligning with his breath.

Drawn by the echoes of distress on the deck below, he turned and continued down.

Stepping off the stairs, he strode toward the aft end of the ship, stopping only when he came to a solid oak door banded with silver sigils. The air in this corridor was dense, close, and carried the faint copper tang of over-strained magic. Beyond the door lay the crystal chamber. Before the door, a young spellblade was pacing back and forth.

Rhyslin took a moment to watch the young soldier. Rembran Du Lac Morn's six-foot frame carried the weight of his concern.

His dark hair was unkempt, his face shadowed from lack of sleep, with dark circles under his eyes. He marched ten feet, paused, turned, and marched ten feet back.

The deck under his feet was silent, the wood holding its breath, as if this part of the corridor refused to betray the unrest beyond the door.

Rhyslin watched the young man for a moment more, then gathering his duster around him, he walked up to the door; the beeswax rising with each step, pressing gently against the silence like a candle in a crypt.

Rembran's steps ceased as he came face to face with Rhyslin, and he snapped out a quick, if sloppy, salute.

The silver sigils on the oak door glimmered faintly at the gesture, then dulled again, waiting.

"You know better than that, Lieutenant," Rhyslin admonished Rembran, then clasped his shoulder. "I'll let it go this once, because of your concern."

"Thank you, sir." Rembran turned to the door. "It's like Ifrinn in there, sir."

"So, I've heard." Rhyslin reached out, closing his fingers around the door latch.

The silver runes pulsed once under his hand, and the scent of beeswax thickened as he pressed down on the lever with his thumb.

The corridor hushed in reply, the deck timbers drawing taut as though bracing for a storm.

Complete silence fell on both sides of the door; then, with a hollow pop, the silver bands shivered and released. The door swung open, exhaling a breath of heat and ruin that staggered into the corridor like a wounded thing.

First came the smell—charred wood, brittle paper crumbling in fire, and air so dry it rasped his throat. Beneath it, deeper, rode brimstone, not just carried but saturating the planks, as if the chamber had been steeped in infernal breath.

Next came the sight: red and orange pulses flashing from the crystal orb at the chamber's heart, light that crawled like flames over walls slick with sweat.

Rhyslin soon understood why O′ Cuire had named it Ifrinn. Even the shadows leaned away from the doorway, reluctant to cross the threshold.

The draoidh shielded his eyes with an open palm, prana flowing outward in a gauze of warding. He had not expected the chamber to meet him as an enemy. Light burst in a violent flare, so sudden it clawed into his vision, searing white. He reeled, covering his face, his staff thrumming in protest against the assault.

When the glare dimmed, he gathered his will, inhaling through clenched teeth, and pressed forward. Each step toward the sphere was like walking into a desert wind: dry air stripping moisture from his lungs, invisible grit scouring skin. \

But he moved anyway, one step, then another, until he stood at the table and stretched his hand toward the pulsing orb.

The instant he touched the crystal, the universe froze. Sound dropped away. Heat vanished. The deck dissolved into an endless field of brittle grass that whispered without wind.

He staggered, staff braced, until the shaking ground steadied beneath him.

"Andros?" His voice rolled into silence, swallowed by the emptiness.

It wasn't like the elementals to stay hidden. The absence itself was a wound, and unease crawled up his spine.

"Ixa?"

The answer came not as words but violence. A boulder screamed through the air, trailing dust like tears. He barely flung himself aside before it shattered against the ground, the tremor rattling his teeth.

Lightning split the silence, jagged and merciless, aimed for his heart. Instinct alone saved him—staff driven into the soil, iron core pulling the bolt into earth. Still, heat surged up the shaft, searing his palm raw.

He hissed, shaking his burned hand, but there was no pause. He traced a rune into the ground, staff carving lines of power, and a half-dome shimmered up around him.

The first impact came instantly—iron ore, massive and merciless, crashing into the shield with bone-deep vibration.

A storm of hail followed, Ixa's fury biting at every seam of the barrier, their ice like shards of grief.

The draoidh steadied himself, eyes closed, breath low. The space disturbed him—always had. Here, there was no natural reflection of sky or water, no balance. Only raw emotion made manifest.

And he could feel it now. Rage, like fire tearing itself apart. Fear, sharp as lightning flaring uncontrolled. Sorrow, heavy as stone collapsing in endless avalanches. The elementals weren't merely attacking; they were bleeding, and he was caught inside their wound.

The dome shook again. Above it, a colossal hand of stone coalesced, fingers curling with intent. He knew the weight it promised. He knew it would break him.

Unless he had help.

Rhyslin lifted his eyes beyond the storm, toward where the crystal linked to the waking world. His voice cut through grit and fire, a call sharpened with both command and prayer.

"Come on, Rembran. I could use the help."

Prana laced the words, sent outward like a beacon, threads of desperation reaching for the young spellblade waiting just beyond the door.

Rembran watched Rhyslin lurch across the room and place his hand on the crystal sphere. The silver runes pulsed once, and the scent of beeswax thickened until it clung to the back of his throat. He stiffened as the older man locked up—as if struck by lightning—and collapsed onto the deck.

Without hesitation, the young spell-blade sprinted forward, boots hammering against planks that shivered beneath him. He pressed his own hand to the sphere. If Rhyslin was in trouble, he would not face it alone.

This time, the shift came faster. The air collapsed inward, thick with pressure. Expecting danger, Rembran felt the temporal drag compress, his breath caught in his chest.

When his vision cleared, he stood in a wide, grassy field–chainmail cold against his skin, sword and shield weighty in his hands. The wind blew sharp, tugging at the iron rings of his hauberk like impatient fingers.

It took him mere seconds to spot the danger. A shadow rose overhead–stone shaped into a colossal hand, poised to crush. Rembran charged, mud spattering beneath his greaves as the field softened under his urgency. He tackled the creature before it struck Rhyslin.

"I don' t think so."

His sword flashed, iron catching what little sun pierced the clouds.

The elemental staggered, its hand dissolving into flakes of dust that the wind scattered with a hiss. A blinding flash lit the sky; ozone stung his nostrils.

Rembran barely raised his shield in time as lightning slammed against it, the impact ringing through his arm, bones vibrating like struck iron.

"What's going on here, old man?" he called, stepping protectively in front of the fallen draoidh.

"I haven't figured it out," Rhyslin rasped, bruised and battered, sinking to one knee. The air around him sagged, heavy with static, carrying the coppery tang of blood. "Immediately upon my arrival, Andros and Ixa ambushed me."

Rembran scanned the field, vision catching only shifting silhouettes at the edges of the horizon. Then he turned back just in time to see Rhyslin collapse face-first to the ground, the earth accepting him with a shuddering sigh.

Standing over him, Rembran lifted his shield against another jagged bolt, the air burning sulfurous where it struck. A flicker tugged at his periphery, he spun, slashing, blade humming as it cut the wind itself.

"There's got to be some way to even the field," he muttered, breath frosting in the sudden chill.

The world answered.

The grassland shimmered, buckled, and drowned beneath a rising tide of rain.

The ground turned sodden, sucking at his boots with each step. Rhyslin was gone—vanished or hidden. Either way, Rembran accepted the change with a grim grin.

This was more like it.

He spun in a slow circle, instincts taut as bowstring. The air thickened. Something slammed into his back—icy talons raked his face. "What the...?"

The attacker shrieked and cursed, a windstorm given voice. Her claws tore skin, cold slicing deeper than steel.

"Hey, stop it! My parents were married!" he growled, dropping his shield with a thud. He reached back, locked his arm around what he hoped was a neck, and bent forward. Using momentum, he hurled the blur of air over his shoulder.

She struck the mud hard, bounced, and rose as her form unraveled. Auburn hair spilled free, and she reshaped into a woman veiled in diaphanous silks, eyes like a storm front. She lunged again, rain gathering in her wake.

Rembran reacted on instinct, tracing a rune with burning precision. "Why don't you just sit down over there and get some Mireth?"

The mud beneath her feet clutched her like chains. She took two furious steps before sinking to her knees. She shook her head, spat curses sharp as hailstones—but the spell held.

The world flickered. When she reappeared, she was bound—silver chain glowing faintly from ankle to stake. The mud bubbled once, sealing the bond.

"I will kill you, if it's the last thing I do!" she screamed. Her voice cracked the air like a gale, her curses spattering like sleet.

Now alone, another figure emerged, the rain parting around him. He stepped forward as if carved from the earth itself. Plainsman's garb wrapped him, spear and buckler coalescing in his hands with a sound like stone grinding.

"Thank you," he said, voice deep as bedrock. "You freed me from her madness. But I must still challenge you. My honor—and our grievance—demand it."

Rembran retrieved his shield from the muck and saluted with the flat of his blade. "Before we do this, I must know. Are you Ixa and Andros?"

"We are."

He glanced toward the bound woman, who writhed and cursed in chains. "She is Ixa. I am Andros." His salute was sharp, spear raised to the storm.

"If you win, I will tell you what befell us—what angered me and broke her. If you lose, we return to our realms, and none will speak of this again."

Rembran shifted into guard, mud clinging stubbornly to his boots. "Those terms are acceptable to me, though Rhyslin might not like them."

Andros paced to his mark, rain sliding from his shoulders like molten stone. "Fight with honor. You are being judged."

Rembran circled. His blade tested with a thrust, then a feint that hissed through the damp air.

Andros deflected both, his spear ringing, eyes flaring with the light of the storm. He stomped the ground, and the mud obeyed.

Behind Rembran, a hulking shape surged upward—mud given monstrous form, limbs sloughing in heavy sheets.

Rembran turned, raised his sword over his shoulder, and barked words not his own.

"Ilun-zai, kael-thera! Vahl′ drek maru Tharn′ ek!"

The air vibrated with resonance. Across the field, Ixa's head snapped up. Though bound, her hand rose, storm answering her instinct. Lightning fell.

The mud-beast exploded—flash-fused, then shattered into blackened shards that sizzled in the muck.

Andros staggered, staring at her, then at Rembran. Shock flared like a crack in granite.

"Using her power against me is dishonorable."

Rembran held his blade low, mud dripping from its edge. "No more than conjuring a mud-beast to strike me down. I answered power with power. I didn't expect her to respond."

The ground vibrated faintly beneath their boots, holding its breath. Then Andros inclined his head. "Fair enough." He raised his spear. "Then–shall it be steel alone, or all we are?"

Rembran shrugged. "Your call."

Andros looked to Ixa–her eyes glassy, storm breaking from within. "She has suffered too much. I fear she's broken." His voice cracked like stone under strain. "I will fight you blade to blade. All I ask is that she receives help."

Rembran nodded once. "So be it."

Without warning, Andros lunged. His spear shot forward like a lightning-struck branch. Rembran raised his shield–the clash rang across the field, echoing into the stormclouds.

He countered with an underhand slash; Andros vaulted, landing in a crouch.

As his feet struck mud, he crooked his fingers—stones rose at his command, streaking through the air.

Rembran swung his shield wide. Each stone slammed with a heavy thrum, sparks leaping from their edges.

So this is how it would be. Steel, grit, and shards of the world itself.

The duel quickened, fell into rhythm—each clash a verse, each dodge a breath between truths. Rain hammered, earth split, wind keened, light seared. The world itself bore witness, line for line.

But then Andros stumbled, mud dragging him off balance. He dropped to one knee, spear wavering.

Rembran hesitated, then stepped into the shadow. When he returned to the light, he sheathed his blade. With a nod to the old ways, he placed his bare hand on the back of Andros's neck.

Andros froze. The spear slipped from his grasp. "Were I a plainsman in truth, you would be the winner." He dropped his buckler and raised both hands. "I yield."

Rembran shook his head gently. "There is no yielding when truth and grievances are spoken." He gripped the Elemental's shoulder, feeling the tremor of earth beneath his palm. "Stand, friend, and be proud of your deed."

Andros rose slowly, the storm quieting around him. Mud solidified, the rain easing.

"You fought well. And have lost nothing." Rembran's words settled like a benediction. "Now, speak of your ills."

# Chapter Eight

## In the Wake of Silence

Andros ran his fingers through his hair as he looked around the mud-spattered battle-site. The air smelled of iron and ozone, as though the world itself had not exhaled since the clash. "Can we speak of it in some other place?"

Rembran, having forgotten where they were, nodded. "Yes, we can." Then, remembering that he wasn't alone, looked around for Rhyslin. No matter how hard he looked, the draoidh remained hidden. The longer he searched, the more the horizon seemed to ripple, as though the field itself conspired to conceal the older man.

Turning back to the Earth Elemental, he gestured. "Can we make this place unmask Rhyslin's hiding place?"

"We can, or rather you can." Andros turned to look at Ixa.

The Air elemental was staring at the silver chain around her ankle. The chain smoked faintly, as if rejecting the very air she once commanded.

"You need but think about the Draoidh in the open, and there he will appear."

Rembran nodded, his eyes drifting closed as he thought about Rhyslin, out in the open, where they could see him. His breath stirred the air—an unnatural silence breaking like a cracked bell.

He opened his eyes to find Rhyslin laying there face down. After rolling the unconscious draoidh onto his back, Rembran exchanged a look with Andros and then turned, watching as the muddy field and grass faded away, color draining as if the world lost interest in its own disguise.

Only the three men and Ixa remained, suspended in that thinning, shifting realm.

The Air Elemental was still kneeling, with her fingers curled around the silver chain that secured her to a wooden post.

Her knuckles were white against the shining links, which pulsed faintly like veins filled with lightning.

Rembran walked toward the wooden post, the absence of stones crunching under his boots making him uneasy, as though the ground itself refused to answer him.

The Air Elemental looked up as he approached, her eyes widening in fear. A sudden wind curled around her body, scattering her auburn hair like dry leaves in a storm.

She scooted back as far as the chain would allow her. When she could go no further, she knelt, her head bowed, her tears falling to the ground like raindrops. Where they struck, the earth hissed, darkening to ash.

Her body shook like the leaves in winter, air moaning through the void around her.

"Please, no more." Her sobs tore at Rembran as he dropped to one knee and wrapped his fingers around the silver chain. The chain pulsed once beneath his touch, as though alive, testing him.

"I've told you everything." Her voice cracked like wind through shattered glass.

When he didn't move, she tried to curl into a ball, her hair becoming a veil that whipped in an unseen breeze. "I did what you wanted. I gave you his soul-name. Please, no more."

At Andros' side, Rhyslin regained consciousness. Not all at once, and not with clarity.

"Oh, my head." The draoidh rubbed at his temple, trying to calm the clamoring bells in the back of his skull. The field itself seemed to waver with the sound, blades of grass bowing as though shaken by invisible chimes.

He held still, half listening to Ixa's tortured cries. Like an iced lake unfreezing, he came to his senses in brittle cracks and spreading lines.

"What is Ixa crying about? What did Meron do to you?"

The wind dropped low and restless, coiling between them like a withheld answer.

Andros looked ashamed—of what they had both done. His head bent, and the ground beneath him shivered faintly, mud fissuring as though it could not hold his weight. "I will tell you, but not here, please."

Rhyslin nodded, lifting his head to watch Rembran. Beeswax traced the air faintly from his coat, trying to soothe the storm, but it clashed with the bitter tang of iron and fear rising from Ixa' s sobs.

The spell-blade listened to her, his mouth set, trying to appear neutral, when all he wanted was to beat the life out of Meron for whatever he had done.

Without thinking, his fingers tightened around the silver chain. At once it hissed, faint smoke rising where flesh touched metal, the air itself recoiling.

Ixa′s eyes followed the chain′s length, traced up to the fingers holding it, then leapt to Rembran′s face. What she found there stunned her.

The trembling air stilled as though waiting. The Elemental tilted her head, studying him, searching memory. Her breath stirred the field into eddies.

The silver chain rustled as she lifted her foot and extended it toward him, tears falling like sudden rain. "Please …"

The spell-blade turned his eyes to hers. "I will let no one hurt you, ever again." His voice resonated low, and the chain dissolved beneath his grip, curling away like ash on the wind.

The scent of torched pine bled into the space, then faded as the bond of pain was broken. "Will you come with me?"

Ixa, haunted, gazed at him, then looked at Andros, who she half-remembered. The earth shifted faintly under his nod, and the wind fluttered weakly through her torn silks.

When he gave silent assent, she reached up and took Rembran's hand. He helped her to her feet, steadying her with a tenderness that made the air around them warm. "Yes. Please take me from this place."

Not saying a word, Rembran walked over to where Rhyslin was on his knees, one hand on the back of his neck, the other wrapped tight around his staff. Ixa walked at his side, stumbling as her shaking knees gave way.

The field dimmed with her weakness, grass bowing toward the ground, until she would have fallen—had he not slipped an arm around her and borne her weight.

Upon feeling his touch, she stiffened, eyes clenched in fear, and the air grew sharp and cold. But when he didn't move to harm her, only steadied her, the sky above softened. She glanced up.

He was looking down at her, holding her with such gentleness that she wanted to cry. When her fears finally ebbed, she nodded at him. "Thank you."

The spell-blade continued to support her, and when she leaned into him, his chest loosened with a breath he hadn't known he was holding.

The grass brightened, a faint shimmer across the field, as the two of them walked toward Andros, who was assisting Rhyslin to his feet.

"Give me but a few minutes. My bones ache." Rhyslin's voice carried the rasp of stone dragged over stone. He moved as slowly as he could, one hand still on the back of his head. "I feel like a mountain fell on my head."

He looked up when Andros let out a low snort, trying to look away, his head bowed in shame.

The ground beneath him darkened with his silence. The draoidh traced a rune in the air, and the faint hum of beeswax rose again, steadying the scene.

Rhyslin traced a rune in the air. The mark shimmered, beeswax thickening on the breath of the field, binding the space with his will.

Time and space distorted—the horizon bowed, the air folded inward like silk dragged through a ring. The distortion drew a groan out of the draoidh as he once again passed out. His body crumpled, staff clattering, the sound swallowed by the shifting world.

When he came to, he and the other three were in the crystal chamber. He lay on the floor, staff under his hand, while the others stood around the crystal.

The air was acrid, heavy with char, as though the walls themselves had been steeped in smoke. "I've got to stop doing that." His words rasped with fatigue, and he drew in a breath of the char-laden air.

"Yes, you do." Rembran shook himself awake, the scent of sweat and iron clinging to his armor. He turned from the crystal to look past Ixa and Andros. "Thank Nan Diathan, we are back."

Andros was gazing down at the crystal with a mixture of resignation and sorrow. The surface of the orb pulsed faintly, its colors muted, as though ashamed of what it had revealed.

Ixa, still in partial shock, stared at it in revulsion. The air around her shivered, threads of cold seeping into the chamber. Turning from it, she fled to Rembran and buried her head against his chest.

"Please, get me out of here." Her voice was a broken reed. Her pleading did not fall on deaf ears.

Rhyslin rose unsteadily, staff ringing once against the floorboards, and led them out of the crystal chamber. The silver runes on the door flared once in recognition as it sealed behind them, muffling the orb's glow.

They stepped back into the corridor, where the smells of warm pine and river-water rolled forward like balm, washing smoke and char from their lungs.

Lost in thought, they followed Rhyslin by rote, steps muted as if the ship itself hushed in respect. First down the corridor, then up two flights of stairs—emerging at last onto the main deck.

Rhyslin closed his eyes, letting the cool breeze wash over his neck and face. The wind played gentle fingers through his hair, whispering relief.

Rembran lifted a hand to shade his eyes from the afternoon sun, its light sharp after the darkness below.

Ixa and Andros drew deep gulps of air, as though surfacing after drowning, their bodies trembling with the sheer gift of daylight.

Ixa shrank back against Rembran as a handful of deck crew greeted them. Her sudden look of fear sent a ripple through the air, sharp and chill. The men, catching it, stepped back at once, eyes turning instinctively toward Rhyslin.

The draoidh held out his hand, beeswax rising steady from his coat. "Gentlemen, please, give them space. They've been through darkness and pain." How much, he did not know. Watching the two, he wondered if he even wanted to know.

The deck crew, seeing and understanding, whispered blessings and prayers as they returned to their duties.

The timbers beneath their boots hummed softly, as though the ship itself approved. They were a good crew—loyal, long-bound to Rhyslin.

Andros recovered first, waving awkwardly at the men. Ixa, still pressed against

Rembran, shook like a leaf in winter. "By my oath, I don't know if I want to hear what transpired in that chamber." His words were breath-fog, fragile in the bright air.

The spell-blade held Ixa loosely in his arms. After the crew left, she let out a soft sigh of relief, the wind easing with it, and turned her face to the sky.

"It has been so long since we've been under the sun." Her very words sundered Rembran's calm, the anger festering in his chest boiling like iron under quench. He hid it, but the air smelled faintly of scorched steel.

Rhyslin wanted very much to ask Ixa to repeat her accusation against Meron, the magi appointed their liaison, the one who was to look after their needs. If he had heard correctly, the magi had broken Saorsa law—and that could not be tolerated.

"Let us retire to my office. We can speak there."

Again, Ixa looked at Andros, who nodded. This was not the Ixa Rhyslin remembered.

When he had assigned Meron to them, she had been so alive and joyous that the crew itself had seemed to brighten, sails fuller, rigging lighter, until every hand loved her. Now, that radiance was gone, the light dimmed to ash.

The two elementals followed Rhyslin across the deck and onto the quarterdeck. The planks beneath their feet moaned low, as though burdened with knowledge. When Rhyslin pushed open the office door, the hinges gave a hushed groan, and the lantern flame bent toward the Air elemental before steadying again.

Rembran followed from curiosity, though not intending to stay. But when Ixa's fingers caught his sleeve, cool as mist, trembling as wind before a storm, he was drawn with her.

The door closed behind them, and the hush of the ship deepened, as if the timbers themselves wanted to listen.

Ixa drifted toward the windows. She dragged a chair across the floor, its legs whispering against the grain, and angled it until she sat in the sunlight.

The light itself seemed reluctant, slipping through glass to touch her with a faint shimmer, as though unsure it was welcome.

Rembran lingered by the door, but when she held her hand toward him, whispering "Please sit with me," the boards beneath his boots urged him forward.

He moved his chair beside hers.

Ryslin sank into the wingback chair at the heart of the office. The air in the room stilled, folding in close around him.

"Ixa, what did Meron do to you?" His tone was even, almost gentle, though the light behind his eyes coiled with storm. He knew that to learn the truth, he must not let the tempest break.

The auburn-haired Air elemental curled in on herself. For a moment, she seemed ready to vanish like mist in sunlight.

But when Rembran leaned nearer, her hand shot out. She seized his, pressed it to her chest with both of her own, clutching as if it were her only tether. Her voice broke, fragile as glass.

"Meron tortured us... did unthinkable things... until our spirits broke and we gave him our soul-names."

The room tightened. The air sweltered. The faint scent of beeswax from Rhyslin′s coat grew sharp and acrid, as if scorched by unseen flame.

He drew a slow breath, fighting the surge that wanted to rend and unmake. When he spoke, his voice was cold iron, every syllable edged.

"Is this so?"

Andros turned from the picture he had been studying, shoulders stone-heavy. "It is so." He bowed his head, and the floorboards groaned as if straining to hold him.

Rembran surprised even himself when he spoke, his words falling calm and flat, like a blade laid on a whetstone.

"If he wakes, he won't live to wish he had."

The lantern guttered once, throwing long shadows across Ixa's face. She did not flinch.

"We struggled not to give in, but Meron would not accept no for an answer." Her voice, no louder than the whisper of air beneath a door, was almost lost.

She lifted her gaze, lips trembling.

"May we ask a favor, Mac Draoidheacd?"

The title caught him. The air stirred, whispering his name as though repeating it through the planks.

"If it is within my power, it shall be so." Rhyslin leaned forward, straining to hear her.

"Let Rembran be our liaison now." Her voice dropped lower still, barely audible.

"I will allow no other magi to come near me. Should any magi other than you and he approach, I will destroy this ship and everyone aboard."

The air in the room collapsed into silence. Beneath her feet, the scent of torched pine seeped from the floorboards, smoke curling invisible through the grain.

The lantern′s flame hissed and dimmed, cowed by her fury.

Rhyslin believed her. He had seen air elementals sunder mountains to dust. His voice steadied with solemn weight.

"You have my word. It shall be done."

Upon hearing his words, the scorching faded, and the air became calm again.

Having gained what they wanted, the two elementals relaxed. The deck itself exhaled a long breath, timbers settling as though relieved. At least they did until Rembran brought something up.

"Sir, do we have cabins for them? I don't know about them, but I wouldn't want to go anywhere near the crystal chamber for a long time, if ever."

The words stirred a faint quiver through the air, like a string plucked off-key.

Andros shrugged. For him, a place to sleep meant little; the scent of raw earth clung to his shoulders, steady and unbothered. He could always sink into a bucket of dirt in the lowest hold and call it rest.

But Ixa... she trembled against that thought. For her, the Crystal had been sanctuary—its glow a hearth where she could dissolve her humanoid shell and scatter into currents.

Without it, the only alternative was to return to Tir Na Noiel every four days, a return that smelled faintly of prison iron behind the sweetness of lilacs.

Ixa clutched Rembran's hand so tightly he lost feeling. Her panic gusted outward in a cold rush, the air itself stiff with desperation. "I'll sleep anywhere. Please don't make me go back to the Crystal." Her voice broke into tears, and the winds around her cracked into erratic drafts.

Rhyslin watched, his eyes soft, the ship's lanterns dimming to match his understanding. "The only open cabins are the two cabins next to mine."

He had three, but he thought he was going to quarter Flur in the one right beside his.

"I can put you in one of them, but that doesn't solve the problem of you actually getting enough deep sleep to recharge your mana pool." The air thickened around the word recharge, humming with what the Crystal once gave—time folded, rest compounded.

The auburn-haired Elemental bowed her head, shoulders shaking. Her tears struck the floorboards, and each droplet raised a faint scent of rain.

"Where would you like to sleep?"

Ixa tightened her grip on Rembran's hand until the blood fled his fingers. He winced, his pulse thrumming like a rope under strain. "If she wants to, she can stay with me." The words came clipped, almost desperate, just to free himself.

"She can take my bunk. I'll string up a hammock."

The cabin sighed at the offer, canvas hammocks whispering in the corners though untouched.

Rhyslin sighed with it. It wasn't ideal, but the ship seemed to accept the compromise, its planks no longer creaking as hard. "We can do that. But eventually we'll have to find something more permanent. Either a new crystal, or visits back to Tir Na Noiel."

Ixa lifted her head and wiped her eyes. The winds about her steadied, though they still carried the brine of worry. "I don't want to go back home, but if I have to, I will." Her fingers slipped through her hair, a nervous gesture that carried the aroma of chilly breezes over distant water.

"I'm afraid that if I go home, Mother won't let me come back." The words left frost along the edges of the room, the faintest shiver settling into the lamps.

"Why?" Rhyslin raised his hand, and the air quieted around it like hounds to a master's call. "When you accepted the contract, the crystal wasn't part of it." A slow smile crossed his lips, and the floorboards warmed with it. "As far as I'm concerned, you are still under contract."

"But if I go back home, you'll have to wait four days before I can come back." Hope and fear tangled in her like storm fronts colliding, her breaths uneven currents.

"We will cross that bridge when we come to it." Rhyslin leaned back, his weight making the chair groan in sympathy. "The crystal has been handy, but it's not that important. If I have to set up an alternate contract with another Air Elemental, I can do that."

Ixa's chest seized with the words, her hiccup scattering a sharp note of ozone through the cabin. "As you say, Mac Draoidheachd."

Rhyslin reached out and took her hand, his touch gentle but deliberate. The beeswax aroma of reassurance spiraled upward, smoothing the turbulent air around her. It worked—the draft eased, the lantern flames steadied, and Ixa's sobbing faded.

"Why don't you go with Rembran and get some sleep? I can't imagine that you've slept well for a while now."

She looked up at him with eyes rimmed in salt but brightened by hope. "Thank you, Maighstir Rhyslin." She raised her hand, covering her mouth to stifle a yawn. The motion carried the faint sweetness of lavender, fragile and drowsy. "I am a bit tired."

"Take as much time as you need. We aren't going anywhere for a while. We have a pier to build and counter sails to mend." Rhyslin tried not to yawn. The trip to the other dimension had been fatiguing.

Most of the tasks slipped past Andros without much thought; they didn't stir his interest. But the mention of the pier rooted itself in him like a seed finding soil, and excitement rippled through his frame. The timbers beneath his boots gave a faint groan as if echoing his eagerness.

"Can I help you build the pier? I can find you the most stable ground to anchor it, and I can shape the riverbed to hold firm."

The air thickened with the loamy scent of fresh earth as he spoke, his voice carrying the weight of stone settling into place.

"That would be very helpful," Rhyslin replied, measuring the offer against the rhythm of their needs. The air around him cooled, sharpening with thought. "I want to wait for the sounding report before we do anything. I might have you deepen the river or widen it somewhat."

His tone shifted with the currents of calculation; all depended on what the depths revealed.

The report came almost two hours later, carried into the cabin by the lead draftsman. The parchment under his arm smelled faintly of ink and brine, and as he unrolled the chart the room seemed to hush, as though the river itself leaned close to listen.

"I've never quite seen a river like this one," he said, his voice thrumming with wonder. He traced the lines of blue with his finger, and the lantern light shivered across the ink like rippling current.

"The major river starts somewhere in the Galiande mountains, breaks apart here, and reforms into three rivers that run to the coast." His finger's path whispered across vellum like water tugging at stone.

"The depth goes from ankle deep at the shore, to ten feet, ten feet out. Then the middle channel plunges to a little over a hundred feet, before rising again to ten feet deep, ten feet from the other shore."

A damp chill seeped into the room, as if the deep trench he spoke of had opened beneath them.

Rhyslin nodded, studying the map while the parchment rustled like reeds in the wind. "How far out does the pier have to be, so as not to ground the Dawn-Breaker?"

The draftsman's eyes gleamed. He pointed to a spot with ink-stained fingers, and the faint scent of pine pitch rose from the parchment, as though wood and water had already agreed to meet there.

"Ten feet from the bank will give us twenty feet under the keel." His words nearly hummed with joy; not every day did he birth a pier from imagination into timber and stone.

Rhyslin inclined his head, his fingers tapping a slow beat on the map—each touch echoing faintly in the air, as though the Dawn-Breaker herself was listening. "Ten feet it is, then. How long will it take us to build?"

The draftsman's grin widened, excitement sparking bright enough to stir a draft in the room. "Usually, it would take about a month to dredge, build up the bottom near the pier, sink the beams, and raise the structure."

When Rhyslin frowned, the man laughed, a sound like stones tumbling over water. "With Andros' help, we can build it in a week."

The earth-scent thickened, as though the walls themselves knew it could be done.

"Ah," Rhyslin breathed, the word laced with relief and calculation. The air in the cabin warmed, then cooled as he weighed time like coin.

"That will give us just two weeks to return for the council meeting."

His gaze lifted toward the window, where the light caught in a shimmer of dust motes, drifting like tiny eddies. "Very well," he said, finality ringing in the timbers as though the ship itself approved. "Let us take the week."

# Chapter Nine

## Threads Unraveled

Rhyslin spent the night aboard the Dawn-Breaker, surprised at how sharply Flur's presence lingered in the bond. Her disappointment pressed against him — deep and cold as the river's bottom. For a moment, he wondered if she could feel his own emotions in return.

He closed his eyes and sank into a meditative stillness, fingers brushing along the invisible thread that tied them. Tentatively, he let his burgeoning love ripple across it, a quiet offering carried on breath and heartbeat. The ship's timbers creaked in answer, as though listening.

For a long moment, nothing came back. He almost dismissed the effort as failure—

Then wonder flared across the bond, startling in its brightness, followed by the sensation of arms enfolding him.

The air stirred in the cabin, cool currents curling around his shoulders as if Flur herself had rested her head upon his chest.

It wasn't what he expected, but it was a beginning.


He stepped out of the great-cabin and paced the main deck, boots whispering across the sun-warmed planks. At the port rail, Rhyslin leaned into the river wind, letting it tousle his white hair.

Below a bent willow, movement caught his eye—three men in measured discussion.

He unlatched a weathered teak box fixed beneath the rail and drew out the far-seer. The brass hinges sighed as he extended it. Raising it to his eye, he found Sloan in black, unmistakable in his stillness. Beside him, Andros gestured with easy animation toward the tall, silent Hîn i-Balanath. A third man, the draftsman, struggled against the breeze, ink-stained fingers smudging parchment that refused to stay still.

A flick of Andros's wrist brought a table from the river stone, smooth and plain. When Sloan gave the barest nod, Andros shaped a second—this one edged with scallops, its surface inlaid with shell and sediment as though honoring the flow itself. The river hushed for a heartbeat, holding the craft in reverence.

Rhyslin clicked the far-seer closed and lingered a moment too long before returning it to its box. His interest ebbed from him like tidewater slipping from a basin. He resumed his walk, boots echoing along the ribs of the deck, but within the half-hour a tight weight pressed against his chest.

It felt wrong. Is this mine? Or hers?

Unease spiraled through him; a sacred thing lay neglected. He stilled, exhaled once, then turned back into the cabin to fetch his staff.

Moments later he descended the gangway to the lower platform, where a lone sailor leaned against a rope post.

"I' ll need a boat to town." Rhyslin' s voice came softer than usual, as if pressed down by the unseen weight.

The sailor straightened, saluted, and set a silver whistle to his lips. Its circling song rose skyward, the notes twining into blue.

A pause followed, heavy and expectant. Then the wind shifted, curling along the dock, carrying lilac and jasmine on its breath.

From the bend in the river, a slender canoe glided into view, sunlight flashing from the oar like molten silver.

"Good morning, Maighstir Darkblade," called the woman at the prow.

Rhyslin smiled, recognizing her. "Back again, are you?"


She returned it with a tilt of her chin. "The river keeps me busy, ferrying those who can't shape stone or bend air, and —" Her smile faltered, softening into honesty, "I may not have introduced myself properly last night. I'm Aewlin."

He inclined his head as he stepped into the canoe, settling on the narrow hwart. "Then the pleasure is mine, Aewlin. I'm Rhyslin."

The hull slipped free from the galleon, and at once the wind eased, as though the Dawn-Breaker's aura had lifted from his shoulders. He drew in a breath, jasmine on the air braided with cattail and river mud.

"Is it true you're building a pier?" Her strokes stayed slow and even, her voice carrying the hush of disbelief, as if naming a myth.

Between each stroke, the river stilled, listening.

"We are," he gestured toward the scaffolding. "Though it's Andros doing the real work."

A flock of green-and-black mallards wheeled overhead, circled once, then skimmed down to water, gossiping among themselves as they searched for minnows.

Aewlin angled her paddle, letting the canoe drift. "I looked at your draftsman's chart. The center runs deep. None of us dive past the reeds. We don't tempt the depths." Her tone dipped quieter. "That depth saved us once—from slavers out of the stone lands."

Behind them, the river gurgled softly. One mallard turned in their wake, drifting closer, as if listening.

"It still will," Rhyslin answered, voice solemn. "Andros won't change what shouldn't be changed."

For a moment he simply watched her—brow serene, arms moving in rhythm with reed and current. "What do you do when you're not guiding strangers across the river?"

Her grin brightened. "I fish and hunt. Sometimes, I sing. The river listens. Sometimes the fish leap in just to hear the end of the verse." She dipped her fingers in the current, tracing a spiral around the curious mallard.

The duck startled, blinked, then resumed its pursuit of bubbles.

"You have a way with wild things," Rhyslin murmured.

Her head tilted, gaze sharpening as the canoe nosed toward shallows. "Why did you sleep on the ship, Maighstir, instead of returning to your newly bonded mate?"

His chest constricted. Caught, by the gods.

"I had business aboard. By the time I finished, the gates were barred."

She didn't press. Her smile carried the ache of truth. "Princess Flur didn't eat last night. She waited for you. When you didn't come, she curled around the silence as though it were you."

The mallard honked sharply, circling once as if to echo her words.

Rhyslin turned aside, climbing to shore. The riverbank felt firmer than it should, the stones too dry beneath his boots. He pressed a few silver coins into her hand.

"Thank you, Aewlin. May we meet again."

But even as he walked away, he wondered—was it the gods who muffled the bond, or himself? His steps fell into a tempo: step, step, thump; step, step, thump. Breath folded into rhythm. He sank inward, searching.

Sensing someone approach, Rhyslin paused, tilting his head to let the cool breeze wash down the street. It carried a trace of familiarity—not Flur, but someone who had brushed close to her.

He opened his eyes as the presence halted before him. Vuuroena stood there with a playful smile.

"I've been looking for you, Nareth'an."

The breeze spiraled around her like a pup circling its mistress, rustling her raven hair and scattering desert-rose perfume into the air.

"You found me." Rhyslin's eyes tracked the rise and fall of her skirt as the wind toyed with it, never more than a few inches. "So—what can I do for you?"

The breeze shifted, tugging the hem of his duster into the roses, stirring the resinous tang of his spell components until the mingled scent went heady. His head swam.

Vuuroena stepped out of the aroma with a quick cough, drawing out a handkerchief. Rhyslin mirrored her, clearing his throat as the perfumed swirl drifted down the street, unsettling passersby.

She dabbed her nose and gave him a knowing look. "Let's find cousin Flur. She missed you last night." Pocketing the handkerchief, she slipped past him.

"So I heard." Rhyslin fell in step, then glanced sidelong. "Were you with her?"

"For a bit. Then I went to bed."
Vuuroena faked a yawn, grinning behind
her hand. "Momma and Aunt Allanagh
stayed until she slept." She caught his arm
in hers, eyes sparkling. "You're going to
have to answer for that." Her tone carried
no anger, only fact, as if judgment were
already sealed.

Rhyslin slowed to match her pace. "I
know." The admission hollowed his chest.
"I've no idea how to make it right."
Bonded life was new ground—he had never
mended the heart of one bound to him. He
lifted a brow toward her, curious. "Any
wisdom you'd care to share?"

From the hedgerow came the warbling call of a nightjar, cold and distant. A coyote answered from beyond the town.

Vuuroena′s perfume deepened, syrupy sweet, as an impish grin spread across her lips—hoarding the world′s most precious secret. "I haven′t been around Flur long, but from what I saw, a hug and a kiss should mend it." She shrugged, feigning boredom. "Though what do I know? A maiden never kissed lacks authority on such things."

A sudden urge flared in Rhyslin—not anger, but instinct. A sharp dominance surged through his chest, the fleeting thought of a playful reprimand.

Heat ghosted across his palm before fading, his fingers loosening one by one.

The breeze, once jubilant, wavered into uncertainty, tugging at his duster like a child testing a boundary.

At his side, Vuuroena glanced from his hand to his face. Something flickered in her eyes – not fear, but recognition, like a key realizing it had nearly turned the wrong lock. A blush climbed her throat, chased by the shimmer of magic tugged too close to a bond unspoken. Her perfume thickened, amber-sweet and edged with mystery, as if her body answered a question she dared not voice.

The longer Rhyslin spent near her, the more uncertain he became of her age. At the Council Hall he had judged her sixteen, perhaps seventeen. Now, under the weight of her shifting presence, he nudged the number higher — eighteen, nearly grown, but not yet fully ripened into her power.

They reached the cottage, where Vuuroena slipped free of his arm. "I'll go in first." Her nudge was half-tease, half-conspiracy. "Flur's in the fourth room down the hall. I think she's claimed your chamber."

Rhyslin arched a brow. "All of you are in the cottage?" The cool breeze off the trees did little to ease the sudden heat rising in him.

Vuuroena's raven hair spilled around her shoulders, silk alive in the air as she nodded. "We are. Allanagh insisted. There's room enough for all. Momma and she take the front rooms, Mayana has the third, and the rest are ours. You've been left the two in the middle." She tilted her head, a sly glint in her eye.

"Be ready to be interrogated by Momma and Allanagh. At least Aunt Mayana is keeping out of it."

The air around Rhyslin shifted, cooler for a heartbeat as though the grove itself offered him mercy. He whispered a prayer to his goddess – and on the wind, he could have sworn he heard her laughter, soft and mocking.

Drawing in a steadying breath scented with pine and Vuuroena's lingering amber, he stepped through the open doorway.

Flur waited in the entryway, as if drawn to his flame. Lavender and clean linen clung to her like a promise, drifting through the warm hush of the cottage. At the sight of him, her smile bloomed soft as dawn before brightening into full light. She stepped forward, pressing close.

"I missed you, my beloved." Her voice was a breath of warmth, the bond between them pulsing like a second heartbeat against his chest, trust seeping into him with every word. "I knew you wouldn't leave me."

She leaned back just enough to meet his gaze, hearthlight dancing in her eyes.

For a moment, his weariness vanished in their sparkled depths.

"Did you stay on the ship?"

Her scent deepened, bond-sickness easing, copper threaded through lavender. The world seemed to hold its rhythm steady. "I did," he murmured, "and I would never leave without telling you."

He gathered her close, threads of draoidheachd tightening around them as if the cottage itself held its breath. His kiss claimed her lips, salt and warmth mingling with the faint tingle of prana sparking against his tongue.

"Well, it's about time you came back."

Allanagh's voice cut across the hush as she stepped from the hall, oak frame creaking behind her. Sage and warmed air followed her in, sharp as memory. She looked at him with an edge that thickened the room.

"Aran Garion often left on overnight trips without telling you," Rhyslin shot back—harsher than he meant, the words tumbling like stones.

Allanagh froze, her foot halting mid-step. Anger flared, but grief overtook it, softening her gaze. A tear welled and she caught it with her hand. "How dare you bring up Garion, as if you knew him."

Mayana appeared from the kitchen and leaned against the wall, silent, her eyes steady on him. Ilyriatri slipped an arm around

Allanagh, whispering comfort. Vuuroena edged closer, studying Rhyslin, dark eyes intent. None spoke further.

Flur lifted her head from his chest, still breathless from the broken kiss. "How is Daddy involved in this?"

Rhyslin whispered a prayer and heard laughter stir in the wind. The floorboards creaked sharp under Allanagh's step as she advanced, regal and unyielding.

"Momma." Flur's voice wove between them, halting her mother. "Let Maighstir Rhyslin speak. He came here to save us—and he's building a pier."

She took his hand, honeyed perfume rising like a protective cloak

Allanagh searched the others for support, but Mayana only folded her arms, and Ilyriatri kept her gaze on Rhyslin. Left with no shield but her pride, she turned back to him. "Then explain, Maighstir." Her calm rang brittle, the air sour with bruised wildflowers.

Rhyslin exhaled slowly. "I recognized you three the moment I saw you in the council chamber." His eyes found Mayana, regret shadowing his voice. "You never told me your husband was Aran Garion, anointed leader of the United Tribes of Ghallende."

She began to answer, but he stilled her with a hand. "I'm not angry. Only disappointed—in you, and in myself. I should have seen it sooner."

The staff in his grip thrummed, iron and wood humming with draoidheachd, as if the truth itself had weight.

Flur looked up at Rhyslin, her eyes wet with unshed tears.

"How well did you know Daddy?" Her voice trembled, torn between the faint memory of a father and the devotion she still carried for his name.

Rhyslin drew her grief into himself and bowed his head.

"I was with him when he died at Bealach nan Iolaire. Marcus and I carried him home on his shield, back to his bond-mates." His eyes closed, the words heavy as stone. "I'm sorry I couldn't save him."

The air stirred only cautiously, as if even the wind dared not break the hush.

Flur turned to her mother, voice steady despite the ache.

"It is as I told you, Mother. Rhyslin came bearing no harm." Then she rose on her toes to brush a kiss across his chin, a soft benediction. "He brought Daddy home, when he could have left him on the battlefield. He deserves our respect."

Allanagh's anger seemed to loosen, unraveling like a storm cloud losing its thunder.

From the side, Vuuroena's curious whisper broke through. "Momma... who are they talking about?"

Ilyriatri drew a sharp breath. "He was your father, lothig."

The words fell like a stone in a still pool. Vuuroena blinked, caught between wonder and sorrow, while her mother's gaze slid backward into memory.

She was there again—twenty years ago—pregnant and grieving, when the draoidh and ranger brought Garion's body home. She had returned to her people by the sands, carrying both loss and new life in the same weary body.

Her eyes returned to Rhyslin, searching his face for traces of that same draoidh who once helped Garion shape the alliances of Hîn i-Balanath. The resemblance unsettled her.

"Come along, lothig." Her hand tightened gently on Vuuroena's shoulder. "There is something we must discuss."

The air shifted again, low and solemn, as though it too understood the weight of what had just passed between them.

# Chapter Ten

## Whispers in the Hush

With the ship anchored in the river's heart, her spars creaked softly to the current's call. Rembran had little to do but long for the sky.

He'd woken just in time to watch Rhyslin depart for the shore. The yawn that followed came not from boredom but from fractured rest. Each time he reached the cusp of dreaming, Ixa whimpered. At first, he tried to ignore it, but as the night deepened he abandoned sleep, dragging a chair from the desk to her bedside.

He watched her shiver as night terrors seized her again, her breath curling upward to the beams, ghosting around the lantern. When she cried out, he brushed a strand of auburn hair from her face.

The air elemental stilled, drifting into fitful sleep that lasted only until the next wave of terror. Sometime in the small hours he surrendered, head pillowed on crossed arms and dreamed of damp mist and cold mint.

A faint rustle broke the room's hush. Turning from the window, he found Ixa watching him. Sky-blue eyes blinked as though she'd forgotten where she was.

His attempt at cheer faltered into a yawn. "Morning, Cailín Ixa."

"Did you get any sleep?" Her voice was slurred, heavy with the same exhaustion that dulled her gaze.

Rembran shook his head. "No, nor did you. Take all the rest you can. We'll be here a week or two—long enough for the river to learn our names."

"I'm sorry I'm so much trouble." Her words fell flat, as lifeless as the air between them. Beneath the covers, her hands stirred the gauzy remnants of the otherworld still clinging to her. Lips scrunched, eyes tight, she fought for memory. "How did I end up wearing these silks?"

He tried to mask his guilt, but the set of his mouth betrayed him. "Mathair, have mercy on me," he muttered toward the ceiling, then lowered his gaze to find her watching. "I'm sorry. When I went into the otherworld to help Rhyslin, you attacked me. Somehow my draoidheachd tangled with whatever power ruled that place and… chained you to a stake dressed like that." The last words tumbled out in a rush, tripping over themselves, half-swallowed.

"I attacked you, and my punishment was to wear this?" A ghost of a smile curved her lips. Her hand slipped from the covers to grip his. "I remember very little. Only anger—and then finding myself here. Thank you for not killing me."

She rested her head on his hand and drifted back into sleep, trapping him in place as mist from the river curled through the porthole, wrapping them in a hush that smelled of rain and dawn.

"Sweet dreams." His voice cracked around another yawn as the lantern flickered once, as if offering its own blessing, before sleep claimed him beside her.

Wood smoke and dried herbs clung to the air, their mingled scents curling through the beams. Flickers of draoidhiel light shifted across the walls like restless spirits, answering the rhythm of Ilyriatri's pacing. Her footfalls creaked against the worn planks, a counter-beat to her sighs, each one steeped in doubt. The thought of visiting Mayana's stone fortress had soured; with every turn across the room, the notion grew heavier, less appealing.

Vuuroena sat curled with a well-worn book, its pages whispering as her fingers turned them. She barely noticed the dappling sunlight outside, or the birds staking claims in the trees. The hero's feats, especially his effortless juggling of lovers, felt impossible, alien to her own guarded heart. She sighed, a soft exhale that fluttered the page.

Her mother's voice cut through. "What is it, Mother?" Vuuroena asked, marking her place with a finger.

"Would you be upset if we didn't go to Mayana's castle?"

Vuuroena pressed back a giggle, the desire to twirl bubbling up through her restraint. She folded it down into composure. "Where else would we go, Mother?" Her heart raced; the Draoidh's image shimmered at the edge of her dreams. Could dreams deceive?

Ilyriatri's hands rubbed together, nervous habit resurfacing. The lights dimmed and brightened in time with her breath. "What if we traveled with Maighstir Darkblade? Would that satisfy your adventurous spirit?"

The warmth in the room pressed heavy, as though testing Vuuroena's poise. Beneath her stillness, joy vibrated through her frame, near-uncontainable. After a pause of feigned thought, she nodded solemnly. "If you think it's best, Mother, I'd have little choice but to travel with you."

Ilyriatri's auburn hair slid across her shoulder as she shook her head. She could see through the ac, her daughter's eagerness ran too deep to hide. She ruffled Vuuroena's hair, drawing a grumble. "Do you have everything packed and ready?"

"Yes, Mother, I do." Vuuroena glanced at her neatly stacked clothes, though her nose wrinkled at the pile of laundry she meant to wash. "I'm not that messy." Then, more quietly: "Does he know we are traveling with him?"

"No, he does not." Ilyriatri drew a sharp breath, skirts whispering as she moved toward the hall. The draoidhiel lights dimmed behind her, as if the cottage itself strained to overhear. "If he's not busy, I will ask him for permission."

Floorboards groaned beneath her departure, her skirts swishing a rhythm that faded into the house's wooden heart.

The cottage's floorboards betrayed Ilyriatri's natural grace, each creak marking her approach. Inside, Rhyslin and Flur sat together on the divan, golden hair spilling across his shoulder as his fingers stroked through it in a rhythm that drew a soft, contented hum from her.

Fear pricked at Ilyriatri—rare for her, but sharp as rejection's edge. She lingered in the doorway, torn between slipping away unseen and stepping into his gaze.

"You may come in, Ilyriatri." Rhyslin's voice, soft as a fine mist, carried across the room. It settled over her skin, calming yet dangerous in its gentleness, much like Garion's once had. She whispered a prayer—*Mathair, don't let me be mistaken*—and crossed to sit opposite him, folding into the chair as if it resisted her.

Flur turned her face toward her aunt, eyes bright, then leaned back into Rhyslin with a whispered word that drew a nod from him. His hand never paused in its stroking.

Ilyriatri's fingers toyed with her skirt's folds, restless, betraying the nerves she despised. This isn't like you. She forced them still, lifted her eyes, only to find his hazel gaze already on her.

Heat thickened the air, dry and oppressive, as though the cottage itself worked against her. Rhyslin's prana brushed outward like a cooling garden mist, meeting the desert-scorch of her unease.

"Is there something I may do for you, your majesty?" His words carried no sharpness, but the weight of observation pressed against her.

She straightened under it, forcing steadiness. "When do you intend to return to your home?" Her own mind snarled at the choice—*Stupid woman, that's not what you wanted to ask.*

Flur's head lifted from his shoulder, surprise flickering across her face. Rhyslin murmured something low, and Flur blushed, nestling back against him.

He continued his gentle caress of Flur's hair, never breaking his regard of Ilyriatri. "The pier's completion is two days away. After that, the counter sails need repairing." The cottage exhaled with his voice, as if it had been holding its breath. He arched a brow, searching her. "Why do you want to know our travel plans?"

Her perfume, desert-flowers sharpened by tension, rose under the pressure of his prana. "I thought I might save you the use of a sky-frigate if Vuuroena and I traveled with you."

Rhyslin bent his head slightly toward Flur, catching the faint shimmer of her bond like a silent thread. Something in her yielded, and he turned back, gaze skeptical. Flur bit her lip, tilted her head into him, and in their wordless communion gave her assent.

Dust motes circled in the sunbeam slanting across Rhyslin's shoulders, drifting like sacred smoke.

"Very well. When we are ready to depart, you'll hear a horn call from the ship." He gestured over his shoulder toward the galleon. "You'll have two hours to board, or be left behind."

"Thank you, Maighstir Darkblade," Ilyriatri said, her voice calm though her restless hands betrayed her.

With permission granted, she rose.
Heat clung to her skin as she slipped from
the room, and at last the house seemed to
sigh in release. Behind her, the air cooled
and softened, flowing back toward the
draoidh and his bhanna as if drawn home.

Rhyslin watched her leave, noting
the sheen on her brow. Did she know she
was the cause? The living land always
answered to emotion—her unease had
stoked the room into a desert swelter.
Now, with her absence, it returned to
damp coolness.

"I'm sorry if I erred," Flur
whispered, tilting her face toward his,
searching his eyes. His body was still, yet
in his gaze emotions flickered like hidden
sparks.

"You didn't err," he murmured. "Further inquiry was inappropriate." His left hand rose, cradling her chin. "What in her request stirred you so?"

Her cheeks colored, not from desire but from shame of thought. "Aunt Ilyriatri desires you." The words tumbled muffled against her hand. "It's been that way ever since she first saw you."

His hazel eyes held hers, patient, as if waiting for her to name the shadow in her heart. "What are you afraid of?"

Flur's gaze faltered, sliding down to the floor, then up past him, unwilling to speak. The room stilled with her silence, as if holding its breath.

At last she let it fall from her lips. "I'm afraid that she'll ask for your bond and you'll grant it." Her hands trembled as they brushed over her arms. "She's so mature and poised. I'm scared you'll love her more than me."

Understanding blossomed in him, steady and certain. "If I bond with other women, as my mathair wishes me to do, you will always be my first bond." His fingers traced her cheek with feathered care. "Is there enough love in your heart for other potential members of a cearcall?"

Her perfume, once bright, dimmed as if the flowers within her faltered. The house echoed her sadness, air heavy and still. "I don't know."

His prana reached out, wrapping her in a tender embrace, a warmth against the cold she carried.

"Are you disappointed in me?" Her question drifted like a breath, fragile, almost lost to silence.

"Why should I be? For doubting yourself? No, Flur Dris, I am not disappointed in you. You are my heart and soul."

The words escaped him unbidden, formed without thought, like water spilling from a cracked vessel. Yet once spoken, they could not be recalled.

Those six words, diamond dust on the air, sifted past the armor around her heart and let the light of his love shine within. Her eyes sparkled with unshed tears before she threw herself into his arms.

He caught her, enfolding her in the cocoon of his embrace, prana weaving around her like silken threads.

But even as their closeness shimmered like bond-fire, no eye of Ananke fell upon them. It was not yet the reciprocation Flur longed for—only the promise that it might come.

# Chapter Eleven
## Song Broken, Song Bound

Ixa, once called ethereal beauty by men, stood at the bow of the Dawn-Breaker wrapped in Rembran's greatcoat. Beneath the heavy wool, diaphanous silks still clung to her. Her fingers combed her auburn hair in nervous rhythm as she stared past the bowsprit into the winter haze.

A gust lifted the ends of her hair, sharp with tar and river ice. She shut her eyes, remembering freedom before Meron's torment, before safety had meant never letting Rembran out of sight.

"There you are."

The voice behind her sent her heart racing. Instinct bent her shoulders, arms half-rising to shield her head.

"I'm sorry, Cailin Ixa," the sailor muttered, hand hovering above her shoulder. "I didn't think that would scare you."

The air tightened. Ropes groaned. She clenched her eyes, forcing back a scream.

The sailor glanced toward the deckhouse, unease flickering across his face. "Is he on his way?"

The air pulsed once, as if in answer, and heavy boots thundered down the planks.

"What is it?" Rembran's breath came quick as his gaze found Ixa hunched and trembling.

"I'm sorry, sir," the sailor said quickly. "All I said was, 'There you are,' and she panicked."

Rembran shook his head. "Not your best choice of phrasing." His voice was steady, though worry threaded beneath it. He stepped closer. The planks creaked, and even the Dawn-Breaker seemed to hush.

"Ixa, it's Rembran. Nobody wants to hurt you." Each step was measured, his prana stretching ahead of him like cool mist over a garden. Her shoulders twitched, hair lifting in the wind. "The bosun meant nothing by it. I asked the crew to watch out for you." Another step, pause. "You don't want to jump. The water below is glacial."

A briny gust curled over the bow, stinging his lips. He reached for his coat, then smirked. She was wearing it.

But she didn't hear him. Only Meron's echo—There you are—filled her skull. Every hand became claws in memory. Fear tasted metallic, and the black water hummed like a mother tongue calling her home. She bolted for the bowsprit.

"No, you don't get to do this."

Rembran lunged, shoulder slamming the deck. His arm snared her waist, dragging her from the brink. The ship's wards flared beneath them, faint blue lines skittering like startled fish across the planks. *By Nan Diathan, Meron, I'll make you wish you had never been born.*

"Why won't you let me die?" Her voice cracked, auburn hair whipping in the wind. Mist coiled thick around them, rising from the sea, the deck pulsing low and resonant beneath her despair.

The cold bit into him, gnawing at his prana. *She's trying to freeze me out.*

"Here ya go, sir." A deckhand, breath steaming, draped a blanket over them both. "Can't have you freezing. Who would fly the ship?" His wary eyes darted between Ixa and the bowsprit, before he backed away, mist licking at his boots.

Rembran tightened his hold on Ixa and hauled her upright, the ship's planks groaning in protest beneath her dragging weight. "I don't want to drag you in front of Master Rhyslin, but you're leaving me little choice."

His fingers sank into her arms, bruises blooming like violets under winter ice. Her empty gaze hollowed him out. "Ah, my lass, it hurts me to see you like this."

He jerked his chin toward the deckhand. "Get a gig ready. I'm taking her to town."

"No! I don't want to go!" Ixa's scream cut through the cold air, sharp as rigging snapping in a gale. She thrashed, the mist answering her with a rising hiss.

Rembran eased his grip but did not let go. "You tried to kill yourself," he growled, low and rough, his breath ghosting frost.

She shoved against him, all the wild fury of the sea in her limbs. "Stop that!" His prana surged in answer, cold and sharp as glacier breath.

"By Nan Diathan, woman, you're going to Rhyslin, period." She strained once more, and he pulled her tight, pressing his brow to hers with a guttural growl. "Don't make me get the nullification bracelets."

Ixa froze. Terror spilled through her, colder than the fog. The bracelets would strip her shape, her song, her element. They would silence her before Rhyslin.

"As you wish, sir." Her voice thinned, brittle as frost underfoot.

Her eyes flicked to the bowsprit—five steps, and the sea would take her.

"Don't think it, Cailin Ixa."
Rembran's eyes flashed, his lips curling
into a snarl. "I will put you in bracelets,
and you will still go speak to Rhyslin."
His prana pulsed, biting into the damp air;
the deck hummed under their feet in
reluctant agreement.

He kept her close as they moved
down the gangway, step by steady step,
until the gig and its crew waited in the pale
morning light.

At the foot of the gangway, Ixa
paused. Five men, one boat, and beyond
them—water's freedom. Four steps was all
she'd need. She tensed, ready to flee—then
Rembran sighed, weary as old timbers.
She lunged.

"I warned you." His grip on her elbow wrenched her back. He didn't even glance at her as he held out his hand. "Hand them here, Bosun."

The cold iron clamped around her wrists before she could cry out. Power drained from her in an instant, leaving her hollow. She looked up, expecting fury, but found only pity and unyielding resolve.

"Get in the gig, Cailin Ixa." Rembran's hand pressed her shoulder, steering her toward the waiting boat. "When you're in the boat's center, kneel and stay still until you receive instructions."

The shame cut deeper than iron. To face Rhyslin bound—betraying Rembran's trust—burned worse than the bracelets themselves. She offered no resistance as two sailors guided her into the gig and set her at the center thwart.

"On your knees, Cailin Ixa." The bosun's command cracked like ice over water. Tears slid down her cheeks, salt stinging her lips.

Rembran sighed again as he stepped aboard, settling behind her. "I didn't want to do it this way, Ixa. You left me no choice."

His hand rested on her shoulder, heavy and dull through the iron's dampening field. *May Nan Diathan forgive me.*

The bond between them felt dead, his prana-song smothered.

"Push us off, Bosun. Take us to shore."

"Aye, sir." The bosun gestured to the men. "Push away there. Look lively."

Two sailors pushed the gig clear with their oars, while the others dipped blades into the current, pulling in clean unison toward the half-built pier. None of them spoke. None of them wanted to look too long at the woman kneeling with iron on her wrists and Rembran's hand on her shoulder.

At the pier's edge, Andros looked up from the stone he was shaping. A flicker in the water had warned him of an approach, and now he saw the gig gliding in.

His eyes caught Ixa first—head bowed, iron biting her wrists. His breath stalled, disbelief cutting sharper than any chisel.

Rembran leaned low, his voice pitched for her alone. "Stand and move to the pier. Once there, hold your place until I join you." His fingers pressed into her shoulder, steel under velvet.

"If you try anything, I will bind you with draoidheachd, and you will still go to Rhyslin. Do you understand?"

"I understand," Ixa murmured, eyes locked to the thwart. This Rembran frightened her—the soldier, not the man who had once offered warmth. She rose, hesitated, then stepped onto the pier, waiting.

"Hold here," Rembran ordered the gig crew before following. His gaze found Andros. The air between them shimmered with cold authority.

Andros stiffened, saluting. "Sir, may I ask why Specialist Ixa is in iron?"

A ripple of icy prana washed over them. Ixa shivered; Andros steadied himself. Rembran's jaw tightened before he spoke. "Specialist Ixa attempted to end her life three times before we left the ship."

Andros reeled, the words ringing like a hammer-strike. *Elementals do not take their own lives.* "Sir, may I accompany you? I may know why. Are you taking her to Master Darkblade?"

"Yes." Rembran moved behind Ixa. "Walk. Don't run." His sigh was tired frost. "I don't want to hurt you, but I will."

"I understand, Lieutenant Rembran," she whispered, shoulders hunched.

"Then go." He nudged her forward. "Stop at the pier's end."

Her gaze clung to the stones as she obeyed. Each step felt like walking the edge of an abyss, the iron clinking with her breath.

At the end, Rembran left her with Andros and addressed the soldier waiting ashore. "Well met. Can you direct me to where Maighstir Darkblade is staying?"

The Hîn i-Balanath scanned him, then Ixa's wrists. His nod was measured. "Well met. I can take you to the cottage where Mac Draoidheachd resides. Follow me, sir."

Rembran gestured. "Bring her." He waited until Andros steadied Ixa, then moved behind them. "Follow the soldier."

They walked through streets patched with snow and slush, the sun breaking weakly through bare branches. Ixa's tears tracked cold down her cheeks. Smoke from hearths mixed with wet earth and iron, choking her as she whispered inwardly: I should have fought harder.

At last the soldier halted before a white-fenced cottage. "Here, sir."

"Thank you." Rembran inclined his head. The man returned it and strode away.

The bracelets clinked again as Rembran marched Ixa to the door. His knock landed heavy on the wood, final as a judge's gavel.

# Chapter Twelve
## The Lady of Chains

Three heavy knocks thudded against the front door, pulling Vuuroena from the list she was making. She leapt at Ilyriatri's offer to take her shopping, eager for any excuse to leave the cottage.

"I'll get it!" The paper was abandoned on the desk as she ran, though she slowed before reaching the oak door, remembering her mother's disapproval of breathless displays.

She smoothed her hair, tugged her tunic straight, and cracked the door wide enough to peer outside. Two figures stood in the snow.

Her gaze locked on the man behind the woman—tall, brown-haired, brown-eyed, his bearing unmistakably military. Not a sailor. A soldier. The sword at his right hip thrummed with draoidheachd, the low hum stirring in her bones.

It took all her will not to bounce on her toes. He was a spell-blade, as she was.

His voice came cool and clipped, all restraint, as he offered her a salute. "Is Master Darkblade present?"

The formality caught her off guard. "He is. Who may I say is calling?"

Rigid, precise, he replied, "Yes, ma'am. Tell him Lieutenant Du Lac Morn has some ship's business for him."

Vuuroena jumped when her mother's presence pressed warm at her back.

Ilyriatri's throat cleared softly. "Vuuroena will inform Maighstir Darkblade you've arrived. Please, step inside out of the cold."

"Thank you, ma'am." The Lieutenant's hand rested on the woman's shoulder as he nudged her over the threshold. Snow melted from their boots onto the boards.

At his feet she knelt, eyes down, the iron bracelet on her wrist giving a muted clink that seemed to chill the air.

Vuuroena hurried away and soon returned. "Maighstir Darkblade is ready for you, Lieutenant Du Lac Morn." Her glance flicked toward Ixa, who stood silent, waiting to be led. The young spell-blade's pulse quickened; she wanted to ask about the iron, but bit her tongue.

Instead, she turned, almost bouncing now, and led the three Saorsans down the hall.

The faint chime of iron followed them, discordant against the warmth of the cottage, until they reached the sitting room where Rhyslin and Flur were waiting.

"Rembra…" Rhyslin's voice cut the room as Rembran guided Ixa forward and pressed her to her knees before him.

Rembran snapped a salute, his tone clipped. "Lieutenant Du Lac Morn delivers Specialist Ixa to the commanding general, sir." Even three paces away, Rhyslin felt the cold of his prana.

Few Saorsan soldiers stood before their general. Rhyslin watched him—emotion locked under iron discipline—then looked to Ixa.

Everything was wrong: diaphanous silks hidden beneath Rembran's coat, head bowed, eyes fixed on the floor, cold iron bracelets ticking softly when she breathed.

"Lieutenant. I accept charge of your prisoner."

Relief eased from Rembran and Andros. Ixa remained soundless, her silence heavier than the manacles. Formality fell away.

"Rembran—what happened? Why chains?"

Rembran slumped, tugging at his hair. "A sailor said something that frightened her. While we tried to steady her, she tried to take her life."

Rhyslin's eyes narrowed. No elemental had ever attempted that. He leaned nearer. "What happened, Ixa?"

Tears rolled from her lashes and beaded on the floor like salt. "I want to die." Her voice scraped the air. "Please, Mac Draoidheacd—let me die."

Flur gasped and leaned forward; to the Hîn i-Balanath, life was sacred and such a plea a grievous shame.

Rhyslin's chest tightened. "Why do you want to die?"

"Because it is better than being bound to Meron."

The word struck him. "Bound? How did he bind you?"

Flur slid down from the divan and knelt before Ixa. "You didn't want it, did you?"

Ixa shook her head, collapsing into Flur's arms. Cold tears soaked through Flur's blouse. "No. He forced himself on me. Then he pressed a knife to my throat and forced the bond."

Rhyslin and Rembran shared a look—horror sharpening their faces. "How did he form it without Ananke's blessing?"

Ixa's eyes went flat, voice thin as ice. "He buried my will. I can feel him adrift in a void. Please — let me die before he wakes."

Flur held her close, eyes pleading at Rhyslin for action.

Rhyslin drew a steadying breath. Pain thrummed behind his eyes; copper rose on his tongue and tinged his skin. Diathan above. The crime was beyond law and faith. He forced his voice calm. "I'll do what I can, Ixa. You have my word."

He touched the bracelets; their iron dulled his draoidheachd. He drew a copper key from his pouch and unlocked them.

Ixa stared. "Why did you release me?"

"I cannot summon aid with those silencing you." He nodded at the fallen manacles. "Rembran, store them."

Rembran slid the irons into a leather holster. Immediately the room inhaled—draoidheachd returning, coiling warm currents around Ixa like a tide coming back.

"Which Diathan will you call?" Flur asked softly.

Rhyslin exhaled, weary. "One who knows bonds and contracts best."

Drawn by the draoidheil currents, Ilyriatri, Vuuroena, Allanagh, and, last of all, Mayana drifted into the sitting room.

Rhyslin lifted his head, watching them gather wordlessly along the wall. The same unheard summons had pulled them, he knew. Seven. The number of invocation, the number that opened the veil to the divine. He exhaled once, heavy. "So be it." He bowed his head.

Ilyriatri's heart lurched. In the stoop of his shoulders and the shadows in his eyes, she saw Garion again, the same weariness, the same burden pressing down. "Is there any way we may assist you?"

When Rhyslin looked up, turmoil burned behind his gaze. "I need frankincense and myrrh; do you have them? I've got the rest in my packs."

"I can find them," Ilyriatri answered, already half-turned. "I think I saw some myrrh on a shelf somewhere."

"The myrrh's near the shrine out back, and you'll find frankincense in my healing bag," Flur said quietly.

Ilyriatri inclined her head and slipped from the room.

Rhyslin rubbed his brow, hiding a groan as he dropped to one knee beside Ixa. He touched her shoulder, steadying himself against the thrum of her pain. "Stay here. I'll be back in a minute."

Her jerky nod was enough. He rose and left, returning with Ilyriatri moments later. Both carried their items with a hush of reverence, as though bearing relics.

"Rembran," Rhyslin said, voice low but edged with command, "move the furniture back against the walls. We'll need room for what I'm about to try."

Wood scraped against floorboards as Rembran and Vuuroena obeyed. The air shifted—anticipatory, tight. Rhyslin closed his eyes, seeking stillness, but the room beat against him: Ixa's pain, Andros' concern, Rembran's anger like iron in his ribs. When a hand brushed his arm, he opened his eyes and found the space cleared, the circle waiting.

He began to lay the ritual: circling Ixa four times, marking the cardinal points. Behind her, he set the myrrh. Before her, the frankincense. To her left, a vellum scroll, blank but hungry. To her right, a silver chain, coiled like a serpent at rest.

Ixa's eyes lifted, wary, fragile. "You're going to call her?"

Rhyslin only inclined his head, then gestured the others into place. One by one, they moved with the gravity of dreamers, pulled to stations they did not question. The hush deepened; even the fire in the hearth dimmed, smoke drawing thin and still.

"I will attempt a ritual to summon Ananke's presence." His voice was steady, but his hand pressed briefly to his temple, betraying the spike of pain behind his skull. "She might decide not to come. We've had a contentious relationship for several centuries."

He bowed his head. Silence gripped the room. Then his lips parted, and the chant spilled forth—not words so much as spidery cadence, threading the air like silk pulled taut.

"Velthis Ahnara sel dor'thar."

Honored Lady, who binds what must be bound.

The silver chain stirred, coils tightening, rattling faintly as though remembering its purpose. The floorboards quivered beneath it.

"Velthis Ahnara sel ereth'karn."

Honored Lady who frees the chained and crowned.

The scroll unfurled with a shiver, pale light seeping across the floor. Spidery letters bled into being, his true name etched in fire. Vuuroena gasped, and the others felt it strike like a pulse through their bones.

"Imora sel kharin—ora velis'ha."

I seek your guidance—draw near to me.

Smoke rose from the myrrh, slow and twisting, curling about Ixa like ghostly fingers. Allanagh shivered, as though the tendrils brushed her skin as well.

"Karnath sel oruh'vela rion."
For what I seek lies beyond my sight.

The scent of frankincense thickened, sharp and resinous, clinging in their throats. Rhyslin inhaled it like lifeblood and nodded once, eyes half-lidded.

"Velthis nahor'ain seth dor'kai."
Let your knowledge set the crooked right.

A shimmer cracked the air, blue-silver, like heat rising from ice. The draoidheil currents shuddered.

Shadows bowed against the walls. Breath faltered in every chest.

Then She was there. Between Rhyslin and Ixa, she stood, eyes like burning constellations.

Her chiton was woven fog and chain, smoky grey layered like drifting fields, hem weighted with circles that rang of judgment and bondage. Raven hair poured free down her back. And her smile, thin, knowing, smug, was a blade slipped between ribs.

"You have need of my help, Mac Draoidheacd? You, who have refused my blessings. You, who have shown indifference to me."

The air thickened until the room felt drowned. Time itself dragged slow.

Each word sharpened into a barb aimed straight at him, the man who had dared to summon what he had once spurned.

Even in the goddess' presence, Rhyslin's pride would not bow. He lifted his head. "I have never hidden what I think about you, Ananke." A small, dignified bow followed. "You've always told us that for a choice to be real, it must be made freely."

Ananke studied him, gaze piercing, finding one-half of the bond in Flur's heart, the other unanswered in his. Her lips curved faintly—there would be need of her again, and next time, perhaps, he would see the truth.

The room itself held its breath, prana stilled, waiting for his answer.

Rhyslin glanced at Ixa's hopeful face, then back to the goddess. "I need your help, Ananke."

The goddess of bonds and contracts leaned close, finger raised. "You, the one born of the weave, need my help?" At his nod, her brow arched. "How may I, the goddess you defied, help you?"

"My friend was bound to another against her will." Rhyslin moved to Ixa's side.

Ananke's certainty rang like steel. "Impossible. I would know."

"You would not, if it was done in a mental plane outside your sight." Rhyslin set his hand gently atop Ixa's head.

The chain on the floor rattled, the scroll with his true name dimmed, and the goddess's chiton whispered as she strode forward. She knelt, eyes bright as stars.

"Is this true, child? Were you bound against your will?"

Ixa trembled, then gave a tight nod. "It is true."

Concern crossed the goddess's face. Smoke from the myrrh framed her like a halo. "May I share your thoughts? I will not harm you. You have my word."

Ixa bowed her head, clutching Rhyslin's hand. "You may."

Ananke laid her palm atop his, closing her eyes. The myrrh and frankincense swelled with her breathing, smoke curling like script across the air.

The others stood in silence, incense searing hidden fears. Bonded women felt their vows pulse under the goddess's regard, remembered and measured.

The unbonded shivered at the thought of such force turned against their own will.

Vuuroena's eyes caught the smoke-light, racing with questions she dared not speak.

Ananke's face hardened. She rose, her voice low with judgment. "Mac Draoidheacd. Someone has shattered the law and must pay."

Rhyslin's reply came rough with conflict. "It shall be done—when the transgressor returns to awareness."

The goddess turned back to Ixa. "I can unmake what was unjustly placed upon you. But breaking will feel like a grievous loss—one that cries to be replaced." Her fingers brushed Ixa's hair. "Do you still wish this path?"

"Yes, Mistress Ananke. I wish to break the bondage." The resolve in her voice drew a rare nod from the goddess.

"I have never stripped a bond from one not native to Crann Na Beatha. There may be pain."

"I will bear it if it means freedom."

"Very well." Ananke gathered her will, incense thickening, chains humming with her intent.

As she pressed deeper, she muttered, "This reeks of incompetence—or malice." Her disgust twisted the smoke. "A cleaner hand could have done this. Instead he filled her with needless prohibitions—commands that would root her like a stone." She paused, shuddering. "This one must go."

Her eyes flicked to Rhyslin. "When you bring this man to your Talla na Draoidheachd, I will testify. His work left her no choice."

The holy spices flared, spiraling upward. With a sound like a chain snapping, the bond dissolved into light.

Ixa inhaled sharply, testing her freedom, then threw herself into the goddess's arms. "Thank you—oh, thank you."

Ananke stiffened, holding her awkwardly, then patted her back with surprising gentleness. "It is well, child."

Ixa turned next to Rembran, tears shining. "Thank you for saving me, Rembran." She wrapped him in a fierce embrace before he could respond.

The goddess brushed her hands together as if dusting off the act itself. Her gaze found Rhyslin, his eyes still fixed upon her.

"Yes, Mac Draoidheacd?"

"I wish to thank thee, Our Lady of Chains, for helping Cailin Ixa." He bowed deeply, hand over chest.

Her raven hair shifted as she inclined her head. "I would call it a pleasure, but it was distasteful. I feel soiled by what he did." A faint shudder ran through her. "I will await your summons." Her smile was small, edged. "Be well, Mac Draoidheacd."

"Be well, Lady Ananke," he answered, as her form dissolved in a glitter of frankincense smoke.

# Chapter Thirteen
## Voices Beneath the Keel

It took the rest of the week for Andros to finish the pier. On the day he set the last beam, Rhyslin and Marcus stood at the river's edge.

"How do we plan on getting the ship over?" Marcus gestured toward the anchored galleon, drifting twenty feet out in the channel.

Leaning against his living staff, Rhyslin considered the water's depth—charted by the sound crew—and the task ahead. Dock her first, then tackle the counter-sails. "Back home I'd use automata to move her."

Marcus snorted. "In case you haven't noticed, we aren't at home."

Rhyslin rolled his eyes. "Must have slipped my mind." His tone matched Marcus's grin. "Besides, Sloan would forbid it. He'd call it a security risk."

"You've got a point." Marcus's gaze lingered on the galleon. "Feels like he's the one casting shadows, not Allanagh."

Rhyslin blinked, the thought cutting new channels in his mind. "I hadn't considered that." He turned to his friend. "If so, we'll need to rework the treaty."

Marcus shrugged. "Later. First we fix those counter-sails."

A cool river breeze swept over them, stirring Rhyslin's cloak. He closed his eyes, savoring the moment. "We could raise one anchor and use the capstan to haul her in."

"By Nan Diathan! Days of hauling—crew too spent for repairs." Marcus shook his head.

Their voices carried across the water, easy and unhurried. Neither man noticed the shimmer rising beneath the hull.

Green eyes opened in the dark current. A limb of water brushed the carved keel, then slipped deeper, where the muted roar of river over stone throbbed like a summons in the throat of the deep.

Rhyslin, Marcus, and the crew did not see the three forms gliding toward the pier.

They lingered in the reeds, one raising a tendril to taste the air. River-light flickered across their gaze, green as moss in shade.

The sound of water through reeds mingled with the hush of melt-ice sinking into depths, their voices eddying in quiet debate.

At last one gripped the pier's edge and pulled itself upward, water cascading from its limbs.

Marcus, ever watchful, caught it first. A soft cough drew Rhyslin's glance; his fingers flicked the ranger's code. Rhyslin shifted, letting his eye catch the shape from the edge of vision while keeping their talk alive.

The being gathered itself, its fluid form reshaping. A man's face emerged from the rippling mass, wary as their own. It leaned forward, meeting Rhyslin's gaze.

"Shaeli, nesa van lishae."

Marcus blinked. "That's not Silvanic." He addressed the stranger: "Fanel lisha nevrin."

Green eyes flared. "No liva, no soreth, vel saeli lisha vana." When silence met it, the being repeated, slower.

It touched a leaf. "No, liva." Shook its head, touched the tree's root. "No, soreth."

Then drew a hand to its mouth, mimicking speech. "Vel saeli lisha vana."

The river hushed around them. Rhyslin and Marcus nodded. "No liva, no soreth."

As Marcus fumbled toward reply, Rhyslin traced a rune against his staff. Draoidheil stirred, reshaping throat and ear with a subtle pressure, as if his breath now carried the river's echo.

"We are not leaf, nor root." Rhyslin tapped his chest. "I am Rhyslin." He gestured to Marcus. "He is Marcus."

The being touched itself. "This one is called Vanloru. We are Aquan." A hand of water rose toward the galleon. "Is that your house that flies?"

"Yes, it is," Rhyslin answered, his mind already threading the translation.

Vanloru's gaze lingered on the hull. "Why is it in the river's heart, instead of bound to the raised stone walkway?"

Rhyslin hesitated, but Marcus spoke plain. "That's the best place we could land here." His brow lifted. "Is it harming the heart of the river?"

The elemental hissed — laughter like steam from stone. "Nothing can hurt the heart of the river." Its eyes swept the ship again. "This one watched, and saw your care for your sky-home."

It sank beneath the surface, ripples curling, then rose once more. "Why can't you move your home to the shore?" With its hand, it drew the shape of an anchor in air. "Can you not lift your iron weights and let the currents carry it?"

"We could ..." Rhyslin faltered, thoughts racing. "It would require us to set the sails and ..."

Another hiss rolled out, this time deeper, like floodwater striking stone. "You do not need cloth spread across wood. We —" it gestured toward its companions, "will guide your house with the currents, and bring it to the raised stone."

The draoidh's fingers tapped the living grain of his staff. O' Cuire would balk at surrendering control, but Rhyslin chose to trust Vanloru's word.

"Master Rhyslin. The pier is complete." Andros's voice came from behind, steady as stone. He stepped forward, palm down, fingers rippling in the ancient greeting. "Greetings, river brother."

Vanloru mirrored the gesture, closing his fist with a soft splash of water. "Greetings, rock brother. This one is Vanloru."

Andros bowed slightly, the timbers creaking under his weight. "This one is Andros Ironheart." His gaze met the Aquan's with quiet warmth. "What brings you from the calm of the heart?"

Vanloru gestured toward his companions, the river's surface dimpling with their movement. "We will guide the House of Nesa Van Lishae to the raised stone walkway." His eyes flicked to the anchored galleon. "Will the Shalu Lorea interfere?"

Andros chuckled softly, the sound like gravel rolling in a streambed. "No. The Shalu Lorea will not interfere." He grinned, amused at their concern over Ixa.

One of the elementals raised a dripping hand toward the ship. "We felt the Shalu Lorea's sadness. Why did she seek the river's heart? Did she not know it would unmake her?"

Andros's voice lowered, the weight of the truth settling like silt. "She was betrayed by one she trusted. In her pain, she wished to be unmade."

The elemental hissed, steam bursting through stone, a sound of dismay. "Such things are not good. What will Nesa Van Lishae do?"

Andros glanced toward Rhyslin, then shrugged. "As ever, he will study all sides and act as the law and Nan Diathan require."

Vanloru turned, his gaze on Rhyslin sharpening like a current against rock. "What if Nesa Van Lishae acted on his own desires?"

The draoidh's eyes met the elemental's, hard and unyielding. "If Nesa Van Lishae acted on his own desires, the world would cease." His breath escaped in a quiet sigh, and the breeze shifted, carrying the scent of riverweed. "It is fortunate he obeys the laws of man and Nan Diathan."

The river stilled around them, as if even the current paused to honor the truth.

The water elementals turned their gaze on Rhyslin and dipped their heads.

"With your permission, we will move your house."

Rhyslin answered with a single nod. The three slipped soundlessly beneath the surface.

A sharp knock rattled O'Cuire's cabin door.

"Captain, there is an emergency."

One brow rose. He stood, shrugged into his greatcoat, and opened the door. "What's the emergency?" He tilted an ear, listening for shouts from the call-stations.

The officer of the deck saluted. "The anchors have come free. We are drifting."

Drifting here meant danger–shoals, hidden snags, a broken keel.

"How long?" O'Cuire asked, stepping onto the quarterdeck.

The galleon eased along at half a knot, rocking steady in the river's main channel. The crew stood unusually calm. Even the leadsman hung over the bowsprit in silence, line slack in his hands.

"Have you tried the aft anchor?"

"Yes, sir. We let her aweigh. It snagged just above the keel."

"And the fore?"

"Same, sir. Something caught it and pulled it forward of the bow."

The leadsman called back. "Clear and free, down to sixteen fathoms!"

O' Cuire closed his eyes, feeling the ship's pulse. "We're under tow, not adrift." His gaze shifted to Rembran. "Is Cailin Ixa aboard?"

The spellblade approached, saluting, eyes uneasy. "Aye, sir. Want me to fetch her?"

"Get her." O' Cuire's tone softened. "I want confirmation."

Rembran hesitated, then nodded. "Aye, sir."

Within a minute, he returned with Ixa at his side, wrapped in his greatcoat over shimmering silks.

"How are you today, Cailin Ixa?" O' Cuire asked lightly, as if there were no crisis.

She combed auburn strands from her face and offered him a bright smile. "Free, Captain. What can I do for you?"

"We' re under tow. Think you can see who' s hauling us?" He almost smiled. "My guess is Master Darkblade arranged it without telling me."

A playful breeze lifted her hair; a sprinkle of mist dampened her cheeks. "Would you have me lean over and call to the deep, like some river-dolphin priestess?"

"If you please." His chuckle came easily. Yet the coat on her shoulders reminded him of wounds the crew had missed.

She bowed. "As you wish, Captain."

Hopping onto the bowsprit, Ixa leaned low and loosed a wild song. A sleek head rose from the depths, answering with a bark-hum that reverberated through the hull. She replied in kind, waved, and dropped lightly back beside O' Cuire.

"Three Aquan are towing us to the dock," she reported, tightening the coat. "The one who spoke calls himself Vanloru. They say they're doing this for Nesha Van Lishea." She scratched her cheek. "That's their title for Rhyslin."

O' Cuire's jaw ticked. "Stand down from general quarters." To the leadsman: "Continuous soundings." Then back to Ixa. "Methinks they said more."

Color crept over her throat. "He remarked on my improved appearance. Then he... invited me for a swim." She flashed a mischievous smile. "Permission to swim, Captain?"

O' Cuire's laugh was subdued. "Only if you promise to come back." He stepped nearer; she instinctively shifted back. His voice lowered. "I'm sorry we didn't see what that blackguard was doing to you. We would have stopped him."

Her blush deepened; fog coiled around her like a shield. "It's okay, sir. You couldn't have known."

The mist dissolved, leaving her bare again. "I only hold Meron guilty."

He read the truth in her tone—no blame for the crew, though they had failed her. The deck trembled faintly beneath his boots.

"Helm, follow their lead. Rudder ten degrees port."

The galleon eased into a wide turn, timbers groaning. O' Cuire kept his knees bent as the river pulled them broadside.

"Come on," he muttered. "Bring us around."

A sudden lurch—the fore anchor catching—jerked the bow leftward. Relief swept him. "Hard to port. Let' s true her up." Across the deck, Rembran had gone seasick-pale. O' Cuire felt it too, deep under his ribs.

The stern cleared; the ship slid parallel to the current. From beneath the prow came a low hum, followed by a guttural bark that rattled the hull.

Ixa grinned. "Vanloru apologizes. He didn't expect the crosscurrent. He says he'll gift you deep-river fish if you don't tell Nesha Van Lishea."

"It's a comfort," O'Cuire allowed, "knowing I'm not the only one who treads carefully around the Maighstir." His voice rose. "Bumpers out—nan Diathan forbid we scuff the paint."

From the pier, Rhyslin and Marcus watched the galleon inch forward.

"What's O'Cuire doing right about now?" Marcus squinted.

Rhyslin's grip tightened on his staff. "Not panicking. He's working down his list."

The ranger leaned forward. "Is that Ixa?" They saw her drop lightly from the bowsprit. "How do you think she's holding up?"

Rhyslin didn't answer, eyes fixed on the ship as it swung broadside. He held his breath until the line caught and the vessel steadied.

"Still think he's not panicking?" Marcus grinned.

Rhyslin exhaled. "Wouldn't surprise me if he did. I nearly panicked for us both."

The ship righted, angling toward the dock.

"See? That's why I don't own a flying ship." Marcus nudged him. "No currents, no docking worries. I get to ride in luxury."

Rhyslin shot him a sidelong look. "Remind me to make you walk the plank once we're back in our lands."

Marcus only laughed.

# Chapter Fourteen

Of Mooring and Messengers.

Rhyslin watched the Dawn-Breaker ease against the pier, her hull steady above the glassy water. Six sailors clambered down, ropes rasping as they looped them around stone cleats and coiled them into precise spirals.

Marcus stood nearby, arms folded, gaze sharp as the crew worked. "I'll go tell the soldiers to load the ship."

"Have them wait two uair," Rhyslin said, gesturing to the rigging. "We don't want the counter-sails damaged."

Marcus dipped his head and strode off, his boots whispering across the damp stone.

Only once the final knot held did Rhyslin move down the pier toward the gangway.

"Permission to come aboard?" He saluted the deck officer waiting there.

The officer returned the salute and lifted a brass bowl, the water within catching the pier's light. "Permission granted, Maighstir Rhyslin. The captain is waiting on the main deck."

Rhyslin cupped the water, rinsing his hands, forehead, and neck. Salt stung faintly as he let the drops fall. "Thank you."

He noted how the officer poured the used water away and refilled the bowl from a nearby barrel before Rhyslin stepped aboard.

He crossed the deck toward O' Cuire. "Report."

O' Cuire snapped a salute. "We're docked and preparing to move the counter-sails to the pier for repair." He pointed to three groups of sailors wrestling canvas and rope into order.

"So I see." Rhyslin's eyes swept the deck, noting the smooth rhythm of labor, the faint thrum of draoidheachd in the rigging. "Let me know when the soldiers can bring their cargo aboard."

He paused, gaze settling on the hatch. "Is the purser below?" His voice caught for the briefest beat. He wasn't ready to name Flur—or the others—yet.

O'Cuire caught the hesitation. "He should be. Want me to send him to your office?"

"That's best. With guests arriving soon, I want us prepared."

The word guests drew O'Cuire short. "Passengers?" In ten years of command, he'd never known Rhyslin to allow it. When Rhyslin offered only silence, O'Cuire stroked his beard. "I'll send for him."

The captain's surprise mirrored what Rhyslin knew would ripple through the crew. Passengers were change; the ship would need to learn.

Alone in his office, Rhyslin slid open the center drawer. A glassine orb rested in its padded recess, humming with raw draoidheachd. He steadied his breath, slid his left hand beneath it, and lifted it free. Power gathered around his palm like fireflies drawn to his skin. With careful reverence, he set it upon the desk's prepared stand.

"Jahns."

Light pulsed within the orb, coalescing into the blue-hued face of a man.

"Greetings, Mac Draoidheachd," the functionary intoned with flawless calm. "How may I assist you today?"

Rhyslin drew another breath. It's not that I don't trust him. "I need to speak with General Yael Oberon. He should be in his office at a' Prìomh-oifis Armailteach in Ause City."

The man inclined his head. "I can connect you. Allow me three standard time units."

Rhyslin knew time meant little where Jahns resided, yet three units always proved no more than minutes. He used them to close his eyes, drawing breath into stillness, until Jahns' voice returned:

"General Oberon is ready to speak with you. It has been an honor to serve you today."

Rhyslin opened his eyes as the orb deepened to blue, then cleared to reveal the scarred face of Yael Oberon.

The general looked to be in his fifties, white threads overtaking black hair, brown eyes narrowed with the weight of long campaigns. His silence demanded precision.

"Maighstir Darkblade. How did your defense of Hîn i-Balanath's fort fare?"

Rhyslin inclined his head. "We intercepted the Orcan war party and killed them all." He paused. "But I believe it wasn't routine."

Oberon's brows drew tight. "What proof?" His tone sharpened, though unlike with other mercenaries, there was no condescension. Rhyslin was a founder.

Rhyslin's fingers tapped a rhythm on the desk. "An Ogren led them. Under interrogation, he named his master—Saldren Halber Drach."

Oberon blinked. "A half-dragon?" His own fingers mirrored the tapping. "That fits other signs we've gathered. We await further reports. When they arrive, I'll contact you again." He leaned closer. "Anything further?"

"I do." Rhyslin bent toward the orb. "I hold a tentative treaty with the United Tribes of Gallande. They wish to join Saorsa."

The general′s eyes kindled. "When you return, we′ll convene council and present it." A wry smile cut through his scars. "How long until Oak Grove sees you again?"

Rhyslin only shrugged. "Unforeseen damage—two sails to repair. With fortune, we depart in four days."

Oberon studied him, knowing what was withheld. "Very well. If needed, I′ll dispatch a cutter. Safe travels, old friend."

"May Nan Diathan keep you safe." Rhyslin′s bow was measured, reverent.

When the orb dimmed, silence filled the cabin. Oberon had spoken of other attacks yet named no places, no numbers.

Rhyslin's fingers resumed their restless drumming, as if the desk itself were a war map. Orcan, Ogren—perhaps even the I Dranneth. Was Saldren behind them all?

In his mind's eye, Saorsa sprawled like a vast gameboard: rivers as veins, forts as points of flame, Despoina's seer whispering of strikes to come. His thoughts were broken by a knock.

"Enter."

The purser stepped in, thin, middle-aged, spectacles glinting. "Chief Purser Posthan, reporting as ordered."

Rhyslin gestured to the chair. "Our supply state?"

Posthan sat gingerly, as if testing fragile wood. "Enough to get us home if we sail straight. But if we're diverted even three days, we'll run out of everything but salt—and wild hope." His dry smile suggested experience. "I request leave to see what town offers—meat, greens, fabric, sundries."

Rhyslin nodded. "Use the vault's resources. Plan for a month." He hesitated, then added, "We'll have three guests aboard when we leave. Ensure you acquire female necessities."

Posthan blinked once, but his face smoothed to neutrality. Rumor had whispered of one woman, never three. "Aye, sir. At once."

When he was gone, Rhyslin returned the orb to its drawer. If he stayed, his thoughts would spiral. Rising to the quarterdeck, he inspected the sails. Everything in order.

And then, like a tide pulling back, he felt it: the hollow stretch of unoccupied hours. A shiver ran his spine before he gave it name. Boredom. Pure, unprecedented boredom. It startled him more than any battle. With a soft exhale, he turned his steps toward town.

Rhyslin paused at the gangway, saluted the deck officer, and stepped ashore. The stone stair creaked faintly under his boots as he descended with care. The moment his feet touched the dock, he turned and left the ship behind.

The path to the cottage carried the faint tang of river mist and rope tar. Before the door came into view, Flur's happiness bubbled through their bond, a warmth so vivid it startled him.

Inside, he found her waiting — golden hair shining, smile radiant.

"Your ship docked without incident?" She wrapped her arms around him, voice soft against his chest. "I could sense you a block away, melethron nîn, heru nîn."[9]

Rhyslin held her, masking his amazement. How can she feel me so clearly when I can barely sense her? "It did," he said, indulging her expectant look. "

___________________________

[9] My Beloved Master

With interesting help. Several Aquan
guided the ship from mid-river to dock."

Allanagh appeared from the hall,
brows rising. "You met the Aquan?
We've heard rumors of them but never
seen them."

"We might not have either," Rhyslin
admitted, "except Andros and Ixa were
present — and my... status caught their
attention."

"Status?" Flur echoed. The word
trembled in her mouth. Realization
dawned, and her cheeks flushed.

"You mean... Mac Draoidheachd." The
title hung between them, heavy. She
dropped her gaze, a rueful smile curving
her lips. "I know the feeling."

Without thought, Rhyslin lowered his head and kissed her, fierce as breath itself. She clung to him until a soft gasp drew his eyes open. Vuuroena stood blushing in the hall; Ilyriatri cooled her face with an opened fan.

Flur leaned against him, flushed and smiling dreamily.

"I heard something about your ship docking?" Ilyriatri asked, folding her fan and sliding it beneath her belt.

"You did," Rhyslin answered evenly. "We'll be here another three or four days, but you may move your luggage aboard."

Flur looked up quickly. "May we visit the ship before we leave? We might need supplies."

"You may," he agreed, already considering the need. "If you wish, we can go now."

"May I go see it too?" Vuuroena burst in, almost bouncing. "I promise I'll do what Rhyslin says."

"Of course," Ilyriatri allowed. She stepped close to Rhyslin, gaze steady. "You will not change your mind about letting us travel with you, will you?"

Flur's smile answered before he could speak. Yet the doubt gnawed — why can't I sense her bond at all? Is it draoidheachd... or me?

"I haven't changed my mind," he said aloud. "You may travel aboard the Dawn-Breaker."

Satisfied, Ilyriatri inclined her head. Vuuroena all but vibrated. "Will you wait a moment?" At his nod, she vanished, returning with her sword at her hip.

Ilyriatri's mouth tightened, but Vuuroena lifted her hands pleadingly. "Please, Momma. Everyone here carries weapons."

She looked to Rhyslin. "If Maighstir Darkblade grants permission, you may."

He traced a sigil on his staff, puzzling at her deference – this was not his town, nor his law. But on his ship? He would disarm no one fit to serve.

"As long as she breaks no local law, I've no objection."

The girl fought to keep composure, voice low though joy all but danced in her eyes. "Thank you, Maighstir Darkblade."

With Flur on one arm, Ilyriatri on the other, and Vuuroena pacing at their heels, Rhyslin led them toward the dock.

The Dawn-Breaker loomed ahead, hull etched in glowing sigils that pulsed like a sleeping heartbeat. The air tasted of salt and oil, undercut with something older — elemental breath woven into timber and brass.

Lines creaked in the river breeze. A sail snapped once, impatient.

"That's a big ship," Flur murmured, ears twitching, the wind tugging at her skirts as if echoing her nerves.

Ilyriatri and Vuuroena stood still, eyes tracking the movement on the deck above. Both agreed with Flur, though neither voiced it. Vuuroena tilted her head, wide-eyed, gaze flicking between the glowing sigils and the floating gangway as if watching a storybook come alive.

Flur shivered, folding her arms as another gust pressed icy fingers down her spine. "How big is it?" she whispered.

"It is cold out here," Rhyslin said, drawing her into his arm. She leaned into his warmth. "Why don't we discuss this in my office?"

Grateful for the excuse to move, Flur nodded. She didn't want to admit how the ship's vastness unsettled her. She had seen sky-ships before—distant silhouettes gliding above the forest canopy—but never this close, where the thrum of power radiated from the hull.

She glanced sidelong at Ilyriatri and Vuuroena. The former's expression was composed, almost disinterested, but the twitch of one ear betrayed her fascination. The latter all but vibrated, a spark waiting to catch fire.

Rhyslin moved up the gangway first, offering his hand as each woman stepped aboard.

Near the entryway sat a copper bowl, water glinting within. Rhyslin dipped his hands, touched forehead and nape.

The women followed, mimicking as best they could. Cool water tingled across their skin, carrying the faint impression of old, unspoken secrets.

"Welcome aboard the Dawn-Breaker." The officer of the deck stepped forward, offering a crisp Saorsan salute.

Each woman returned with an elegant nod. The air itself seemed to shift, as though the ship acknowledged their presence.

"Any news?" Rhyslin asked, returning the salute.

"No, sir. Nobody's left anything for you. Will you be in your office?"

"Yes, I will." He started aft. "There may be trunks arriving before nightfall. Be sure someone is ready to receive them.

Find me when they arrive and I'll tell you where they go."

"Aye, sir."

They left the officer behind and followed Rhyslin through the corridor. He paused now and then to trade nods and clipped words with passing sailors. The Dawn-Breaker felt alive—responsive, attentive. Vuuroena trailed a hand along the railing, eyes wide with wonder.

At last they entered the captain's cabin, broad and airy, spanning the ship's aft. A desk was bolted to each wall, surfaces bare, while a wing-backed chair faced the stern windows like a sentinel steeped in shifting light. The scent of lemon oil and vellum ink lingered in the still air.

"Do you sleep here?" Flur asked, voice no louder than the creak of her boot. Her scent thinned with quiet apprehension.

"No," Rhyslin said with a soft smile. "But let me show you where you'll be staying."

He opened a door set into the bulkhead. Hinges creaked. "Here's your room."

Flur stepped inside and stopped. Ten feet by ten, functional to the point of austerity. A bolted bed, a desk, nothing more. No books, no warmth.

She turned, eyebrow raised. "This is my room?"

She traced the edges of the space, noting what she'd need to make it livable.

Nothing of Rhyslin lingered here—not his scent, not his presence.

She returned to him, searching his face. "Why aren't I sleeping with you in your cabin?" Her voice was quiet, but heavy.

*Or are we bonded in name only?* The thought curled cold in her chest. Her perfume, once warm and floral, faded to bruised stalks and broken green.

Rhyslin cursed himself inwardly. He hadn't meant to wound her. "I didn't intend to cause you such pain." He hesitated, unable to put his existence into words. "I sleep so little these days." He slipped his arms around her, gesturing toward the wing-backed chair. "When I do, it's in that chair I sleep the few hours granted me."

The golden-haired bhanna raised a skeptical brow. "All creatures sleep, even you." She leaned closer. "Don't you?"

Before he could answer, Ilyriatri's calm voice cut in. "Where will my daughter and I sleep?"

Rhyslin cleared his throat, pointing to the door beside Flur's. "Your cabin is through that door. The one next to it is where Kiesha and Kietha sleep."

Ilyriatri opened it, gaze sweeping with practiced authority. "This space requires a mirror—and two proper chairs," she said, tone final.

Rhyslin almost corrected her, then stopped. Let her call it what she pleased. "You may order anything you require from town. It can be delivered until the hour we cast off."

Vuuroena peeked in, shrugged—she didn't care where she slept; adventure mattered more. She paced the great-cabin, pausing by a sealed door. When her mother emerged, she caught her eye and pointed.

Ilyriatri examined the varnished wood. "Maighstir Darkblade. What lies beyond this door?"

The cabin seemed to shrink. Rhyslin faced it as though facing death. "That is the cabin I never use."

Flur tried to mask her disappointment, but it clung to her like dusk to frost. He said he slept little, yet what lay hidden behind this door? What part of himself did he keep sealed? She longed for him to feel her as she felt him: a blazing sun cast into her long winter. Quietly she padded over, resting her hand on the latch. When it didn't yield, she turned back, eyes soft with silent plea.

Rhyslin went to the door, laying a hand against it. Without thinking, he traced the world tree's sigil across the wood.

"Thank you," Flur whispered, brushing his cheek with a kiss before pushing the door open. Dust spiraled into the air; she sneezed, then steadied her breath.

The cabin dwarfed hers and Ilyriatri′s, threefold in size, yet lay barren. Only a single painting broke the emptiness.

Vuuroena and Ilyriatri slipped in behind her, careful not to disturb the dust. After a moment, Ilyriatri leaned close and whispered, "This room awaits your personal touch. Make it a place he can use and enjoy."

Flur nodded, already planning. Measuring out a square of space with her steps, she glanced back toward the great-cabin where Rhyslin sat in his chair. A devious smile curved her lips.

# Chapter Fifteen

## Change Creeps In

The next four days unfurled in a flurry of sound and scent. Hammers rang on oak, sawdust hung in the air, and the Dawn-Breaker shivered under the touch of change. Above, the huge counter-sails creaked as they were repaired; below, Rhyslin's unused room filled with the pulse of life.

During the bustle, the Hîn i-Balanath's traveling trunks arrived, heavy-latched and smelling faintly of cedar and rosewater, set down in Rhyslin's great-cabin by the officer of the deck.

Together, Ilyriatri and Flur turned the "Mystery Room" into something livable. The master carpenter and the purser became constant figures in the hallway, slipping in and out with blueprints curled like scrolls and samples that carried the tang of fresh varnish. When not aboard, they scoured the village markets for fabrics and fixtures that matched Flur's vision.

When the room emptied for an hour, Vuuroena planted herself on a folding chair outside, book open across her knees. She guarded the door with a grin so smug that Rhyslin, passing, only shook his head. Better her joy unbroken.

Above, sailors labored on the counter-sails. Metal sang against metal as booms were raised, spars set, and curved masts tested against the wind. When a vital part couldn't be found in the cavernous stores, a deckhand sprinted off into the village in search of a smith. The whole ship breathed industry, its ribs groaning with it.

Nor was the Mystery Room the only place altered. Rhyslin's great-cabin acquired an eight-place dining table with folding chairs that smelled faintly of oiled wood. He had asked the women not to too quickly change what he called his own. Yet even then, the air tilted, balance shifting beneath his notice. Change had already entered.

When a cushioned divan appeared beneath the aft windows, soft as surrender, Rhyslin gave up.

Vuuroena saw him shake his head at the intrusion. When she asked what bothered him, he only murmured about change creeping in and retreated to the quarterdeck with the weariness of a man losing ground he hadn't meant to defend.

She shadowed him, light-footed, watching him pace against the quarterdeck rail. When pacing failed him, he strode down the main deck. Vuuroena bit her lip. She had promised Flur to keep him out of the cabin, but her curiosity itched. He stopped mid-deck, falling into a low-voiced conversation with Ixa, Andros, and Rembran. Vuuroena pressed against the cabin door, arms crossed. So boring.

She wanted to roam the ship, but Ilyriatri had forbidden it.

A sour tang rose from the lower decks — water, sludge, something fouler lurking beneath. Her nose wrinkled. *What is that nasty smell?* A shift of air warned her too late. The door swung open, nearly knocking her off balance. Heat flushed her cheeks; she glanced around to be sure no one saw. Then a hand touched her shoulder. She stiffened, slipped under it, and spun, palm brushing her sword-hilt.

"Momma, don't do that," she groused, flipping her hair with a pout.

Ilyriatri smiled. "Where is Maighstir Rhyslin?"

Vuuroena pointed to the small knot of men. Her mother followed her gaze, then her posture, and nodded. "If only we could hear what they're planning down there."

Vuuroena grinned, hugged her mother quick, and darted off. She crept toward the group, feet whispering, eyes sharp for cover. A sail shifted with the wind, offering her a shadowed nook. She slid into it, ears twitching as the air carried Rhyslin's words.

"How are you feeling, Ixa?" Rhyslin leaned against his staff, eyes scanning the elemental's veiled form. "I see you are still wearing the veils."

Ixa's cheeks flushed. Her fingers brushed down the greatcoat concealing her garb. "I'm not ready yet."

Rhyslin inclined his head. "Very well. It's only a little chilly here on the river, but when we reach higher altitudes, you'll want warmer clothes." He drew the crisp river air into his lungs. "You should know better than most."

Ixa pulled her hair forward, strands veiling her eyes. "I know — it's just that I'm not ready to go on yet."

Rembran, off to the side, gave a small nod but said nothing. As Andros had put it: Ixa is the only person who can help herself.

Rhyslin shrugged. "Don't come crying to me if you get cold." His lips softened into a smile. "I have warned you. Even air elementals get cold."

Ixa studied him, tasting his prana as she did. "You could order me to change clothes."

Rhyslin's eyes did not waver. "I could, but I won't." The unspoken yet hung between them.


Hidden in the sail's shade, Vuuroena clenched her fists — torn between defending Ixa or cuffing Rhyslin. When the elemental dipped her head in deference, Vuuroena felt her chest ease. Is this what having a family feels like?

Rhyslin's smile faded as the sourness in the air tugged at his attention. The stench below had been growing for days, and though the crew swore nothing was amiss, his instincts said otherwise. He turned, prana brushing over a familiar spark.

"Come along, Vuuroena. There's no need to hide." He didn't look back as he strode toward the mid-deck ladder.

The girl squawked, caught again, and scrambled to follow. She glanced to her mother's nod, then sprinted to Rhyslin's side. "Where are we going?"

The draoidh gestured toward the downward stairs. "There is a foul stench from below."

She caught the taut lines around his eyes. "Don't you usually send someone else to poke at the filth?"

The frown tugging his mouth betrayed him. "I needed to step away from my office." His voice was clipped, then softened. "Things are shifting faster than I can keep pace with."

Vuuroena studied his face, careful. "Is it Flur?" A faint smile flickered. "Is it what they are doing to your office and unused cabin?" She saw the curve of his lips vanish behind neutrality.

Rhyslin exhaled as he started down. In his mind: Rowena's going to blaze like a bonfire when she finds out.

"I'm sorry they are messing up your sanctuary," Vuuroena whispered as she trailed him to the next deck.

He sniffed the air, shook his head. "Life is all about change. This was inevitable. If it weren't Flur and your mother, it would have been something else."

The second deck stank thicker. Vuuroena breathed shallow through her mouth. "That doesn't smell right. What died?" She clamped her nose. "I asked a couple of sailors about the —" she sounded the unfamiliar word, "bilge and wastewater. It was educational."

"I'm sure it was," Rhyslin muttered, sniffing again. Not here. He turned downward.

On the lowest deck, the air shifted —
forward holds smelled of spice, flour,
alcohol. That left only bulk storage, where
soldiers' plunder was kept.

Surely they didn't bring a corpse
aboard. Rhyslin traced a spell, unlocked
the ward. He glanced at Vuuroena, saw her
jaw tighten. Then he cracked the door.

The reek of rotten flesh, dried blood,
and filth rushed out like a wave. He
staggered a step back. By Nan Diathan,
that's foul.

"Run back up to the main deck. Find
Captain O'Cuire and Rembran. And have
them bring a work crew."

Her eyes went wide, then she bolted,
boots hammering the planks.

Rhyslin pressed his back to the door, drew a sigil in the air. A current stirred from the bow – sharp, clean, cold. It rolled down the corridor, thinning the stench, giving him breath enough to wait.

The corridor air thickened with rot.

"What did you find in there?"

Rhyslin looked up to see O' Cuire and Rembran approaching.

"Vuuroena said you' d found the source of the stench," Rembran offered with a nod.

"I know where it comes from, but I haven' t entered." Rhyslin stepped aside from the door, the planks beneath him groaning. "I was waiting for you."

The captain moved forward, hand brushing the latch. His grimace said more than words. "The quicker we see it, the quicker we get it off my ship."

Pride ran through O' Cuire as deep as a keel through water—every polished rail of the Dawn-Breaker bore it.

"Whatever it is, it's had time to ripen."

Rhyslin's dry humor found no welcome. O' Cuire only grunted, shoved the door, and stepped through.

"Bloody Ifrinn!" His curse rang against the timbers. "Did someone bring a body back from the battlefield?"

Rhyslin and Rembran entered to find the captain bent double, hands braced on his knees. After drawing a long draught of air, O' Cuire jabbed a finger at him. "Don' t you dare say a word."

"I wouldn' t dream of it," Rhyslin replied calmly. "Why do you think I waited outside?"

"Fair point." O' Cuire pulled a handkerchief from his coat, muttering, "By Nan Diathan, that' s foul." He tied it over his face and drew shallow breaths. "Where is it coming from?"

Rembran raised his hand, pausing for the captain' s nod before tracing a stylized canine nose in the air. The rune shimmered, then backfired—Rembran turned pale, coughing, while Rhyslin hid a grin behind his hand.

The spellblade steadied himself, drawing slow, ragged breaths until the trail of rot resolved.

His steps led to a black chest shoved into a far corner, iron corners rasping against stone as he dragged it into the light. The sound was like a warning—metal against bone.

O' Cuire laid a hand on his shoulder. "I don't recognize this coat-of-arms."

Rhyslin studied the sigil: a shield circled by curved draconic horns, Auvrik darastrixi – Vargach scrawled beneath. His brow furrowed. "I have never seen this language." From his belt he drew a yellow crystal. "Shai' velen thu orach?"

The crystal flickered and went dark. Rhyslin blinked, shaking his head.

"Strange." He stroked his beard, unsettled.

"What did it say?" Rembran asked, knowing the spell.

"I don't know." Rhyslin's voice carried a rare edge. "It is untranslatable."

"That's impossible."

"Apparently not." He turned his palm upward. "I can't decipher this."

The captain circled the chest. "What exactly were you planning to do with it?"

Rhyslin's brow knit. "A fair question." He looked toward the bulkhead. "I plan to move it. If something goes wrong, we can't afford to be sealed in with it." His decision came cold and certain. "Secure it on the main deck, just forward of the bowsprit. I need time—and space—to study it."

O' Cuire nodded, already picturing the spot. "I' ll have it moved in half an hour. How heavy a watch do you want?"


"None." Rhyslin was already turning toward the door. "Just see that no one disturbs it. And if you can find out who brought it in..." His voice cooled like steel in water. "I' d like a word."

# Chapter Sixteen
## The Counsel of Ashes

Rhyslin returned to the main deck in time to hear cheers rise from the pier-side. The sound carried over the river water like gulls calling at dawn, bright and sudden. He moved toward the port rail, gazing down. Below, the two counter-sail teams clapped shoulders, their victory written in tired grins and tar-blackened hands.

"It's about damned time," O'Cuire muttered as he joined Rhyslin at the side rail. His jaw was tight, but pride glinted in his eyes. "I'm tired of sitting here."

The draoidh nodded once. He, too, felt the itch of stillness. Dockside air tasted of stone dust and river mud; he longed for clean sky pressing under the ship's hull again.

"Let me know when we can lift ship." Before O'Cuire could answer, Rhyslin turned on one heel and strode away, his cloak catching the wind like a restless wing.

He had no desire to return to his cabin. The air in it no longer felt his—it smelled faintly of sawdust, varnish, and someone else's touch. The loss unsettled him more than he would admit. When Marcus intercepted him on the companionway, Rhyslin welcomed the pause.

"What brings you to me, old wolf?"

"The chest you found, I think." Marcus's tone was cautious, as if the words themselves were uncertain.

Rhyslin tilted his head. "Black wooden chest with iron hinges and a strange coat-of-arms on it?"

"That's the one." Marcus folded his arms, posture broad and braced. "I found it in the Ogren's campaign tent after the battle." He gestured toward the bowsprit. "Why was it brought up?"

Rhyslin lifted a brow. "I'm surprised you couldn't smell it from there."

"Smell what?" Marcus closed his eyes, drew in a long breath—and coughed as the rot hit him like a blow. He staggered a half step, eyes watering.

Rhyslin's mouth quirked in faint humor. "Now you know why we moved it."

---

Ilyriatri sat in her cabin with the mirror of silver and crystal before her. Its polished back caught the river-light and fractured it into shards along the ceiling beams. Garion's gift.

Once it had bridged their partings. Now it linked her to the only advisor she trusted.

Her fingers tapped an anxious rhythm on the desk. *What will he think of me traveling with Maighstir Darkblade?* The thought was as heavy as the silence.

"I would like to speak to Makar Lann Neimh."

Mist bloomed across the mirror's surface before clearing. The face of the elder Hîn i-Balanath appeared, bone-white hair combed neat, crystal eyes alive with quiet concern. On his brow, ash clung in the mourning mark.

"Ilyriatri," he said softly. "Are you well?"

He had seen the fatigue in her face, the weariness she hadn't hidden well enough.

"How many did we lose?" she whispered.

The elder drew a hand down his face, sighing as if each word scraped against stone. "We lost everyone in Aelin Silivren. The sands devoured them before they could escape." His eyes grew distant. "The Fîr Lithren couldn't even find them to administer the rites."

The prayer rose from Ilyriatri's lips without thought, light as breath: "Despoina, guide them." Then, sharper, more urgent: "Makar, we have to find someplace else to live before we are no more."

His shoulders slumped. Even across the glass, she felt the weight he carried. "Mathair Astinmah summoned you, didn't she?"

"She did."

"What did she want?"

"She wanted Mayana, Allanagh, and me to sign a treaty with Na Saor-shealbhaichean nan Raointean Mòra."

Makar frowned, searching memory. "I don't know them. Did you sign?"

"I did." Her admission carried both defiance and weariness. Then, softer: "Makar, Vuuroena has seen their leader in her dreams. I have met him. He seems… honorable."

The elder ran a trembling hand through his white hair. "Be cautious, Ilyriatri. We do not know these people. And this man she dreams of—who is he?"

She bit her lip. "He said he knew Garion… and apologized for not being able to save him."

The elder's jaw dropped. "Describe him."

"He is unremarkable to the eye. Your height. Close-shaven white beard, hazel eyes flecked with gold. A Draoidh."

Makar leaned forward. "Ilyriatri. His name?"

"Rhyslin—" she hesitated, as though giving away a secret.

"Darkblade?" The name snapped from him like a lash. His eyes widened. He breathed fast, as if memory rushed through him too quickly to bear. "It's been a long time since I last heard that name." His voice broke, then steadied. "Yes. He knew Garion. If this is the same Rhyslin Darkblade… he helped Garion build the United Tribes. We used his ideas as the bones of our laws."

Ilyriatri listened, a trace of smile touching her lips. The thought bloomed within her—wild, sudden:

*Perhaps this is the path to survival.* But she gave Makar no more than a whisper.

"Makar, I may have found a way for us to dwell among the Saor-shealbhaichean."

He pointed at her, sharp as a spear. "Be careful. Don't act in haste."

She arched a brow. "Have you ever known me to act in haste?"

"No… but you have done things without mulling them over." He sighed, shoulders bowing. "Promise me you'll be careful."

Blush warmed her cheeks, unexpected, unwelcome. "I'll be careful." They both knew it was an empty promise. Destiny bent no knee to will.

"I will speak with you later, old friend. Keep our people safe."

"I will do my best." The words rang hollow. He could no more hold back the sands than halt the turning of the stars.

Just before the mirror dimmed, she caught his face again, carved with helplessness. She lifted a hand to her cheek, whispering into the empty room: "Forgive me, Flur, for what I'm about to do."

The words hung in the cabin like incense, whispered more to the gods than to her absent companion. The air smelled faintly of oil and pitch, yet beneath it lingered the stench from the chest—a sour rot that no prayer could banish. She drew a long breath, trying to center herself, then left the room in search of her daughter.

The great-cabin was empty. Silence pressed around her, broken only by the creak of timbers and the faint shiver of sailcloth. Unease stirred within her chest. *I hope you don't grow to hate me.*

On the quarterdeck she found Vuuroena at the port-side rail, her face pale, tinged green, breaths coming shallow and quick. The younger woman clung to the wood as though it alone kept her steady.

"What happened?" Ilyriatri asked, draping an arm around her shoulders, feeling the tremor of her body.

"We found the source of the stench. The smell made me sick." Vuuroena whimpered as she leaned into her mother. "Even Rhyslin turned green."

The sea air tried to sweep the rot from their lungs, but its trace clung stubbornly, like a curse. Ilyriatri guided her daughter back toward the great-cabin, each step heavy with the knowledge of what must follow—and the cost of it.

Inside, she eased Vuuroena into a chair and pressed her hand briefly against her cheek. Then, gathering her courage like a mantle, she crossed the room and rapped on Rhyslin's door.

"Is it time to—" Flur began, but the grief etched across Ilyriatri's face stilled her words as surely as a hand upon her lips.

"What is it?"

Ilyriatri's throat closed. No words came, only a lifted hand beckoning them both to the table.

The lamplight flickered as though reluctant to witness what was about to be spoken.

When they were all seated, Ilyriatri turned to her daughter. Her voice was soft, but it carried the weight of a dirge.

"The burning sands have devoured Aelin Silivren."

Flur blinked, gaze darting between mother and daughter. Silence fell—thick, heavy, sacred as a temple veil. Even the ship's timbers seemed to hush, listening.

Vuuroena bowed her head, whispering a prayer to Despoina. The name of the goddess seemed to still the air, as if the ship itself bent to hear the plea.

"Did anyone survive?" The question was fragile, childlike, the echo of a girl she had once been.

Ilyriatri's lips trembled. No sound emerged. Only the faintest shake of her head.

Vuuroena broke then, sobbing for the lost. "Yana and her family lived there." Her voice cracked, and she rocked as though to cradle her own grief. Longing welled in her for comfort, and Ilyriatri—mother as much as queen—spread her arms wide. Vuuroena collapsed into them, curling against her lap.

"Momma, are we doomed to die?"

"I don't know, Mîr nîn," Ilyriatri whispered, holding her tight. She kissed her daughter's brow, her lips brushing sweat and salt. "I don't know."

The silence between heartbeats stretched. At last she spoke again, voice low and tremulous. "I need to ask you about the dreams you've been having about Maighstir Darkblade. What do they show?"

Vuuroena lifted tearful eyes. "He would find me when I got lost and care for me." She scrubbed at her cheeks, leaving red streaks where tears had been.

Ilyriatri closed her eyes briefly, steeling herself. "I'm considering doing something that might anger you," she confessed. "And you as well, Flur." Her gaze returned to Vuuroena, almost pleading. "What do the dreams show you, Mîr nîn?"

The young spell-blade blinked, then surrendered to the weight of memory. She closed her eyes. "In my dreams, I am taken prisoner by a man I've never seen before. I'm taken far from home and enslaved. In some dreams, I fail to save the others they stole. Other times, I succeed—but only at great cost." Her breathing slowed, steadying itself. When she opened her eyes, they locked on Ilyriatri's with unsettling clarity. "The only constant is that Maighstir Rhyslin saves me from death."

"Are you —" Ilyriatri hesitated, the question cutting against her daughter's dignity. "—bound to him within any dream?"

Vuuroena shook her head. "No, Momma, why?"

"Are you sure?" The queen's voice carried both urgency and reluctance. "When Maighstir Darkblade was unconscious in the cottage, you said—"

"That I'd bond with him if I could. Yes, Momma, I remember." Vuuroena's stomach clenched, a knot of dread coiling tighter. "But why?"

The truth was a blade. Ilyriatri unsheathed it without ceremony. "I'm thinking of giving Rhyslin my bond."

The words struck like thunder in still air. Silence answered first, no screams, no fury, only shock. Vuuroena stared wide-eyed, her mouth open, disbelief written across her face. Flur, golden-haired and quiet until now, let a single tear slip down her cheek. She exhaled a sigh that trembled on the edge of sorrow.

"Who am I to tell you no?"

Vuuroena slipped from her mother's lap and drifted to the divan, folding in on herself like a shutter against the wind. Her silence pressed the cabin close, leaving space for the older women to speak.

"You are his Bhanna. The old code gives you the choice — to accept or to refuse."

Flur's head bowed, her voice breaking on the words. "We haven't even consummated our bond. I used to think being a bhanna would feel like love — like home." She buried her face in her hands. "Now, I'm not so sure."

The lantern light trembled with her sob, as if the Dawn-Breaker itself grieved with her.

Ilyriatri leaned across the table, her fingers brushing Flur's arm. "What's wrong?"

"It's been four weeks since we bonded." Flur's hand flicked toward the small chamber Rhyslin had given her. "We haven't shared the same bed. He sleeps in that chair, while I sleep in there." Her eyes shimmered, rimmed with unshed tears. "What's wrong with me? Why doesn't he want me?"

The deck creaked, timbers bowing like an old heart under strain.

"I wish I knew, Flur." Ilyriatri's voice softened to a hush. "But maybe someone wiser does."

Flur lifted her head, hope and despair caught in the same fragile breath. "How?"

The queen exhaled, as if steadying herself against her own grief. *Perhaps it's time I turned to the one soul who's never failed me.* "I'm going to ask Chantico."

Flur raised her head from her hands, eyes wide. "Why not Ananke?"

Doubt rimed her tone like frost on glass.

Ilyriatri's gaze did not waver. "Because I don't worship Our Lady of Chains."

The last word hung heavy in the air. A silence settled so profound it seemed even the lantern flame dared not crackle.

# Chapter Seventeen

## The Dryad and the Sky

Under Captain O' Cuire' s orders, the sailors labored to rehang the counter-sails. Work faltered when a dryad strode down the pier, drawing every gaze.

She moved like summer shadow, long black hair rippling with the scent of rain-soaked leaves. Her crop-top clung across her breasts but bared her stomach; a black leather skirt brushed between hip and knee, while moccasins coiled up her calves like ivy on stone.

A sailor elbowed his mate. "Is that Kiesha?"

"Aye," the other squinted. "Heard Lady Astinmah borrowed her for a week." The first sighed, hunger thick in his tone. "Looks good on her. She looks good enough to eat."

At the gangway's crest, Kiesha paused, searching for the officer of the deck. Not finding him, she sighed — a weary sound, more grief than breath.

"Lady Kiesha, is that you?" The officer dropped his line and hurried over.

"It's me," she said flatly, waiting for the ritual bowl.

He set water before her. "May I help you in any way?"

Her dark hair swirled as she shook her head. She dipped her hands, brushed water over her wrists, face, and neck.

"Do you know where Rhyslin is? I need to talk to him."

"He just came up from the lower decks. Likely heading to his cabin."

She spotted him moving toward the quarterdeck stairs. "Thank you." She bowed and hurried, her steps quick and desperate.

"Rhyslin!" She caught him at the stair-bottom, clutching his cloak with trembling fingers. Tears streaked her cheeks. "Look what she did to me!"

He reeled, startled. "Kiesha?"

"Yes!" she growled, lifting her head. "Who else could I be?"

His brow arched. "Why are you growling at me? I didn't do that to you."

"She turned me into an old woman." Kiesha spun, graceful even in sorrow, baring new lines in her body as if they were scars.

"Twenty-two is not that much older than you were." His words pressed the air sharp with burnt rosemary as her glare seared across the space between them. "She only aged you four years."

"You don't understand." Her voice cracked. "If I'm four years older, I can't fit in my tree. Where will I sleep?" A tear slipped before she felt his arm settle around her shoulders.

"Let's not discuss this here." He placed a foot on the stair, then hesitated, remembering. "Let's use my—office."

She followed him up, light-footed but relentless, into the hush of the great-cabin. She froze, wide-eyed at the refurbished space she had not seen since her absence. Fingers brushed the oak table as though tracing what she'd missed. "I've missed everything," she murmured. "Tell me all about it."

Gasps sounded behind her. She turned, eyes widening. "What's going on here, Maighstir Rhyslin?"

He sighed. "Kiesha, these are my guests—no, that's not entirely true." He beckoned Flur forward. "Kiesha, this is Flur, my bond-mate."

The dryad stilled, words lost, then whispered, shocked, "Rowena's gonna be livid."

'That's understating it,' Rhyslin thought grimly. "There's no help for it." He gestured to the other women. "This is Ilyriatri, and her daughter, Vuuroena."

Kiesha's gaze locked on Ilyriatri, memories not her own rising unbidden. "Sira' Talaneth." She offered as stately a courtesy as her weariness allowed.

"I have not been a Rian since Garion died." Ilyriatri bowed half-low. "I am merely the representative of Hinnath i-Lith. My daughter and I travel with Maighstir Darkblade."

Vuuroena, bright-eyed, hurried closer. "You are the dryad I-Banwen en-Taur chose as vessel for her divine spirit."

Shaken, Kiesha nodded. "I am."

"You're beautiful," the girl gushed. "I love your hair. I wish mine curled like that."

Kiesha flushed beneath the sudden praise. "Do you truly believe so?"

"Oh yes, truly." Vuuroena leaned in. "So—who is Rowena, and why will she be livid?"

Rhyslin muttered, shaking his head, unwilling to name her.

Kiesha's eyes narrowed knowingly. "You haven't told them about Rowena yet."

"I haven't had time," he growled low.

Flur, already unraveling from his silence, slid her hand into his. *Bêl nîn o gûr nîn—* "Who is Rowena?" She felt guilt coil through their bond but held her tongue.

Still unable to sense her feelings, Rhyslin's chest tightened. *Why can't I hear her soul?* He curled his fingers around Flur's as though holding a relic too fragile to risk breaking. "Rowena is—well, she's a seer of Despoina. She lives in the manse."

Flur searched his eyes. "How long has she been living with you?"

The question carried no accusation, only the ache of wanting truth. She could feel his reluctance, his effort not to wound her, and found comfort that even in hesitation, his love for her did not falter.

Rhyslin guided her toward the table, taking the head seat. Flur followed, her hand still locked with his, clinging like ivy on stone. While the others drifted closer, she pressed inward, testing her own heart. How long had this seer dwelt under his roof? Did his affections lie divided?

When Ilyriatri, Vuuroena, and Kiesha had taken their places, Rhyslin finally spoke.
"Rowena has been living in my home for almost five years."

His eyes flicked over the women, bracing for betrayal, anger—disgust. Instead, he met thoughtful, measured faces, their stillness carrying more weight than any outcry. The candle flames held steady, as if waiting for the next truth.

Ilyriatri met Flur′s gaze before asking the question her cousin could not. "Has she given you her bond?"
Her voice was gentle, steady. Sharing did not frighten her; she only sought clarity.

"She has offered," Rhyslin admitted, voice low. "I have refused her, for reasons of my own." He squeezed Flur′s hand, as though her touch alone could steady the ground beneath him.

Ilyriatri frowned, setting aside the sharper questions.
"And now?"

His posture stiffened. He tried for indifference but failed; the timbre of his voice betrayed him.

"Now, the next time she asks, I cannot deny her."

The words trembled into the air, the sails above creaking as if burdened with the weight of them.

Vuuroena's chest burned with a flicker of jealousy. Rhyslin haunted her dreams, yet where could she fit? He already had Flur, a waiting seer, and even her own mother's shadow pressed toward him. The thought broke loose from her lips before she realized:

"Why does that scare you?"

The room stilled. Rhyslin looked at her as though she'd torn away his last defense.

Before them all, the draoidh's mantle slipped. A man sat in his place, weary-eyed and stripped bare. His gaze flicked to Flur.

"You can feel how my soul sings for you."

Flur nodded, her bond affirming it, though his voice faltered.

"I cannot do the same. I cannot hear your soul, and I don't know why." His fingers gripped hers so tight she felt the tingling ache. "I fear you've bound yourself to a broken man."

The words fell heavy, and the chamber seemed to bend with them, the lantern flame guttering, the wood groaning as though in sympathy.

Flur met Ilyriatri's eyes, her heart caught between fear and devotion. The older woman gave a single, curt nod. Silent promise. She would speak to her goddess before the night ended.

---

With a final tap of the hammer, the port-side counter-sail locked into place, canvas folding tight against the hull. The Dawn-Breaker shivered once, like a creature waking.

Captain O'Cuire let his gaze sweep the rigging. He prayed the new sails would hold. The only way to know was to risk the skies. He gave a short nod to the waiting sailor.

"Call them home."

The sailor lifted a brass horn and blew four long, brazen notes. The sound carried across the river like a summons. From the barracks on the west side of the village, Saorsa soldiers came marching, boots striking in rhythm, debts paid and favors called, every man ready to return.

Drawn by the horn, Allanagh and Mayana drifted to the dock, skirts stirring in the river wind, to watch the ship make ready.

On the deck, O' Cuire stood rooted in the timber. He could feel the tension in the planks under his boots, the ship yearning forward. He turned to the officer of the deck.

"Is everyone aboard?"

he officer double-checked the manifest, then saluted. "Sir! All crew and contract soldiers are aboard." The salute held until O' Cuire pressed a hand to his chest. "Ship and crew are ready to get under way, sir."

The captain raised his hand to test the wind. A shift of breeze stroked his palm, steady as a promise. "Man the masts. Get ready to lift ship."

The handlers swarmed like gulls, climbing rigging, unlacing gaskets, shaking canvas loose. Sheets cracked open to the river air. The ship pulled against her anchors. At the helm, the pilot braced as the rudder bit deep.

"We have bite, sir."

O' Cuire nodded. "Weigh the fore anchor."

The fore crew strained at the capstan, the deck humming with effort until the bosun barked, "Anchor is up and hanging free, sir!"

"Helm, rudder two points to starboard."

The helmsman swung the wheel, watching over his shoulder as current and wind nosed the ship into the river's heart. "On course, straight and true. Bringing the rudder back amidships."

"Weigh the aft anchor."

"Aft anchor clear and free, sir."

The captain's lips curved. The Dawn-Breaker was loose. "Hold course with the river until the mainsails draw."

"Aye, sir."

Wind streamed through his hair as O' Cuire turned to the elementals. "Ser Andros, Cailin Ixa, are you ready?"

Andros dropped to one knee, palm spread flat to the deck. Ixa bit her lip, eyes flicking to Rembran before nodding. "I think so, sir."

O' Cuire' s frown cut sharp. Dockside, he could accept hesitation. In the sky, doubt meant death. He leaned closer. "Cailin Ixa. If you aren' t sure, we can' t safely make the flight home. Are you ready?"

She shrank back toward Rembran.

"Stop that." His hand steadied her hips, then pushed her forward again. "The captain's right. If you can't handle it, we'll follow the river until it grows too shallow to sail."

Her pout trembled like wind against canvas.

"If you can't handle it, nobody will blame you." His voice stayed firm, though his thoughts wrapped her with care.

She studied him, then turned back to O'Cuire. "I'm ready, sir." Her voice rang crisp now. "Give me a minute to check the cargo stowage." She closed her eyes, pulse of draoidheacd rippling through timber and rigging. "Cargo storage is optimal. We are ready to lift the ship."

The captain inclined his head. Ixa sagged back into Rembran's side. "Thank you for pushing me."

He chuckled low. "You won't be thanking me when we clear the clouds. I'm going to take my coat from you. If you're still wearing those veils, you'll freeze."

Heat climbed her cheeks. "You wouldn't let me freeze. You're too much of a gentleman."

"Keep thinking that. The moment I feel cold, you're losing the coat." He poked her side, drawing a half-suppressed laugh. "Change now or at altitude. Your call."

She crossed her arms. "Is that an order?"

"Only if you need one."

Her breath stilled. *Surely he won't take it by force.* One look at him stole that illusion. She stomped lightly. "Fine, I'll change."

She closed her eyes. Beneath the shelter of his coat, veils shimmered away, replaced by cotton, wool, and leather. When she turned, the new clothes peeked from the folds. "Are you happy now, Lieutenant Du Lac Morn?"

He raised a brow, uncertain whether to read her tone as play or rebuke. In the end, he let it pass, unsettled by the strange current running in his blood.

Ixa smiled faintly and pressed back against him, then let her spirit sink into ship and river. As the sails filled, she drew the winds upward, guiding the Dawn-Breaker's hull from water to sky.

The vessel strained, then rose. Treetops fell away beneath. Counter-sails dropped and steadied her climb.

"Good job, Ixa, you did it." Rembran's arm curled around her waist. "Now, give me my coat."

She gave a theatrical shiver. "But it's so cold."

He muttered a curse. She giggled, delight sparking like a child's bell.

"Don't make me take it. You won't like it if I do."

She was about to press the game further when O' Cuire's voice cut in. "If you two are through, I'd like the distance under the keel, please."

"Of course, sir." Ixa closed her eyes. "I estimate six hundred feet from the keel to the treetops. Though Andros could be more precise."

The Earth Elemental looked up from the desk and nodded. "This is true." A deep pulse of draoidheacd rolled through the hull, down into the bones of the ship, and spilled into the air until it touched the earth far below. The timbers answered with a low hum. "It is exactly one hundred three fathoms from curve of keel to the ground below."

The helmsman steadied himself against the wheel as the ship shivered with life. "All sails are set, sir. The counter-sails are functioning as intended.

We are making five knots with a favorable tail wind." He glanced down at the compass in its raised binnacle box, its needle quivering like a bird's wing. "Our course is sou'–by Sou-west. If the winds hold favorable, we should be home within a week."

Above the clouds, the Dawn-Breaker sang softly in her rigging. Canvas snapped like laughter in the sky, the hull creaked as though eager to run, and the wind sharpened the air with a taste of resin and salt. With the ship secure, Captain O' Cuire ignored it when Ixa and Rembran's voices rose again in easy banter.

The spellblade leaned into Ixa, his shadow falling across her veils. "Are you going to give me my coat?"

The Elemental smirked playfully as she shook her head, the ship's planks thrumming faint approval beneath her bare feet. "No, I don't think I will. You'll have to take it from me."

Rembran gave a mock sigh, his breath curling white in the cold air. "You had a chance to save face and give me my coat." Slipping his hands around her waist, he crooked his fingers and started to tickle her.

The ship itself seemed to echo her laughter, rigging trembling as Ixa tried to swat his hands away but quickly fell to giggling. "I yield — I yield."

Still giggling, she surrendered his coat and watched as he shrugged into it, warmth spilling from him like fire against the chill.

Feigning a shiver, she gave him a pout. "It's so cold, may I—?" Then, without giving him a chance to refuse, she slid under his coat and curled into him. The hull beneath them gave a long, satisfied sigh as though approving the fit.

"Little Chit," he whispered affectionately, his hand resting against the small of her back, steady as an anchor.

"I'll admit to that, where you are concerned." Ixa reached up and cupped his cheek, her touch as light as falling snow. "Have I thanked you for saving me?"

"Not as such," he said with the hint of a grin, though his eyes softened, betraying the weight behind the jest.

She brushed a soft kiss across his lips. "Remind me tonight and I'll thank you appropriately." Ixa winked at him, her thoughts flashing with silks and candlelight, the image warming her more than the coat.

The sails overhead bellied full, carrying the ship steady through the endless white. Rembran held her closer, silent, his heart tightening in response to her promise, though no words left his lips.

# Chapter Eighteen
## The Grove and the Hearth

As the Dawn-Breaker reached for the sky, its sails swelled with borrowed winds, yet its master did not stand on deck to command it. Rhyslin remained in his great-cabin, the air thick with candle flame and the lingering musk of oak resin, speaking quietly to the women who defined the orbit of his life.

Flur squeezed his hand, her warmth a tether against the storm within him, and leaned to brush a kiss against his cheek. The scent of wildflowers and hearth-ash clung to her as she turned, her golden hair swirling like a banner in the lamplight. "I didn't realize you couldn't hear my soul."

Her glance toward the closed chamber door found Ilyriatri's eyes, and for a heartbeat their silent understanding filled the space more strongly than any spoken vow. She caressed Rhyslin's cheek, her touch soft as velvet. "Will you excuse us for a moment?"

Rhyslin nodded, leaning into her palm as though savoring the last warmth of a hearth before winter. "Of course. Take all the time you need."

The air stirred faintly as Flur crossed the cabin, Ilyriatri and Vuuroena falling into step behind her. When the forbidden door closed after them, silence rushed in, a hush so profound that the wood of the cabin itself seemed to hold its breath.

Rhyslin waited until he and Kiesha were alone. He gestured for her to sit beside him. Instead, the young dryad slid the chair aside and knelt gracefully at his knee, the earthy scent of moss rising with her. "Rhyslin—what am I going to do?" Her bright eyes searched his face, wide with the ache of displacement. "If I can't fit in my tree, where will I live? What will I do?"

Rhyslin laid his right hand upon her head, fingers brushing through strands like new spring shoots. A subtle weight settled in the air as though the cabin's beams leaned closer to listen. "There may be a tree you can live in." His voice held gentle secrecy, for the truth had been entrusted to him in confidence.

Kiesha wiped at her eyes, leaving dewdrop-like trails on her cheeks. "You do?" Wonder quickened her breath. "Which one?"

Rhyslin's fingers curled in her hair, and the faint, unmistakable fragrance of oak spread through the chamber, as if the very grove leaned through him. "The towering dair that rules the grove's heart."

Kiesha froze mid-motion, her nuzzle against his palm stilled by revelation. Her next breath shivered with sap and leaf. "That dair is Matron Foghar's tree. Why would I belong there?"

Closing his eyes, Rhyslin spoke from a place beneath words, his voice resonant with the hush of age. "Matron Foghar is looking for a young dryad to train."

"Training? For what?" Her question quivered between fear and awe.

"For her place." His words bore the cadence of seasons turning, of autumn leaves surrendering to winter.

Reverence widened Kiesha's gaze. She bowed her head as if in the presence of something holy. "Is Matron Foghar going somewhere?" She already feared the answer.

"Mathair na doire Foghar has been hearing Gair an Doire." Even the candle flame guttered at those words, as if stirred by a distant breath.

The Call of the Grove. For a dryad, the invitation into paradise.

"How long does Matron Foghar have left?" Kiesha's voice was the voice of a child meeting death for the first time, fragile and breaking.

Rhyslin traced a tear down her cheek, his touch reverent. "Only long enough to guide the next grove mother."

She nuzzled deeper into his palm, her spirit clinging to the shelter of his presence. "But, Rhyslin. I'm not old enough. I'm eighteen, just as is my twin sister, Kietha." Her earlier complaint lay forgotten like a shed husk.

A wry smile softened his lips. "Kietha is indeed eighteen. You, however, are not. A Mathair gave you the gift of maturity—a burden and an honor most never receive so young."

Under his hand she grew utterly still. Even her breath halted, as though time itself waited with her. "She did, Rhyslin." The whisper trembled. "I'm old enough to enter training to be a grove mother."

Yet her heart beat wild beneath the gift, demanding not only destiny but the fire of knowing a man.

Her voice cracked into fragile hope. "If I become a grove mother and take Matron Foghar's place, would you be my maighstir an doire?"

The question brought pause. Shadows seemed to thicken in the cabin as Rhyslin weighed the truth. If Kiesha inherited the grove, she would seek bond with him, and Flur's heart must bear it. He chose careful words, tinged with irony. "The grove sits at the center of my holdings. By default, that makes me the grove master." And with it, the inevitable bond.

Kiesha sat back on her heels, her heart pounding so loudly she was sure he must hear it. "Did you and Matron Foghar ever—you know—join in the mating dance?"

"Sadly, no." His eyes softened with memory. "She was beyond seed years when I enclosed her grove."

Before sense could catch her tongue, Kiesha blurted: "If I become the grove mother, would you dance with me?" The words struck like arrows loosed too soon. She covered her mouth, crimson flooding her cheeks, and buried her face in her hands. *What did I just say? I've offended the grove master.*

But Rhyslin only shook his head, his patience as steady as stone. He did not fault her youth or the fire Astinmah had placed in her veins.

"All in good time, Kiesha. It will happen if A Mathair wills it."

Flur perched on the edge of the new bed, back straight, her gold-flecked eyes narrowing as if her aunt had just stepped into the room wearing a drake's skin. The lamplight caught in her hair, scattering fire across her shoulders. "Why do you worship Chantico instead of Ananke?" She had always assumed Ilyriatri followed the goddess of chains, as she herself did. The thought that her aunt might bow to another felt strangely disorienting, like standing on a deck that shifted beneath her feet.

"I've always kept a house, both my mother's and the one I had before Garion." Ilyriatri paced the narrow walkway between the king-size bed and the desk.

Her steps were measured, almost meditative, the sway of her auburn curls catching the glow of lantern-flame. "It was only natural to worship the Hearth-Mother." She glanced toward Vuuroena, sprawled diagonally across the center of the bed like a victorious huntress, one arm draped across her brow. "When I joined Garion's house, being a hearth-maiden let me smooth out the wrinkles between your mother and Mayana."

Flur's brow furrowed, shadows gathering beneath her lashes. "Mother never mentioned any marital problems."

Ilyriatri's laugh was low, like an ember catching fire after long slumber. "Your mother hasn't always been so calm. She and Mayana were like fire and oil. Garion asked me to be a mediator."

With a fluid motion she climbed onto the bed, the mattress dipping beneath her weight, and gave her daughter's foot a playful shove. "Move thy feet, thou bed-hog."

The raven-haired spellblade groaned, but scooted upward, her back thudding against the carved headboard. "I am no bed-hog," she muttered, her pout just shy of theatrical. "What are we doing in here?" Her glance slid toward the window where pale light slanted in, wistful and restless. Her spirit clearly wanted to be outside — near Rhyslin.

"We are here—" Ilyriatri pointed first at her daughter, then at Flur, "—so I can speak to Abuela Chantico and find out what's wrong with your mate."

Flur half-turned toward her, the sharpness in her eyes softening to hope. "Will the Hearth-Mother be able to help?"

Ilyriatri's shrug carried both honesty and the illusion of confidence. "If Abuela can't, she'll know someone who can." For years she had wondered whether Chantico's teachings on the Nan Diathan's bonds were mere metaphor, or something far deeper.

Flur leaned forward, curiosity tugging at her despite herself. "How do you speak with her?"

Ilyriatri brushed auburn curls over her shoulder, her sigh warm as a settling hearth. "I sit still and meditate." A grin curved her lips, a sudden flare of mischief. "You should try it sometime."

Flur settled back, folding her hands neatly in her lap, the air of a chastened student. Beside her, Vuuroena shifted to watch, her amber eyes bright beneath her veil of feigned disinterest.

Ilyriatri closed her eyes. The air in the room hushed, as though the very boards of the floor leaned in to listen. A faint heat rolled outward from her body, smelling of clay dust, warm earth, and distant woodsmoke. Candle flames steadied, shadows retreating to the corners as if pressed back by unseen hands.

And when she opened her eyes—

—she was home. Not her own, but the Hearth-Mistress's. Walls of sun-warmed adobe rose around her, holding in the crackle of firelight.

The scent of fresh tortillas mingled with peppered beans and chili smoke, the kind of warmth that seeped into bone and memory alike.

Even before her eyes adjusted, Ilyriatri knew where she stood. The clay hearth's breath filled her lungs, earthy and real, carrying the sound of crackling flame and the fragrance of food prepared with love.

"Welcome back, child. It's been seasons since you last visited me." The voice was a woman's, warm as bread taken from the oven.

Ilyriatri smiled, eyes opening to the sight of a middle-aged Aztec woman at the hearth, black hair cascading down her back as she pressed corn flour between practiced palms.

Rising quickly to her feet, the Hîn i-Balanath all but danced across the kitchen, skirts swaying like embers, and wrapped her arms around the goddess.

"I'm sorry I haven't visited you, Abuela." Ilyriatri leaned into Chantico's embrace, the scent of flour and smoke clinging to her skin.

The goddess, voice deep and steady as a winter hearth, inquired, "What troubles you, nieta? If that man of yours has wronged you, I will have him—" Chantico's words faltered as her gaze touched the sorrow in Ilyriatri's eyes. Understanding softened her, and she cupped the Hîn i-Balanath's cheek, thumb brushing away the weight of memory. "I am sorry, nieta — I did not know he was gone."

Her voice dropped, reverent. "That's not what brings you here, is it?"

Ilyriatri wiped her tears of longing with the back of her hand. "No, Abuela, I've come about something else."

Chantico touched the stool beside her, flour-dusted fingers beckoning. "Come, help me make tortillas as you tell me about this problem that has brought you to me."

Ilyriatri nodded, gathering a mound of corn flour. Her fingers pressed and shaped it, grounding her in the goddess's rhythm. "My niece, Flur, recently offered her bond to a man." Slowly, she flattened the dough into a circle, her movements steady. "She can sense his soul. By his own admission, he can't sense hers." She glanced up, flour streaking her hands.

"Would you know what's wrong with him?"

Chantico looked at her, eyes dark as polished obsidian. "Why not go to Ananke about this? Why come to me?"

"I'm not a follower of Our Lady of Chains, and I thought you'd know how to help Flur," Ilyriatri admitted, her voice threaded with both reverence and resolve.

Chantico mumbled something under her breath as she closed her eyes. The hearthlight pulsed in rhythm with her words, heat rising in waves.
"Ananke, me Hermana, I need your help for a moment. I've got hot, spicy beef and bean tortillas for you."

Before she could finish, the doorway flared with starlight. A portal bloomed like a wound in the air, its edges shimmering with constellations and faint, silvered chains that clinked against the silence.

Through it stepped a dark-haired beauty, her Grecian toga whispering across her legs as if the stars themselves carried her. She all but skipped toward the hearth, her presence bending the warmth of the fire as if flames leaned to greet her.

Without ceremony, she plucked up a tortilla, steam curling upward into the scent of pepper and cumin. The first bite drew an ecstatic shiver through her frame, her eyes half-lidding.

"Mmm—mmm!" Her voice purred in pleasure, velvet against the crackle of the hearth. "You always know how to get my attention, sister." A low laugh followed, warm and sly, tugging the very air into ripples. "If folk knew this was the way to summon me, I'd never know a moment's—" She broke off mid-breath, her gaze catching on Ilyriatri.

Starlight pooled sharp and intent in her eyes. "Well, hello there."

Chantico accepted the praise with a smug little tilt of her head, the fire dancing higher in agreement. "This is my nieta, Ilyriatri. She has a bond question."

Ananke snagged another tortilla, devouring it with unselfconscious relish, the crumbs scattering like sparks. "Do tell," she invited, her words muffled by food but threaded with unmistakable authority.

When Ilyriatri explained the problem, Ananke's gaze sharpened, the chains on the portal behind her tightening as if echoing her focus.

"You said your niece offered her bond, and the man accepted it."

Ria nodded.

"Did he offer his bond as well?"

The pause stretched. The fire dimmed, shadows thickening. Ilyriatri shook her head. "No. I don't recall him saying anything."

"Gia ónoma tou theoú." Ananke threw up her free hand in mock disgust, the other still clutching her tortilla like a priestess gripping a relic. The hearth spat sparks at her exclamation. "And there it is. Your problem. He hasn't reciprocated. Without mutual offering, the bond's only half alive." Her tone dropped into dry, almost fond contempt. "Typical male — takes the gift, forgets the giving."

Her eyes narrowed, glinting like blades under moonlight. "And who, exactly, is this man?"

Ilyriatri hesitated, throat tight. "Rhyslin Darkblade."

The kitchen's warmth seemed to still, every ember holding breath. Both goddesses stared, silence deep enough that the hearth's crackle rolled like distant thunder.

"Mac Draoidheacd?" Ananke's voice softened, reverent as temple incense. "She offered her bond to Mac Draoidheacd — and he accepted?"

Ilyriatri nodded.

Ananke tipped her head back and laughed, bright and unrestrained. The star-flecked portal trembled, chains rattling in mirth. "Des is going to be livid."

"Yes," Chantico agreed with quiet certainty, her fire casting long, swaying shadows. "She's been chasing the threads of his destiny for years."

Ilyriatri's breath caught. *There was something Despoina couldn't see?*

The Hearth-Mother's amusement ebbed, embers settling into a steady glow. "Typical man," she murmured again — but this time her eyes clouded, reaching outward into the ether. Her voice dropped low, vibrating the clay walls. "Nieta… we may have another problem."

A coil of unease twisted in Ilyriatri's stomach. "What kind of problem?"

"My Taghta mentioned he fell unconscious after a battle. Do you know why?"

Ilyriatri recounted the interrogation and Flur's account of what followed. Chantico tapped her fingertips against the brick, each sound like a spark flaring to life. "If I'm right, Astinmah may have interfered with his prana control — though I can't be certain."

"Which of the Nan Diathan would know for sure?" Ilyriatri asked.

"None," Chantico said, her voice steady as the hearth itself. "We are not Diathan of Draoidheacd. That knowledge lies with the draoidhiel guardians."

Ananke's head shook once, slow and deliberate, the star-light dimming at the motion.

"Why is that a problem?" Ilyriatri pressed.

"Mac Draoidheacd," Ananke said, her words carrying the weight of a verdict, "is the only draoidhiel guardian on this continent. The next nearest is buried deep in the old Nahuatl empire."

A humorless laugh slipped from Ilyriatri, brittle as burnt wood. "Of course he is. It's never easy, is it, Abuela?"

"No, Nieta," Chantico said, her gaze lingering on her granddaughter with heat that was almost protective. "It never is."

Ilyriatri stood and dipped into a deep courtesy before Ananke, firelight catching in her auburn curls. "Thank you for your help, Mistress Ananke."

The goddess of chains, bonds, and contracts waved her right hand, her left still busy with tortilla. The portal pulsed in rhythm with her movement. "Give Mac Draoidheacd my regards."

"I will." Ilyriatri turned and hugged Chantico tight, breathing in the clay-and-woodsmoke scent of her Abuela. "Thank you, for everything."

The Hearth-Mother held her close, warmth radiating until it blurred into the edges of waking.

"Don't fret, Nieta. I don't think you'll be alone for much longer."

Before Ilyriatri could question the prediction, the fire surged, and she was pulled back into the waking world.

# Chapter Nineteen
## The Entangling of Souls

With a deep breath, Ilyriatri opened her eyes. The warmth of Chantico's presence had faded, leaving only the muted creak of timbers and the low hum of elemental prana coursing through the Dawn-Breaker.

Outside the window, the sun had fallen two fingers toward the horizon, painting the clouds in a wash of molten copper. Nearly two hours gone. She stretched carefully, bone and sinew aching but willing, coaxing her body into motion with the same patience she offered her kin.

Vuuroena slumped against the headboard, chin resting on her chest, breath soft as drifting ash.

Beside her, Flur lay curled in repose, golden hair scattered like spilled sunlight across her folded hands. The air carried the faint salt of the upper winds mixed with the resinous tang of the ship's wards, a scent that always reminded Ilyriatri of pine smoke and ocean spray braided together.

She reached out, tapping Flur's right foot. "Wake up, thou slug-a-bed." When the bhanna only burrowed deeper into the quilt, she crooked her fingers and scratched lightly at the sole. "Up, lazy-bones."

Flur jerked her leg away with a gasp, kicking toward Vuuroena, who squawked and nearly toppled from her seat. "Stop, for mercy's sake, stop! I'm awake, you cruel shrew!"

Ilyriatri hid her grin behind a composed hand, feigning matronly dignity. "If that's how you greet kindness, I won't tell you what's wrong with your mate."

Flur froze as if a string had been plucked inside her chest, then scrambled upright, eyes wide with hope. "Chantico figured it out? Come on, Aunt, please tell me. What's wrong with him?"

Ilyriatri lingered a moment, turning first toward her daughter. She brushed a stray lock from Vuuroena's brow, letting her know without words that her well-being mattered. The girl's lips twitched upward in quiet satisfaction, though her eyes, like Flur's, brimmed with eagerness.

Ilyriatri fixed her niece with a mock glare. "There's nothing wrong with your mate that a well-placed strike to the back of his head won't fix."

Her tone sharpened, but a glimmer of humor softened the edges. "When he finds out what's wrong, he's going to feel a proper fool." She let her gaze shift to the door, where the timbers thrummed faintly as if the ship itself awaited their choice. "Would you rather do this now, or later tonight?" She inclined her head toward Flur. "Well, when shall we—?"

"We?" Flur's voice faltered, crestfallen. "I had hoped—."

Ilyriatri slipped an arm around her, drawing her close in a gentle press of comfort. "I know, Flur, but I have a plan. I wish to be present to witness his reaction." She tweaked her niece's cheek. "Should he act with honor, I will leave the pair of you alone for tonight." One eyebrow arched like a bowstring. "Which is it to be? Now, or later?"

Flur thought but for a heartbeat, then fanned her flushed cheeks with her hand. "Now. I don't think I can wait until tonight."

"Now it is." Ilyriatri rose, pulling Flur to her feet as Vuuroena trailed behind. The air in the cabin shifted — a low stir of elemental current, like breath held in expectation. "Come along. Let us finish this. Before I lose my courage." She drew the younger two toward the opening, pushed it wide, and stepped into the great-cabin.

Rhyslin stood at the far side, speaking with Keisha. The draoidh's voice carried low and steady, his shadow stretching long in the lantern-light.

The wards of the room flickered subtly, the ship responding to his cadence. When at last he finished, the three women moved forward as one.

Ilyriatri advanced, her eyes narrowing, each step echoing faintly against the planks. Rhyslin blinked, cleared his throat, and began to rise. She gestured sharply, and he slumped back, his glances darting between the women like a stag aware of the hunt. A growl rumbled in her throat, her fingers tapping her thigh in a rhythm of judgment. The fire in the nearest lantern guttered as if caught in her disapproval.

"According to Lady Chantico, there's nothing wrong with you."

Rhyslin met her approach with calm shaded by caution. His right eyebrow arched, curiosity tempered with unease. "Go on, I'm listening."

Vuuroena lingered just within the door, breath caught in her throat, eyes wide at the tableau. Flur had taken two steps forward before stopping, torn between awe and fear as she watched the confrontation unfold.

Ilyriatri closed the distance, planting herself two feet before him, hands on her hips. The air between them grew taut, charged like the stillness before a storm. "Should I repeat Chantico's words, or make it simple enough for a child to grasp?"

The smug curve of his mouth vanished, replaced by a flicker of concern. Her invocation of the Hearth-matron struck deeper than any scold, cutting him to the quick. He tilted his head up, eyes steady, voice subdued. "Chantico's words will suffice."

"You, sir, are a typical man, always receiving a gift, never giving one in return."

Her voice lashed like a whip, and for a heartbeat she feared she had broken the fragile thread between them. But then, shock, guilt, sorrow,  his emotions cascaded across his face, bare as a sky stripped of clouds.

Slowly, deliberately, Rhyslin rose. The floorboards creaked, but the elemental hum of the ship stilled, as if all the vessel's listening wards leaned closer. He walked to Flur, each step heavy with recognition.

"Mo Flùr bhòidheach. I have wronged you so." He gathered her into his arms, holding her close enough that the sound of her sighs trembled in his chest. "Can you ever forgive me?"

She could only nod, surprise silencing her tongue.

"I accept your freely given bond. I promise to protect you from all harm, to provide you with all that you wish, and to love you till all in this world turns to dust at my feet."

For one dread-filled minute, he thought the Hearth-Matron mistaken, feared he would remain hollow forever.

Flur's gaze met his, pity softening her eyes — or so he thought. Then, without warning, their souls twined together, surging like river-rapids loosed from stone. The air sang with prana, the lantern flames bending inward, as if every element bore witness to the union.

What he mistook for pity revealed itself as deep and abiding love.

[**I never imagined that it would feel thus.**]

Flur pressed close, tears streaking her cheeks, savoring the echo of her devotion. [**You'll never be alone again.**]

Ilyriatri hid her smile behind a composed mask, but her eyes glistened with pride. She stepped back, ceding the space, as Rhyslin swept Flur into his arms and carried her through the doorway into their new cabin.

The wards of the Dawn-Breaker pulsed once in quiet affirmation, as though the ship itself had witnessed the sealing of their bond.

When Rhyslin and Flur emerged from the cabin hours later, the air of the great-cabin felt hollow, like a hearth gone cold. The lanterns swayed with the ship's slow breathing, their light spilling across empty chairs and a table laid bare. Rhyslin paused, gaze moving over the room as though he expected the others to rise from the shadows.

"I expected to find them here, waiting for us."

Flur tugged at her blouse, the fabric refusing to sit neat; with a soft sigh, she gave up. "Maybe they've all gone to eat."

"Mayhaps." The draoidh frowned, listening to the creak of timbers and the muted song of the wind against the hull. He had grown used to Ilyriatri and Vuuroena hovering near, their presence a steadying rhythm.
Without them, the silence seemed too deep, like a missing note in a familiar song. He was about to voice the thought when the hallway door groaned open.

The two Hîn i-Díath women stepped in, each bearing trays from the galley. Warm scents spilled into the room, roasted root and herb, spiced beans, the faint sweetness of baked honey-bread. The timbers near the galley door seemed to hum in welcome, as if the ship itself approved of hearth and table returning to their place

Ilyriatri stilled mid-step, her keen eyes catching the draoidh and his bhanna. For a long heartbeat, she studied them, the bond-light between them shimmering in the air like heat over stone. Then, soft as falling sand, a smile touched her lips.

The way Rhyslin and Flur mirrored each other's pauses and glances brought back memories of Garion, Mayana, and Allanagh, a harmony she had once known by heart. She cleared her throat, and both turned toward her.

"How does it feel, being — so entangled?"

The draoidh inclined his head with rare humility. "Different, but good. It's as if I'm —"

"—Complete and will forevermore be." Flur's smile shone bright as candleflame. "He can feel my soul, and I can feel it as well." She glanced at Rhyslin; his answering nod confirmed more than words. "It feels like I'm seen and known."

Vuuroena shifted her tray onto the table, her chest tightening.

The warmth between her mother and cousin was like firelight glimpsed through glass — beautiful, but distant. She bit down the ache, telling herself it was petty.

"I don't know about you, but I'm famished." She placed one of her plates in the center of the table, waiting for her mother to sit before she chose her own place.

Ilyriatri caught the flicker in her daughter's eyes and gestured to the chair beside the draoidh. "Sit, Mirnoth-lin. Show Rhyslin what we brought back from the galley."

Vuuroena obeyed, her shoulders loosening as she set a plate before him. "For you, Maighstir. The cook was sure you'd like it."

Rhyslin arched a brow, the corners of his mouth twitching. "If I don't like it, will you eat it?"

The spellblade's brows pinched as though she were bracing for a snare. She had chosen carefully, thinking only of what might please him. "I will." She set her tray aside, eyes fixed on him, hoping.

The draoidh glanced at Flur, who radiated quiet amusement through their bond. He lifted the plate, gaze sweeping the table for utensils.

Flur caught his thought and nearly laughed at the smirk ghosting his lips. "Are we to eat with our fingers?"

The words sent a ripple through the room. Even the lanterns seemed to flicker, holding back laughter of their own. Flur bit her lip, the air taut with shared humor.

Ilyriatri paused mid-motion, her own trays settling onto the table. One brow rose, sharp as a hawk's wing, as she noticed her daughter's face fall. "It looks like we forgot to pick some up in the galley," she admitted, though her tone carried a tightness, as though the omission thinned the very air.

Vuuroena shook her head quickly. "No, we didn't, Momma. I didn't see any cutlery anywhere in the galley."

Ilyriatri leaned toward her, unwilling to yield. "Are you absolutely sure?" She searched her memory, but found only the blur of her own haste.

Rhyslin hid his grin, watching her lips curve downward. She held herself like polished stone, yet even a small crack revealed the fragility beneath.

"Vuuroena's correct. The galley didn't hand out cutlery." He gestured to the cabinet behind her, the wood catching lamplight like a living ember. "Every crewmember handles their own tableware. Some are simple copper or wooden bowls, cups, and spoons. Some officers save up for silverware."

Flur drew a slow breath. Her gaze fell to the cabinet: redwood polished deep, silver filigree tracing the edges, a croabh-na-cruinne glowing faintly at its heart. [May I?]

Rhyslin's answering nod stirred the very air. [You may.]

Flur's lips curved in tender delight as she stepped forward. Both hands pressed to the doors, she pulled them open with reverence. The cabin filled with a hush, broken only by her soft gasp. Within lay electrum tableware gleaming pale as dawn, golden chalices that seemed to breathe sunlight, pewter cups dulled with age, and mithril plates shimmering with their own inner light. "Maighstir, may I get Ilyriatri to help me?" Her voice trembled with awe.

"You may." The draoidh's gaze warmed. The wonder in her eyes glowed brighter than the mithril itself.

He leaned back, reflecting that if this astonished them, they would scarcely believe what lay in his home. He watched Ilyriatri approach, saw her composure falter. A soft gasp escaped her lips, like stone struck and cracked by water's persistence.

Flur bit her bottom lip for a moment, then leaned toward her aunt. The candles guttered with her breath, their smoke curling upward like shy spirits. "Have you eaten from this kind of dishware?"

If Rhyslin tilted his head just a shade, the low timber of her whispered question carried through the wood grain of the table to him.

The Hîn i-Díath matron gave a small shake of her head. "No. Nothing this grand." She reached out and picked up one of the electrum plates, the gold-light glinting against her fingers. "I may have been a bereth, but after leaving the castle—," she took a deep breath, a tremor of grief stirring the air between them, the ship's timbers creaking in soft sympathy. "I moved back to a small manor-house at the edge of the desert." Her fingers traced the delicate scrollwork on the plate, the cool metal almost humming beneath her touch. "I couldn't afford anything better than metal tableware and pewter cups."

The golden-haired bhanna leaned into her aunt, warmth radiating like sun through leaves. "I never knew." She wished she could pour her feelings straight into Ilyriatri's heart. "Momma moved us into a house built high in a dair tree. We used wooden tableware." Flur picked up a handful of silverware, its chill pricking her skin. "If we were anywhere but here, I'd be afraid to use these."

Ilyriatri nodded as she carefully placed the plate back in the cabinet, the air sighing as if relieved of its weight. She picked up four crystal cups; they caught the lantern light and scattered it across the table like fragments of starlight.

Rhyslin waited until each cup was full, and each plate was ready. The scents of roasted meat and herbs swirled with the salt-breath of the airship. "Before we partake of this meal." When he had all their attention, he bowed his head. "Thank thee, Mathair Astinmah, for this food which you have given us. May it nourish our bodies, as your love nourishes our spirits."

A hush followed, deep enough that the boards beneath their feet seemed to hold still. He waited until each of the women had thanked Nan Diathan for the meal, then brushed his fingers across his lips, ritual soft as a breeze. "May it always be."

The four ate the meal in silence, save for the rustle of cloth and the occasional, "Please pass the—" or "Thank you." The airship seemed to sway more gently, as though easing itself into the rhythm of their communion.

Throughout the meal, Vuuroena kept sneaking peeks at Rhyslin to see if he liked what was on his plate.

The draoidh let her peek for a few minutes, then caught her attention. "You need not worry, Vuuroena. Were I not to take joy in what you've brought, I would speak it plainly." He took a bite of carrot and graced her with a smile, warmth rolling like a current through the room. "You have done well."

Not used to being praised, Vuuroena stared at him for a minute. The set of her mouth suggested she was putting his words through a sieve, straining for any trace of falsehood. "Thank you, Maighstir Rhyslin."

The draoidh's brows furrowed at Vuuroena's hesitation, then raised one as he caught Ilyriatri's attention. Sparks flickered quietly in the air between them, an unspoken promise that he would speak with her later. For now, no drop of food would go to waste.

After finishing her dinner, Flur leaned over to Ilyriatri, the ship's lantern-light catching the pink on her cheeks. "Do you mind helping me with something?"

When Ilyriatri raised an eyebrow, Flur looked down, a blush creeping up her face. "This is my first full night with him. I want him to remember it."

The Hîn i-Díath stared at her niece, her heartbeat echoing faintly through the timbers. 'What's she playing at?' She leaned toward Flur. "You're no blushing gell. I know you've had melethronnath." When her niece nodded, Ilyriatri shook her head, the air tightening with disapproval. "How many?"

It wasn't possible for Flur's blush to get any brighter, but it did. "Four." She admitted while covering her face with her hands.

"Why are you so nervous?" The elder Hîn i-Díath couldn't understand why her niece was acting this way. "It's not as if you don't know how to please a man."

"You're right." Flur looked at Ilyriatri through her fingers, voice small but steady. "But he's not just any man. He's Rhyslin Darkblade." She wanted to sink through the floorboards; the air itself seemed to warm with her confession.

Ilyriatri nodded once, then reached over and placed a hand on Flur's knee.

The gesture steadied the space around them, like a stone dropped into rippling water. "Maighstir Darkblade, may we have your permission to leave the table?"

Rhyslin briefly glanced at the two women, saw that they had finished eating, and nodded. "You have my permission." He turned his attention back to Vuuroena, the room holding its breath around them.

"Hannon le, Heru Rhyslin." Ilyriatri stood and waited for Flur before following her into the newly refurbished cabin. The door closed with a hush of wood and fabric, as if sealing a secret.

Vuuroena watched the two women disappear and couldn't decide whether she wanted to be in there with them, or stay out in the Great-cabin with Rhyslin. Her fingers fidgeted against the table, curiosity gnawing louder than her restraint.

The draoidh noticed her furtive glances toward the cabin, the air around her humming with indecision. He understood more than Vuuroena thought he did; it was only natural for a young woman to long for the counsel of other women, especially when secrets were being whispered.

"You may join them if you wish. It won't bother me if you do."

Vuuroena fixed him with another of her narrow-eyed looks, sharp as a drawn blade.

Rhyslin met her gaze with one of calm, the steady warmth of a hearth-fire answering her storm.

When she was sure of his motives, she stood and curtsied. "Thank you, Maighstir Darkblade." Then, without a second look, she walked over to the door and knocked.

The door opened just wide enough for her to whisper something, then a little wider for her to slip inside. The air in the Great-cabin softened at her leaving, as if the ship itself leaned closer to its master.

# Chapter Twenty
## In the Chamber of White Satin

Vuuroena slipped through the half-open door and pressed it shut with a soft click, the iron latch whispering into place. The faint scent of lavender hung in the air like a lingering prayer, weaving with the glow of the lamplight. The boards beneath her feet stilled, and for a heartbeat the whole room seemed to hold its breath.

The hush was thick with unspoken expectation. Vuuroena's blue eyes lifted toward her Hîn i-Balanath-a-taur cousin, but it was her mother's voice—low, steady, carrying the weight of hearth and storm—that broke the silence.

"Before we help you prepare for your unforgettable night, we need to understand why you need our help."

As Ilyriatri crossed the floor, the timbers beneath her feet creaked in a rhythm of inevitability.

Her hand came to rest on Flur's trembling shoulder, and the air warmed at the touch, as though the bond-thread itself stirred to listen.

"What is your real reason?"

Flur could not meet her aunt's eyes. Her breath hitched, thin as a torn veil, her fingers twisting knots in the folds of her skirt.

"I want tonight to be perfect for him."

The words shivered into the stillness, fragile yet carrying the strength of truth. Her hand pressed against her heart, and Vuuroena felt the faint answering tremor in her own chest.

"I don't understand why I'm so nervous."

Her swallow was audible, her voice soft as falling rain upon leaves.

"He loves me. I know that."

Her body sagged then, surrendering to the weight she carried, and she folded into Ilyriatri's embrace.

The matron's presence steadied the air; the hearthfire hissed as if in sympathy.

"Then why—why am I so nervous?"

Ilyriatri stroked a calming path down Flur's back, her fingers tracing circles that soothed more than flesh. The bond-thread between them brightened faintly, answering her touch.

"It is difficult, knowing that someone loves you and will never be disappointed in you."

Her hand lingered, then patted Flur's back in reassurance. A sly curve touched her lips, the mischievous spark of youth not yet gone.

"The key to an unforgettable night is to relax and enjoy it."

Her eyes gleamed, catching the lamplight like polished amber. "Tell me, who among your previous lovers let you just be yourself, without judging?"

The question hung in the air like incense. Flur blinked as memory washed over her; Vuuroena saw her cousin's gaze unfocus, saw the flicker of past faces in her expression, each smile a ghost-light. Slowly, a satisfied smile curved Flur's lips, fragile but true.

Without a word she slipped from her aunt's arms. The floorboards sighed beneath her bare feet as she crossed to the nightstand. Her hand found the drawer, and without looking, closed around the familiar shape.

When she turned, the black leather gleamed in her palm like liquid shadow, the silver lock winking in the lamplight as though alive. The air thickened.

Vuuroena′s breath caught as Flur′s cheeks warmed, and the nervous tremor in her breath quieted, replaced by a steady calm.

"Raw a-Charn..." Her voice softened, reverent. "He was the lover who accepted me for what I am—and didn′t judge me."

She lifted the collar, and the lamplight kissed its edges like a benediction.

Ilyriatri took it without hesitation. The smooth leather yielded in her fingers, warm and supple. She turned it over with an appraising eye, as if she weighed not the object, but the truth it represented.

"Why am I not surprised?"

Amusement colored her tone, light as smoke.

Vuuroena tilted her head, caught by the shadow of a smile that played across her mother's face, unreadable yet full of meaning. Fascination curled in her chest. Beside her, Flur's wide eyes betrayed hope and fear tangled together, braced for judgment that never came.

The elder matron pressed the collar back into Flur's hands with quiet confidence, her voice unshaken.

"Why didn't you mate with Raw a-Charn?"

Flur′s pulse shuddered. Her lashes lowered as a single tear traced her cheek, glittering in the lamplight like molten silver.

"Even though he loved me adorned in it, he couldn′t see himself mating with a woman who would give herself to him and him alone."

She raised her gaze, trembling, searching.

"Why aren′t you surprised? More importantly, why aren′t you disappointed? Mom would be."

Ilyriatri′s scoff cracked the air, sharp and dry.

"Allanagh has always borne too much pride. Her being Garion' s first bond only made it worse. She could never understand submitting to his wishes. She was fire."

Her eyes softened, drifting closed as memory rose like curling smoke, wrapping the room in echoes of the past.

"Mayana moved through life laid-back, but with lightning in her veins, she reveled in teasing your mother."

Her words lingered in the air like ancestral song, and Vuuroena felt her chest tighten as though she had glimpsed a door into a world half-lost and half-promised.

Vuuroena listened, rapt, her chest tightening with the quiet revelation of things her mother had never shared.

The lamplight bent toward Ilyriatri's lips as they curved into a small, wistful smile, as if the room itself wanted to hear the confession.

"Garion invited me into the cearcall to bring balance to his family." She paused, her voice quieter, tinged with the ache of loss. "My nature allowed me to act as a bridge between Allanagh's pride and Mayana's teasing."

The air seemed to thicken around them, as if remembering with her. She pressed the choker back into Flur's hands. "You aren't alone, Flur Dris. Being a melthrad is a joy."

Her gaze flicked to her daughter, unreadable but piercing, as though wondering what seeds these words might plant.

Vuuroena felt her heart quicken, as though some unseen current stirred beneath her skin.

Flur's breath shuddered as she slipped the choker around her throat.

"Would you...?" Her voice trembled as she turned, golden hair spilling like molten silk down her back.

The lock clicked shut—soft, final. The sound rang like a quiet chord in the air, the bond-thread itself quivering. Ilyriatri's fingers lingered against Flur's skin for a heartbeat, warm and steady, grounding her.

"That looks good on you," she murmured, pride and affection threading through her husky voice. Then her lips curved into a sly smile.

"But," she teased, "you should probably wear more than that when giving yourself to Rhyslin. We can't give him an unwrapped present."

Heat rose in Flur's cheeks until her skin glowed a rosy hue. She pointed toward the chest in the corner, her voice shy yet eager.

"Momma and I went shopping before we left. Would you — could you help me pick out something to wear?"

"Of course I will."


The deck timbers beneath Ilyriatri's feet groaned softly as she strode to the chest and knelt. One by one she lifted garments into the air, the lamplight playing along their folds before she set them aside. Now and again she gave a low sound of approval, like a purr of the earth itself.

"You did a great job of packing. You've got a good balance of casual and other wear."

The Hin-a-diath matron smiled as she drew out a length of white satin, holding it high so that it shimmered like water under moonlight.

"This will do very well. Come here, Flur bess i-dael. Let's array you for your mate."

The golden-haired Hîn i-Balanath drifted toward her aunt, a dreamy smile softening her features. Vuuroena's breath caught as she watched her mother turn Flur this way and that, undressing her with gentle practicality before wrapping the satin gown around her. The air around them seemed to brighten with each approving murmur Ilyriatri gave, until the girl stood arrayed in silver-white.

Ilyriatri had just finished painting delicate lines of color onto Flur's cheeks when the air shifted. Flur's hand flew to her stomach, and a groan tore from her lips. Her head rolled back, eyes flashing white, and the glow of the room dimmed as if a shadow had crossed the lamp.

Ilyriatri′s gaze sharpened. She narrowed her eyes and reached forward, but already the scent of burned garlic cloves spread on the air like a warding fire gone wrong. She laid her palm against Flur′s brow, and the skin beneath it burned too hot.

"Oh, I see."

Her voice carried both certainty and dread. She turned, seeking her daughter — and found Vuuroena pressed flat against the door, her wide eyes mirrors of shock.

"Lell nîn bain beleg." She beckoned with her hand, voice steady against the rising storm. "I need you to do something for me."

The young spell-blade stepped
forward, each pace reluctant, the air
pulling at her heels. She froze mid-step
when Flur's lips peeled back in a snarl, a
low growl vibrating from her chest.
Vuuroena's blood chilled; she longed for
her sword as fear tangled in her veins.

"What's wrong with Flur,
Momma?"

"It's something that, hopefully,
you'll never have to deal with."

The air thrummed as Ilyriatri squared
her stance before Flur.

"Flur is suffering from a bond-
fever."

The words made the walls seem to
contract. Flur answered with another
growl, the sound feral, edged with hunger.

Ilyriatri leaned forward, her aura flaring with quiet dominance.

"All will be well, Flur, bess i-dael."

Her hand closed firmly around the leather choker, tugging with the weight of command.

For a moment Flur fought her, panic flashing wild in her golden hair and pale gown, but Ilyriatri's grip did not falter.

"Oh no, you don't." The auburn-haired matron growled back, her tone carrying the bite of iron. "If you fight me, I'll lock you away and take my turn with your mate."

The air froze. Flur stilled mid-struggle, a whine breaking from her lips, thin and desperate.

"Please, must get to Maighstir, Rhyslin — need him — can't live without him."

Vuuroena furtively watched her mother as she listened to her cousin. The air in the chamber thickened, her blood racing hot, fear warring with reason until her pulse felt like a war-drum in her throat.

"What can I do?" she whispered, desperate. She would do anything to help Flur.

Ilyriatri's breath came steady, but the lamplight quivered against the walls as she tightened her grip on Flur. "Go get Rhyslin. Tell him I need his help."

"Yes, Momma!"

Vuuroena sprang for the door, the floorboards groaning beneath her haste.

She vanished into the hall, returning moments later with Rhyslin a step behind, the air shifting around him like the quiet wake of a storm.

"Vuuroena said you needed—"

Rhyslin stopped cold.

Flur knelt in the center of the room, satin clinging to her curves, the bond-thread between them gone strange—wild, electric, feral. The lamplight guttered low, shadows lengthening as if drawn to her.

"What in Nan Diathan..." His voice dropped to a wary growl.

Her head snapped up, eyes blown wide, pupils sharp and dark. A sound rumbled through her chest—not quite a word, not quite a growl, and then she crawled toward him, each slow movement hitching the gown higher along her thighs. The boards creaked beneath her palms like a predator's drumbeat.

"Flur," he breathed, "mo gràdh— is that you?"

She tilted her head back, sniffing the air. A feline purr rose, thrumming through the bond like a living chord.

By the time she reached him, her hands pressed against his chest, her body clinging, satin whispering against him. She rose, nuzzling at his throat, and when her teeth grazed his skin, heat flared—sharp, immediate, dangerous.

Rhyslin's breath caught. His hand fisted in her hair, tugging her gently but firmly back. His gaze cut to Ilyriatri.

"What's wrong with her, Ria?"

The sound of her name—shortened, claimed—slid over her like ice melting to fire. Heat raced up her spine, her breath faltering, her body answering before her mind could. Her head turned instinctively toward him, eyes wide, pulse fluttering.

"She has bond fever."

"Bond fever?" Rhyslin's other arm locked around Flur as she coiled against him, purring louder now, the sound vibrating through the floorboards. He realized what he had done, how he had claimed with her name, and shook his head. "Ria, out with it. What is this fever?"

Driven to her knees by the repeated shortening of her name, Ria's voice trembled as she fought for composure.

"The bond-fever happens when a Hîn i-Balanath woman undergoes a partial bond for a length of time. When she completes the bond, there's a one in one-thousand chance her chemistry goes out of balance, and she reverts into one of our first ancestors." She bowed her head, shame burning her cheeks.

Rhyslin's eyes narrowed as he studied Flur's trembling form, her feral grace. "How do we get my Flur back?" His voice was flat, certain. He hadn't bonded with this creature, not yet, and no matter how beguiling she was, he would not settle for less than his Flur.

Ria's voice faltered, low and raw. "You must claim her as the males of our people did long ago. If you can't show your dominance, Flur won't return." She swayed on her feet, then whispered, "May I please leave?"

"No, Ria. You may not."

The growl began deep in his chest, primal, until it rolled outward like distant thunder. The lamplight dimmed. The air itself tightened.

Both women shivered.

"You will stay." His words struck like iron, low and commanding. "Until Flur returns to me. Do you understand?"

"Yes, maighstir."

Ria backed against the wall, her arms curling around herself as she shivered. *What has he done to me?*

"Momma, what should I do now?"

Ria's eyes flicked to the door—Vuuroena's head peeked through, her body hidden. Her blue eyes were dulled with shock.

"Go to bed, Lell nîn bain beleg. I'll be along when I can." She did not know how long it would take Rhyslin to tame this Flur.

"Yes, Momma."

Vuuroena lingered just long enough to see Rhyslin draw Flur's body into a bow, her back arched, her golden hair spilling like molten light.

When his teeth grazed her neck and a raw, feral yowl split the air, Vuuroena froze.

Heat rushed up her throat, into her cheeks, until even her ears burned. She didn't understand the rush in her chest—fear, awe, something dangerously close to longing—but it stole her breath and made her knees weak.

She fled before either of them could look her way, the slam of her heart loud in her ears as the door clicked softly shut behind her.

# Chapter Twenty-One
## Where Soul-Songs Entwine

The sound of wind threading through the sails greeted the dawn, a low and constant hymn that filled the cabin with the pulse of the sky. Ria drifted in that strange country between wake and sleep, half-dreaming, half-aware.

"Go away. Let me sleep."

Her hand brushed lazily at the thin blade of light that pierced the muslin curtains, a golden spear intruding on the shadows she clung to. The warmth of the hearth wrapped around her like a second quilt, mingling with the heady scent of beeswax and papyrus, a fragrance that tugged at memory and belonging. *That smells like Rhyslin.*

Her eyes flew open. Panic rose sharp as steel. She reached out, fingers clawing at empty air, needing to anchor herself in the unfamiliar space.

*How did I get here?* The heavy comforter weighed across her shoulders and down to her feet, a barrier both comforting and strange. She ran her hands frantically beneath the cover, and only when she felt the fabric of her clothes against her skin did relief flood her like water poured into a parched vessel.

The last memory that came to her was of Flur, fevered and trembling, Rhyslin's presence a steady wall as he tamed the storm in her bond-sick soul. *Did he get her back?*

Her gaze found them.

Rhyslin sat in a wide-backed chair, its carved arms a twin to the one in the outer cabin. Flur perched on his lap, turned toward him, her golden fingers tracing the fresh scars carved into his chest.

"How did you get these?" she asked, her voice thin, bewildered.

"You gave me those last night." His tone was quiet, matter-of-fact, and his eyes never broke from hers.

The golden-haired Hîn i-Balanath frowned, confusion flashing like a sunbeam across her face. "I did? I don't remember doing it." She bent and brushed her lips over one of the raw marks, a kiss both tender and ashamed. "Why did I do it?"

The old draoidh drew her in, his arm a band of iron and comfort alike. "You were suffering from a bond-fever."

Flur's breath caught, sharp and pained. She did not want to believe. But his scent did not shift, did not sour with deceit. The beeswax clinging to his skin carried only truth. Her head bowed, her cheeks aflame. "It's been centuries since the last reported bond-fever."

The bruised-apple tang of her sorrow bled into the air, striking Rhyslin like a bruise against his chest. His fingers threaded through her hair, the golden strands sliding like sunlight over stone. "I bring you nothing but pain and anguish."

The words shook her from her shame. She raised her eyes, wide with sudden fear, and the whole room seemed to still in that fragile moment.

Before her protest could rise, he spoke again, voice heavy with the weight of choice. "I understand if you want to have nothing to do with me."

Flur's horror came swift and fierce. She buried her face against his chest as if to anchor herself in his heartbeat. "No — I don't want to go. Le melin!" The cry broke in Sindarin, wild and unrestrained. "ú-istathon cuinar ú-chegin!" Her scent soured with grief, sharp as vinegar. Tears came, the salt of her despair carried on the air.

With a soft sigh, Ria rolled her eyes and slipped from the warmth of her bed.

The wooden planks beneath her feet carried the chill of the morning sea as she padded across the floor. She placed her hand on Flur′s trembling shoulder, grounding her with a sister′s weight.

"Stop crying, Flur. Rhyslin couldn′t toss you aside any more than he could chop off his own foot." Her voice was calm, steady as stone beneath a storm. "Listen to him before you lose your mind."

"Na, Tetheneth." Flur blinked, forcing the tears away, her gaze searching Ria′s face. "Did I, in truth, suffer from bond-fever?"

Surely, surely, Rhyslin was jesting. But when he did not deny it, her eyes widened with dawning horror.

"Did I regress into a —?" She could not speak the shame.

"Into a wild purring mess of a woman?" Rhyslin lifted his brow, unflinching. Flur hid her face in her hands and gave the smallest of nods.

"Yes, you did." He gathered her close once more, his voice a balm. "Are you well, *mia amare?*"

Her mortification burned like embers in the air. "I will be, *guren o guren nín.*" She cupped his cheek, her hand trembling yet sure. "I'm sorry I broke down. All I could think was that you didn't want me anymore."

"I'll have to admit I wasn't expecting our souls to sing to each other. I have no intention of sending you away."

His nose brushed against her palm, and the smallest laugh slipped from her lips like sunlight breaking cloud.

Ria lifted her hand from Flur's shoulder and knelt at Rhyslin's side. Her teeth worried at her lower lip; thoughts tangled like threads caught in a loom.

All her carefully spun plans for the future lay in flux. She had meant to wait, to give Flur time to settle into her bond before daring to speak with Rhyslin.

Yet he had already gone and claimed her, not with ritual, but with a single syllable, the shortening of her name. Even Garion had never done that, and the sound of it still shivered through her bones. She wondered if the draoidh knew what he had wrought.

How could he not? The moment had seared her, felt all the way to the soles of her feet. Even now, the name *Ria* pulsed within her like a low drumbeat, insistent and unyielding.

Her thoughts pressed so tightly on Rhyslin, on the paths ahead, on what her place at his side would mean for Vuuroena, that she did not hear her name being spoken. Not until a warm hand touched her shoulder and his whisper wrapped around her like smoke.

"Ria."

She looked up, caught in the quiet snare of his hazel eyes. Her breath stalled, as though the ship itself had slipped into a dead calm.

When his brow quirked, she flushed scarlet and bowed her head, wishing he would leave her to her thoughts. But Rhyslin would not leave her.

When he brushed a fingertip across her cheek, lightning coursed through her, and when he said her shortened name again, she shivered to her marrow.

"Ria."

She trembled, her plea soft as moth-wing against fire. "Stop that, please."

Rhyslin blinked, scratching at his head. "Stop what?"

"Calling me Ria." She leaned toward him despite herself, following the song that coursed through her body. "You don't know what you are doing to me."

A sly curve touched his mouth, born half of mischief, half of testing. "Pray tell, Ria, what am I doing to you?"

Her blush burned so hot it seemed the cabin air thickened with rose-petal heat. She could not keep from crawling toward him, unable to resist the pull. "You are claiming me as your own." Before sense could intervene, she had climbed into his lap.

His smug smile faltered, replaced by startled breath. "Ria, what are you doing?" His voice caught as she smiled at him, eyes bright. "What do you mean by I claimed you?"

Ria lifted a trembling hand and pressed a finger to his lips, silencing protest. The room seemed to still,  timbers hushed, hearth dimmed,  until only the drum of her heart marked the silence. She drew three breaths, steadying herself, her gaze locked with his.

"I wanted more time," she whispered, truth aching in each word. "Truly, I did. But after you claimed me last night... I haven't been able to think of anything else."

Confusion flickered across his eyes, but she met it with a quiet, enigmatic smile.

Rhyslin nipped her finger, and gooseflesh rippled down her arms. "That' s not amusing, Ria." His voice softened, the air tightening around his words. "But I don' t think you are being amusing. You' re being serious."

Ria swept her fingers through her hair, her laughter light but edged with longing. "I am. Flur' s generation can only think of finding a mate and having children. Many, many children."

When Rhyslin paled, she laughed outright. "Does that scare you?"

He shook his head, though unease curled his scent. "No, I expected that from Flur." His eyes steadied, inscrutable as deep water. "How did women of your generation pick a mate?"

Ria's lips lifted in a wry smile as she dropped her gaze. "We didn't. Men chased us until they caught us." She raised her eyes again, a spark dancing there. "One way they caught us was to shorten our names until they sang.."

"So I gave you one of these song names?" His brow furrowed, as though the past night blurred at the edges.

Ria's eyes never left his. "Do you remember what you called me last eve, when you forbade me to leave?"

Realization dawned with reluctant admiration. "I called you Ria."

Her smile widened as she leaned against him, letting silence hold the weight of her triumph.

At last, she relented, voice teasing. "You can relax, Maighstir Darkblade. Just because you claimed me doesn't mean you have me. According to ancient rite, I can still say no."

The growl that rumbled low in his chest carried the scent of storm and cedar. Shivers coursed through her.

"Are you?"

She tilted her head, feigning innocence. "Am I what?"

"By Nan Diathan, you are infuriating." His voice dropped to a husk. He leaned down, his presence pressing heavy as thunder. "Are you going to say no?"

She lifted her chin in mock hauteur. "I have my daughter to think about." Beneath the mask, delight danced; she reveled in the game.

With a tortured groan, Rhyslin shifted, growl deepening, and in one swift motion tossed her onto the bed. The timbers shuddered with the force of it.

"I'll bet I can get Rana to agree with it."

"Rhyslin!" she squealed, rolling toward the center of the mattress. "You just claimed my daughter as well." Her laughter rang like bells, and his eyes rolled in mock exasperation.

When he crawled onto the bed, she lifted her arms, an unspoken invitation.

He caught her easily, his arms closing around her with a certainty that stole her breath. Her body fit his as if it had always known the shape. His scent, beeswax, papyrus, and the undercurrent of his soul, filled her lungs until no room remained for fear or doubt.

Her voice came soft but sure, threaded with tremor: "No," she whispered, tilting her face up to his. "I won't say no."

For a heartbeat the world hushed, bond-fire glimmering unseen in the air. Then, only then, did she notice that Flur was missing.

"Rhyslin? Where is my niece?"

"She'll be back." His voice was low, almost lazy, but his fingers crept between Ria's shoulder blades, each brush sending tingles down her spine like sparks skipping across harp strings.

"She and your daughter—"he shaped the full length of *Vuuroena's* name with care, refusing to shorten it, "have gone to the galley for breakfast."

The ship gave a gentle roll beneath them, timbers creaking as though to affirm his words. The faint scent of baking bread and dried fruit drifted from the passage, carried on a warmer draft.

Ria refused to let him slip away so easily. She leaned in and caught his lips with a playful nip. "Rana. You've already made her name sing."

A flicker of gold sparked in his hazel eyes, quick as firelight on bronze. "Not to her face, I haven't." His breath warmed against her neck as he buried his face in the crook of her shoulder, his voice muffled and stubborn. "Nor will I. You can't make me."

Her laughter came soft and sure, the sound of running water over stone. "I won't have to. You'll do it. You won't be able to help yourself."

Her certainty settled over him like a prophecy. Rhyslin groaned theatrically, the sound rumbling low in his chest, yet beneath the mock despair he knew she spoke true.

All it would take was one unguarded moment, one careless breath, and Vuuroena's nickname would spill from his lips as easily as honey slides from the comb.

The ship seemed to hush in agreement, sails straining faintly in the morning breeze, as if the world itself awaited the moment when he would give voice to the name.

# Chapter Twenty-Two
### Where the Hearth-Mother is Honored

Flur and Vuuroena walked down the corridor, their hands full of plates of breakfast food. The ship's timbers creaked with the slow breathing of the Dawn-Breaker, the faint scent of cedar oil rising from the planks beneath their feet. Light spilled through narrow slats, gilding dust motes in drifting columns.

"How do the serving girls in taverns do this without spilling food?" Vuuroena's arms trembled as she tried to balance two trays, her steps uneven, the hum of the ship exaggerating each sway.

Flur carried hers with practiced calm, balancing the trays at their center points. Her hips swayed in rhythm with the galleon's pulse, a soft grace that made the motion seem effortless.

"Like this, I think." She lifted one tray, testing its weight, and brought it closer to her body. Joy illuminated her face like morning sunlight breaking through clouds.

*Why am I so jealous because she's happy?* Vuuroena's chest ached with the question. She frowned at herself. She was on a beautiful galleon, her mother weaving permanence into their fate with Rhyslin, and still her heart twisted at the sight of Flur's ease. The trays quivered as if reflecting her unrest. "Flur, I'm about to lose a tray."

"Can you hold it until we get closer to the cabin?" Flur's golden hair caught the corridor's light as she looked ahead. "We're almost there."

"I don't know." Vuuroena shifted her weight, trying to steady herself. Her tongue flicked across her lips, tasting salt where anxiety had gathered. "No, it's no good. It's going to fall."

She shut her eyes, bracing for the crash that never came.

"I've got it."

Opening one eye, she saw the younger dryad's fingers wrapped around the top tray, lifting it away with effortless grace, as though the ship itself had steadied her hand.

"Thank you." Vuuroena blinked, trying to remember the dryad's name.

"Kietha." The dryad dipped her head, a movement as fluid as wind stirring leaves. She fell in step beside Vuuroena. "You've already met my sister Kiesha."

Vuuroena nodded, recalling the elder twin's calm presence. "Is it strange?"

Kietha's eyes sparkled as she tossed her head, a grin spreading like dawnfire. "Having my twin be four years older?" Her laugh rippled down the corridor, carrying warmth that eased Vuuroena's tight shoulders. "It is strange, and I'm happy for her. It's an honor to be chosen as Astinmah's avatar."

Her joy was so bright it seemed to spill into the timbers themselves, and Vuuroena felt her own jealousy scatter like snow carried off by a sudden gust.

She watched Kietha balance the tray on her palm, the movement so natural it looked like dance. Hesitant at first, Vuuroena imitated her, lifting the tray to her shoulder.

The ship rocked gently beneath her feet, yet this time her body found the rhythm. One step. Then another. The tray stayed steady.

Her grin bloomed as she realized she was moving as fluidly as when she practiced a kata, her body remembering balance in motion.

Flur's lips curved, pride shining in her eyes. "Now you've got it."

Side by side, they walked, their steps aligning, trays balanced like offerings carried to a hearth. The corridor seemed to hum with them, floorboards resonating as if recognizing the shift. Vuuroena moved now with the grace of a dancer, her clumsiness melting away.

Flur blinked, watching the spell-blade transform before her eyes into a young woman marked by poise. *What will Rhyslin think?*

The door ahead opened as if in answer, the great cabin waiting for them, its threshold brightened with morning light.

The door swung open before they could knock, as if the ship itself anticipated their arrival. Vuuroena stepped into the great cabin and found Kiesha already waiting, her hand resting on the latch as though she'd been guided.

"May the sun's kiss grace thee, Vuuroena." The older dryad's smile shimmered like dawnlight through leaves.

The raven-haired spell-blade returned it, her voice soft but steady. "Good day to you as well, Kiesha."

She swayed into the room, her steps catching the rhythm of the ship's slow breathing, and set her plate at the center of the table.

Kietha and Flur followed, their trays releasing the warm fragrance of biscuits and stewed fruit. Flur moved toward the cabinet, her bond's golden thread humming faintly in the air. "Kiesha, can you come over here and help me?"

The dryad skipped over, her movements fluid as water over stone, and lifted plates and bowls with easy grace. "Can I help you set the places?"

"Certainly." Flur's voice rang clear as she carried mugs and utensils to the table. Without thinking, she began to hum. The melody spread like fire through tinder, catching each woman in turn until all of them were humming together. The ship's timbers seemed to resonate with the sound, prana vibrating in the air as though approving the harmony.

When the table was finished, they counted the empty seats.

"All we need are Rhyslin and—"

"My momma." Vuuroena's glance slid toward the master cabin, her pulse stumbling.

"What do you think they're doing in there?"

Flur closed her eyes, sinking into the bond. Warmth brushed her spirit like sunlight across skin. "Not what you think."

Vuuroena blushed, lowering her gaze.

Kiesha nudged her sister with a sly look, then asked outright, "Last night was your bond-night, yes?"

When Flur reluctantly nodded, the dryad's brow arched in mischief. "Why did she—?"

Flur fidgeted, her blush blooming like rose petals. "She was helping with my—" Her voice faded into a mumble.

Vuuroena embraced her cousin, shielding her from further teasing. "I'll tell them breakfast is ready. Be back in a minute."

The golden-haired bhanna sank gratefully into the chair beside Rhyslin's, while Vuuroena lingered by the cabin door.

She stared at it, the polished wood gleaming like the surface of still water, and for a heartbeat it seemed less a door than a threshold into something irrevocable. Her hand trembled as she raised it. *Will my life change if I cross through?*

The ship's lanterns flickered low, their flames bowing as if in expectation. Vuuroena bit her lip, then knocked twice. The sound echoed down the corridor like a drumbeat marking passage into fate.

---

Inside, the air was heavy with warmth. Rhyslin sat in the wingback chair, Ria curled in his arms.

"Do you know how long it's been since someone held me like this?" Her voice was the hush of doves at dawn. When Rhyslin said nothing, she lifted her head, her gaze searching his face. "It's been almost nineteen years."
The silence beneath her words trembled: *I've missed it every day since Garion died.*

"I wish I could spend the day like this."

Rhyslin's fingers stroked her hair, his prana threading comfort through her. "There is nothing stopping you." He felt Flur's contentment pulsing in the bond outside, warm as honey, and smiled.

Ria sighed, soft as falling ash. "You'd think so, wouldn't you?" Her fingertip traced the curve of his lips. "But if I stay much longer, someone will come knocking on that door."

Rhyslin arched one brow. His prana stretched beyond the cabin walls, brushing the figure who waited just outside. *You don't know how right you are.*

The knock came. The ship's frame creaked in answer, as if acknowledging the truth.

Ria shrugged, resignation written across her face. She shifted to rise, but Rhyslin's arms held her still. "What are you thinking?" she hissed, half-dreading discovery.

"Don't move, Ria."

Fear trembled through her voice. "But it could be anybody." She struggled faintly, panic fluttering like a trapped bird. "Rhyslin, let me up."

He looked down, his hazel eyes steady, his voice iron wrapped in velvet. "I told you to stay put."

The dominance rippled through her, sinking to her marrow. Candle flames stilled, air tightening.
With a shiver, she surrendered, settling reluctantly back onto his lap.

At his calm, resonant, "Enter," the door creaked open.

Vuuroena stepped inside.

"Breakfast is ready—" Her voice fractured as her gaze fell upon her mother, held in Rhyslin's arms. She froze, jealousy gnawing sharp as ice, echoing the sting she'd felt when Flur had bonded. She prayed it did not show.

She would have fled, but Rhyslin's voice caught her mid-step. "Shut the door and come here, Rana."

The name struck her like a bell tolling her fate. The ship hushed, beams groaning low, the air thickening with unseen weight. Shivers cascaded down her spine as if the very world had claimed her.

Numb, she obeyed. She shut the door, her hand slow, and crossed the space with measured steps until her knees bent of their own accord. She knelt at his feet, head bowed, heart hammering against her ribs.

For a long moment, silence ruled.

Then Ria, voice gentle but insistent, leaned up to Rhyslin's ear. "May I have a moment with my daughter?"

When he inclined his head, she slipped from his lap and knelt beside Vuuroena, her hand resting lightly on her daughter's back. "We'll be along when we've spoken. You have my word."

Rhyslin's gaze lingered on the two Hîn i-Balanath women. His words fell like a judgment that could not be undone. "Very well. We will wait for you before we break our fast."

Once they were alone, Vuuroena sagged against her mother, her voice trembling. "Momma, he just—" The words broke apart in her throat, like shale shattering under a storm.

"I know, sweetling—he just claimed you."

The words seemed to ripple in the air, as though the ship itself marked them. A faint creak of timbers, the soft sigh of canvas above, even the air within the cabin pressed closer, as if listening.

Ria folded her daughter into her arms, heart aching with the need to shield her from the unseen weight that had just settled on her. She pressed her cheek to Vuuroena's hair, tasting the faint salt of her skin where tears had already risen.

How had he claimed her? As a daughter, an apprentice, a mate? Or was it something older, stranger, the Draoidh's way of weaving souls into his orbit?

The not-knowing gnawed at her, and for a moment she wondered if even Rhyslin himself understood what he had done.

Rana trembled in her embrace, the fine shiver running from her shoulders down to her fingertips. The bond between mother and daughter hummed faintly, a counter-song to the deeper pull Rhyslin had stirred.

Ria kissed her brow and whispered against her skin, "I think I love him."

The confession, quiet as a dove's wingbeat, was meant only for her daughter's ears. Yet even so, the prana of the room seemed to quicken, as though the ship itself drew breath with her.

Vuuroena tipped her head up, eyes wide, confusion glimmering in their depths. "Does he love you?"

"I don't know, sweetling," Ria admitted, brushing a lock of hair from her daughter's damp cheek. "But I want to find out. But I won't, not if—" She faltered, groping for words that wouldn't wound. "Can you tell me about your dreams? What part does Rhyslin play in them? Are you and he — bonded?"

Rana's breath hitched, her lashes lowering as she shut her eyes, sifting through eight years of restless visions. The cabin grew hushed, even the steady thrum of the Dawn-Breaker's heart seeming to dim as she spoke.

"I'm scared, Momma." The words came like a child's prayer. "I'm taken from you, marked as a slave, and forced to be with men. I escape, and I free others when I do —" Her open hands pressed against Ria's back, anchoring herself. "I'm left to die alone and afraid. Rhyslin saves me somehow, but I don't know if we bond or not." She buried her face in her mother's shoulder, voice muffled, breaking. "I don't want to die, Momma."

The words pierced Ria like iron through flesh. She rocked her daughter, skirts whispering together with the rhythm of a lullaby. "Shhh, sweetling. I'm here."

She offered the only comfort she had, presence, steady and warm, a flame in the dark.

When her daughter's sobs eased, Ria took a shaky breath, voice almost playful in its attempt to ease the weight. "Shall I bond with the man?"

Rana sniffled, swiping her sleeve across her nose, then looked up with reddened eyes. "If he makes you happy, I think you should." Her gaze softened, catching the tangle in her mother's hair and the clothes she still wore from the day before. "Can I help you with your hair?"

Ria blinked at the sudden turn, surprised. "Of course you may. What did you have in mind?"

Rana's tentative smile brightened like a shaft of light through storm-clouds. "I was thinking of a waterfall braid, the kind that will take his breath away." She only wanted this moment to last, to steal a little more time with her mother before Rhyslin, and Flur, claimed her fully.

"That sounds wonderful." Rising slowly, Ria held out her hand. "I can't wait to see how it looks."

Together, they moved to the desk. As Ria sat, Vuuroena stood behind her, gathering the sun-warmed silk of her mother's hair. Each strand slipped like water through her fingers, carrying the scent of salt and lavender.

With steady, reverent movements, she wove the outer locks into a delicate braid that framed Ria's face like a coronet, leaving the rest to tumble in loose waves down her back.

The air in the cabin softened, as though time itself had slowed to honor them. Only the whisper of hair through loving fingers and the distant sigh of sails disturbed the silence. In that fragile space, mother and daughter clung to each other, making a sanctuary of the moment before the world, and fate, pressed in again.

Ria and Rana entered the great cabin, arm in arm, the glow of reconciliation clinging to them like morning mist. The timbers of the Dawn-Breaker seemed to sigh with them, the low hum of elemental prana echoing faintly along the hull as if acknowledging the bond between mother and daughter. They moved to the table where everyone was waiting and sat down together, their grace making the act feel like ritual already begun.

Rana reached toward the biscuits, but the weight of Rhyslin's gaze—measured, immovable, gold-specked—caught her hand mid-motion. Heat flushed up her cheeks, her fingers curling back to her lap in guilty obedience.

The bond-hum from Flur warmed the air, not reprimand but reminder, and Rana felt both seen and chastened. Her eyes lifted again, finding her mother and Flur expectantly watching the draoidh.

When he had all eyes upon him, Rhyslin inclined his head toward Ria. "Ria, you may offer our prayers to the gods."

The auburn-haired Hîn i-Balanath blinked, clearly unprepared, yet the cadence of his voice left no room for refusal. "May I gather some items?" When Rhyslin nodded, she rose with the grace of a queen restored and walked toward the room where her property was stored. "Come, Sweetling, I require your help."

Rana's pulse quickened. She hurried to her mother's side, whispering, "Momma. Are we going to—?"

Ria's serene nod steadied her. "Yes, we are."

She opened one of the traveling cases, the clasp clicking open like the strike of flint. Reverently she lifted the lid and drew forth a copper bowl that gleamed with a soft inner light.

At her goddess's prompting, her hands found each offering in turn: sacred ash, cedar chips in their beaded pouch, two chili peppers, five kernels of corn, three cacao beans, a reddish-silver flame construct that pulsed faintly with draoidheachd, and a scatter of marigold leaves.

The air thickened around the case, as though even the galleon leaned close to listen.

"Would you carry these for me?" she asked, handing the bowl and the flame construct into her daughter's trembling hands.

"Yes, Momma," Rana breathed, awe shimmering in her voice. The flame construct vibrated faintly, resonating with her heartbeat as she pressed it to her chest.

Ria replaced the case's lid, the lock clicking shut like a seal. Gathering the remaining offerings, she nudged the door open with her foot. The scent of cedar rose in the air as mother and daughter returned together.

All eyes in the cabin turned toward them. Silence deepened, reverent and expectant, until the galleon's very timbers thrummed low with anticipation.

Ria nodded to Rana, who stepped forward with measured care and placed the copper bowl upon the table, setting the flame construct beside it. Ria laid the offerings within, then crossed to the hearth.

The iron tongs hissed as she withdrew a live ember, glowing deep orange.

"Abuela Chantico, blessed hearth-mother, we create this sacred space for you."

The ember's glow brightened as she raised it, trailing heat across the air. Shadows bent toward her hand. She laid the ember in the copper bowl, and it flared like a heart remembering its first breath.

"Abuela, she who guides our family. We honor your hearth by offering ours."

Ash fell in a pale circle, soft as snowfall, around the ember.

Ria raised her hand toward her daughter. Rana exhaled reverently as she untied the beaded pouch, pouring the cedar chips into her mother's palm.

"Abuela, we pray for harmony as we sit at your table."

The cedar hissed as it met the ember. Fragrant smoke curled upward, twining like invisible song through the rafters. The bond-hum between Flur and Rhyslin shimmered faintly in response, their joy mingling with the prayer.

Ria kissed the flame construct before circling it once around the table. Its silver glow traced a line of light in the air, sanctifying each face, before she set it into the flames. Chili, cacao, corn, and marigold followed, each hissing their own voice into the fire.

"Abuela Chantico, we ask that he who leads us be wise, never straying from the holy ways. We ask that our family bring honor to Nan Diathan, and we ask that you bless the food before us and let it nourish our bodies as your words nourish our souls."

For a heartbeat, the entire galleon stilled. The hull's creak faded. The prana currents hushed. Even breath seemed held.

Then the air bloomed with the unmistakable scent of tortillas, warm and fresh from an unseen hearth. The blessing rolled through the cabin like sunlight after storm, and every heart remembered to beat again.

Rhyslin beckoned, permission given. Flur filled a plate and passed it left, her smile tender. The circle of family began to eat, laughter and comfort threading into the sacred silence that remained.

Rhyslin leaned back, savoring the rare peace, letting his gaze linger on the women gathered under his roof. For a brief, fragile moment, it felt like eternity's hearth had opened for them.

Until Kietha's voice broke through, soft but edged with reality:

"What are you going to do about Rowena?"

The fire in the copper bowl guttered as if the goddess herself leaned in to hear his answer.

# Chapter Twenty-Three
## Of Bonds and Banishments

Under the compulsion of ancient eldritch magic, the veil between worlds buckled and tore. As if in protest, the living skein of reality groaned, a hollow crack echoing like thunder through marrow and stone.

The jagged seams bled light, stitched and unstitched by hands unseen, until the sundered sky split wide. Through the wound descended the ancient one's servant, trailing a wave of chaos that sent a shudder through hill and hollow.

The Crannic Diathan turned their watchful eyes, heaven and earth alike catching the pulse of intrusion.

For a breathless moment, the world itself seemed to hold still. The wind dropped. Leaves clung unmoving to their branches. Rivers slackened in their flow as if refusing to bear witness. Suspended against the dying light, the Skelettdrache hung in the sky—decayed wings stretching wide, their membranous tatters whispering against the cold air.

When its ruined pinions beat, the taste of ash and grave-dust rode the currents, silencing the wild things below. The forests hushed, birds dropping from branches to crouch trembling.

The beast circled, as if hunting, while the wound it had torn in the heavens sealed behind, chains of law binding the intruder to this plane.

Like a shadow with a purpose, the rider shifted in his saddle. His scorched, unrecognizable armor cloaked him like a tomb. No gaze could mark him; no prayer could name him. The grass beneath their shadow withered, and frost rimed stones not touched by winter.

When he raised the visor of his helmet, a gout of ghostly blue fire burst from the empty sockets where eyes had once been. Oaks cracked as their sap chilled, and field-hares bolted in terror.

"We have arrived," the knight rasped, his voice stone grating against steel, "for better or worse. Did the ancient one choose to reveal our purpose on this desolate plane?"

The drake's charred leather wings stirred the air as they flexed. Habits learned over a lifetime lingered beyond death; the old reflexes of predator and mount still bound them. The air reeked of burned hide and iron.

"All the spider said," the beast rumbled, its voice hollow thunder that rattled root and branch, "was that one of his converts no longer answers his call."

As if borrowed from the drake, a faint unease, a foreign feeling, ghosted through the rider. The soil beneath them quivered, as though the world itself sought to shake them off.

"We need to be quick." There was a hint of strain in the hollow timbre of his tone. "This realm′s laws are already pulling at me, trying to chain me to its wheel."

"Right, you are." The knight lowered his visor, the steel clicking home like a closing tomb. "Did the spider at least give us a way to find our quarry?"

As its left wing folded toward the saddlebag, the drake moved with a wry, familiar motion that mocked its ruined state. The clouds above them recoiled, parting in thin streaks like torn cloth.

"The tracker is in the bag."

With his gauntlet, the knight reached into the black, scaly hide. The air hissed as if resisting the act. His fingers closed around something brittle, glass-like. When he drew it forth, the crystal pulsed with a sickly inner glow, the essence swirling like ink in water. The hedgerows below curled inward, their leaves shriveling as its light spilled across the land.

Then it flared bright as day to his hollow sight.

"There." Grim satisfaction filled his voice as he lifted the crystal, its glow washing his scorched helm. He turned his gaze northward, where the horizon darkened under gathering cloud. "North. Take us north."

The *Cloud-Dancer* slipped southward, her sails whispering with the steady breath of the winds.

Below her, the land stretched wide and living, patchworked fields drinking in the last light, villages exhaling smoke from their hearths, towns humming like hives, and stone keeps rising like old bones from the earth. The ship hummed in answer, timbers creaking with a rhythm that matched the pulse of the world she rode above.

On the quarterdeck, Rembran leaned over the binnacle box with Ixa, their fingers tracing the course etched in glowing lines. Andros held the wheel, his hands steady, the magnetic veins of the world thrumming through his bones like a song only he could hear.

"If we keep on this course, we'll reach Oak Grove in two days." Ixa's fingertip glimmered faintly as she followed the line across parchment, her voice airy as the breeze that curled playfully through her hair.

Rembran chuckled, his mirth deep as mountain stone. "As if we ever travel a straight course. When have our trips ever been clear of detours?"

The wind caught Ixa's hair, lifting it in silver ribbons as she laughed and nudged him. "Would you rather be stuck on land?"

"Diathan, no!" His vehement reply struck the air like a drumbeat, and the sails above swelled with a sudden gust, echoing his certainty.

Ixa's laughter rang brighter, the wind dancing with her voice as though delighted to share in her joy.

At the wheel, Andros's lips curved into a small, rare smile. The earth beneath all things spoke to him in low, patient tones, but here—on this ship, in this household, he found another kind of steadiness.

Seeing Ixa's joy was like fresh loam under roots: grounding, vital. His old misgivings about her and Rembran had long since crumbled, washed away like sand in the tide of their easy fellowship.

Footsteps on oaken planks announced Captain O' Cuire. The ship's bones creaked in greeting as he stepped from his office, his eyes glancing upward to read the sails as if they were stars.

He strode to the helm with a seaman's surety. "Ser Andros, what is our current course and speed?"

Andros barely needed to blink. The veins of the world tugged through him, magnetic lines like taut cords beneath his skin. "South by a little west. Speed is just shy of eight knots."

O' Cuire clapped him on the shoulder, the sound sharp as flint against iron. "As always, I'm amazed at how easy you make that look." His voice carried both humor and warning, the seasoned weight of a man who had once bled for every degree of the compass.

Andros shook his head. "It's nothing, Captain. Just reading the magnetic field." The world whispered its secrets freely to him; it was no feat, merely listening.

The sky stirred. Ixa's blue eyes glazed, her breath catching as if she heard words the others could not. "There's a storm heading our way. What order will the captain give?"

Rembran squinted at the horizon, the clouds brooding like beasts gathering their haunches. "Depends. If it's not too bad, we'll power through it. If it's a bad one, he'll climb to get out of it."

Ixa tilted her head, listening to currents above currents. The clouds above the storm gleamed with calm light, a higher refuge calling to her. "The clouds above the storm are calmer."

As if her words had summoned him, O'Cuire's voice cut through the air, firm as a hand on the tiller. "Cailín Ixa. If you can, take us up."

The winds curled around her ankles like eager hounds. The air elemental grinned, lifting her hand, and the *Cloud-Dancer* shivered with anticipation as though the ship herself was ready to climb.

"What are you going to do about Rowena?"

The look the old draoidh gave the young dryad carried the weight of mountains. Weariness shadowed his features like dusk on stone. "I will do what must be done." His voice was a monotone, the stillness of deep earth.

Yet the river of his thoughts ran swift and troubled, eddies of time and distance tugging at him. Since the soul-bond with Flur, the future had ceased to wait.

The golden-haired bhanna glanced up at Rhyslin, her heart catching on the tremor beneath his words. This time she caught the flash of pain that flickered like a wounded star when the seer's name rose between them.

Not pain of making or receiving, but the sharp ache of uncertainty, of fear unvoiced. She doubted Rhyslin even recognized the shape of it in himself, and silently resolved to speak to Ria later. The bond hummed with her undying love, nearly sent across the veil to steady him—

—but Rana's voice broke in, quipping like a spark on dry grass. "Just how many women have you claimed?"

The draoidh's reply bore a thread of irony, a smile hidden beneath the weariness. "From what I understand, the only people I've claimed are you and your mother."

The expected result followed. Rana blushed crimson, her cheeks bright as dawn, stammering about him being mean. The air about her quivered with embarrassment, as though the very timbers of the ship leaned closer to share in her fluster. Rhyslin only shook his head, the corners of his mouth tugging.

From Flur came wry amusement, the bond's silver laughter brushing him like wind through meadow-grass.

Ria's feelings were quieter, a feline patience that curled around him—her half-smile a cat batting a bird without striking the final blow.

Never one to let Rhyslin slip from the snare, Kiesha sang her words in a lilting tone. "You know what she wants."

The air stilled. Rhyslin groaned, his hand rising to cover his mouth as if to keep the thought from leaking into the world.

The bond shimmered, betraying Flur's quiet intuition of Rowena's desire. A sharper flicker crossed—naughty, playful, wicked in its daring. He blinked hard. *By Na Diathan. She doesn't know Rowena, but she's thinking of—surely not.*

His sudden glare at Kiesha might have cowed another, but she only smirked, a dryad's knowing grin that bent the air like greenwood under strain.

"I am very aware of what she wants." His gaze flicked to Flur, searching, testing. "Now that Mo Flur Dris has claimed me, I won't be able to refuse her request."

Flur's pained smile echoed Kiesha's, shadow and sunlight meeting on water. Rana's confusion rippled sharp and bright. "What do you mean? You won't be able to refuse—?" She turned, eyes darting to Flur, who was trying, failing, to smother her giggle.

Recognition dawned like a torch flame; her mouth fell open in mute shock as the realization struck of who might be next to join the circle. "Oh." Her face deepened to a shade beyond crimson, and she hunched down, wishing the air itself would swallow her.

*Oh, indeed.* Rhyslin's stomach clenched. He saw the storm that might break if Rowena could not find accord with Flur and Ria. The timbers around them groaned as though echoing his unease, the room's stillness grown taut with tension.

His gaze swept to Ria. Her smile was calm, untroubled, the steady rhythm of a hearth-fire against winter winds. A quiet counterpoint to the storm that pressed against the walls. *Why is she so calm?* It took him a moment to recall: she had walked this path before. Her composure held him like an anchor, and after a slow breath, he moved to the couch and sank into its waiting embrace.

When he saw the shock lingering in Rana's wide eyes, he gestured gently for her to join him. The spell-blade wavered, torn between pride and yearning, before settling beside him.

She was quiet, her voice low as falling snow. "Are you going to bond with Momma?" Uncertainty coiled in her tone, as if afraid he might dismiss her.

Rhyslin's answer was steady, the truth bare as stone. "I believe that in time, I will ask your mother to bond with me." *Unless she asks me first,* his private thought rang in the bond, muted but real.

Rana looked up, still stiff at his nearness. "What about me? You put a claim on me."

Rhyslin's eyes closed briefly, pain furrowing his brow. "I've got to pay attention to what goes through my mind." He slipped an arm around her shoulders, slow and deliberate. She sat rigid, breath caught—then softened by degrees, the tension easing from her frame. "You have choices," he said, voice low, words steady as a vow. "I can claim you as a future mate."

Her blush burned hotter, crimson flooding to her ears, her very soul aflame.

"Or I can claim you as an apprentice."

Rana's eyes flicked up, thoughtful beneath the storm. "Would it help me survive the prophecies?"

The air itself seemed to lean in at her question. Bonds thrummed, the walls listening, the very weave of Saorsa pausing as though the land wanted to hear the answer.

"Prophecies?" Rhyslin raised his left eyebrow. "What prophecies?" He couldn't remember if Rowena had mentioned a Hîn i-Balanath under prophecies. But she certainly hadn't mentioned his getting bonded by ambush either.

Rana bowed her head, shoulders tightening as though she feared the words themselves might lash her. "I've had the same dreams for years. I get taken by force. I am forced to please men." She shuddered, a ripple of shame crossing her frame. "I help slaves escape and am left for dead. Somehow you save me."

The chamber dimmed as if listening. Shadows drew long across the beams, and the hearth's flame guttered once, offended by the taste of cruelty in her words. Outside, the wind pressed against the shutters, low and mournful, as though the Diathan themselves bore witness to her telling.

Rhyslin listened carefully, his silence not absence but weight. When she was through, he gathered her trembling form against him, his arms becoming a shield. "How long have you had these dreams?" His voice carried the tone of a man testing chains he could not yet break.

Rana slumped down, her head bowed, her voice small. "Eight years."

The walls creaked, carrying the sound like an echo of disbelief. Somewhere in the stone, the old wood groaned as though time itself mourned what she had borne alone.

"I'm so sorry." Rhyslin knew the words were fragile vessels, hardly fit to carry the weight of her suffering. Yet as he spoke them, the bond flickered with sincerity, and the hearthfire flared, as if to say that acknowledgment, even when frail, mattered.

At first, Rana held herself still, taut as a bowstring strung too long, as though waiting for scorn or dismissal. But slowly—bit by bit—the tautness unwound. With each breath, the world's edges softened.

The scents came first: beeswax and warm parchment, notes of a scholar's refuge; sage and wild root rising from the hearth, grounding her in earth's embrace.

The air thickened with those fragrances until her eyelids grew heavy, the invisible lullaby of a household that had decided she belonged.

When Rhyslin felt her burrowing into his side, he lowered his gaze. She was drifting, lashes trembling against her cheek, surrendering to sleep at last. His hand rested gently at her shoulder, fingers brushing strands of hair from her face.

*Sleep well, mo phr ìseil. You deserve it.* The words were not only thought but vow, and the land seemed to take them as such.

The timbers eased their creak. The fire settled into a steady glow. Even the restless night winds hushed their keening, as if granting this fragile moment its sanctuary.

As he held Rana close, Rhyslin realized the truth: prophecy spoke of chains and violation, but here, in the quiet heart of his cearcall, the world itself bent to cradle her. For the first time in eight years, Rana did not dream alone.

He only half-listened to Flur and Ria as they conversed, content to keep watch while she slept.

The lamplight in the great cabin softened to a golden glow as Flur hesitated, her words faltering in the hush. The air pressed close, scented faintly of beeswax and roses, as though the ship itself leaned in to listen.

"How do you do it?" The hesitation in Flur's voice prompted Ria to raise her right eyebrow in question.

"Do what?"

Flur rolled her eyes, knowing her aunt wasn't stupid. "Just accept that a man might bond with more than one woman, and that one of them might be your daughter, or you?"

A current stirred through the timbers, a low creak like an elder clearing its throat. Ria put her hands on the table and slid one forward to cup Flur's, her touch warm and steady.

"There have always been more women than men. Not even Nan Diathan know why."

The air brightened with a faint shimmer, as though unseen blossoms had opened in the rafters. "You can either hope to find a man who wants only one woman, or you can try to build a larger cearcall of sisters that you get along with."

When Flur appeared thoughtful, Ria patted her hand. "Would it be so bad if others joined your cearcall?"

The air between them filled more thickly with the scent of roses, petals seeming to brush against Flur's cheek as her heart twisted. She nibbled her lower lip. "I guess it wouldn't bother me much."

She drew a slow breath and held it. "It's just — that when Kietha mentioned Rowena, Rhyslin got worried." She cast a glance over at Rhyslin. "I don't want him worried about things like that."

"He's a man." Ria bluntly stated. "He'll always worry about things. You can't stop it." She paused for a moment. "But you can limit the things he worries about."

The floor hummed faintly beneath their feet, as though the ship approved the wisdom spoken aloud.

She paused for a moment. "The old ways give the first bond the right to talk to a new woman before the man accepts or initiates a bond. It's one way to bring balance to the cearcall."

The golden-haired bhanna gazed at her aunt, the rose-scent deepening until it was nearly cloying, pulling memory and longing to the surface. "Did you know all this before entering Garion's cearcall?"

Ria's silence stretched, a pause like the breath of wind before rain. Then she shrugged, her voice low but steady. "My clan doesn't hide the past. We live it. So, I've known about cearcaill all my life. My mother was part of one, just like yours was." A nod of her head sent her hair swirling over her shoulders, copper catching the lamplight like fire. "Garion explained the old ways before he ever asked me to join his cearcall."

A faint grin crossed her lips as she tweaked Flur's nose, eliciting a low growl that made the shadows on the wall quiver like startled birds.

"Cut that out," Flur protested, swatting at her aunt's fingers.

"If you love Rhyslin, you'll have to get used to it. He's bound to draw other women, especially now that he's bonded to you." Ria cupped Flur's cheek, softly caressing.

"If he loves you, he'll let you talk to any woman who wants to join the cearcall, but he may dismiss your concerns. The old ways give you the right to talk to potential bondmates, not deny them."

The golden-haired bhanna's blue eyes fluttered shut at the touch on her cheek, and in that silence, the creak of the hull deepened into a heartbeat rhythm. The ship carried their conversation like a witness sworn.

"It won't be easy, will it?"

"It never is." Ria leaned in and placed a kiss on Flur's forehead, the faintest shimmer of starlight glancing off her hair. "All you can do is ride the rapids."

As her words fell into the air, a low susurrus echoed through the timbers, like river water rushing unseen below the keel—reminding them both that life, bond, and cearcall were currents no one woman could hold still.

# Chapter Twenty-Four
## Fear's Tide upon the Dawn-Breaker

"How much further is our quarry?" the skelettdrache rasped, vertebrae grinding as its skull turned toward the flickering crystal. Frost eddied from its teeth as it spoke, shadows dripping from the hollow of its sockets. The air curdled where its breath touched, grass below blackening to ash in silence.

The Todesritter slapped the beast's neck with a gauntleted hand, the strike ringing like steel on stone. Mountainside moss recoiled, shriveling as though scorched by sound. "Eyes on the sky. Leave the guidance to me."

Death held no fear for him — only delays. A mountain′s flank would not end him, merely splinter his frame and slow his regeneration. Inefficiency. Unacceptable.

The drache′s ribcage flexed with a hollow grunt before it faced forward. The clouds over their heads rippled, as if even the firmament winced at its obedience. "Well?"

"Sometimes you are worse than a coffin full of noisy rats." The Todesritter shifted the crystal, its shard pulsing in his grip, its pointer quivering toward the wall cloud hanging low like a curtain of ash. The winds around the shard thrashed like caged things. "According to the spider′s tracker, our quarry waits ahead. In there."

The drache's jaws snapped shut with a crack that echoed like broken bones. Pine boughs far below shivered violently, though no breeze stirred them. "The spider didn't say our quarry could fly. I wonder what we're chasing."

Flame vented from the knight's helmet, wreathing his head in a sulfurous glow. The air tasted suddenly of brimstone and burnt copper; birds screamed and veered from their perches miles distant. He leaned forward, voice thick with hunger. "Let's find out."

The beast angled its ruined wings toward the storm, and as it descended, it exhaled Drachenfurcht — a psychic tide rolling outward, metallic on the tongue, cold as a grave.

The very sky convulsed. Clouds shrank from one another as if torn by unseen claws. Lightning quivered sideways, its light bending, and thunder stumbled in its own throat. Far beneath, rivers surged against their banks, churning as though the land itself rejected the intrusion.

The warmth of the great-cabin, mingled with Flur and Ria's soft exchange, lulled Rhyslin toward sleep. Rana's desert-rose scent curled upward from beneath his cloak, tugging him toward surrender.

At first, the hum of his staff whispered like a breeze stirring leaves. He ignored it.

But the resonance thickened, thrumming through the timbers until it struck like a bell against his skull. His eyes snapped open.

The hum swelled into a trumpet's peal, short, brassy, relentless. Each note carried the taste of iron across his tongue. With the sound came weight: pressure on his chest, a tide of dread not born of Crann Na Beatha. Alien. Chaotic. Closing fast.

Rana bolted upright before he could rise, breath hitching as her pupils widened. "Something is out there."

He nodded once, already on his feet, staff in hand. Its crystal flared, threads of white light trembling outward like roots searching for ground. Rana rose after him, blade in her grip, her aura stretched taut as bowstring.

"Rhyslin, where are you—?" Flur half-rose from her seat.

"Stay here until I call for you!" His words cracked over his shoulder as he strode for the quarterdeck.

The moment the door swung wide, the Dawn-Breaker groaned as though it feared what stalked the sky. The air outside was heavy, salted with ozone, ropes quivering like bowstrings under strain. Deck-planks swelled and flexed as if resisting a hand pressing down from above. Even the lantern flames guttered sideways, shrinking from the pressure.

Rhyslin turned starboard. His senses crashed against the rolling tide of Drachenfurcht. Chaos seeped like oil across water, smothering air currents, muddling starlight.

The clouds themselves bent wrong, lightning staggering sideways, thunder stuttering as though robbed of breath.

O′ Cuire, Rembran, and both elementals already stood at the rail, jaws locked, bodies tensed with unspoken recognition. The air elemental′s hair lifted despite stillness; the earth elemental′s hands clenched as if bracing against invisible stonefall.

Boots hammered the stairs. Marcus erupted onto the deck, longbow drawn, a draoidheil arrow blazing at his string. His wolf-shadow rippled along his shoulders and spine, ears flattened, hackles up. It growled without sound, muzzle lifted to scent the chaos-stench rolling in.

Rhyslin met O'Cuire's eyes, raised his hand, fingers outspread at waist height, then swept it aside. The command rippled like wind through tall grass. O'Cuire and his officers echoed it, and the deck obeyed, not as wood and iron alone, but as if the Dawn-Breaker herself stirred.

Loose gear vanished below in a hush of hidden doors and swallowed crates. Silver tubes, rimmed with draoidheil sigils, locked into place along the rails with a sigh like iron drawing breath.

More yawned out from the gun-ports below, their runes glowing faintly in defiance. The timbers groaned, not in protest but in readiness, the creak of a warhound bracing against a storm, teeth bared, hackles rising.

Ixa caught O' Cuire' s gesture and nodded. Her crystalline eyes flared with light, and the Dawn-Breaker nosed down through the mist. The clouds resisted, clinging like cobwebs, but peeled back at the ship' s insistence, as though even the storm feared what lurked in its heart.

Beneath, Andros leaned into the keel, spiraling the vessel clockwise. His will pressed into the wood, and the Dawn-Breaker' s bones answered, angling her weapons toward the darkness with the precision of a predator narrowing its gaze.

Then the enemy tore through. Marcus blinked as the skelettdrache and its rider burst from the cloud bank — bone and iron gleaming against storm-light, every motion a wound upon the sky.

The clouds buckled around their passage, lightning faltering, thunder catching in its throat. The pair began a slow, deliberate circling of the ship, their presence pressing like a hand on every chest.

His bowstring creaked as he drew tighter. "I thought we got them all!" The wolf inside him growled in chorus, claws raking memory. Old prey. Old enemies. Things that should have stayed buried. The storm growled with him, thunder rolling low like a beast remembering.

"We did." Rhyslin's voice was quiet, steady, iron laid against fear. His eyes locked on the circling figures, reading them, measuring.

Then he caught the movement of cloth snapping in the wind — a pennant streaming from the knight′s spear. Its sigil writhed against the storm′s light, wrong against Crann Na Beatha, as if it repelled the gaze of sky and earth alike.

"Look at his pennant."

Marcus′s eyes narrowed as he tracked it, wolf-shadow flickering. A sigil unknown, alien. "I don′t know it. Where is he from?"

"I believe he is a visitor," Rhyslin said. His tone was sharp with certainty, a note that steadied the crew as surely as the deck beneath their boots. The storm leaned closer, listening. "If he were of this world, Nan Diathan would already have sent their taghta to bring him down."

The drache angled closer, skeletal ribcage creaking. Its hollow chest expanded — and then it exhaled Drachenfurcht.

The aura struck like a hammer of ice. Breath seized in lungs. Chests tightened as though invisible chains had been thrown over every heart. The Dawn-Breaker herself cried out, her timbers groaning like a wounded hound, rigging lines quivering as if the ship had been seized by unseen claws. The sky convulsed: clouds shuddered backward, lightning staggered sideways, thunder lost its voice.

Elementals flared in protest. Ixa's crystalline body blazed until the mist itself refracted her brilliance, scattering blue fire across the storm.

Andros bent into the keel, his iron shell bowing under the weight, sparks dripping from his form like falling stars.

Marcus's wolf snarled, claws raking the soil of memory. In his mind, the grave yawned, iron chains dragged him down, bones whispered beneath the earth. For a heartbeat, he nearly bent.

But then warmth unfurled through him, subtle, golden, like five hands pressing steady upon his shoulders. A hearth's glow in midwinter. Blossoms opening in a gale. Bells pealing faintly in the marrow of the wind. It was not his strength, not Rhyslin's alone. It was Nan Diathan.

The dread did not vanish, but it broke like waves on granite. The wolf quieted. His fear was met and stilled. Marcus straightened, breath catching, eyes hard.

Beside him, Rhyslin's staff burned with mirrored gold light, threads of radiance tangling with the gods' calm until the quarterdeck itself gleamed. The draoidh stood unflinching, aura spread like a bastion around them all.

"Should we attack, Rhyslin?" O'Cuire asked, cutlass half-drawn, his voice trembling against the storm's hush.

"Are you kidding?" Rhyslin's tone was iron. "We do nothing except defend ourselves. We don't have the weapons to take on those two."

Marcus grunted agreement, bow never wavering. "Best bet is to let them leave — and wave as they do."

The crew held fast, shoulders pressed into the weight of the moment, charms clenched in fists, breaths ragged but unbroken. The hunters circled, shadows scraping across the cloud-walls, then vanished back into the storm, Drachenfurcht collapsing behind them like a slammed shutter.

The pressure fled. The air loosened. A bitter ash-taste clung to tongues, but beneath it lingered the warmth that had steadied them — the unmistakable proof of divine witness. The Dawn-Breaker exhaled with them, her timbers easing, ropes falling slack as though even she had been braced by the hands of gods.

Rhyslin lowered his staff, breath fogging the air. "Back on course."

Above, the skelettdrache hissed through its ribs as they turned away, the sound grinding like stone dragged across bone. The clouds sagged in its wake, bruised violet and black, their edges fraying as if they wished to flee. "Who are these people? Did you feel it — the energy of those two on the deck?"

The Todesritter's helm tilted, its guttering flames throwing green reflections across the storm-wrack. Even the air around his iron frame quivered, torn between cold hunger and a force that blunted it. He had felt it — not only draoidheachd, but a barrier stitched into the world itself.

Golden threads pulsed faintly along the Dawn-Breaker's hull, interlaced with the timbers like veins of living light. A calm that dulled even his dread.
"I did."

The drache's wings faltered mid-beat, casting down a spray of frost that hissed against the storm-clouds like acid. Below, the forests whispered uneasily, their leaves curling though no wind stirred them. "But they did not fear us. Our aura should have broken them. Were they not afraid?"

The knight's flames dimmed, then flared green, the storm answering with a flash of lightning that split and recoiled, as if unwilling to strike too near. "If they were, their gods drank the fear before it surfaced.

I sensed not less than five signatures guarding them. That is no mortal courage."

His gauntlet flexed, grasping the unseen weave. Even in the hollow air, he could still feel it: woven light tangled with mortal magic, a net that rippled through the very aether. It was not merely a defense, but a warning. For the first time since his resurrection, his hunger thinned, edged back by something older, sovereign.

"Then they are not prey," the drache rasped, its unease rolling down like grave-dust into the world below. The farmland beneath their shadow fell still, oxen halting in furrows, birds frozen mid-flight.

"No." Smoke coiled from the knight's helm as he admitted, voice low. "What we do next is not ours to choose."

He gathered the residue of his power, clutching the cold between his fingers until the storm itself stiffened. Words left his helm like shards of frost, threading upward into the aether. The air around them tightened, sticky and cold, like strands of web stretching across the heavens. "The Spider will decide."

The two vanished into the cloud bank, the storm swallowing their forms like a mouth snapping shut. The heavens stitched themselves closed behind them, but the land below exhaled only slowly, tremors running through oak and stone.

Yet on the Dawn-Breaker's deck, warmth still lingered — faint, golden, pressing steady against bone and heart. It clung to crew and vessel alike, proof that the gods had not only seen, but chosen them.

The Dawn-Breaker seemed to breathe again only after the drache vanished. Wind returned to the rigging in hesitant sighs, and the timbers stopped their low groan of protest. But Rhyslin's thoughts did not settle. A quiet ache tugged through his bond until curiosity drove him across the deck.

He found Rana pressed against the cabin wall, knees drawn tight, shivering so hard her teeth clicked. Shadows clung to her skin as if they too feared to lift. When he dropped to one knee before her, the ship's planks warmed faintly under his palm, as though the Dawn-Breaker herself wished to reassure.

"It's gone. You can come up now." Rhyslin's voice was calm, stripped of judgment. He gave her no blame, only the soft gravity of initiation.

But Rana could not look at him. Fear still bound her limbs like iron bands. Then, all at once, she hurled herself forward. He staggered but caught her, cloak and staff pressed awkwardly between them.

Her tremors passed through his ribs like a drumbeat. "What was — that thing?" she gasped. "The one with the tattered wings?"

"That was a skeletdrache." His hand settled instinctively along her spine, tracing small circles. The words he whispered were more draoidheil cadence than comfort, and the deck beneath them steadied in time with his voice.

"How did you face it? I was so frightened that I couldn't even stand up."

Rhyslin bowed his head, breath close to her ear. "I have faced them before, the drache and ritter. We faced them," he amended as Marcus' step pressed into the deck behind him, "and sent them to the wheel. We had to, you see."

The wind shifted then, a low moan against the sails — as if even the storm remembered the Bone War.

Marcus crouched, his hand landing on Rana's head with a steady weight. "You did better than most. When Drachenfurcht bends your will, most people run and never stop."

"I couldn't stop shaking. All I felt was terror." Her eyes lifted, wide and wet, to him. She reached out as if to anchor herself. "You didn't run."

Rhyslin let out a humorless chuckle, the sound rolling like gravel across the boards. "Old wolves don't run; they stand and die."

"Old wolves that run only die quicker," Marcus countered with a stretch, his wolf-shadow flickering faint against the rail. He glanced toward the cabin. "I wonder how your bond took it."

Rhyslin closed his eyes, sinking into the bonds. For a moment, the ship's lanterns swayed as if carried on his exhale. "Shaken but not broken. It appears that Ria helped brace her." He stood slowly, Rana still clinging as though the timbers themselves might fall away. "Let's go inside and see how your mother is doing."

The cabin welcomed them in warmth, the hearthstone pulsing faintly brighter as they crossed its threshold. Rana gave only the barest nod but leaned on him still, half-child, half-ashamed woman.

Ria saw at once, and the air seemed to hush around her. She swept her daughter from Rhyslin's side, cradling her close. "What happened out there?"

Flur was already against him, her golden hair catching hearth-light. "Your emotions were all over the place." She burrowed into his chest, the bond trembling like taut strings. "You haven't been that nervous since I've known you."

He slid one arm around her, silence weighing heavier than the cabin beams. The question burned in Flur's eyes until he relented.

"We were being hunted." The words dropped like stones into water. He searched for a gentler telling, but none came. His frustration sharpened until the fire popped, sparks echoing his strain.

"Whatever was out there scared Rana to death." Ria's hold tightened. "What was it?"

"A Lhûg góren and a Rochben Gorthren."

The matron's breath hitched. She drew Rana closer, pale as frost. "How did you survive the Glaur Lhûg?" Her hand reached for him. Rhyslin gathered her in, cloak and cloak overlapping until they stood locked in a four-fold embrace.

"Marcus and I have faced them before." His breath slowed, trying to soothe not only Rana but the timbers that creaked faintly with each quiver of dread. "Rana survived it by putting her back to the cabin wall."

"I was so scared, Momma," Rana whispered, still shivering though the hearthstone glowed bright. "I couldn't move at all."

Ria pressed her brow to her daughter's. "All we felt was fear that stole our breaths." She raised her gaze to Rhyslin, voice threading with awe. "Was I imagining it, or did Nan Diathan assist us?"

"You didn't imagine it. I felt a Mathair's calm." His certainty softened the hearth-light to gold. "The others, too. They guarded their children."

"What were the hunters after?" Flur's voice was low, echoing the same question that gnawed at him.

"I do not know." His admission pulled at the rafters like a draft. He swore, silently, to learn what prey those creatures had sought.

# Chapter Twenty-Five
## The House of Fourfold Warmth

The Dawn-Breaker clung to her last heading, timbers creaking as though still listening for pursuit. Breath and heartbeat lingered taut across the decks until O' Cuire judged enough distance lay between them and the skeletdrache. Only then did the tight coil in his chest ease.

When the silence had worn itself into something resembling safety, he gave the order to set their course for home. The elemental core shifted its hum, the sound more like a sigh than a change in pitch. Restless, unwilling to sit idle, he left the bridge in search of Rhyslin.

He found him in the great-cabin. Firelight breathed warmth into the paneled walls, pressing back the memory of bone and shadow. Rhyslin sat upon the divan, Flur curled against his right shoulder, Rana folded close to his left, their breath steady as though drawn to the rhythm of his heart. The hearth crackled low, pine resin scenting the air until even the storm glass on the shelf seemed to loosen its tension.

"Sir," O' Cuire called, poking his head inside.

Rhyslin lifted a hand, weary, but steady, and the captain stepped in. The sudden contrast made him blink; the great-cabin glowed alive, a pocket of sanctuary carved from darkness.

"It's been three bells since we've seen the drache and ritter," O' Cuire reported.

Rhyslin nodded, gaze steady. "Put us back on course for Oak Grove."

"Figured you'd say that, sir. We already carried it out." He shifted, uneasy, not yet ready to return to the cold corridors outside.

Rhyslin gestured toward the hearth's warmth. "Something's troubling you?"

"Yes, sir." O' Cuire leaned back against the door, shoulders bowed under thought. His hands slipped into his pockets, fingers restless. "Could we have beaten them?"

The question hung like smoke. Even the fire stilled for a breath, crackling softer, listening with him as Rhyslin walked back through memory.

"Marcus and I brought one down once. It took a month to prepare the ambush, and two taghta fought beside us. Still, we lost half our number."

His gaze lifted, brushing the captain, then lowered to the women curled at his sides before straying across the cabin to Ria's quiet presence. "Could we have beaten that pair? Perhaps. But the Dawn-Breaker would not have come through undamaged." His hand tightened on Flur's shoulder. "It wasn't worth it. We'll meet them again — unless the taghte claim them first."

O' Cuire, deep in thought, nodded. "That's what I thought." He inclined his head and moved to the door. "Thank you for the time, Rhyslin."

As he stepped into the passage, the shift struck him at once, hearth-warmth fading into chill, lanterns dimmer, planks groaning with the sea's breath. He paused a heartbeat, glancing back at the glow spilling through the half-shut door, then closed it behind him. The cabin kept its fire-lit peace; ahead stretched corridors of shadow and duty, and the long watch home.

Flur waited until O' Cuire had gone. Then, with a languid stretch, she pressed her body against Rhyslin's side, her breath feathering his jaw before she nipped at his lips.

The draoidh tilted his head and caught her mouth in a kiss that burned with lazy hunger. When she drew back, his eyes half-lidded and smiling, a slow grin curved his lips. "Did you want something?"

Her golden hair spilled forward, whispering across skin already bronzed by sun and spellfire. "Want?" She wriggled against him, voice husky. "I need—" The words dissolved into a moan as his fingers climbed the back of her thighs. Heat coiled low in her belly when his hand cupped her and thought scattered like leaves in a gale.

Beneath his left arm, the spell-blade stirred. Dreams filled with moans not her own, and she growled in protest as she was nudged from her warm place. "Hey!"

Rana' s complaint broke into a flush
as she blinked awake to find Flur arching
back in ecstasy. Blood rushed to her
cheeks; she scuttled to the far end of the
divan, curling in on herself.

The fire cracked sharply, echoing the
gasp that slipped from Flur' s lips.
Shadows trembled, dancing with the
cadence of her breath as Rhyslin' s hand
traced her spine, ribs, and higher still.
Whimpers laced with sighs spilled from
her throat, rising into the air like a hymn.

Rana squeezed her eyes shut, but the
world offered no escape. Every honeyed
gasp and dripping sigh seeped into her
ears, igniting warmth she could not master.
She bit her lip to stifle the sound that
wanted out — only to hear another gasp,
softer, from the table.

Daring a glance, she found her mother watching, eyes fixed on the lovers as though upon a sacred rite.

Through the haze of fire and desire, Flur remembered they were not alone. Panic fluttered in her chest; she clutched the bond as if shaking his shoulder. {We need— to stop.} Yet even as she thought it, her hips pressed against him.

{Why? Am I hurting you?} Concern pulsed through their link, steady as his hand's slow exploration.

Her answering moan betrayed her. {Ai Rodyn, no — but Ria is watching.}

Rhyslin lifted his head, lips grazing her throat with feather-light kisses. {Then let her join us.}

Flur′s breath caught. She had expected restraint, not a bold invitation, and the shock thrilled her to the core. Shivers coursed down her body, unraveling the last of her protests. {Rana is—} His fingers brushed the curve of her breast and her thought fractured into a cry. {Rana is—Ai Rodyn, yes!}

{Then Rana can watch.} His smile was slow, inexorable, as Flur collapsed against him, trembling.

The air itself pulsed with their bond, wrapping heat and shadow around the four of them. Rana, cheeks aflame, could not tear her eyes away. Ria′s gaze never wavered.

Flur was so lost in the moment she didn't see Rhyslin beckon Ria to his side or hear what he whispered in her ear.

When the Hîn i-Balanath matron assisted her to her feet, Flur whispered, "I'm sorry."

"For what?" Ria asked, guiding her onto the bed. "I remember what it was when I first bonded with Garion." Once Flur was settled, Ria climbed onto the bed and leaned against the headboard, her presence steady as a pillar of flame.

Flur rolled onto her side, propping her head on one hand. Firelight played across her bare skin, painting it in shifting hues of bronze and gold. "Will it always be like this?" She waved her hand down her body, the gesture half-wonder, half-vulnerability.

Ria offered her a warm smile. The hearth′s glow softened the fine lines of her face, lending her the look of a woman both aged by wisdom and renewed by memory. "So long as your love holds, everything else will only get better." Her eyes lit with remembered joy, bright as embers stirred to flame. "You will be fine."

Flur′s gaze faltered. She looked away, then back again, her doubt clinging to her like a thin blouse against chill air, offering scant protection. "How do you know?"

"Because you blaze like a fire." Ria′s hand found Flur′s arm, her touch warm, grounding. "You′re a lot like Allanagh."

She had the satisfaction of watching Flur's eyes widen, surprise spilling across her features.

Flur scoffed, the sound brittle. She could not see the fiery woman Ria described in her mother. "Mother? Fiery?" The word felt alien. She could not recall her mother ever raising her voice, let alone burning with temper.

Ria's laughter rose low from her belly, a hushed warmth that seemed to ripple the shadows on the walls. "Allanagh has changed a lot since I first met her." She tilted her head, brushing fingers through her hair, memory carrying her voice. "She and Mayana did not get along at all."

Her smile turned wistful, as if she were seeing ghosts dance in the flames. "Garion likened it to being caught between fire and lightning."

Flur blinked, trying to reconcile this version of her mother. "Really? Was it that bad?"

The wood behind Ria's back cooled her skin even as her smile softened, half-hidden behind her hand. "Allanagh was afraid Garion might spend more time with Mayana than with her. She barely spoke to Mayana, and when she did, she practically screamed at her."

Flur's heart climbed into her throat. "What changed? Mother and Mayana are thick as peas."

"They are now." Ria's lashes fluttered closed, her voice spilling out like honey softened by heat. "They weren't a family then, only three people bound together, and they were miserable."

She exhaled slowly, a sigh that stirred the air. "When I became part of his house, I prayed to Abuela for guidance, and she showed me they needed structure."

Her fingers moved as though marking lines on invisible parchment. "I made a schedule for Garion, giving him time with each of us individually, as well as time together as a family."

Her smile settled into a contented glow. "When Allanagh and Mayana found they were not fighting for his attention, they settled down, and we became a real family."

"All that from just a schedule?" Flur raised an eyebrow, doubt mingling with curiosity.

Ria reached out, tapping her shoulder with a fingertip. "No, Neth-gwelwen." The word — little flame — hung between them like a blessing. Her smile never wavered, but her tone carried the weight of law.

"It was a reminder that Garion led our home, and that no bond outweighed another." She stretched her leg, wincing faintly as a muscle pulled, the gesture grounding her words in lived truth.

"How did Mother and Mayana take it?" Flur grinned, leaning in, caught now by the thread of the story.

Ria heaved a dramatic sigh, rolling her eyes at the memory. "At first, they accused me of getting more time with him than they did." Her tone mocked the old accusation, but the curve of her lips gentled. "When they saw that we all had equal time, they settled down."

She leaned back, her smile softening into tender warmth. "It wasn't long after that we started spending every day together. We became a family in truth."

Flur looked down at her hand, curling her fingers as if to hold onto something unseen, then looked up at Ria. "Will we have problems?" Her voice wavered; beneath her words, the fear whispered that Rhyslin might love Ria more than her.

"You won't even know I'm around." Ria's answer came with quiet certainty. "Garion called me his sheltering oak tree." She reached out, curling her fingers around Flur's, her grip a steady anchor.

"What about Rowena?" Flur's voice held a plaintive beat, the name carrying all her hidden dread.

Ria's grip tightened, steady but not harsh. "I would like to withhold my judgment until we meet her." Her lips pursed as thought drew its lines across her face. "There may be a way to talk to her before they bond."

Flur searched her aunt's eyes. "Do you think he'll let us talk to her first?"

Ria gave a slow, deliberate nod. "If he follows the old ways, he will." Her fingers brushed through her hair, a habitual gesture. "Do you want us to try it?"

Flur's throat tightened. Fear strangled her voice, but her nod was answer enough.

They would speak to Rhyslin about it soon.

Ria lingered against the headboard until Flur curled into sleep, small as a kitten, her breath soft and even. She eased herself from the bed and paused to brush an errant strand of golden hair from Flur's forehead.

Her whisper, "Sleep well, neth-gwelwen" spread like a fine mist through the cabin, leaving behind the faint hush of blessing. With a last look at her niece, she cracked the door and slipped into the dim corridor beyond.

Stepping into the darker cabin, the Hîn i-Balanath matron blinked, brushing the damp warmth of the adjoining chamber from her brow. The lanternlight here burned lower, throwing long shadows across the beams.

The hush of the ship wrapped around her like a shawl, the timbers groaning in rhythm with the sea's pulse.

It took her a moment to see them: Rhyslin settled on the divan, her daughter curled small in his lap.

Ria stilled. She had known he was fond of Rana, but not until now—seeing the old draoidh's hand moving in patient circles down her daughter's back, steady as a blessing—did she feel the weight of it. His hold was no casual comfort. It was protective, almost paternal, threads of bond-light weaving unseen through the air.

"You care about her," she whispered in awe, her voice catching as she crossed the room. Caution tugged at her ribs even as joy pulled her forward. She lowered to her knees beside him, the boards warm beneath her palms.

"Did you think I wouldn′t care?"
Rhyslin′s quiet reply carried no reproach,
only curiosity. One eye opened, its pale
gleam catching hers.

At Rana′s soft moan, he bent and
murmured into her ear. The sound was so
low it seemed to fold into the wood around
them. At once, the girl slackened back into
sleep. "Let me put this young lady to bed,
and I will be back."

Ria only nodded, her throat tight, and
watched as he rose with careful grace. The
old draoidh cradled her daughter as though
she were made of light itself, then crossed
the floor, toeing open the cabin door.

The ship seemed to hush as he entered the smaller berth. He laid Rana upon the bed as if laying an offering at an altar, drawing the covers high about her shoulders. His fingers brushed her brow with a tenderness that made the air itself hold still. "Sweet dreams, mo phrìseil," he whispered, the words lingering like incense smoke.

When he returned, silent as shadow, the cabin seemed subtly warmer. Rhyslin sank into his chair. Ria, who had not moved, found herself inching toward him, as if the boards themselves urged her nearer.

"Why did it surprise you I care for your daughter?" His brow lifted, the question carrying a faint weight.

Her heart jolted at the thread of accusation. She dropped her gaze, shame stirring. "I wasn't sure," she confessed softly. "Back home, the men treated her as if she were only a child pretending at spell-blade games. I was afraid that you would do the same."

Her eyes lingered on the shut cabin door, picturing his hands tucking her daughter in. Was that what a benevolent father looked like? "Rana had faith in you before she ever met you."

She looked back to him, uncertain. "Is it true that you dueled with her outside the council chamber?"

Rhyslin leaned forward, his gaze leveling with hers, steady as the horizon. "Do you have a problem with that?"

The amused glint in his eyes told her he thought it no transgression. Neither, she realized, had Rana.

"No," she said at last, slowly. The admission eased something in her chest. "Nobody took her spell-blade training seriously."

"Really?" His surprise flickered bright. "Rana is exceptionally skilled for her age. If we hadn't agreed to first touch, she could have seriously hurt someone." His words carried no condescension, only recognition.

"Rana's blade skills are above average, while her mastery of Draoidheachd is exceptional for someone not trained by a dedicated Master Spellblade."

As he spoke, pride flushed through her like heat. Her body betrayed her before she could guard against it–leaning, seeking, her head coming to rest against his lap as though it had long belonged there.

"I was going to ask you to work with her," she whispered, her voice nearly lost to the timber's sigh. "That prophecy has me worried."

His hand slid into her hair, fingers combing slow. A purr rose unbidden in her throat. His smile was half-play, half-command as he tapped her crown. "Come up here, Cuddle-cat."

"I'm not a cuddle cat," Ria complained, though good humor threaded her words. Still, she obeyed, climbing into his lap, curling close.

"Of course not," he murmured, the corners of his mouth unconvinced. "And yet here you are—curled in my lap, purring like one."

The ship rocked them gently, cradle-like. Shadows stretched and settled as though the whole cabin breathed with them. Before long, their eyes slipped closed, his arms folding around her, her breath syncing to his. Wrapped in timber, tide, and bond-thread, they drifted into sleep.

# Chapter Twenty-Six
## Of Windless Skies and the Water Below

Attunement to nature comes in many forms. Some can smell the shift before a storm and name its hour. Others can unerringly find what has been misplaced. Still others carry in their marrow a quiet kinship with beasts.

Rhyslin's attunement, however, went deeper — so deep it sometimes drowned him. When change came, it struck like the silence after a drumbeat, the void louder than sound.

He felt it first in the absence: the wind's song faltering, the sheets falling slack. The rustle and groan of canvas, the creak of cordage, the humming rise and dip of the hull, all gone, like breath snatched from a sleeper's lungs. The Dawn-Breaker herself seemed to hold still, waiting.

By the time the cutter's flight ceased, the draoidh was already awake, his hand resting lightly against Ria's shoulder, urging her from dreams. A faint furrow between his brows betrayed what his lips had not yet said.

Before Ria could even open her eyes, Rana burst from the cabin, blouse half-fastened, skirt gathered in her fists. The deck timbers betrayed her urgency, drumming beneath her moccasins.

She rolled her eyes at the sight of her mother's drowsy blinking.

"Wake up already, Momma. Something's wrong with the ship." Her words cut sharp, then she rounded on Rhyslin as though the fault were his. "Why did we stop?"

Ria rubbed her eyes with the back of her hands, her yawn soft as a child's. She half-heartedly pushed away from Rhyslin's warmth. "What do you mean, something's wrong with the ship?"

Rana stamped her foot, the plank beneath her ringing with her impatience. "How could you not feel it? We've stopped dead. We're not moving." A flare of bond-born heat trembled outward from her, loud and raw in Rhyslin's senses.

Not for the first time did she wonder if grown folk dulled to what was right and wrong in the world.

Ria blinked again, her daughter's words sinking in, sobering her faster than morning Kafe. "Rhyslin?"

She saw him then, not his calm, but his listening. His eyes roamed the chamber as though chasing the echo of something just out of reach.

"Rana's correct." His voice came low after a long pause. "We aren't moving." He shifted, and Ria caught the subtle tilt of his hand: *May I rise?* She nodded, sliding from his lap. Only then did she notice it too, the absence of the ship's gentle lift and sway, the silence where once had been breath.

Rhyslin rose, his shadow lengthening with the lantern-light as he strode to the double doors. The timber groaned faintly under his boots, like the ship herself yearned for motion. He flung the doors wide, the air heavy and still beyond.

"We are becalmed." The words struck like a ritual pronouncement, more than mere report. A concerned look crossed his face. "We've got to find a place to set down. Ixa won't be able to hold us up for very long."

The ship seemed to exhale in sympathy as he stepped onto the quarterdeck, already searching for command.

"Ah, it's you, Rembran." Rhyslin halted in front of the spellblade, the silver gleam of dawn-light catching on his staff. "Report, please, Lieutenant."

Before Rembran could reply, O'Cuire stepped out of his cabin, his overcoat loose about his shoulders as he took his place beside Rhyslin. The quarterdeck lanterns burned with a steady but subdued flame, as though the still air pressed their light downward.

A quick sweep of the deck brought the situation into his grasp, but he did not speak. He caught Rhyslin's slight gesture — a tilt of hand, a narrowing of eyes — and held his tongue. The draoidh was shaping this as a lesson.

Rembran seemed to feel it too. Instead of blurting out what he already knew, he paced the length of the quarterdeck, listening to reports from the deck officers one by one. The timbers beneath his boots murmured in faint complaint, as if resenting their stillness.

When he was ready, he returned, saluted first the draoidh, then the captain.

"Maighstir Rhyslin, we have come to a complete stop. There is no reported damage to the ship, hull, or sails." He gestured to the three masts, shadows of still canvas looming above. Then to the counter-sails lashed below. "We are becalmed." He leaned closer, lowering his voice. "I've already ordered Andros to find us a place to set down."

His expression said what his words did not: *he did not expect to find one.*

Rhyslin inclined his head, acknowledging both the report and the growth in the lieutenant's patience. "Thank you, Lieutenant, that was an excellent report."

He crossed to where Andros knelt midship, the elemental's hand already pressed flat to the planks. The air above him quivered faintly, shimmering with the hum of power spiraling downward. "Anything to report?"

"Not at the moment, sir," Andros replied, his voice a low resonance like stone rolling through a cavern. A pulse of draoidheil energy leapt from him, winding through the hull and plunging toward the hidden ground below. Lantern-light stuttered as the energy went, and when it rebounded, it carried strangeness with it.

"That's odd," Andros murmured, his black-on-black eyes narrowing. "How accurate are your charts?"

O'Cuire, steady at Rhyslin's side, glanced once toward him before answering. "As accurate as can be. It's been some time since we've done a complete survey from the air and ground — why?"

Andros's brow furrowed, as though translating a language only he could hear. "If I'm not mistaken, there's a body of water below that shouldn't be there." His eyes slid closed again as he loosed another pulse. This one came back heavier, colder.

Rhyslin's gaze sharpened. The stillness around him grew heavier, heat pressing down as if the sky itself disapproved. A bead of sweat traced his cheek, though his expression remained steady. "Just how big is this body of water?" His tone was deliberate. He would not leap blindly, not even into providence.

Andros opened his eyes, black within black fixing upon the draoidh. "About a mile in circumference and almost nine hundred fathoms in depth." He shrugged with an odd, earthen grace. "As for life, I can't sense any from this distance."

A hush rolled across the deck at that — even the rigging above seemed to groan more softly, as if the ship herself disliked what she'd heard.

Rhyslin exhaled slowly, the sound carrying into the silence like a ritual. He glanced toward Ixa, the air elemental swaying faintly with strain. Her auburn hair clung to her temple with sweat, her breath shallow. She could hold the vessel aloft, yes, but not without the wind to carry her.

His voice, when it came, was calm and firm as iron driven into earth. "Take us down, Lieutenant. Put us in the water."

The apprentice pilot straightened, voice carrying sharp as steel across the deck. "Aye, sir."

Orders spilled from him in a steady cadence, and the crew obeyed. Counter-sails folded and locked along the hull with the groan of wood settling into restraint. Canvas whispered as the sails were furled and bound against the spars, as though even they knew the sky had abandoned them.

When the deck stilled, he gestured to the waiting Elementals. "Take us down."

Without wind to cradle the descent, the Dawn-Breaker's fall was less flight than burden.

The ship sagged through the air like a stone guided by trembling hands. Ixa's breath came ragged, Andros's arms pressed hard to the planks, their power holding the galleon steady against gravity's demand. The wood of the hull quivered as though in sympathy with their strain.

*I know you can do it. I have faith in you.* The thought was not merely Rhyslin's, but seemed to thrum through the crew, the ship itself, and into the straining elementals.

By grace or providence, the great galleon met the water with a hush instead of a crash. No spar cracked, no plank screamed, only a soft settling, as though some unseen hand had laid her gently down.

"Excellent landing," Rhyslin said, voice calm but carrying warmth. He inclined his head to the trio, acknowledging their effort. His gaze found Andros. "A mile deep you said?"

At the elemental's nod, calculation flickered across the draoidh's eyes. Anchors of iron and chain were useless here; they needed something that would grip an abyss.

The order went out. At once, the deck shifted into motion, but not with the jangle of metal. Instead, they drew out the storm-sheet, a canvas broad and heavy as a burial shroud. Weighted spars were lashed to its corners. The men worked in silence save for the rasp of rope through calloused palms, their movements urgent yet reverent, as if preparing a rite.

At Rhyslin's nod, they cast it overboard. The cloth kissed the water with a hiss and bloomed outward, white against the black glass before being swallowed beneath. Lines groaned and blocks creaked, taut as drawn bowstrings. The Dawn-Breaker shivered from mast to keel, then steadied, no longer adrift, but braced against the abyss as though clinging to the bones of the earth itself.

The silence that followed was deeper than before. No flutter of rigging, no sigh of wind, only the slow, thrumming pull of canvas buried in nothingness.

Rhyslin closed his eyes, the soles of his boots registering the faint resistance, as if the ship herself had sighed in relief. "Hold fast," he murmured. Whether to the crew, the sheet, or the heart of the Dawn-Breaker, none could say.

The stillness was broken by a soft gasp. Rana leaned far over the port rail, hair falling like a black banner into the void. Her breathless words trembled when she returned to his side. "I can see all the way to the bottom. There's not a fish or frog in there at all."

Her shiver needed no explanation. The absence was palpable. The lake was no lake, but a vessel of void disguised as water.

The twin dryads padded up behind, bare feet soundless on the deck. Their unease whispered like leaves wilting in drought. "How long are we going to be on this—body of water?" Kiesha asked, trying to bury her fear.

"I do not know."

It was not the answer they hoped for. Kietha's voice was barely more than a breath. "This isn't natural. We shouldn't be here."

Ixa, pale with fatigue, added her own verdict as she and Rembran returned. "Neither should this—whatever it is."

The spellblade's hand lingered on his hilt as his eyes swept the unbroken surface. "Is this Lady Astinmah's doing?"

Rhyslin's shrug was heavy with unease, gaze fixed on the black glass below. "Mayhap—indirectly."

O'Cuire approached, practical as always. "Should we fire the galley?"

"Might as well; we're likely to be here a while." Rhyslin's answer was flat, distracted, his eyes still on the water. "Besides, food is always better when heated."

The hearth-fire lit below, but instead of comfort, its smoke seemed to war with the silence pressing down upon them. The aroma of oil and bread, salt and broth rose defiantly into the air, yet it could not mask the absence beneath. No hearth could banish that void.

Rhyslin turned from the rail at last, choosing not to linger in its stare. The great-cabin welcomed him with the murmur of familiar voices. Rana slipped in after him like a shadow clinging close.

Ria looked up from her place beside Flur, her hand still gesturing mid-conversation. "What happened?"

Rhyslin caught Rana's glance, an unspoken exchange that drew an amused tilt from Flur's lips. He answered at last: "We lost the wind and had to set down in this—lake."

The word felt wrong, hollow.

Ria cocked her head, frowning at the unnatural hush. "Why is it so quiet?"

The shared look between Rhyslin and Rana deepened. It was the younger who spoke, her voice thin. "It's not a living lake."

Ria froze. Flur blinked. "What do you mean it's not living?"

Rhyslin's hand flexed on the table, his tone flat with disbelief. "It's a pool of fresh water with no living things in or around it. No trees, no plants, no fish, no birds." He shook his head once, unwilling to linger on the thought. "I know it's not quiet time, but they're going to fire the galley. Who would like to go get dinner?"

The chance of escape, any excuse to leave the weight of silence, was seized at once.

"I'll go," Rana said quickly, eyes flicking to the dryads.

"Uh, yeah. I'll go as well," Kietha muttered, relief betraying her voice. Kiesha gave a silent nod.

Together the three of them slipped away, eager for the warmth of food and company, anything that smelled of life.

Rhyslin waited until the three of them were truly gone, Rana's eager footsteps fading, the dryads' laughter drifting down the passage, before moving to the divan. The galleon creaked low in its moorings, as if aware of the stolen privacy. Sinking into the cushions, he whispered, conspiratorial as a fire crackling low, "We have the cabin to ourselves, if for a short while."

Ria and Flur traded a look across him. The words sank like stones into still water, sending ripples through both women. Slowly, deliberately, their expressions curved into predatory smiles. They resembled stalking cats, lithe, graceful, eyes bright with mischief, as they prowled to his side and curled into him. The lantern flames leaned inward, as though the ship itself bent closer to watch.

Ria snuggled against his chest, her breath stirring his tunic. "What did you want to talk about?" Her voice carried the teasing edge of temptation, though restraint coiled beneath it like a leash she held tight. She knew they hadn't long. The timbers beneath them groaned softly, marking the fleeting quarter hour like a ticking clock.

When Rhyslin looked down at her and said, "You," the single word fell with the weight of an oath. The air itself grew warmer, a shimmer rising off the oil lamps. A delightful shiver racked Ria's frame, and she flicked her tongue across her lips, her pulse thudding like a muffled drumbeat in the bond.

On his other side, Flur stiffened. A sharp pang pricked her heart, and the bond flared with it, jealousy, fear, love twined in confusion. She had known Ria would join them. She had told herself she was ready. And yet hearing it spoken so directly stole her breath. The lantern flame nearest her guttered low, as though it felt the tug of her sorrow.

*I won't cry. I won't cry.*

Rhyslin turned at once, his senses attuned, drawing her against him. His voice was a balm. "It's okay, mo chridhe." His hand smoothed through her golden hair, and the faint scent of wildflowers rose as if the world itself tried to comfort her. "You have but to say the word, and it shall be only the two of us for eternity."

Flur trembled, then steadied, her heartbeat syncing with his. The warmth of the bond wrapped her like a hearthfire. His words were impossible, and yet they healed her. In her deepest heart, she had already accepted Ria, and even whispered to herself of Rowena, waiting somewhere in the weave of fate.

"Thank you, my beloved," she murmured, nestling closer. "Our home will only be complete when we welcome everyone properly." She lifted her head, brushing her lips across his. The kiss deepened, and a low moan escaped her throat.

The lantern nearest them flared high, then dimmed, as if in time with her blush.

{Are you sure?} Rhyslin's calm mental voice flowed through her like a cool spring.

Flur's reply was steadier than she expected. {I'm sure.} And to her surprise, she was sure, and hopeful.

When Rhyslin at last turned to Ria, her breath caught as though she had been waiting her whole life for this moment. The cabin hushed, even the creak of timber pausing.

"Ria, I have given you time to think about what you want. I've given you time to discuss your future with Rana." His gaze softened. "You've said that I claimed you."

Her cheeks warmed, a flush stealing across her face. "You did," she admitted, glancing toward Flur, who watched with bright curiosity.

Rhyslin, who had never known a family, felt the bonds of one twining around him now. "Ria, I, Rhyslin Darkblade, offer you my bond. I will love you and protect you. Our house will be your house, our hearth, your hearth."

The goddess Ananke's name hung in the air like incense. The timbers of the Dawn-Breaker groaned deep, the lanterns flaring in resonance.

Ria gazed into his eyes and saw her future unfurl, not as queen, nor as object, but as a woman claimed, cherished, whole. Joy so fierce it nearly undid her welled inside, but she mastered it, drawing a steady breath.

"I, Ilyriatri oran roinnag, accept your bond. I offer all that I am to you. I will be your Ria till the dust of time takes us from this world. In Ananke's name, I do vow."

The blessing fell like starlight. The goddess stirred through the bonds, a warm breath that set every lantern flickering in time with Ria's heartbeat. Rhyslin caught his breath as her bond twined with Flur's, not weakening but strengthening in love.

{I've waited so long for this,} Ria's mental voice surged through the bond, strong and certain.

Flur blinked, startled at the clarity.
{How did you do that so easily?}

Compared to Ria's, her own voice felt a whisper.

Ria laughed softly and tweaked Flur's nose. "I've had more practice. It's like any other muscle — the more you use it, the stronger it gets."

Flur's eyes gleamed with sudden mischief. "I see. How about we—" She leaned and whispered into Ria's ear. The grin that spread across Ria's face answered for her.

"Yes, let's."

Together they turned their shared mirth on Rhyslin, setting upon him in a delightful torment. The divan rocked under their play, the ship itself groaning like an old friend in laughter.

When at last the three came up for air, breathless and glowing, they found two wide-eyed dryads and one red-faced spellblade frozen in the doorway.

Kiesha, impudent as always, clapped her hands. "More, more!" Her eyes twinkled like stars. "Nothing like a pre and post dinner show."

"Oh, hush," Rhyslin groused, adjusting his clothes as Ria and Flur sashayed away, hips swaying like dancers. They busied themselves at the table, laughter still glittering in their eyes.

Rhyslin stood, shaking his head. "I see you've got dinner. Why don't we eat before it gets cold?"

# Chapter Twenty-Seven
## The Stillness Before the Shimmer

Rhyslin was halfway to the table when a flicker of motion caught his eye — Rana, fidgeting in the shadows near the bulkhead.

If they' d been on soil rather than deck planks, she would have buried her toes in the dirt to hide her shame.

Here, the timber betrayed her, creaking under her shifting weight. Her blush rippled up her frame in waves that tugged faintly at the air around her, like heat wavering above a summer road.

The bond-thread that linked her to him quivered with the same restless rhythm, a tautness that spoke of words unsaid.

Dinner could wait. The Cearcall's meal might fill the body, but Rana's unrest pressed on the soul.

He caught Ria's gaze and tipped his head. The Hîn i-Balanath matron read her daughter as easily as she did the weather. Ria's eyes danced knowingly over Rana's small, betraying gestures.

She gave a nod that was both permission and blessing. "We'll save you some. Take as much time as you need."

Rhyslin smiled at her, then turned to Rana, offering his arm. "Care to take a walk?"

She nodded mutely and slipped her hand into the crook of his arm. The ship seemed to hush as they stepped out into the night air.

Lanterns swayed gently on their hooks, their flames dimming in sympathy with her hesitation. No wind stirred the sails. Even the strange lake below had gone flat — a glass-dark mirror, waiting to receive the girl's confession.

They made one circuit of the deck in silence before Rana halted, her moccasin toe dragging arcs into the planks, as though she could carve her confusion into the ship's very bones. When she finally looked up, her voice was so faint it nearly vanished into the stillness.

"Aren't you going to ask me?"

Rhyslin turned, measured and patient as the eerie lake itself. "Ask you what?"

She ducked her head again. "What I'm feeling." The hush deepened with her sigh, and lantern light caught the sheen of a tear. "Momma loves you."

The admission struck him harder than he expected, like a bell rung in a sacred hall. The lake below shivered with a ripple, echoing the shock.

He had known her feelings already — could feel them through the trembling bond-thread — but the question was not his to answer. It was hers.

"Why am I jealous?" Her words cracked the silence, raw as thunder before a storm. She paced, moccasins thudding against the planks, each footfall echoing into the hollow dark.

"You are good to Flur. You didn't have to let us travel with you, but you did, and you put up with us changing your cabin, invading your space."

Rhyslin said nothing. Even the rigging overhead gave only the faintest groan, as if the ship itself understood that he was holding silence open for her.

She stared down at her moccasins, shifting again. "You claimed me, and yet I' m free to do what I want." Her gaze rose, anguish written in the tightness of her lips. "I' ve seen you in my dreams for years, helping me, saving me. You said you' d save me if I needed it." A tear slipped free, glittering as the lantern flame bent to it. "Why can' t I just be happy with what I' ve got?"

She broke. The girl hurled herself into his arms, and the ship pitched with the violence of her sobs, timbers shuddering as though even oak and iron could not bear her grief alone. Rhyslin drew her close, steady as stone, his voice low against her hair.

"I don't know what happened in your dreams, nor do I know what you want — but I will do everything I can to provide you with what you need."

Her question came muffled, fragile against his chest. "Is it okay to feel this way?"

He breathed in, long and deep, until his chest pressed against her crown. The breath left him slow, ruffling her hair, and the lantern flames along the deck wavered with it.

"It's not my place to tell you—" He tilted his head so his words touched her ear alone. "Rana, the answer depends upon how I'm answering. Are you my daughter, my lover, or my apprentice?"

She blinked once, twice, then stilled, her thoughts plunging deeper than words could follow. Her whisper trembled. "Now what do I do? I need to talk to Momma."

She hugged him tightly before running back toward the great-cabin. Her footsteps echoed once, twice, before the still water below swallowed the sound.

Left alone, Rhyslin closed his eyes. The air cooled around him as he cast his thoughts upward, where Astinmah might hear. "If I've ever treated you badly, I'm sorry, Mother."

The lake gave a single ripple, as though the goddess had brushed its skin.

The ripple had barely stilled when the scream tore the night apart.

Rhyslin's eyes snapped open just as a shimmer flared on the deck. The form, half-seen and half-smelt, swept one sailor off his feet and flung him into the black water. Lantern-light shattered across the distortion, as if the air itself were breaking.

"Man overboard!" Rhyslin's voice cracked the silence, sharp as a whip. He raced to the rail, the planks drumming beneath his boots. Below, the lake boiled and stank like open graves.

Another shimmer lunged, stretching unnaturally toward a second sailor. His scream rose as the water swallowed him, then cut short. A wet hiss rolled up, and the stench of rotting kelp and acid burned the nostrils.

"Wait! Don't jump!" Rhyslin
barked, catching the shoulder of the
nearest man who had leapt to the rail.

"Whatsa sayen?" the sailor snapped,
fear thick in his throat. His hands clenched
the railing as if it might save him.

The lake answered instead. It
bubbled, releasing a pale vapor that stank
of bone and bile. Through it, Rhyslin saw
— and wished he hadn't. The sailor
already lost was dissolving into white
threads of marrow, his skeleton drifting
down like brittle weeds.

Rhyslin's stomach turned. He
yanked the living man back with all his
weight, retreating a step as the shimmering
cloud surged across the deck. The lantern
flames guttered, and the air turned sharp
with cold.

"He's dead," Rhyslin said flatly, ducking beneath the vapor. His voice was iron over dread. "We're not floating on water anymore."

He spun toward the quarterdeck, catching Rana's wide eyes. The bond carried her terror to him as surely as the stench filled his lungs.

"Get to the bell!" His command snapped like lightning. "Ring for your life. Don't stop ringing until we're airborne."

Rana froze only a heartbeat, then bolted. Her moccasins slapped the planks as she vaulted the steps two at a time. At the bell she seized the rope and wrenched it with all her strength, the bronze throat of it crying out again and again, each toll reverberating against the shimmering horror pressing in.

The sound was no longer just a warning. Each strike rang like defiance, like the heartbeat of the Dawn-Breaker itself.

At the bell's call, the crew came scrambling from below, looking for all the world like an ant colony kicked from its mound. Boots struck the deck in a discordant rhythm, the timbers shivering beneath their weight as if the ship herself felt the alarm.

"What's the alarm?" O'Cuire called from the wheel, half-dressed, his overcoat thrown on over bare shoulders. His breath steamed in the cold night air, vanishing into the gusts rolling across the lake.

"The lake is alive!" Rhyslin's voice cut sharp against the wind, his eyes locked on the shimmering clouds rising off the black water. The frost in the air seemed to recoil from the sight. "Get us airborne now!"

Before O' Cuire could issue the command, Rembran was already gesturing, his voice rough as salt air, urging sailors to hack at the sea-anchor lines.

The deck shuddered as Andros dropped to one knee midship, his palm pressed flat, delving the deep currents below. Ixa stood beside Rembran, her auburn hair lifting on an unnatural wind, blue light kindling in her eyes as she coaxed the cutter into motion.

At the stern, a sailor stared in horror at the frayed end of the sea-anchor line. Acrid smoke stung the night air. He lifted the ruined cord overhead. "The Sea-Anchor is gone!"

O' Cuire gave a single nod, his tone terse but iron steady. "When we rise, bring us to starboard. Ixa, hold her at a hundred feet."

The elemental' s gaze turned skyward, her voice straining. "It' s hard going, sir. Something' s got us tight." The air itself seemed to drag against her will, every gust fighting her command.

Rhyslin planted the butt of the singing staff on the deck, the runes along its length shimmering faint silver in the lantern light. He let his senses pour downward, through the warm, living planks, past the crowded holds breathing of iron and salted meat, to the keel and into the cold black beyond. There, his will brushed against something oily, greasy, hungry. The lake water around the hull quivered as if trying to warn him, and the air turned foul with the tang of brine and rot.

The black pearl atop his staff pulsed dimly. Rhyslin's voice carried low but firm. "Ixa, I need a lightning strike on my staff."

Her sky-blue eyes flashed toward him. She raised her right hand, the wind gathering like a tide. Static pricked the hair on every neck as she aimed, her fingertip trembling with raw charge.

Then the clouds above split. A blinding strobe lashed down from the heavens into the draoidh's staff, thunder chasing it close behind.

The bolt cracked through him, down the staff, and into the keel. The ship sang in protest, timbers thrumming as though alive, before the energy surged out into the dark water. Steam hissed up around the hull.

From below came a high-pitched squeal that rattled teeth and bones, a sound so sharp even the iron nails in the deck seemed to shiver. Sailors clapped their hands to their ears, grimacing.

The lake released them. Smoke rose from the water, spiraling upward like a soul torn loose, before the depths swallowed it whole.

Before anyone could speak, Ixa heaved, and the ship leapt skyward, breaking free in a burst of air and frost. The cutter rose above the treetops, sails catching clean wind at last, while below the lake lay still, as though nothing had ever stirred its black surface.

As the Dawn-Breaker steadied above the lake, Rana lowered her hands from her ears, the ringing fading like the last chime of a struck bell. She blinked away the afterimages of lightning still strobing behind her eyes.

Her breath came ragged, drawing in the sharp scent of singed oak and brine, and she forced it out in a long exhale until the fear left her chest. Then, without thinking, she sprinted across the deck to Rhyslin.

"What was that thing?" she gasped as she reached his side. Only belatedly did it strike her that she had not run from danger this time, but into it.

"I've never seen anything like it," Rhyslin said, brushing smoke from his duster as if batting away gnats. The faint glow still lingered on the runes of his staff.

He extended his hand toward her, palm steady despite the tremor in the planks beneath their boots. "You did well raising the alarm."

Rana blushed under the praise, her eyes darting down to hide the heat in her cheeks. When she dared look up again, he was smiling at her, and the warmth of it steadied her more than any lightning strike. "I didn't even think about running," she confessed. "I just did what you told me." She took his hand and tugged gently, like a child yearning for safety. "Can we go back inside?"

Rhyslin inclined his head but stilled, his eyes drawn to Andros.

The elemental's gaze was turned downward, pupils wide and unblinking. "Something stirs below," Andros murmured, voice shifting to a register that carried across the deck.

He reversed Rana's tug, guiding her with him to the starboard rail. The timbers were still warm underfoot, humming faintly as though remembering the lightning that had coursed through them.

Below, the lake was no longer still. The crew gasped, some crossing themselves, as the water dragged its own shores inward. Frost-rimmed reeds bent and disappeared, swallowed by glassy folds.

The lake tightened into itself, curling like a cloak drawn over shivering shoulders.

Rhyslin quirked a brow, studying the uncanny sight. It looked less like a retreat than concealment, as if the land itself wished to turn its face away.

Behind them, O' Cuire' s voice cracked out sharp orders for a damage survey, but his own boots carried him swiftly back into his office, the door thudding shut.

The crew remained silent on the deck, staring at the vanishing lake, until the only sound left was the hiss of snow against the sails and the faint groan of timber, unsettled by what it had carried through.

Knowing that O' Cuire would share the damage report with him, Rhyslin squeezed Rana's hand as he turned and led her toward the warmth and safety of the great-cabin.

# Chapter Twenty-Eight
## Of Bonds Tested and Sanctuary Found

The warmth of the great-cabin enfolded them as Rhyslin and Rana stepped inside, a balm after the night's ordeal. Lantern-light pooled golden across the broad table, flickering in ripples like reflections on water. The ship's timbers creaked in long, contented sighs, the hum of the elementals threading through the grain of the oak as though the vessel itself was settling into rest.

Flur and Ria sat close together, voices quick and hushed in intimate cadence.

Rhyslin tried to follow their words but let them slip past the edges of his weariness; the rhythm of their talk washed over him like wind in reeds, soothing but beyond his grasp.

The sharp edge of battle-born alertness drained from him, leaving only weight. He yawned, shoulders heavy, and the air stirred softly with his exhale, lantern flames dimming in sympathy.

At his side, the young spellblade matched him breath for breath. She drifted to the divan with careful steps, her moccasins whispering against the planks as though asking permission of the cabin itself. She curled neatly at one end, making herself small, unwilling to intrude.

He looked from his chair to the cushions she had claimed, then shrugged with a faint smile. The bond-thread between them tugged gently, carrying a pulse of permission. He followed her down, taking half the space.

The timbers underfoot eased their groan as he sank into the cushions, as though approving of his choice. His eyes stayed open right until his head touched the backrest; then sleep claimed him in one long pull, deep as undertow.

Rana lasted only moments longer. Too tired to read, she let her book fall aside, parchment whispering against wood. She crawled into him without thought, curling with her cheek pressed to his lap. Her breath evened out quickly, rising and falling in rhythm with the slow tide of his chest.

At the table, Flur's question about the ship's sudden leap met only the hush of the room. She turned to see them sleeping, folded into each other like ivy around stone. Her breath caught at the sight—the quiet rise and fall of their chests, the peace that had so eluded them of late— and she nudged Ria.

The auburn-haired Hîn i-Balanath matron regarded them for a few heartbeats, weighing the moment like she might weigh the weather. Then she rose. Her bare feet made no sound as she crossed the cabin. She bent to Rana, eyes tracing pulse and color. Both were steady. Whatever had happened outside had left no mark upon the girl.

Circling to the head of the divan, Ria leaned close to Rhyslin, her voice warm with quiet authority.

"If you aren't too tired, would you carry Rana to our cabin and then join us? We'd like to speak with you about our Cerin Gwedh."

He cracked one eye, his lips quirking with weary humor.

"Can it wait until tomorrow?"

Ria glanced back at Flur, lifting one shoulder. "Maybe. We' d rather settle it soon."

He followed her glance and saw the worry written plain across Flur' s face. His sigh loosened into the bond, conceding.

"Give me a moment to move Mo Bhòidhchead Cadalach, and I' ll be there."

Ria stepped back, giving him room.

He bit down on a groan as he drew Rana closer, her warmth soaking into his chest as though she meant to root herself there. A shallow breath steadied him, then a careful lean forward. He rose, balance found in the hush that fell across the room. Even the lanterns seemed to hold their flames steady as he bore her weight.

Step by step, he carried the sleeping spellblade down the narrow corridor. At her cabin, he laid her in the center of the bed, drew the covers up beneath her chin, and lingered a moment. She murmured something soft and curled tighter under the blankets. The timbers beneath his boots creaked once, like a lullaby, and fell still.

He cocked his head, the smile tugging his lips unbidden, warmth rising through him like a hearthfire. The smile faded as he closed the cabin door behind him.

It was time to hear what his bhannaichean wanted.

Worn to the bone, he lingered at the Master-Cabin door, heart tugged by the question of what Flur and Ria wished to share. The timbers seemed to listen with him, holding their groans as though curious.

Removing his duster, he folded it across his left arm and laid it upon the back of the divan, the leather's weight settling like a sigh as he crossed the great-cabin.

He paused before the door, no longer his alone, but theirs, and reached into the bond, searching for a thread of meaning, a glimmer of what waited beyond. Ria had told him only that it touched upon their circle, nothing else. The bond met him with a brush of calm, tinged with quiet concern, cool as river-water over stone.

He almost rapped on the wood, then halted mid-motion, exhaling as he shook his head. He didn't have to knock; it was still his cabin. Rhyslin set his hand to the latch. From within, that calm pressed again against his chest, like soft moss, steadying his pulse. Whatever it was, it couldn't be that dire—could it?

Before entering, he breathed a prayer for steadiness. The air in the great-cabin hushed in answer; even the floorboards, prone to their creaks and pops, seemed to still in reverence. The lamplight upon the table leaned toward the door, flame bowing like a benediction. Taking the silence as a blessing, he opened the door.

The first thing he saw was Flur, seated at the edge of the bed in a short red nightgown that caught the lamplight like banked embers.

Behind her, Ria—draped in gossamer-thin cloth—moved a brush through Flur's long golden hair, each stroke shimmering as though spun from sunlight. The hush of bristles across her locks seemed to set the air itself thrumming, soft and low as harpstrings.

At the door's whisper, Flur lifted her head and smiled. He returned the smile as he kicked off his boots and set them neatly by the jamb, leather falling against wood with a muted thud that seemed swallowed by the warmth gathering in the room.

"If you'll give us a few more minutes, we'll join you at the table," Ria said, drawing the brush down to the middle of Flur's back.

Her voice flowed like silk through still water, the brush's rhythm falling into step with her words.

Rhyslin closed his eyes as warmth stirred in the cabin, a rising current that spoke of the goddess's blessing. Without looking away from them, he crossed to the table, the lamplight stretching his shadow long across the boards, and lowered himself into a chair.

Flur tilted her head back, baring the pale line of her neck, and he accepted the tease with a faint smile, leaning into stillness to watch. Ria caught his gaze, green eyes glinting, and gave a slow, conspiratorial wink before setting the brush aside with deliberate care. She pressed a gentle hand on Flur's shoulder, urging her forward.

"Thank you for helping me with my hair," Flur whispered as she rose, her nightgown shifting to reveal fleeting glimpses of her inner thighs. She moved with liquid grace, rosewater scent curling in her wake, and brushed past him to take the seat at his side. The bond carried her affection with the fragrance, cool and sweet, filling his lungs.

Then Ria stood, unhurried as a spring afternoon. Her auburn hair fell loose in waves as she crossed the cabin, lamplight catching copper fire in each strand. She leaned down to press a kiss to his cheek, warmth filling his senses like sun-kissed hay, before seating herself on his other side. "Thank you for waiting, mo ghràidh," she murmured, voice soft as silk drawn across the heart.

Rhyslin nodded, fixing his gaze on Ria. "What can I do for you, mo rionnagan brèagha a thuit às na nèamhan[10]?"

---

[10] My beautiful stars that fell from the heavens.

The cabin seemed to hold its breath. Blushes rose slowly and visibly across both women's bodies. Flur's pleased sigh joined Ria's, their pulses quickening in the bond until the very air leaned closer to listen, timbers thrumming faintly like distant drums.

Flur leaned forward, her hand light upon his. "Mo ghràidh, your words fill my heart with joy." Her eyes flicked to Ria, hesitation pulling her lips taut.

Rhyslin's brow lifted as he looked between them.

Ria exhaled, a sound that carried both exasperation and resolve. "We wish to talk to you about something that brings you discomfort when spoken of."

Her look toward Flur stung of cowardice; the golden-haired bhanna′s downcast gaze conceded it.

"What would that be?" Rhyslin cupped Flur′s hands and squeezed, warmth flowing back through the bond like sunlight pressing through stained glass.

"Rowena." Flur′s whisper barely stirred the air, yet the name landed with the weight of a spark upon dry tinder. Rhyslin′s eyes shut, a muttered word lost in the hush. The lamplight guttered once, then steadied.

"That′s what we mean," Ria said gently, laying her hands over his. "We don′t want you to feel as if we or she will become a source of strife."

He breathed deeply of their mingled scent—rosewater and hay, summer and hearth—and shook his head. "It isn't Rowena who troubles me—it's what might happen if the three of you do not find peace with one another." His voice dropped low, eyes turned upward to the ceiling planks that seemed suddenly heavy with listening. "It was she who urged us toward Trì Aibhnichean. Her visions showed battle and loss, and she thought we might blunt them."

Ria's left brow arched. "Visions?"

Rhyslin nodded. "Rowena is a seer. Her goddess guides her." His fingers twined with theirs, steadying himself. "Despoina has never led her wrong."

At the goddess's name, a faint curl of frankincense drifted through the cabin, spiraling from nowhere, carrying judgment and mystery.

"I see." Ria's whisper carried the weight of revelation. "You fear we will not welcome her—that discord will grow between us."

Flur bowed her head, her heart pressing hard against his through the bond, like waves breaking against a cliff. "Are you fond of her?"

Rhyslin paused, thoughts scattering like chaff in a gust. "I cannot answer that simply. She has lived with me for eight years, and her counsel has never failed us." Even as he spoke, he felt the words fall short, brittle things in the face of their question.

The air thickened, heavy as summer rain before it breaks. Ria's fingers tightened over his. "She is not a piece of equipment, Rhyslin. How do you feel about her? Will you invite her into our Cerin Gwedh?" When his silence lingered, the Hîn i-Balanath matron sighed softly. "Then let us speak with her before you bond."

Flur bit her lip to keep a sob from breaking free. She had always yearned for a great household, but not at the cost of peace. Blue eyes lifted to his, love pouring into the bond like stained-glass light, dazzling and fragile.

Rhyslin steadied himself against the tide of her feeling, then nodded. "That would be for the best."

His gaze lingered on the woman who had surprised his heart. "When we return home, you may speak with her."

The cabin seemed to ease, timbers relaxing as if the ship itself exhaled. With understanding on steady ground, Ria playfully tugged on the fingers intertwined with hers, and the bond hummed like a chord struck. She led her bond-mates toward the bed, where the lamplight bent low, drawing a veil of warmth across them all.

Evening yielded to night, and night to silence broken only by soft cries that ebbed into sleep.

Bells later, dawn's first light slipped between the curtains of the master-cabin, painting the air in pale gold that mingled with the lingering scent of sweat and roses.

Wrapped in warmth, the old draoidh woke slowly. His first thought, rising through the fog of dreams, was why his right arm would not move.

Awareness came by degrees: his forearm was pressed between warm, steady breasts, his palm flattened to a taut belly, fingers pinned by another hand curled tight around him. A leg had been thrown across his own, anchoring him as if he were a thing precious, not to be lost.

He stilled, breath softening. Through the bonds he reached, and found no alarm, only the shimmer of quiet laughter: Flur and Ria in the great-cabin, their amusement like sun-dappled ripples across the back of his mind.

Memory turned until the truth settled. If not Flur, nor Ria, then only Rana remained.

{When did she come here?}

Flur's reply rippled with mischief. {Sometime in the night. We found her when we woke.} A teasing pause lingered. {Is something amiss, mo ghràidh?}

{I'll let you know in a moment. She's waking.}

Ria's steadiness joined them, grounding as earth. {Be gentle. She trusts you enough to come to you in the dark.}

His chest loosened. It was not mischief that had drawn the girl, but hunger for warmth, for safety, the presence that stilled her fears. That was a bond deeper than flesh.

As if to answer, Rana shifted in sleep, hips brushing against his leg. Heat stirred through the bond, quick and bright, tempered by the innocence folded in her spirit. He wondered what battle of the heart had driven her to cross the shadows into his bed.

Her pulse leapt as she surfaced from slumber. He steadied his own, feeding calm into the bond while she woke against him. Her hand slipped lower in drowsy wander, brushing across his stomach before resting, bold, unknowing, on the heat of him.

A groan climbed his throat, desire flashing like struck flint, but he bound it down beneath will, prayer pressing against his teeth.

*Oh, Mathair, this is your weaving.* His thought cracked with strain. The goddess' s laughter shimmered like chimes stirred by a hidden breeze.

Beside him, Rana stilled. Awareness caught her. She looked down, saw her hand, and froze. A sharp breath shuddered through her chest as color flooded her cheeks. Eyes wide, startled, darted to his, then fell, auburn hair cascading like a curtain pulled in haste.

The bond trembled with mortification, innocence scorched by sudden heat. Yet beneath it pulsed something older, wordless: the cry that had carried her through the dark. Not lust. Not mischief. A soul's plea for sanctuary in the only place it felt safe.

At last she gathered herself. Her gaze rose, twin currents braided too tightly to part: fear and longing, both shining. Her lips trembled, breath breaking across them like prayer.

"Master Rhyslin — I don't know what to do." Her voice wavered, terror of rejection knotted with the hope of belonging, as though one step might send her fleeing, and another bind her forever at his side.

"What do I do?" Her whisper came almost reverent, fragile as spun glass.

Taking her hand, Rhyslin brought her up to his side, whispering, "Only what you want to do, mo phrìseil."

When she settled against him, her warmth sharpened the desert-rose scent that clung to her. He curled an arm around her shoulders. "What brought you to my bed?"

Rana pressed her body to him, drew a long, deep breath, and wondered why he always smelled of beeswax and papyrus. Eyes fluttered closed, a sigh slipping past her lips. "The dream again. I wanted to — needed to —"

"I understand, mo phrìseil." His fingers traced gentle circles on her back, steady as a prayer. Rana gave another sigh, easing deeper into him until slumber reclaimed her.

Rhyslin waited until she rolled away before slipping from the bed. He lingered for a moment, gazing at the sleeping spellblade, then stepped silently into the great-cabin.

"How is she?" Ria asked, offering him a cup of juice. Concern shone in her eyes.

"Asleep." He took a sip. "She had the dream again."

The auburn-haired matron weighed her words. "Will you take her as an apprentice and teach her to survive?"

The old draoidh didn't hesitate. "Of course I will. She's part of our cearcall."

Love burst from Ria like sunlight through cloud, and he quickly set the cup aside before she flung herself into his arms. He had only just embraced her when three sharp knocks rattled the door.

"Come in," he called, gathering her close.

At his word, the door opened and Rembran stepped through. "Here's the report from the captain."

Rhyslin scanned the parchment with a weary glance. "Tell him to set a watch. I want us on our way when the wind picks back up."

# Chapter Twenty-Nine
### The Home Beneath the Ash Trees

Ria tried to peek over Rhyslin′s shoulder, the parchment rustling faintly in the hush of the great-cabin. Her brow furrowed as the cramped, technical hand blurred past her eyes. "What does it mean? How bad is the damage?"

The draoidh let the report slip from his fingers into hers, shoulders bowing under a weariness that went deeper than flesh. The beeswax scent that usually clung to his clothes seemed dimmed, smothered by the cabin′s stagnant air.

A faint groan ran through the timbers, low as a grief-stricken sigh, as though the Dawn-Breaker herself still remembered the shadow-creature's touch. "Whatever that thing was, it was eating the ship."

"Eating the ship? In what way?" Flur's voice lifted from across the table. She looked up from Rana's book, the thin pages trembling slightly as she closed it. The candlelight guttered with her movement, throwing restless shadows against the walls.

"According to the report, the strakes have been dissolved from the outside in." Rhyslin's voice caught, chilled by the thought. "Unless—" His eyes narrowed, dread tightening his jaw.

The cabin seemed to draw still, the flame leaning toward him as though listening. "Could it have been trying to get to my people?"

The possibility fell heavy into the air, so weighty even the candle's flame seemed to falter.

Ria followed his thought, her auburn gaze hardening. "If we had stayed one more day, would it have—?"

Rhyslin nodded, a cold crawl rising his spine. "Yes. It might have eaten all the way through."

A tremor shivered beneath their feet, the hull answering his words with a muted ache. Flur drew in a breath, her golden hair stirring as if touched by the same chill.

"I'm glad we lifted when we did." She reached across the table, her fingers brushing his. "I'm sorry you lost two men."

He closed his hand over hers, steady but worn. "We all know the risks when we sign up. Their families will be compensated."

The words were calm, but the Dawn-Breaker groaned again, softer, like a mother keening in her sleep. Flur's lips pressed tight, her frown half-hidden, until he added, "We aren't regular army. My crew are mercenaries."

Her head lifted, confusion clear in her eyes. "How does that work? Do you love your realm?"

"We all do," Rhyslin answered, tone easing. His breath stirred the flame, steadying it again. "There are ten full-time companies in the military. Every male above the age of seventeen must serve five years."

Ria leaned into him, her weight a warmth against his side, grounding him like earth beneath roots. "Where do mercenaries come in?"

He tilted his head back until it brushed hers, the ship's slow rocking carrying them together. "The Saorsa is vast. The regular military can't be everywhere. That's where we come in. Mercenaries fill specialist roles, carry out special assignments, and carry the diplomatic flag."

He felt her nod against his temple, her hair brushing him like a seal pressed on his words.

Tracing Flur′s fingers, he coaxed a soft sigh from her lips. "The regular army might have dismissed your people′s problem as your own. I am allowed more leeway. Hence, I could help your people."

"I′m glad it was you who came to help us," Flur murmured, her smile sultry as the candle′s flame steadied once more, burning low and sure.

Rhyslin caught Ria′s soft snort. He teased Flur with a crooked grin. "We can′t spend all day in bed, you know."

The golden-haired bhanna stuck her tongue out at him, her mirth like a spark against the gloom. "Why not? You're magical in bed."

"You insatiable Huiel," Ria muttered, just loud enough. The candle sputtered at her words, almost in agreement.

Flur's lips curved predatory. "I am just as you are a miul melethron."

Ria stretched closer, curling into Rhyslin's side, the heat of her body warming the cabin's stale air. "Not going to deny it."

The master-cabin door opened on a whisper, unheard over their banter, until Rana's bright voice cut the tension like dawn through cloud. "I'm bored." She slipped beneath Rhyslin's left arm, her lightness scattering the heaviness from the room. A stray beam of morning pressed through the porthole, striking her hair so it flared like spun bronze. "Can we walk the deck?"

"Of course we can," Rhyslin said, half-hugging her, the cabin itself brightening with his smile. "In fact, why don't we all go outside?"

He hid a smirk as all three women scattered to dress. The timbers eased with their laughter, the floorboards creaking like a sigh of relief. Moments later, they stepped into the quarterdeck mist.

Cool air wrapped them, salt and dew cleansing away the heaviness of beeswax and smoke. The Dawn-Breaker breathed easier with them, her planks damp but steady beneath their feet.

The sun and moon graced the sky thrice as the Dawn Breaker rode her favorable winds toward home. Her sails drank deep of the currents, each canvas breathing as though alive, while her hull creaked with steady heartbeats against the waves. The air smelled of brine and pine-resin pitch, warm with sun, cool with the night's passing mist.

Her steady trek faltered when a cutter burst from the clouds like a hawk stooping on prey. The very wind seemed to recoil at its sudden plunge, spilling from the Dawn Breaker′s sails in startled shivers.

It skimmed across the galleon′s prow with unnerving precision, its bright pennants snapping like talons spread wide. The Dawn Breaker answered with a low shudder in her timbers, an uneasy groan that trembled through deck and mast alike.

"Well, it′s good to see the border patrol sharp as ever," O′Cuire said, reading the challenge flags with practiced calm. "They′re asking the usual—who we are, where we′re bound, what cargo we carry."

Rhyslin narrowed his eyes as the cutter wheeled around them, its shadow flitting across the Dawn Breaker's sails like a predator circling. "They should be sharp. They're paid well enough." The wind tugged at his cloak, carrying the faint salt tang of foam, but he hardly noticed.

Marcus, beside him, counted the glitter of spyglasses catching the sun from the cutter's deck. Each flash felt like a pricking arrowhead, the light striking like steel against their hearts.

Then O'Cuire frowned, the shadows shifting with the crease of his brow. "Strange. They want to know who owns the ship—and if he's aboard."

The Dawn Breaker's rigging thrummed, ropes quivering as though she bristled under the question. Rhyslin arched a brow, gaze fastening on the smaller vessel. "Fly my pennant."

Marcus gave a crooked grin, though his eyes stayed sharp. "Why would they care who owns her? Did you forget to pay a tax or something?"

"No." Rhyslin's answer came quickly, then softened with a shrug. "At least, I don't think I did. If it were tax, a revenue agent would be waiting at the dock."

"True enough." Marcus nodded up as the rectangular pennant unfurled high in the rigging. The silver branches of the Croabh na Cruinne caught the light, shimmering as though alive.

For a heartbeat, the air itself seemed to still, roots and boughs spanning sky and sea alike in radiant symbol.

The cutter answered at once, fresh flags running up its yards like a sudden breath. O' Cuire read them swiftly. "Their captain requests permission to deliver a message."

Rhyslin felt the weight of a dozen lenses still fixed upon him, as though their gazes pressed like fingers on his skin. The Dawn Breaker's hull swelled under the scrutiny, her sails whispering their unease. He set his jaw.

"Pull in the stun sails and extend the gangplank," he ordered. "Let's see what the man has to say."

The galleon's motion shifted, her stunning sails sheeting home with a heavy sigh as her yards drew to centerline.

Up on the quarterdeck, Rembran's stance was taut as a drawn bow. He watched the cutter's careful turn toward the port-side gangplank, his voice low to Ixa. "Be ready to push us away if they try something foolish."

The elemental inclined her head, her eyes glinting with reflected starlight though the sun still held the sky. The smaller ship came to an immaculate stop, a ship's length off, drifting with predatory grace, like a hawk that knew exactly where its shadow fell.

Rhyslin had been so fixed on the cutter that he didn't notice Flur, Ria, and Rana until they stepped onto the deck. The older women came to his side, their presence warm as sunlight through a break in cloud, while Rana darted straight to the rail, peering over with eager eyes.

"Why did we stop?" Flur asked, her voice soft as she took in the sleek vessel. A thoughtful hum slipped from her lips. "Oh. I see. Who are they?"

"Border patrol," Rhyslin answered, sparing her a smile before returning his gaze forward.

The golden-haired bhanna leaned into him, satisfaction lighting her face. "So we're in your lands at last?"

He nodded, and she sighed with contentment, resting her head against his shoulder. "Do they always stop you like this?"

Marcus, arms folded, grunted. "No. Looks like they've got a message for him." He tilted his chin toward Rhyslin.

"How do they deliver it?" Ria asked, tone curious but cautious.

"You wouldn't believe me if I told you," Rhyslin murmured.

As if on cue, a slight figure appeared on the cutter's deck. He accepted something from the captain, then broke into a sprint. His boots drummed on the planks, beating like a war-drum as he raced the cutter's full length toward the gangway.

At the last four feet he leapt, his weight bowing the timber low before it snapped back, catapulting him in a perfect arc toward the galleon.

At the apex of his flight, white wings snapped open with a crack like a sail catching sudden wind. The Dawn Breaker's sails shivered in echo, and the sunlight caught his feathers, dazzling bright, scattering silver motes across the deck like stars shaken from heaven. He glided toward the galleon, each downstroke stirring the air with a sweet ozone tang.

"Oooh," Flur breathed, unable to hide her wonder. "Where will he land?"

"Right on, Rana, if she doesn't move," Rhyslin replied dryly.

The girl froze, eyes widening as she realized. She squawked and stumbled backward, tripping over a coil of rope.

The hemp sang against itself as it tightened, and down she went with an undignified thump, arms flailing just as the winged courier flared to a graceful stop in front of her.

The ship timbers gave a hollow chuckle at her fall, rigging trembling with it.

"Feas gar math," he greeted, folding his white wings neatly. The feathers rustled like sails catching breath, their edges glimmering faintly where dawn spilled across them.

Extending a hand, he smiled. "Could you point me toward the owner of this magnificent ship?"

Rana eyed him like a cornered cat, the flush already heating her throat, but reluctantly took his hand. The warmth of his palm and the faint, wild-air scent of mountain peaks unsettled her more than she wished.

"Maighstir Rhyslin is on the quarterdeck. Can't miss him—he's the one with the black staff." She hauled herself upright with his help, rope coils shifting as though reluctant to release her.

The messenger's eyes glimmered as he bent and kissed her knuckles. A whisper of wind brushed across the deck in time with the touch, and the candles guttered below in the great-cabin.

Rana went crimson to the roots of her hair and yanked her hand back as though scalded.

Up on the quarterdeck, Flur nudged Ria and giggled behind her hand. The sea itself seemed to echo the sound, lapping playful against the hull. "Is he a celestial?" she whispered.

Rhyslin shook his head, his cloak stirring faintly though no wind touched him. "Celestials rarely manifest here. He's an air magaidh."

Flur tilted her head, eyes fixed on the folded wings. "The wings?"

"Draoidheachd," Rhyslin said simply, watching the messenger climb the steps toward them. The boards creaked softly in rhythm with the youth's stride, as if acknowledging a guest.

"Maighstir Darkblade?"

When Rhyslin inclined his head, the young courier gave a half-bow and drew a small silver orb from his jacket. Its surface gleamed like polished moonlight, and the air grew cool as though the dawn had slipped behind a cloud. He offered it forward with both hands.

Rhyslin accepted the orb, its weight unsettlingly heavy, like stone cut from the deep earth. A hush ran through the quarterdeck; even the gulls wheeling above went quiet.

He braced his staff against his shoulder and laid his left hand gently atop the rounded crystal.

At his whispered words—"*Leigh domh faicinn*"—a hum vibrated through the planks beneath them, the Dawn-Breaker herself answering the draoidh's command.

The orb kindled with pale fire that licked the edges of their shadows and washed the rigging in ghostly light.

The shimmer coalesced into the lined face of a grizzled warrior, hair salted with grey, voice carrying the clipped cadence of command.

"Maighstir Darkblade, we received your report of the battle at the Three-Rivers fort.  On your forecast, we reinforced the border keeps at Arn, Belgra, and Tula. Each was infiltrated by Orcan companies; each held. Far-northern Saor-shelbhhaidean were struck by bands of an fheadhainn a thuit—repelled with minimal losses."

He raised his hand in a farewell wave, the light flickering as though passing through smoke. "We will see you at the council meeting next week."

The image dissolved like mist, sinking back into the orb until only Rhyslin's tired reflection wavered on its polished curve. A faint sigh seemed to escape the timbers, the ship herself easing once the voice was gone.

Rhyslin exhaled through his nose, the pale fire's afterglow dimming from his skin, and returned the sphere to the messenger without ceremony. "Well. That should be interesting."

The courier bowed again, then sprang from the deck with impossible lightness, his boots striking sparks of salt-light as he launched. Wings snapped wide, scattering droplets of morning dew into prisms, and he glided back toward the cutter.

The sea wind sighed in relief as his shadow lifted from the Dawn-Breaker's deck.

The cutter peeled away into cloud, its wake scattering like torn silk across the air.

"What will be interesting?" Marcus asked, squinting after it as the smaller ship vanished into the mist.

Rhyslin's gaze did not follow. It drifted past the Dawn-Breaker's prow, as if his eyes could already pierce leagues of sea and see the council hall rising on the horizon. The sea-wind stirred his cloak, tugging at the black staff balanced against his shoulder, and the bonds carried the slow heaviness in his chest.

"Next week′s meeting. They′ll expect three beraith Hîn i-Balanath — queens. Not Two beraith and a bhanna." His tone carried no bitterness, but inevitability pressed on every word like stone upon stone.

Sensing it, Ria laid her hand upon his shoulder, warmth spilling into the coiled tension there. "Worry not, maighstir mo ghràidh," she whispered, her voice steady as prayer.

At her touch, the ship′s timbers gave a low, sympathetic sigh, as though the Dawn-Breaker herself sought to ease his burden. Rhyslin turned to her, eyes searching.

In her gaze, he glimpsed his own longing reflected—his fierce desire to keep peace: between clans, between realms, even between the hearts bound now to his own.

And for a heartbeat, the burden eased.

The vessel carried their silence with her, sails trembling against the hush of wind, until Ria lifted her eyes to him once more. "Do you remember what we discussed before I offered my bond?"

Rhyslin inclined his head, black staff catching the last light like a blade of shadow. "You no longer wished to be a queen."

When she nodded, his brow arched. "What did you do?"

Her auburn hair stirred with a faint gust, the breeze tugging away the last fragments of a crown that no longer bound her. "Several years ago, I created a council of ministers to assist me in governing my small—" her voice faltered, and a small, embarrassed laugh escaped. "I suppose you would call it a county."

The timbers shifted beneath their feet, settling with the weight of her confession. She gazed into Rhyslin's eyes, voice softening. "I gradually stepped back until the eight of them were dealing with almost all the day-to-day duties."

Her gaze dropped like a faltering sail, afraid she had disappointed him. "I'm sorry that I didn't mention it sooner," she whispered, lifting her eyes again.

"It's okay," Rhyslin replied, his voice steady as the sea's heartbeat. The staff at his shoulder gave the faintest hum of Draoidheacd, echoing his calm. "I should have asked more questions when the accord was written." His eyes searched hers with gentle gravity. "Will your council still accept the accord?"

The sails above stilled, as if the ship herself leaned closer to hear the answer. "They should, if Minister Makar honors my wish." Sorrow quavered in her tone. "Had I not been so selfish, you wouldn't have to worry about this."

Her tears shimmered in the lamplight, scattering like drops of starlight. At once, Rhyslin extended his hand–not reaching for her but waiting. When she stepped into his shelter, curling into his side, the wind returned, salt-sweet and warm, drawing her hair across his cheek like a benediction.

"It's okay," he whispered at her ear, his breath carrying the scent of cedar smoke. "I know Makar Lann Neimh. He was Garion's chief lieutenant. He'll ensure you want this, and then do what's best for his people."

Ria's pulse slowed, her heart falling in rhythm with the seas, and she stood quiet in the strong crook of his arm. "I can't wait to see our new home. What's it like?"

The word *home* seemed to awaken the vessel herself. The figurehead groaned low, as though remembering the place she was bound to, and the rigging thrummed like harp strings yearning for port. Overhead, the stars brightened, scattering across the sky like lanterns lit in welcome.

Flur, hearing it, drifted nearer, golden hair catching starlight. Rana followed too, the bond tugging her close, until the three women stood together within the circle of Rhyslin's presence—bound not just by oaths, but by hope, longing, and the promise of hearth yet unseen.

"How does one describe his home?"
Rhyslin's voice softened, and for a
heartbeat, the salt air and creaking lines
dissolved. Memory drew him through the
bond—until he stood again before his own
gates, wind cool upon his face, ash trees
bending in welcome.

"The locals call my saor-shelbh Am
Mansa Flur. Once you see it, you'll
understand why." His words carried pride
and longing both, and when he opened his
eyes, three pairs of eyes held fast upon
him.

"My home sits atop a hill
overlooking fields of grass and flower
beds, with groves of uinnseann, darach,
agus craobhan measan. In spring,
blossoms drift like snow; in summer, the
air hums with bees. It is..."

He faltered, voice thickening. "...a place made for rest.."

Flur sighed, golden hair brushing his shoulder as she slipped beneath his arm. Her palm pressed to his chest, her pulse quick through the bond. "That sounds wonderful," she whispered. "I would love a proper bath. It's been ages since I had one."

"You mean a sit-down tub of water, don't you?" Ria teased, though her own eyes betrayed the same hunger.

Flur's eager nod made her hair spill like sunlight. "Oh yes, that was all we had at the manor house. What about you?"

"The same," Ria admitted with a shrug. "Large tubs when there was water to spare. More often, a wet-cloth bath."

Rhyslin's deep chuckle rolled through them, steady as distant thunder. "I can do better than tubs of water and wet cloth." At his tone, the bonds sparked with anticipation. "On the first floor of my manse, there is a bathhouse."

Flur gasped, kissed his cheek. "Then you are the wisest man on Crann na Beatha."

Ria pressed closer, her lips brushing his shoulder. "Cruel, to speak of paradise when we cannot touch it for days. You've cursed us to longing."

"I don't understand," Rana cut in, her voice sharp with honest curiosity.

She leaned forward, eyes darting between her mother and Flur. "What's the difference between a bathing tub and a bathhouse?"

Ria faltered, words slipping. "It's — larger. A place where — ah—" Her cheeks pinked, and she buried her face in Rhyslin's shoulder.

Amusement rippled through the bond, and Rhyslin took pity. "Rana, do you remember Dearg's pond?"

Her blush deepened at the dryad's name, but she nodded. "Yes. Stones at the bottom, water lined to hold."

"Good." Warmth brushed her thoughts as his approval steadied her. "Now imagine that pond doubled, contained within walls, the water ever renewed. That is a bathhouse."

Her eyes narrowed, weighing his words. Then widened, incredulous. "That much water? How can you—?"

"My saor-shelbh sits atop an underground lake, refreshed with each rain." He smiled faintly. "The garden is carefully tended so that not a drop is wasted."

Still, Rana crossed her arms, skepticism bright. "I don't believe you."

Ria stiffened, bristling. "Vuuroena Seilmatt—apologize at once—"

[Be silent, Mo Ria.] Rhyslin's thought cut across the bond, firm as hammered iron. She drew breath to protest, but his will pressed deeper: [Will you defy me, after asking me to take her seriously?]

Her rebellion melted into chastened quiet. [No, Maighstir,] she whispered, submission heavy as velvet against his will.

[Then let her stand,] he reminded gently, tracing her back. [Let her test herself.]

Rana muttered, "I'm sorry, Maighstir Rhyslin." The bond revealed hollowness.

"No, you're not." His gaze pinned her. "Are you sorry?"

Her chin lifted, grateful for the chance to stand firm. "No, sir. I don't believe you."

A grin tugged his lips. "Good. Never apologize unless you mean it." His voice dropped to a wolf's challenge. "I can't wait to see your face when you find the bathhouse."

Rana's smirk answered, challenge accepted.

Through the bond, he pressed the same truth to Ria: [That goes for you as well. If you truly mean it, it will never be a lie.]

Her breath shuddered. Pride and humility wrestled in her gaze until she turned to Rana, stepping free of Rhyslin's arm. "I spoke without thinking, Mo Flur Alain. Can you forgive me?"

The girl searched her mother's face, found only sincerity, and flung herself into her arms. The bond filled with quiet joy, blooming like dawn. Rhyslin's heart eased at the sight of Ria's happiness.

The days that followed flowed in peace. Wild forest gave way to ordered groves, then farmland, then villages—each ring of civilization folding into the next. Fortresses crowned the hills like guardians, while saor-shelbhs gleamed on horizons like jewels set in green.

The Hîn i-Balanath watched in wonder, voices alive with questions. Marcus and Rhyslin answered each in turn, their patience and laughter weaving the company ever closer to hearth.

At last, the Dawn-Breaker slowed, her sails folding like wings at rest. The elemental lines pulsed steady beneath the deck, guiding her descent.

The air grew still, heavy with anticipation.

Below, Am Mansa Flur waited. Their journey was over.

Their homecoming had begun.

Don't worry, Rhyslin's Cearcall
will return in The Draoidh's Gambit.